"BRILLIANTLY
DONALD WESTLAKE

"When it comes to combining a thick and shifting layer of double-crosses with a witty prose style, Perry is right up there with Ross Thomas and Elmore Leonard."
The Boston Sunday Globe

"Perry tells a story at once terrifying and amusing. He enriches this story with fascinating characters on both sides of the law and has them speak in crackling, dead-on dialogue."
Chicago Tribune

"The cross-country flight is made up of pure thrills, plenty of wit and humor, and eventually ends with a climax you'll have to read yourself."
Rocky Mountain News

"The Butcher's Boy is back! And his skills as the cunning and efficient Mafia hit man are still honed as sharply as before. . . . Readers will quickly start rooting for this precision instrument of destruction, relishing his cool escapades and grace under fire—and there is a lot of fire. . . . SLEEPING DOGS is a solid page-turner."
Mostly Murder

"Slickly executed and well written."
Daily News of Los Angeles

SLEEPING DOGS

Thomas Perry

IVY BOOKS • NEW YORK

Ivy Books
Published by Ballantine Books
Copyright © 1992 by Thomas Perry

All rights reserved under International and Pan-American Copyright Conventions. Published in the United States by Ballantine Books, a division of Random House, Inc., New York, and simultaneously in Canada by Random House of Canada Limited, Toronto.

Library of Congress Catalog Card Number: 91-27137

ISBN 0-8041-1160-X

This edition published by arrangement with Random House, Inc.

Manufactured in the United States of America

First Ballantine Books Edition: June 1993

For Alix
with thanks to Jo
and the Leschers

"At my coming back, I shot at a great bird which I saw sitting upon a tree on the side of a great wood. I believe it was the first gun that had been fired there since the creation of the world. I had no sooner fired, but from all the parts of the wood there arose an innumerable number of fowls of many sorts, making a confused screaming, and crying, every one according to his usual note; but not one of them of any kind that I knew. As for the creature I killed, I took it to be a kind of a hawk, its color and beak resembling it, but had no talons or claws more than common; its flesh was carrion, and fit for nothing."

—DANIEL DEFOE, *Robinson Crusoe*

On August 14 at three in the afternoon, Michael Schaeffer noticed a small poster on a board inside the front window of a small teahouse. It said THE AMAZING POWERS OF THE INTELLECT in bold letters at the top, and this attracted his attention. He hoped that there were amazing powers in the intellect, although his dealings with others and many years of self-examination had revealed none that he thought much of. In smaller letters at the bottom, the poster said 14 AUGUST, FOUR P.M. and LYNCHGATE HOUSE, BATH.

He had a little trouble finding it, because in England "Lynch-gate House" could mean anything from a private cottage to the corporate headquarters of a conglomerate. By asking directions he discovered it to be a country house not, strictly speaking, in Bath, owned by someone not named Lynchgate. When he arrived, he found a pair of pink, beefy young women at the entrance to smile at everyone and presumably to shut the door when their number approximated the capacity of Lynchgate House. Inside, he followed a middle-aged woman in a flowered dress to a large room with leaded-glass windows that reached from the fifteen-foot ceiling nearly to the floor, and looked out onto a garden with a foreground of topiary trees shaved and worried into the shape of gumdrops and a background of hedges nearly twenty feet high.

The room contained about thirty-five people, all very British and all apparently from the class of British people who always seemed to be busy doing things that couldn't possibly bring in any money, but didn't necessarily cost much, either: gardening and bird hikes and lectures. He wondered how many of them knew Latin, and decided that probably all of them did. His eyes settled inevitably on a pretty young woman who was arranging some pamphlets on a table at the front. She bent over as she worked, and he appreciated the curve of her hips under the light silk dress she wore. At this moment The Honourable Meg came in, scanned the crowd and sat down next to him.

The first thing Schaeffer noticed was her skin. It was fair, and appeared to have an even, uniform smoothness like natural ivory, its only variance a slight flush to her cheeks. Her shining dark brown hair made the skin seem to glow, and her bright green eyes looked amused. What she had wasn't exactly beauty, but perfection, and this was unnerving because it tempted him to scrutinize her for flaws. He sat stiffly in his chair to keep from violating the expanded amount of space that seemed her due.

The girl he had been watching turned around and announced, "Mrs. Purvis will open the meeting with a few announcements on our autumn trip to Atlantis."

Schaeffer barely breathed. Maybe it was the name of something else, or maybe he had heard the word wrong.

Mrs. Purvis was a slightly plump, enthusiastic blond lady in her forties, and she dispelled his doubts. "After the experience we had last year on our trip to the alien landing strips on the Plains of Nazca, I'd like to beg everyone to pay attention to the instruction sheet when packing this year. We'll be establishing our base camp on Grand Turk Island. It is tropical, but we'll be there in hurricane season. During a hurricane, between twenty-five and fifty centimeters of rain may fall in two days, and the winds may be violent, so dress accordingly."

Michael Schaeffer felt distinctly uncomfortable. He wondered for a moment how this group of people would go about dressing for twenty inches of rain and 150-mile-an-hour winds. The girl who had introduced Mrs. Purvis now launched into a few more details. "Everything we know about ancient Atlantis suggests they wore bright colors, probably lots of reds and yellows. So please try to respect that scheme. There will be ever-so-many lingering spirits about, and it won't do to offend them."

Schaeffer slipped out of his seat and moved toward the door. As he made it past the two beefy girls, one of them asked, "Something wrong, Meg?" and he heard a soft voice at his shoulder. "Sorry, dear. We've just got to leave. My friend has another appointment." Then she slipped her arm in Michael's and pulled him out of Lynchgate House.

Outside the door she didn't let go of his arm. "Thank you. I'm sorry I had to hitchhike, but when you left it was my last chance. Two persons might have to leave at once for some perfectly benign reason, but if they leave one after the other, it appears to be a trend and they get very upset."

"Do they?" he said. "You're welcome." He tried to turn toward her to remove his arm from her grasp subtly.

"Don't do that," she insisted. "They'll think I just grabbed you for a convenient exit, and they already resent me."

"Who are you, their psychiatrist?"

"Meg Holroyd. The Honourable Margaret Susanna Moncrief Holroyd. Does that mean anything to you?"

"Where I come from, it would mean you're a politician, so the 'Honourable' would be a lie. Here I suppose it means something else."

"No, it's a lie here, too. It means that hundreds of years ago there was a man in my family whose homicidal tendencies got him a title. My people are from York, but nobody goes up north anymore except to sweep the cobwebs out of the family battlements. Where do you come from, by the way?"

"Arizona." Automatically he fed her the first half of his prepared story.

She demanded the other half. "What's your name?"

"Michael. Would you like to go for tea or something?"

"Charmingly put. Who could refuse? Macready's isn't far."

"Good. When we get there you'll have to let go of my arm. Why do those people resent you?"

She smiled proudly. "I did something cruel to them for fun."

"You did?" He watched her as they walked. "What?"

"Something horrible. Afterward, at the next meeting, they voted a formal reprimand and made speeches saying how irresponsible I was about taking care of the hidden secrets vouchsafed to the initiates." She laughed happily.

"In other words, you're not planning to tell me."

She studied him for a moment, or pretended to. "Yes, knowing you as I do, I suppose I'll have to. You'll make me, won't you?"

As they entered Macready's tea shop and he followed her to a table in a dark corner, he had a moment to evaluate the risk he was taking. But then they were seated, and he decided to defend himself with questions. "You don't seem to take your friends very seriously. What are you doing with them?"

She shrugged. "They're one of my hobbies. I give them money, so I get to play with them. I inherited them, actually. My grandfather was a scholarly sort, and all his life he supported study groups and lectures on scientific topics. But late in life when he was beginning to think a lot about dying, and was getting a bit dotty, he lost interest in geology and archaeology and flora and fauna, and became obsessed with this sort of thing.''

''Expeditions to Atlantis?''

''Well, it's a whole range of things, all mixed up and linked together. There's Atlantis, but some of them think it was an ancient civilization and others think it was people from outer space. There's a smaller faction who think it was an ancient civilization destroyed by people from outer space, and another that think it wasn't destroyed at all, that they're still underwater, waiting for us to be worthy of their company before they'll come out. I hope they're not holding their breath. It's pretty easy to get an expedition together: if you're a lunatic you have to hold some theory that accounts for Atlantis.''

''Why?''

''Because lunatics are systematic thinkers. If they have a secret history of the world to put forward, they can't have other lunatics shouting, 'Then, how do you account for the pyramids? What about Stonehenge? Easter Island?' They have to include these things.''

''What did you do to them?''

''I'm ashamed to tell you.'' She stared into her teacup, then added, ''But of course I will. I assaulted them. Sexually.''

Schaeffer looked at her. ''All of them?''

''Every last one. All of the people who were there today, and a few more who were otherwise engaged. Attendance is down today; you were the only new one. A month ago, I came in and took the podium. I'd been in Paris for some time, but I'd told everyone I was going to Bolivia. I was supposed to tell them about my research at Tiahuanaco. I went on for some time with slides of the ruins, the weeping god and all that, and then told them about my greatest discovery: I'd found a true aphrodisiac. I told them that in a tiny village I'd found a *curaca*, and paid him eight hundred pounds for a small vial of the stuff.''

''Don't tell me you sold it to them.''

''Oh, no. It wasn't anything so crass as wanting their money. I just wanted to play with them. I told them I'd put it in their punch at the reception before the meeting.''

''And had you?''

''Of course not. There's no such thing. I'd slipped in a little powdered Valium mixed with cognac so they'd feel *something*. I said I'd just put some in so they could help with the experiment.

But I'd prepared rather well. I'd hired two very attractive and respectable-looking prostitutes in London on the way home, and had them come to the meeting separately as interested beginners. Around this time they began to show symptoms that something was very wrong, if you know what I mean."

"No, I'm afraid I don't."

"Well, I don't know how to say this delicately. They began to adjust their clothing and wriggle in their chairs a bit. When that began to attract some attention, they started to make rather brazen advances to their male neighbors. Then, when the response was positive and visible, they both moaned with a certain urgency and insistence."

"And it worked?"

"Not immediately. At first the emergency struck some people as medical rather than erotic, but then they both tore off their clothes and began to attack the men around them. There was a good deal of pawing and clutching. They were also extremely good at disrobing others with an economy of movement, and when a man's trousers are suddenly around his ankles, he feels very silly. He must decide immediately either to pull them up, or not. Several of them delayed the decision until too late, and very soon some kind of line was crossed. It was like a riot. I ran to the door, locked it and shouted that it was a gigantic disaster—things had gone terribly wrong, all the while unbuttoning my dress as though I couldn't help myself. But it was unnecessary. By that time both of the Hartleby sisters—the plump ones who take attendance—were uniformly naked, and Eunice Plimstall—the one you were ogling today—had convinced herself she'd fainted, and the poor dear had fallen with her skirt up to her waist, so old Mr. Capshaw was giving her an esoteric form of artificial resuscitation. She came to herself rather quickly, I have to say, and then she was up in search of a comforter with more stamina. Mrs. Purvis went to her hands and knees to help the fallen, but within seconds the vicar had lifted her dress and was helping her to free herself of her underclothes. It didn't seem to cure her hyperventilation, but she appeared to be grateful for the thought, and the orgy was fairly begun. Afterward, they considered having me arrested, but thought better of it and settled on a reprimand."

"That's a wonderful story," he said, then sipped his tea.

She looked disappointed. "You don't believe it, do you?"

He shook his head. "Not a word of it. But that doesn't matter. I don't know any of those people. Why would I care if it's true?"

"The stories are better if you believe in them," said The Honourable Meg. "I always tell them to be believed. I hope you aren't going to mind."

"Not at all," he said. He looked at her thoughtfully. "It ensures a certain level of quality. A story has to be pretty good before you can tell it as a lie."

It was at this moment that things were settled. The Honourable Meg had found someone who would listen with fixed attention to her stories, and she was content to spend the next two years cherishing him for it. The time simply happened, without anything unpleasant to make her notice its passing. Michael Schaeffer was competent and solid, an American businessman who had done something so thunderously dull to earn a living that as soon as he had gathered enough to satisfy the dictates of respectability, he had retired to England and stopped talking, or even thinking, about it. Of course, marrying a man like that would have been unthinkable.

The Honourable Meg, as a young, healthy, attractive member of the aristocracy, was the property of an invisible national genetic trust. Her only duty as a loyal subject was to be scrupulously careful not to be impregnated by the American. She helped him to assuage his curiosity about music, art and the other pursuits of the rich, but after the first year, she became accustomed to the fact that his curiosity wasn't strong enough to lure him far afield. He wouldn't go to London for the theater or even for the food. This was acceptable because it enabled her to move among her equals and let her life proceed unimpeded by the presence of an embarrassingly unacceptable lover.

It wasn't that she was worried that one day he would show up in a terrible necktie and disgrace her before all England. He was without personal preference, and so he would pay the best shops to dress him in the way other people dressed. He was unacceptable only because of who *she* was. The Honourable Meg would have to marry a young man with a name her family had heard of, and she was certain that it wouldn't matter to Michael Schaeffer when she did. He wouldn't expect their relationship to change at all, because as nearly as she could discern, that kind of morality was simply not something that occurred to him. It was something that other creatures had, like the desire to migrate or hibernate or lose their feathers.

2

At the end of the two years, a morning came and Schaeffer opened his eyes to evaluate it. He'd had the window in his bedroom knocked out and replaced with glass bricks before he had allowed himself to sleep in the room. The effect had been to provide him with a view of the quality of the light without the distraction of objects or images. The position of the wall of light was high: a rifle shot would have to come from a helicopter, pierce the translucent glass bricks, and then would hit a lone man standing inside only by chance.

The gray ceiling of clouds that had covered Bath for the past week must have gone, because now the light was gold and blue. He sat up and looked around him. Nothing of the years of working had left him. When his eyes opened he was awake and alert. Without thinking about it, he knew at any moment where the nearest weapon was hidden. It had been a simple matter when he had established himself in the house to present himself as a gun collector. He had bought a collection intact at an estate sale: handmade Purdey shotguns, engraved presentation revolvers, the worn .455 Webley pistol that the former owner had carried in the trenches at Verdun, even a delicate set of dueling pistols that looked as though they would crack into fragments if they were fired. Thereafter he had been able to add a few more modern and functional weapons without alarming the housekeeper or her husband. The precautions he had taken had never been elaborate or inconvenient; they were simply the normal, sensible things he had been doing since the days when he had started working.

He remembered that Eddie Mastrewski would not sleep in a bed when he was working: he would rent a room, move the mattress to the floor and sleep there with a pistol beside him.

Once he and Eddie had taken a motel room and slept in the car, and that night Eddie had been right. At three in the morning two men carrying shotguns had burst into the room. Until Eddie had started the car he could hear the two of them in the dark room blowing hole after hole in the twin beds—a blast, then a metallic slide and click, then another blast. Even as they pulled away, he could still hear the firing and see the muzzle flashes through the open doorway, lighting the walls and leaving a bright orange afterimage floating behind his eyes.

As Schaeffer stepped onto the floor he heard a quiet clicking sound, and realized that someone was trying to turn the handle on the bedroom door. He walked toward it and listened.

"Oh, damn." It was the voice of The Honourable Meg. Then there was a small thump on the door. It was a steel fire door that he had bought from a restaurant-supply warehouse in London, so the sound of her fist on it carried no resonance. "Ouch. Damn it, Michael. I know you're in there. Mrs. Satterthwaite said so. Get up and open this door."

"Just a minute," he called. It was only at times like this, when he had been asleep and had wandered in the places that dreams constructed for him, that the name still sounded strange to him. He put on his bathrobe and moved to the side of the door. There was no telling who she might bring: members of the entourage of overbred young aristocrats she swept along with her, or the regimental band of the Thirty-Eleventh Welsh Borderers in full battle regalia. He opened the door and saw that she was alone. She wore a wide picture hat and a thin, sleeveless dress of yellow cotton. She had calculated today's costume as striking, the bold and direct look of the big-eyed young girls in nineteenth-century paintings who had such oddly curly hair. Was that Turner? No, he was the one where the sky looked as if a nuclear war were being fought somewhere in the suburbs. It was somebody else. As soon as he opened the door, she snatched the hat off her head and marched into the room, already talking.

"There's not much time, so you'll have to be quick about it. This place is ridiculous. You know that, don't you? Of course you do, but you don't care at all. It was a perfectly decent old house, and you've made it look as though Hitler had escaped and built a bunker in Arizona, then went even madder and moved it intact to Bath. How can anyone be expected to surprise you?"

"I don't like surprises. I like sleep."

She looked at him slyly. "It's because you wake up with an erection, isn't it?"

"I beg your pardon?"

"It is. Don't deny it. You're afraid Mrs. Satterthwaite will walk in and set a tea tray on it and you'll be discovered. Hurry up, now. Your secret is safe with me."

"Hurry up with what?"

"We're going to Brighton for the races, and the horses are only going to wait so long for the likes of you."

Schaeffer had only a vague notion of the whereabouts of Brighton. It was near the sea somewhere in the southeast. "Isn't that a little far?"

"No problem. Jimmy Pinchasen has offered to take us all in his Bentley, and he drives as though he'd signed a suicide pact. His family was really named Pinchausen, but they changed it when they came here with George the First because he was German too, so Jimmy has a genetic desire to drive the way they do on the autobahn."

He sat back down on the bed. "I don't think so."

"If you don't believe me, then ask him."

"I mean the other races." He thought for a moment. "I'm not much of a gambler." It was true. He never gambled, and yet he'd had terrible luck at it. After he had done his last job, he had gone to Las Vegas to collect. They had sent him to a casino to pretend to play blackjack, and he remembered the sight of the dealer's perfect, paraffin-white fingers making face cards appear from the shoe in front of him. The dealer had been a mechanic they had brought in just to pay him with chips, so that he would go out into the darkness loaded down with money, his senses dulled by the warm, fat, stupid feeling that winners had.

"We'll talk about that in a few minutes, when you're finished and can be expected to think clearly."

"Finished with what?"

She tossed her hat and purse on the nearest chair. "With me, silly. I'm wearing only the kind of undergarments that the worst sort of woman wears to inflame the jaded desires of men like you. See?" She lifted her skirt, and showed him that she was wearing only a garter belt and stockings, then dropped the skirt again.

He looked up into her eyes, but the flash of white thigh was fresh in his memory. "Well, you've got my attention."

"Come on, Michael. I sincerely hope this pleases you, because I've been thinking about it ever since I woke up this morn-

ing, and walking over here feeling secretly naked, and—well,
it's gotten me into rather a state. So, if you don't mind, I'd just
as soon forgo some of the preliminaries I'm entitled to in favor
of immediate gratification.'' She looked down at his bathrobe,
which was beginning to slip open. "Thank God," she said. "So
would you."

Lying on the bed, he stared up at the glass-brick window. The
sun was higher now, and there were squares that looked like
small golden containers of sunlight. The Honourable Meg was
in front of the mirror, slipping the yellow dress over her head.
"Look sharp, old fellow," she said. "They'll be waiting for
us."

"I thought you said we'd talk about it."

"Of course we will, while you're getting ready. If you like,
we can talk about it all the way to Brighton." She glanced at
him, then shook her head. "I agreed to go because I know you
have only two emotions: curiosity and lack of curiosity. I thought
you'd be curious about horses."

He stared at the ceiling. It wasn't as though he were about to
walk into one of the gambling clubs in London with a beautiful
woman on his arm and two or three loud, half-drunk young
Englishmen drawing attention to themselves. Brighton probably
wasn't the sort of place he had to be wary of. And he'd seen
Pinchasen's Bentley. It looked quiet and conservative, almost
absurdly so, with slightly tinted windows in the back seat. He
could tell from the wall of light that the sun already had warmed
the earth and dried the dew on the grass. He sat up, walked to
the bathroom and turned on the shower. Like everything else
in the house that was intended to perform a function, he'd had
it installed. It had Swiss fixtures and Italian tiles and French
porcelain, and looked as though it had been assembled in a co-
op in Manhattan. As soon as he felt the hot water on his skin,
he admitted that he already had a high opinion of the day. The
decision was behind him; he was going to please Meg. After
ten years the surviving capos in the United States wouldn't be
thinking about doing each other favors by spotting people like
him in remote places. Instead they would be worrying about
some DA hauling in their children's baby-sitters as witnesses to
convict them of conspiracy. He could afford to relax a little.

"Do you go back to the States often?" Peter Filching asked it
as though he were stating a fond wish. They could feel the car

accelerating relentlessly as the long straight stretch of road seemed to be getting used up.

"No," Schaeffer answered, then sensed that he needed to elaborate or become the subject of conversation at a future dinner, where an American who was dull-witted and reticent wouldn't be particularly surprising, so that Peter would have to add entertaining details. He glanced at the windshield and felt the same sensation he often felt in airplanes: would the vehicle lift up in time, or hurtle into the woods at the end of the runway? "Years ago, there was an advertising campaign built around the slogan 'See America First.' So I did. I'd planned to see the rest of the world second, but now Jimmy's driving, and I'm glad I didn't pay for any tickets in advance."

Jimmy Pinchasen's pointed jaw dropped and he bared his long white teeth to bray, "Haw." There was a moment of pronounced deceleration as the big sedan drifted into the turn at the end of the road, and all the passengers braced themselves to keep from sliding into one another.

"Too bad," said Peter Filching as he shrugged to elbow his way off the door, where the centrifugal force had plastered him. "I've heard you can now pick up bargains there on certain things that used to be expensive."

Meg let out a groan. "Michael doesn't want to buy you cocaine, Peter." She squeezed his arm. "It's passé in America now anyway."

"Is it?" Peter's jaw tightened. If he hadn't been forced into exile in a place like Bath for the past two years, he would know these things. But the disasters he had suffered at the hands of the Frenchwoman he had met in Cap Ferrat had been impossible to hide from his father. In a year he had exhausted the careful husbandry of generations of Filchings who had made themselves blind fiddling over ledgers in the East India Company headquarters in Calcutta and then had patiently awaited the rewards of compound interest in the family stronghold outside Bath. And that was the worst of his luck, to be born in a place that had glittered with celebrity and social lightning a hundred and fifty years ago.

Jimmy Pinchasen executed a sedate approximation of a power shift to bring the old Bentley out of the turn. The beautifully meshed gears survived the experiment and the car rumbled to reach its former cruising speed, and soon there were hedgerows slipping past the window again in an exciting blur of green.

Jimmy glanced in the mirror to catch a glimpse of Meg and

her middle-aged American in the back seat. The Honourable Margaret Holroyd certainly wasn't interested in the man's money, if he had any. The thought intruded on Jimmy's complacent consciousness that perhaps the fellow was some kind of sexual athlete. Those fellows—Indian mystics and Jamaican ska singers and South American Marxist poets—all seemed to flock to the south of England to debauch high-born young Englishwomen. It seemed as though every few weeks he was hearing that the daughter of the Twelfth Earl of Something was temporarily not being invited to things because she was having it on with a Masai warrior with great beaded gewgaws hanging from his ears. Jimmy glanced in the mirror again. This time he slouched to the left so that he could see himself in the foreground. He studied his beloved and familiar head, the shape of the nose and chin and the complicated molding of the noble brow, and above it the thin blond hair. When it was time for marriage, they would have to come to men like him, the Last Englishman on Earth.

Jimmy was distracted when they all felt the subtle change in the air and the sudden drop in temperature signifying that the ocean was near. "Are we there?" asked Schaeffer.

"No," said The Honourable Meg. "This is just Southampton. Now we hurtle along the M27, then careen onto the A27 to Brighton. By the time we get there you'll feel as though you'd ridden a horse yourself."

"Are you a horseman, Michael?" Peter Filching's voice carried some dim hope.

Schaeffer didn't like to remember the horse. He had been trapped in the barn at Carlo Balacontano's house outside Saratoga. He had found himself beside a huge beast, all taut muscles, distrust and outrage because a smaller, two-legged animal had slipped into its stall. The big white eyes had rolled in their sockets, and the long face had swung around, the nostrils frantically twitching and sucking in deep breaths as it prepared to hammer him against the wall of the stall with its iron-clad hooves. He had opened the gate, clambered onto the big animal's back, cut the rope and clung to it as it shot out of the warm building and across the pasture over the thin blanket of snow, then flew over a fence. The pair of them had been combined into a single mass of terror and energy, his own fear of being shot by Bala's soldiers merging with the beast's fear of everything and everybody, and his fear of being thrown to the frozen ground from this height and speed working to spur the horse's fear that it couldn't run fast enough to free itself of the vile creature clutching its back and mane. Then, unaccountably, the horse had come to a stop at the second fence, some dim and cloudy memory reminding it that on the other side was the road, which it feared more than the night, the cold or the intruder on its back. He had slid off and muttered, "Thanks for the ride, you big, stupid bastard," and slipped through the fence into the darkness while Bala's men were still fishtailing their big Cadillacs down the icy driveway to intercept his nonexistent car on the road. Months later, when he was already in England, he had read that one of Carl Bala's horses had won a big race in Florida. He had always thought it might be this one. It had been granted brief fame not because it won the race but because by then it was the property of the Internal Revenue Service. They had attached Bala's visible assets during the murder trial, but by then it had been too late for even the IRS to reclaim the entry fee, so they'd had to let the horse run.

"Not me," Schaeffer said. "I haven't been on a horse since the pony rides when I was a kid. How about you?"

The car sped along the highway, floating past other vehicles as though they were laboring against a thicker medium, like water. "We don't keep horses anymore," said Peter regretfully.

The conversation became intermittent and tentative, as conversations involving Michael Schaeffer often were. There were always questions that required answers about his life before Bath, or that might reveal something about his education, income or past acquaintances. Schaeffer was quick and responsive, but his mind always seemed to be full of observations about the present. He never introduced the past except as a way of prompting someone to talk and thus divert attention away from Michael Schaeffer.

Meg sidled into the void as they reached the outskirts of Brighton. "Michael needs a Baedeker tour. He's never been to Brighton before." The two men in the front seat were silent. "All right, then," she said. "I'll do my best."

They cruised slowly past the Royal Pavilion. Its vaguely Arabic spires and domes made Schaeffer think of Disneyland, but Meg supplied the commentary. "The Prince Regent built this as a playhouse where he could get away from it all."

"Which prince?" asked Michael. He had accepted his responsibility to feign interest.

"Later he was George the Fourth. But all his friends built houses here too, and that was the start of the carnival mess you see around you. What you can't see is in the palace—the reason why Peter and I have always been so close, like brother and sister, almost.''

''We have?'' said Peter Filching. ''I wasn't aware.''

''You know. The mock Oriental bed in the red bedroom.'' To Michael she said, ''Most of the place was refurnished in Regency furniture from the Royal Collection. But that bed was bought by the National Trust from my father only ten years ago. It used to be in the family digs in Yorkshire, but it was moved to Bath during some massive housecleaning a couple of generations ago. I was conceived on it, and I've always suspected Peter was, too. My father probably felt guilty . . .''

''Nonsense,'' Peter protested.

Jimmy Pinchasen coughed and cleared his throat. ''I think I'll drive up and let you two out right at the track. Peter and I will put the Bentley where they won't crash a lorry full of horse fodder into it, and then catch up.'' He pulled the big car over into a crowd of pedestrians, letting them grab each other and sidestep to avoid the gleaming machine's inexorable progress into their midst. Once out of danger, they glared into the dark windows impotently.

''That won't be necessary,'' said Meg. ''I'm a very good walker and I wore sensible shoes.''

''I insist,'' said Jimmy. He glanced at the silent Filching. ''I really do.''

Meg opened the door and stepped out onto the grass. ''Come on, Michael. We'll go tell the horses what we want them to do.''

Schaeffer got out of the car and stood beside her as the vehicle resumed its deadly progress through the crowd. ''Your story offended him.''

''Peter? Don't worry. As soon as he's served his time as the Monk of Bath and his father frees his trust fund, he'll return to Babylon and tell the story himself, after altering it to his taste. I've always done this to him.''

''I wonder if anyone will believe it.''

''He doesn't have the conviction I have, but they might,'' she said. He noticed that she was assessing him as though she were trying to decide how far she could push him. ''I taught him to lie when we were children, just in case I wanted him later as a lover.''

Beside the grandstand, several small wooden structures had been erected that were not much more than desks with awnings. They looked as though they had been clapped together in haste, but the apparent age of the wood argued that they had been assembled on the grass for the races and carted off each season for generations. The awning over one of them bore a printed sign that read B. BALDWIN, TURF ACCOUNTANT. When the Bentley had knifed its way into the crowd, Mr. Baldwin had grinned and displayed the peculiar arrangement of his teeth, which were straight and even, but had small, regular spaces between them as though they had once belonged to a much smaller person. In fact, they had: Mr. Baldwin, a man in his forties whose face had already acquired a permanent, wizened squint, still had his baby teeth. The others had never grown in to displace them, and when he'd had his jaw X-rayed, he had learned that he was the victim of a minor genetic disorder. One theory expressed by the scientific minds around the betting circuit was that he was so greedy he couldn't bear to give up anything he had. But another theory that gained more popular credence was that Baldwin was like a shark, growing row after row of sharp little teeth, each row moving forward to replace the last as he wore them out on the victims of his voracity.

Baldwin's grin caused the two men with him to follow his gaze to see what was causing the commotion. They saw the beautiful girl get out of the Bentley and listened to Baldwin's appraisal: "I'd give five hundred pounds."

"For one of her earrings," said Mack Talarese. "That's a Rolls she just got out of." His name was Mario, but nobody called him that anymore except his relatives. One of them was his uncle, Tony Talarese, whom he called Uncle Antonio with the greatest humility and a hint of gratitude. Uncle Antonio lived in New Jersey, but he had managed to get young Mario a chance to make his bones as a soldier for the Carpaccio brothers, two entrepreneurs who were trying to establish a business in England. Someday, Uncle Antonio hoped, his nephew would wear Savile Row suits and carry a briefcase into a two-hundred-year-old building, where he would manipulate the computers and fax machines Antonio thought of as the instruments of power, buying and selling and controlling the immense flow of cash that would be coming from America. The money would be translated into investments of incalculable value and unassailable strength. But first Mario would need a few years to make himself into the man who could do it. He needed the experience that would make him different from the other men in tailor-made suits in the old, gleaming offices. He had to know without faltering what he would do when a man tried to avoid him on the day his loan was due, what he would do when one of his hookers withheld a portion of her earnings, what he would do when a rival appeared to be surpassing him. He had to know that when the time came he would not hesitate to act with force and certainty. He had to know where all that money came from.

Now Mario saw something that struck him as the greatest good luck. The man who had emerged from the Rolls-Royce looked familiar. Mario couldn't remember his name, but at home they would sure as hell remember. He was the hired specialist who had gone crazy years ago and whacked all those guys. He had killed even Mr. Castiglione, who must have been eighty at the time, living like a withered emperor in a fortress on a manmade oasis outside Las Vegas. Mario considered how to use his good luck. He could call his uncle Antonio on the telephone and tell him what he had seen. But then his uncle would be the one who would get the credit; he would put a couple of men on a plane. If Mario could just handle this himself, take a careful grasp of the good luck so that it wouldn't slip through his fingers, he could take years off his apprenticeship. Somebody would hear about it and elevate him to a place of respect that was rare for a man of his years, and free him from dependence on the meager patronage of his conservative uncle.

Mario took inventory of the assets at his command. There was Lucchi, the young Sicilian who was making the rounds with him. Lucchi had been a waiter in a small, dirty London restaurant that the Carpaccio brothers owned. They had brought him here from Sicily and given him a job to pay off some debt they owed someone through the complex and prehistoric accounting system they carried in their heads. Lucchi still dressed like a waiter in tight black pants and loose, bloused white shirts with ancient stains on them, and he walked like a woman.

But Mack also had Bert Baldwin. "See the guy with her?" asked Mack. "He's somebody we want." When he had said it, he felt a wave wash over him; it was as though he could feel a huge infusion of heat pump into his blood. What if he were wrong? He had seen him only once, by chance, and he had been a kid then.

"What do you mean, you want him?" asked B. Baldwin. "Does he owe you money?"

Mack gritted his teeth in fierce urgency. "He's a psycho, so we have to be careful. And I think he had two guys with him in the Rolls."

B. Baldwin squinted at him. After a moment he was satisfied

that he understood, and thought he might be able to wrest something significant out of this. After all, he had been the one who had pointed the victim out, or at least seen the bird, and that was the same thing, wasn't it? "Well, good luck to you. I've got a lot to do before the first race if I'm going to pay you after the last one."

Mack clutched his arm. "This is bigger than that. It's bigger than a hundred damned races. If we get him I'll pay the Carpaccios myself." When he saw Baldwin's sawtoothed smile, the wave washed over him again. He remembered that he had no idea how much Baldwin actually owed the Carpaccio brothers. The two Sicilians kept everything in their heads and told him how much he and Lucchi were supposed to collect from each of their fish. They didn't even let him carry it. Lucchi was supposed to deliver it, and they talked to him in rapid, low-voiced Italian that only a native-born Sicilian could understand. He still didn't know if he was in charge and Lucchi was his bagman, or if Lucchi was in charge and he was sent along only because Lucchi's English was so bad. But it didn't matter now because he was going to make his bones on the Butcher's Boy.

Baldwin winked and nodded to a man in the crowd Mack recognized as a pickpocket. The man sauntered over to the booth, and while Baldwin handed him his stack of betting slips, Mario turned to Lucchi and searched his memory for the Italian words. "It's a question of honor. This man has acted like an animal." In fact, Mario had only a vague idea of what the Butcher's Boy had done, except that he had somehow managed to kill a large number of men and at the same time get Carlo Balacontano convicted of one of the murders, and Bala was still serving a life sentence for it and sending embarrassingly inflammatory reminders through channels to the outside. Mario watched Lucchi's face as he exhausted his vocabulary. "He violated hospitality, threw loyalty out the window and made my uncle ashamed."

Lucchi's eyes flickered in a faint reaction. Mack hoped that something in his stammered litany had meant something. "Si," said Lucchi quietly. The Carpaccio brothers had not brought Lucchi to England to save him from the endemic poverty of Sicily, but from a sudden manhunt launched by the national police in Rome. When he had killed the banker Giovanni Parla in his bathtub it had been to expunge an insult Parla's grandfather had committed against Lucchi's grandmother before Lucchi's father was born. And since Lucchi's father had died attaching

an oversensitive pipe bomb to a Parla's automobile, Lucchi had
not felt he could honorably stop there. After he had left Parla
bleeding to death in the bathroom, he had gone to the other
rooms of the house and killed the wife and two children. Now
he said in English, "How do you want it done?"

3

Meg pulled Schaeffer into the stands and sat him down in the center near the bottom. "Okay, Michael. Let's appraise these horses. My system is to ascertain which are the tallest, and then place large wagers that they'll win."

Schaeffer stared out at the broad green lawn. There were a few horses being exercised on the track, which was little more than a white railing cordoning off a portion of the expanse of grass that stretched from the road to the hills where buildings began. It wasn't like American tracks, which were almost like freeways for horses, bordered by huge concrete structures for crowds of bettors, electronic tally boards and the subterranean bunkers where money was pushed through windows and machines pumped out tickets. He liked it. Things in England always seemed to him faintly amateurish. "I wonder what's keeping the others."

"Jimmy's always been like that about parking. He cares about machinery. Have I ever told you that's something I like about you? You don't care at all about machines."

"Are you sure you haven't offended Peter?"

"Positive." She turned to him and gave him her most enigmatic smile. It looked so open and guileless that he knew it was a practiced artifice. "When we were young, he talked me into taking off my clothes—one garment at a time, of course. He took Polaroid pictures of me. I could see that I was beautiful from the first ones, and I got rather caught up in the whole thing, mainly from the pleasant surprise and narcissistic curiosity. So I kept unbuttoning things further, and letting the cloth slip lower to reveal a little more. When there was nothing left to take off, I found I wanted to see myself from angles I hadn't seen. Peter still has the pictures, I'm sure. I was just reminding him that I remember too."

"Why do you tell these stories?" Schaeffer asked.

"Because it should have happened," she answered. "Or *something* should have. Something shameful and scandalous. In fact, we were a sad, gangling lot with running noses who were lonely and bored and cold most of the time, but were afraid to speak to each other. It would have been nice if something had happened, and if I tell it that way it will make it seem true. Who does it hurt?"

"No one. I'm going to find them."

"What on earth for?"

"So when we want to go home they'll allow us in the car."

He stepped carefully down the wooden bleachers, then made his way through the people on the ground. As he had since he was young, he avoided looking straight into their eyes when he moved past them, always looking at the place where he would be after a few steps. In the street he turned in the direction Jimmy had taken when he had let them out of the Bentley. A small feeling of discomfort lodged in his throat as he scanned the straggling trail of men and women strolling toward the track. In the years since he had gotten off the airplane at Heathrow carrying a passport in the name of "Charles F. Ackerman," he had come to depend on an orderly sequence of events that could have passed for a sense of decorum and conformity. He had an instinctive dislike of walking toward a large herd of people, presenting his face for each of them to notice and wonder about.

When at last he saw the Bentley, it was parked at the curb under an ancient walnut tree. Already, the black skins of nuts had specked the mirror finish, and a couple of leaves were plastered on the windshield. Jimmy Pinchasen was an idiot. If the car was so important to him, he should at least have parked it in the open. He walked to the car, stopped and looked around him. If they had come this far, why hadn't he passed them on the way? He squinted to see through the smoked glass, and froze.

He could dimly see Pinchasen and Filching inside the car. Pinchasen was lying on his side in the front seat, as though he had simply toppled over. Filching was lying facedown in the back seat, and his pant legs had ridden up to his calves. Someone had dragged him by the ankles to his present position. From the quantities of blood that had seeped into pools on the leather seats and the floor, he judged that their throats had been cut.

He straightened, looked to the right up the street and to the left down the street to see that no cars were coming, then started across. The steady stream of people kept coming, a little faster because the races were about to begin, and now he looked at them differently, staring into their eyes, searching for a sign of recognition. All his old habits came back automatically. At a glance he assessed their posture and hands. Was there a man whose fingers curled in a little tremor when their eyes met, a woman whose hand moved to rest inside her handbag? He knew all the practical moves and involuntary gestures, and he scanned everyone, granting no exemptions.

He and Eddie had done a job like this one when he was no more than twelve. Eddie had dressed him for baseball, and had even bought him a new glove to carry folded under his arm. When they had come upon the man in the crowd, he hadn't even seen them; his eyes were too occupied in studying the crowd for danger to waste a moment on a little kid and his father walking home from a sandlot game. As they passed the man, Eddie had touched the boy's arm, and he had opened the webbing of the glove so that Eddie could pluck out the pistol with the silencer attached to it. Eddie then turned and put a round behind the man's ear. He remembered the man taking another step and then toppling forward to the sidewalk. As Eddie hustled him away, he had heard people saying something about heart attacks and strokes. Bystanders had made way for them, apparently feeling sorry that Eddie's little boy had seen some stranger at the moment when a vessel in his brain exploded.

Schaeffer felt his pulse beginning to settle down now. In the first glance into the parked car, he had known it all as though he had seen it happen. His mind hadn't raced through a series of steps, or shuffled through the possible implications of the sight to his own survival. In an instant he had been jerked back ten years to the old life: somebody had spotted him. They never forgot, and they never stopped looking.

Mack Talarese leaned his back against the side of the curio shop and tried to catch his breath. He looked at Lucchi with horrified awe. The little waiter had turned out to be something else, and Mario was not entirely comforted by what he had seen. Mario and Baldwin had come up on the driver and the bodyguard from the front of the car as the driver eased the big Rolls into the curb. Mario had formulated a notion of taking the two of them somewhere and shooting them. But then Lucchi came up on the right side of the car behind the driver, and his right hand appeared from behind his thigh, and there was a gravity knife already open, and the hand went inside the open window, and when Lucchi drew it back it was bloody. Then Lucchi had the back door open and was inside the car doing the other one. The man had managed to clamber into the back seat and unlatch the door, but Lucchi was already on him. He was already dead when Lucchi grasped his ankles and hauled him back inside.

Then the little Sicilian walked casually ahead of Mario and Baldwin back toward the racetrack. But Talarese had caught the look on Lucchi's face as their eyes met. When Mario was a child on Long Island, his dog had caught the scent of a rabbit in the field and run off after it, interpreting Mario's calls as some kind of exhortation to greater speed. Then the dog had brought the broken, limp thing back with him in his mouth, his eyes looking proud and hopeful, returning for the approval he knew he had earned. Lucchi's eyes had looked like that.

Baldwin leaned close to Mario as they followed Lucchi. "Ferocious little bastard, isn't he?" Talarese nodded. Lucchi was dangerous. He was something Mario had never anticipated, a throwback, a Sicilian like the ones who had gotten off the boat at Ellis Island before the First World War, lean, cunning, ambitious and utterly without compunction or reluctance.

Mario decided to let the implications of his discovery wait until the day was over. He was operating on his own already. The Carpaccio brothers would have no idea who the man was. When it was over Mario would be the only one in a position to take advantage of the accomplishment, and he would be transported to the United States and raised to the heights appropriate to young men who had initiative and decisiveness. Lucchi would be a fond memory.

"Come on," Mario said. "Now that he can't leave, he's ours." He walked out from the side of the shop onto the street, and he could hear the others' footsteps following. He didn't look back. He concentrated only on moving through the crowds of people toward the racecourse, where the Butcher's Boy—Jesus, that was the best part; he must be forty by now—would be sitting in the grandstand with his girlfriend, never suspecting that the forces he had set in motion years ago had already stripped him of his soldiers and cut off his only means of escape. It was like that Shakespeare play they made everybody read in tenth grade. The bastard felt like a king, sitting there in the sunshine with a woman who wore the kind of jewelry a queen might have. Well, today was the day that Birnam Wood was coming to Dunsinane. The trees were closing in on the bastard. Mario smiled, and felt an impulse to say something about it to the others, but of course it would have been pointless. Baldwin was English but probably hadn't made it to the tenth grade, and Lucchi wouldn't even know who Shakespeare was.

Margaret Holroyd was fighting disappointment. She looked out across the field to where the beautiful horses were being steadied and reassured by jockeys and trainers. They were festooned with silks in gorgeous, gaudy colors, and the jockeys wore oddly clashing combinations, probably cut from the same ten bolts. They were so far away that she could see very little except the tiny spots of emerald, pink, crimson and gold. What in the world was she going to do without Michael? He had been gone for only ten minutes, and already she missed him and was feeling angry with him. She couldn't go on playing with him much longer. Soon she would begin to get little wrinkles at the corners of her eyes like Aunt Caroline, and then she would have to be responsible and act as though she'd never had a time like this in her life.

There already was no doubt that she could change, and this was a sign too. Not so long ago, she wouldn't have believed she could; people would have recognized the hypocrisy immediately and laughed about it. But now she was perfectly competent to carry it off. What a shame. If she had been at home now, she decided, she would have spent the afternoon in the big leather chair by the library window, wallowing in poetry, probably *Ubi sunt* poems: "Où sont les neiges d'antan?" And she would have let the bright afternoon sun deepen to amber, then darker and darker shades of blue, as the light slowly dimmed the page and finally left her in darkness, a little rehearsal for getting old and dying. No, she wouldn't, she admitted; it was a lie. She stood up and stepped quickly and recklessly down the steps to the grass. It felt good on her open toes, a little damp and tickly, and there was Michael already.

He was striding quickly toward her, as though he wanted to head her off and say something before she wandered away to the loo or the betting booths. Well, fine, she thought. She was perfectly willing to be distracted from whatever she would have found to pass the time. When he reached her, he didn't stop walking, just took her arm and swept her along. She kept up with him, conducted smoothly by a gentle pressure that changed directions subtly, telling her where to go. "I was getting bored," she said.

His face was empty, and he was looking ahead as they walked. "Don't talk, just listen. We've got to get out of here right now. Some people are here to kill us." He looked at her for a second. It sounded impersonal, as though he had overheard a weather report.

"What is it?" she whispered. "The IRA?"

Schaeffer didn't understand the question at first. Even after all the years in England, the whole endless, bitter struggle had remained as remote to him as the wars in Lebanon or Mozambique or El Salvador. People had talked at dinners about The Irish Question and he had only been puzzled by what they thought the question was. "No," he said after a moment. She certainly would know more about it than he did. "It's my problem, but I'm sure they've seen you."

"Are you trying to make me feel silly because I told you stories?"

"No," he said. There was no change in his expression. He was still staring at the people they passed. In spite of her resolve not to be duped, she began to feel afraid. It was impossible, she told herself. Here they were, walking along in the middle of a huge gathering of perfectly respectable people on a sunny afternoon in Brighton. Working women and clerks in London shops loaded their children onto the train and took them here to toss pebbles into the sea and eat the dreadful candy.

But then she made the mistake of reaching to gather more evidence to bolster her cause, and thought about Michael Schaeffer. She knew nothing about him except what he had said. A cold feeling settled in her stomach. She had somehow gone too far, foolishly strayed across some invisible line, and now she was on the other side of it wishing she could scramble back. But she was already too far away, sinking with this man into some horror. She felt small and weak, and the world was sharp-edged and full of eyes watching her.

When Michael led her around the stands and up the road toward the city, she had a moment of relief. "Are Peter and Jimmy bringing the car?"

"They're dead," he answered.

It hit her senses like a loud, sharp noise, and she felt herself fall another step downward into the horror, as though her foot had slipped on a ladder, before she stopped herself. When she did, she was surprised by her thought: Well, I'm alive. What it meant she didn't know, but it reassured her in some simple-minded way. After a moment, she realized it had been a question, and since nobody had contradicted her, she began to feel stronger.

They walked along the road until they came to a row of curio shops. There were five of them, and the windows seemed to contain crowded troves of identical china souvenirs, postcards and embroidered placemats, all having to do with the seashore at Brighton. When Michael didn't go inside the first shop or the second, it occurred to her that whatever was after them was too big for that: it wouldn't wait, foiled by the simple ploy of hiding in a shop while they ordered a taxi on the proprietor's telephone. It would roll over them like a tide, not delayed at all by the fear that the old ladies buying china would see it. The thought crossed her mind that Michael was being pursued by the police. But he had said, "Some people are here to kill us," and the Brighton police didn't do that; they lived in the same world she did. They tipped their hats and gave people directions. When the bomb had gone off in Mrs. Thatcher's hotel, they had expressed the same surprise and distress that Margaret had felt. They didn't think in those terms either.

Michael led her down a long passage between the second and third shops. The buildings were so tall and close, she could feel that the sunlight never fell here. The air was cool and damp and dark, and the stone foundations had a tracing of deep green moss up to where the clapboards began. At the end of the passage, Michael stopped. He put his hand on her shoulder, and she felt affection for him, but then he surprised her by grasping the shoulder strap of her purse and slipping it off.

He stepped forward into the sunlight, and she saw the white flash. It was a man's arm, and it had a white sleeve on it, and the hand was in a fist. It punched at Michael, fast and hard, like a piston, but Michael had somehow known it was going to do that. He clutched her purse in both hands and caught the punch on it. Then it was all too fast. He had already wrapped the shoulder strap around the white arm, and now he tugged with all his strength.

She saw the man dragged across the entrance of the passage. He was thin and dark, and his hand was still in a fist, but somehow stuck on her purse. There was a strange, alert look on his face as he passed, and for that instant his eyes seemed to stare down the passage at her. She heard three distinct noises, hollow and sharp, like a croquet mallet hitting a ball. Then she heard a scraping sound, as though something were being dragged on the ground along the back of the next shop.

Michael reappeared. Now he was sweating and his hair was hanging in his eyes. He had her purse, and he jerked a knife out of the side of it and hung it on her shoulder. He swept his hair back with his hand. She looked at his face, but there was no expression she could identify as fear or remorse or disgust, which amazed her because she could still hear the three cracks and knew that they had been the sound a man's head made when it was broken on concrete. Michael was already thinking about something ahead of them in time or space, like a cricket batsman anticipating where the bowler was going to throw the ball.

She turned and took a step back toward the other end of the passage. She was ready to run now, her heart pounding in her chest. They would have to get out of this dark place, and she was willing to keep up with him by running as fast or as hard as he wanted her to. But his hand shot out and held her arm. She looked into his eyes, but they weren't looking at her. He only shook his head and pushed her back against the wall. Then she could tell it was too late. She could hear the footsteps of a man running, and Michael was tensing his muscles, his knees bent a little, one foot ahead of the other, and his arms out from his sides.

Mario stopped running when he saw the legs protruding from the space between the third and fourth stores. Lucchi had done it. The little bastard had stalked the man behind the buildings and cut another throat, and this was the one that counted. Mario was going to be rich. He was going home. He fought an impulse to turn and go back to the street. This was the time when he would have to control himself, if he never had to again. He looked around for Lucchi and felt a little tingle of annoyance. The nasty little faggot could be anywhere. Then Mario remembered the girl. Something occurred to him and he began to sweat. There was no question that Lucchi had gone off after the girl. But what if he was that kind of psycho too? He might be doing something to her, something that Mario didn't want to think about. He decided that the revulsion was something else he would have to control. These few minutes were the ones that were going to make all the difference for the rest of his life. Nobody back home was going to take his word that he had done this. He had to have something to carry away from here that proved he had found the Butcher's Boy and killed him. He didn't have much time.

He walked toward the body. As he passed the opening between the first two stores, then the next one, he turned his face away and moved faster. If people passing on the street happened to see him, they saw nothing. He controlled the impulse to go back to the front of the stores and look for Baldwin on the street.

Now he was close enough to see the legs clearly. His mind took inventory: black, shiny shoes; black, tight pants—Lucchi! Then he heard a footstep behind him. He reached inside his coat for the pistol, but then abandoned the intention because an arm was already around his neck. In the instant before consciousness left him, he felt a sharp pain move up under his ribs toward his heart.

B. Baldwin strolled along the sidewalk in front of the shops, using his peripheral vision to peer into them and around them as he went. He had seen the little dago go around the corner to check behind them, and he calculated that Mack T. would be covering any spillover onto the side street.

When he had come to the racecourse today he had been in a foul humor. He had known that they would show up before the sixth race to see how much cash he had taken in before he could chance handing it off. The life of a debtor was something he wasn't accustomed to, and he hated it. To owe money was to place everything at someone else's disposal, from your betting booth to your spectacles. But to owe money to the Carpaccios was to sell yourself into slavery. You couldn't decide to take a day off and go to London instead of working the football outings, because that night they would send someone to pick up the rake-off. Until they had their money, you were theirs.

But Baldwin's mood had brightened considerably since then. Young Mackie T. had spoken without asking for the numbers. B. Baldwin was going to be his own man again, a man with a debt of eight thousand pounds that was about to vanish.

Baldwin kept his hand in his coat pocket as he walked, running his fingers along the big sailor's clasp knife that he carried there. He had bought it years ago in a pawnshop in Southampton and had it sharpened like a razor, and then spent hours taking the tarnish off the blade with jeweler's rouge. It shone like a sliver of mirror now. A man who used his knife would have tried to darken the blade, but Baldwin didn't worry about an opponent seeing the sudden reflection in his hand. He didn't use his knife. He would just sit facing a man across a table and open it to clean his nails or idly scrape the dirt off the sole of his shoe. He would watch the man's face, and try to catch a bit of sunlight on the blade so that a flash of the reflection would hit his eye. That sort of thing worked with the small shopkeepers and restaurant help who made up his usual clientele.

Baldwin had once thought of himself as a man ready for anything, but time and a few blows with heavy objects had made him calm and helped him to find his natural niche in the hierarchy of the universe. He was a predator, but too small to take in everything he wanted in one bite. Time gave a man's luck a chance to kick in.

He was beginning to wonder if Mackie and the little ferret had simply done their work behind the shops and run off. It wouldn't do for B. Baldwin to be found standing here not fifty yards away with a razor-sharp sailor's knife in his pocket, not with his previous life history. The police would see him as a gift from heaven, and he suspected they wouldn't be above giving his knife a little dip in the gore to make sure the gift wasn't taken away.

He sauntered by the first passageway, then sidestepped into it without missing a step. He moved quietly down the space between the buildings toward the light, feeling a little disappointed in young Mack Talarese. Taking off and leaving a man on the scene was something that just wasn't done. It was probably his own fault for involving himself with foreigners who didn't know any better, but it was going to be the last time, he swore. Unless it was Packies, who were for all practical purposes Englishmen with black faces.

B. Baldwin would just take a quick peek to be sure the bodies were there, then go back to work. When he reached the end of the passage he heard a sound. He knitted his brows and held his place, listening. It wasn't loud enough for a struggle, just a single footfall somewhere in the courtyard behind the shops. Baldwin took his knife out of his pocket and opened it. Could they have walked right past the victim and his woman? Could they still be hiding in the shadows between the next two shops? Well, if, when he stepped into the light, Mackie and the little rat terrier were busy going through the dead woman's purse and taking the diamond studs out of her ears, he would lose nothing by having the great gleaming knife in his hand. It would make them feel he had been one of them, in on it from the beginning and still ready at the end.

Baldwin crouched low and leaped out of the passageway, his eyes taking in the scene at once. There was the man, kneeling over Mack Talarese's bloody corpse where it lay on the ground. His hand was in the coat pocket. The man looked up at Baldwin and his face brought Baldwin very bad news; it showed no fear or anger, and, worst of all, no surprise. The eyes weren't looking at him to size him up as an opponent in a knife fight. They were aiming. The man's hand was on its way up from Mackie Talarese's chest, and there was Mack's little black pistol in it. B. Baldwin noted this with displeasure, but his mind troubled him no longer, because by then the bullet was already bursting through the back of his skull, bringing with it bone fragments, blood and even a tiny bit of the brain tissue that might have cared.

The shot was too much for Margaret. She sprang out into the sunlight in time to see Michael pressing the gun into the hand of the dead man on the ground. The sound had been loud in the passageway, and it still rang in her ears. It seemed to propel her forward, as though it were still sounding behind her.

Michael stood up and took her arm, not slowing her momentum at all, just guiding her in the direction she wanted to go. She was barely aware of him now. She was only thinking about putting space between herself and what lay back there. She wanted to run and he let her, the cloudy sense of the design of the city she carried in her memory taking her across the court-yard to the next passage between two houses, and along a quiet lane away from the ocean and toward the Royal Pavilion. Then he stopped her. "Do you know where the train station is?" She nodded. "Go there."

4

In Alexandria, Virginia, Elizabeth Waring Hart stirred in her sleep and opened her eyes. She waited for the whisper to come out of the darkness again. She lifted her head a little from her pillow so that she could hear with both ears, and stared into the shadows near the door for a shape that she hoped wouldn't remind her of a man. Her muscles were rigid, held in tension more to keep her from moving than because she had any way of fighting or anyplace to run to in her closed second-floor bedroom.

Then she realized that she had already given a name to the voice she had heard, and the name made it impossible that there was a voice. It was Dominic Palermo, and he had been dead for ten years. She collapsed back on the pillow and let him come back, and the room in the Las Vegas hotel came back with him.

When she had awakened that night it was dark, but she'd had the disconcerting feeling that she was already late for something. It was a feeling of urgency: something had begun and she was still in bed. It was then that she had heard the knock on the door, and knew that it had been going on for some time. She turned on the light, but it hadn't helped, and she had put on her bathrobe and slipped the standard-issue .38 police special into its pocket, but that hadn't helped either, because she had been a novice in those days, and the Justice Department had hired and trained her to analyze information that might result in a trial, not to shoot people.

But she had opened the door, thinking somehow with sleepy logic that if people were banging on her door at four-thirty in the morning, it had to be urgent, and nobody she didn't know who had urgent business would bring it to her.

And there he was, standing in the hallway, and that was when she had heard the whisper. He had said, "You're Elizabeth War-

ing,'' and then, ''Please, can I come in?'' This was the sound
that haunted her now. It was the saddest sound in the whole
world, a man saying, ''I'm dying out here. Let me in.''

Now the rest of him came back too: the way he looked, his
dark hair beginning to turn gray, the wide shoulders made less
menacing by the big belly, the big, sad brown eyes protesting
that he didn't deserve this. ''For Christ's sake, look at me,'' he
had said. ''I weigh two-thirty and I'm five-eight. I'm over fifty
years old. For the last twenty years I've cleared over two hundred thousand a year. Do I look like somebody who takes on
wet jobs? Hell, they hired somebody to do that. A specialist.''

Even then, Elizabeth had instinctively understood that what
he had told her was immensely important, already more important than anything else about Dominic Palermo. The specialist
was the one the Justice Department wanted, the one who would
know things. She tried to prompt Palermo. ''But we don't know
what to do about a professional like that. Look at all the assas-
sinations. We can't protect you from that kind of killer unless
we know who he is, or at least what to look for.''

Palermo shook his head solemnly. He said, ''Jesus, you must
think I'm stupid, pulling that on me. The specialist? Shit, him
I'd give you for free if I could. Problem is, I can't. I never saw
him, and I don't even know his name. When they talked about
him, they just called him 'the Butcher's Boy.' ''

She remembered what she had said: ''Nice name.''

''Yeah,'' said Palermo. ''Isn't it?'' He was trying to make it
sound sarcastic: Look at the sort of thing I have to put up with.
But he couldn't carry it off at four-thirty in the morning, still
talking in a whisper because he was afraid.

And that was what she was feeling now. It was Nicky Palermo's fear. He had died of it. Nobody would ever have said it
that way, but it was true. He had gotten scared enough to decide
in the middle of the night to be a witness for the Justice Department, and the only way he could think of to go about it was
to turn himself in to the agent who had been visible serving
papers and taking depositions that week. Only he couldn't know
that the agent had been visible not by accident but by choice and
foresight, because Justice Department thinking at the time was
that the only agent on the case whose anonymity was expendable
was the one who shouldn't have been in the field in the first
place: Elizabeth Waring. And this had killed him; not the man
he was so afraid of, but his own friends, because he had talked
and she couldn't protect him. Nobody would have said it, but

she knew it, and Nicky Palermo knew it, even though he had been dead for ten years now, and was not even a ghost, but an uncomfortable memory.

Elizabeth sat up and turned on the light beside her bed. It was four-thirty again, only now it was Alexandria, Virginia, and Las Vegas was a long time ago. She looked over at Jim's empty side of the bed. It was four-thirty, the coldest, darkest hour out of every twenty-four, and Nicky Palermo was dead, and her husband was dead, and her career was dead. No, her capacity for having or wanting a career was dead. Next week or a year from now, she would be going through it again. There would be a new office that was almost like the last because it was in the same huge building, and new people, some young and eager, and the others quietly and unofficially burned out but carrying too much rank to be randomly reassigned somewhere to fill in for a GS-7. There would be some new special problem the Justice Department thought it could solve with a crack task force—stock fraud or banks or imported flea collars with so much poison in them that they made Rover roll over with convulsions—and Elizabeth Waring would volunteer for anything except Organized Crime.

She listened to the baby monitor beside the bed. Above the static she could hear Amanda breathing the slow, regular breaths of the innocent.

5

As the train added power, slowly clacking out of the station, Margaret sat stiffly, willing it to go faster. She timed her breaths to the precise moments when it passed the poles along the track, and found that she felt smothered, until they were floating past too often to have anything to do with her breathing.

Cautiously she pretended to look out the window, but craned her neck to use the reflection to look at the other people in the car. In the very back were two elderly ladies in flowered dresses who had raised a redoubt of oversized purses and shopping sacks to repel any smokers who might try to sit nearby. They were wisely returning from a morning at the shore early enough to miss the crowds of horse fanciers and gamblers and be in their flats in time for tea. There were three young boys in the front who could be misidentified as representatives of the very element the old ladies intended to avoid; they had hair cropped in peculiar patterns of tufts and lawns like little dogs, and sported clothing of leather and denim held together with metal rivets. But they were well mannered, merely nudging one another at intervals and pointing out landmarks and milestones that were invisible to Meg. She guessed that these must have some significance in their lives, perhaps scenes of early exploits as they had widened their range away from Brighton and closer to London.

"Why are we going to London?" she whispered.

Schaeffer studied her and acknowledged the injustice of it. She looked small and young, her bright green eyes even greener because her pumping heart had brought more oxygen than she had ever breathed into her, and even now something hard and admirable was keeping her from going limp and gray from the shock. She had first approached him out of a sense of adventure, and had stayed involved out of some notion that liveliness was better than torpor, but she hadn't signed on for this. "It's the sensible thing to do," he answered. "Most people leaving town will be going to London, and once we're there, they have to pick us out of millions of people."

"Of course," she said. "I'm not sure that was what I meant to ask you. I was hoping you'd tell all, as they say."

He thought about what had happened. She had come to his house this morning in the full and delighted confidence that she was the wildest creature in the little universe she inhabited. Now the walls had shattered and let real monsters in. "I'm sorry," he said. "I never should have let this happen. You were very brave."

"I'm trying to hold on to my sanity," she said quietly. "Michael, I can't even believe this is happening, has happened—no, it's still happening, isn't it? I'm afraid, and I want to know if I'm just being weak, or if I'm right to be afraid because in a minute they're going to stop the train, drag us off and . . ." She stopped, and he could see her making a conscious effort to beat down the terrors that were spontaneously taking on specific shapes with hard, defined lines. She failed, but he could see she was holding them on one side of a line for the moment. "Or will I always have to be afraid because it's never going to be over?"

Schaeffer searched for something that would make sense to her. "Sometimes in the newspapers you read that somebody in Parliament made a speech demanding that the warmonger Americans get out. Well, I guess I'm one of the ones they mean."

It gave him a morbid fascination to watch her mind grab for this little bit of comprehensible nonsense and clutch it to her. "I should have known it," she said. "I even thought about it, but I told myself there really weren't any such people, or anyway that I'd never see them. CIA. What could you be but one of them? You move into a big old house all by yourself and never talk about anything that could even begin to give anybody an idea of who you are or what you did before."

In her mind's rush to gather evidence to support the lie, she had begun to forget that there were other people on the train. He put his hand on her forearm and moved his eyes toward the three boys at the front of the car. "To answer your question, I think the bad part is over now," he whispered. "We just have to be sure we aren't followed."

"Where are we going? MI5? Your embassy?"

He shook his head. "All of the obvious places will be under surveillance. We're on our own." He tried to remember which it was: "in the cold," or "out of the cold." "We're going to have to stay out in the cold for a while." Then he remembered that he would have to prepare her for the future. "Or I am, anyway."

"One more thing, and I won't ask for any more secrets," she said. "Those men weren't English, except maybe the last one. They looked like Italians. What has Italy got against you?"

He had to block that avenue of thought. "They were Bulgarians. They probably came in from Yugoslavia across the Adriatic into Italy; that's the way they usually do it. They look the same, and lots of them speak the language. It's only a few miles." He was quoting a travel brochure he had seen once: "An hour or so by boat on a calm, sunlit sea." Or was that Coleridge: "Down to a sunless sea"? He had been reading some of the books in the library of his house again, and it sounded familiar. He felt a small prickle of alarm. Books were a trap. If he accidentally quoted from one of them, she would recognize it.

Her face retained its look of intense concentration. "But why were they after us—after you? You were in Brighton only for the day, and even I didn't know we'd be there before this morning."

He looked as puzzled as he could. "That's something I've got to find out. I came to England ten years ago, and since then I've been in the deepest cover. Even the chief of station in London doesn't know. I'd say our troubles must have started in the United States."

"A mole?" she said. "A Bulgarian mole inside the CIA?"

He let his puzzlement turn to frustration. "That's the hard part. There's no telling the nationality in a case like this. The information could have come to the KGB, and they may have passed it on to Bulgarians in this area."

She looked very sad. "Poor Peter and Jimmy. They weren't up to this sort of thing at all."

He stared out the window at the flat green countryside sweeping past, and strained for something to give her, like a present. "I'm going to tell you something that's absolutely secret. Very few people even inside the Western intelligence community have heard it, and I'm not cleared by your government to be one of them. There's a special room inside a building near Whitehall. It's a big room in a basement, and outside the door there are always two sergeants of the Royal Marines, fully armed and at attention on two-hour shifts. Inside the room are hundreds of identical black-velvet boxes, with little gold plates on them engraved with the names of the heroes of the secret wars. When a member of England's intelligence services does something spectacular, there's a quiet ceremony where he's given a medal. Because who he is and what he did must be kept secret, the medal is put inside the little velvet box and kept in trust by the government. But years later, when the man dies and the secret is no longer crucial to national security, the Queen invites his family to the Palace for an audience and gives them the box. But it's not just for professionals. A lot of the boxes in that room are set aside for people like your friends, just regular citizens who maybe got involved by accident, or performed some service when the need arose. For the moment their families and friends are going to think that Jimmy and Peter were killed by robbers or something—whatever story the government puts out for the press. But someday they'll get a little printed invitation to come visit the Queen, and then they'll know.''

Margaret stared at him, and in her eyes he could see that she wanted to be able to tell the story, to go to Peter's sister or Jimmy's mother in some private room of the gigantic old country houses they lived in and whisper the lie he had offered her. Then there was no telling where it would go, and he knew it wouldn't hold up. ''You've got to keep that to yourself,'' he said. ''If it ever got out, the Russians would do anything to get into that room and read the citations—the ones for the last fifty years, anyway.''

''But you know, and now I know,'' she said. ''Michael, if I could tell just one or two people . . . and after all, it's their secret, theirs and mine, not yours.''

He wavered as he thought about her. If she told it, she would probably make up lots of details that would make it sound more authentic, but he couldn't chance it. ''It's a deep secret. None of them would ever have told an American, even one who's been here for years trying to protect their country.''

''Then, how do you know?''

He sighed, as though he were giving in against his better judgment. ''A few years ago, a man from MI6 managed to get inside a Soviet communications post in Afghanistan. How that happened, and how he got out, I can't go into. But he ended up with me. He'd seen some things: the specification plates on the equipment, written texts on the computer screens and so on. The problem was, he didn't speak Russian. He'd looked at them, but there was no way he could remember them because they meant nothing to him; just gibberish. His own people tried hypnotism, locking him in a sensory-deprivation chamber, everything. But they knew that we'd experimented with certain drugs. I can't name them, but chemically they're several generations beyond truth serums.

"This Englishman came to my house and met a doctor we'd flown in from Langley. The doctor shot him up, and he started to draw. He drew for days. He drew the Russian letters he'd seen on the computer screens, and made diagrams and maps. He saw everything all over again, and traced it on paper. But he also started to talk. It was endless, compulsive talk about all kinds of things that he'd kept secret. He told me about sexual experiences, childhood lies and things his parents hadn't caught him at, secret fears and worries that he'd never resolved. It turned out he was from an old family that had been involved in British secrets for generations. The way it sounded, they were recruited by their fathers about the time they left Eton for Oxford, so they'd be sure to study hard and read the right books. Anyway, one thing he told me about was the room with the velvet boxes. When he'd been in the service only a few months, they called him in and showed him around. There were boxes in there for his father, who had helped crack some German code, and his great-grandfather, who'd done something or other in the Boer War, and I think somebody was in the Crimea. He kept raving on about the medals—the Victoria Cross, the Distinguished Service Order and I don't know what else.

"The whole thing seemed to bother him a lot. At first I thought it was because when he got the tour he was so green. He couldn't have been more than twenty-two, and seeing all those medals made him think he could never amount to anything compared to all of his ancestors. After the drug wore off, I asked him about it, and he said that wasn't it. By now he had a few medals and citations in a box of his own. It was the secrets that bothered him. A lot of the things from a hundred years ago are still current: secret family contacts in Russia and East Germany, for instance, that have been kept up for generations. If those got out, the Russians would have whole families put up against a wall. Things change on the surface, but not underneath, in the world where spies live. It all seemed to him like a string that might unravel. If one thing came out, it could be traced to something else, and so on."

"But this is different," she muttered. "What can it possibly hurt to give their families something to hold on to?"

"It's not different," he said. "Knowledge is dangerous. You'd be doing them no favors." He wondered if he had sounded ominous enough, but it made her stop asking, and he had to be satisfied with that.

As the train rattled on toward London, he stared out at the grass and trees. He wondered if he detected in himself some annoyance at her for luring him out into the world where they could find him, but decided he did not. She had made such a small, innocent offer, and the consequences had been huge and abrupt. It wasn't even a problem she could have imagined. But now he had to work his way out. He had done exactly what he had promised himself he would never do. He had become lazy and comfortable and forgetful. It had been so stupid that it now struck him as a kind of miracle. For some time, maybe for years, he had kept up a few hollow rituals and observed a few minimal precautions, but it was only out of habit.

He remembered a day nearly fifteen years ago in New York, when he had waited for a man named Danny Catanno to come home from a night at the theater. He had sat in the dim light the man had left burning in the huge living room and contemplated the nature of human beings. This man no longer called himself Danny Catanno. He had been an accountant for a friend of the Castiglione family in Chicago, changing a few dollars into apartment houses and putting particular people on the payroll as managers or handymen or gardeners. But one day Danny Catanno had bought himself a BMW and paid for it in cash. Somehow the IRS had gotten curious about it because it had cost sixty thousand dollars that had not come through a bank account. Within a few days Catanno was sitting in a room somewhere that was full of men who could not afford BMWs but were good enough at arithmetic to prove to Danny that he couldn't either.

Years later—maybe seven—somebody had seen Danny Catanno in New York. The Castiglione family, by now run by the son and his two sons since the old man had retired to the Southwest, had quietly made inquiries. It wasn't that he had done any real damage to the family reputation. The name had been famous since before the son was born. And the family friend had gotten off with a small fine and a wordy warning about fraudulent business practices and shady connections, because he had never been arrested before and had other friends besides the Castigliones. But the Castigliones were curious about the same thing that had attracted the IRS—the BMW that wasn't attributable to any of Danny Catanno's personal bank accounts. Danny was a thief.

A contract had been offered for Danny Catanno as soon as he had disappeared, but it had produced no satisfaction. After he had been spotted, the Castigliones had decided to hire a specialist.

Schaeffer had known that the Justice Department had some kind of agreement with Castoria College, which granted degrees to people on the basis of oral examinations given in courtrooms thousands of miles from its campus in New Hampshire. The government lawyers also gave their graduates false birth certificates and driver's licenses and social security numbers, and then they said, "Good-bye and good luck." All he had to do was to keep checking Danny's mother's mailbox for a month to see that Danny was beginning to forget his troubles. About once a week there was an envelope from a brokerage in New York with a check in it. When he had gotten to New York, all he'd had to do was to pick up a little brochure the company put out advertising the qualifications of its brokers. Among the dozens of brokers who had gone to places that meant nothing to him, he had found David Cutter, an honor graduate of Castoria.

He had looked around the apartment a bit while he waited for David Cutter to come home. It was the sort of place that cost a million or more up front, and another half-million that had to be paid to decorators, furniture dealers and art galleries. In the antique writing desk he had found a pile of credit-card receipts for expensive restaurants. He had been astounded. The man had even gone on a trip to the Bahamas a month before. People had a way of pushing things out of their minds, like the ones who built fancy houses in the floodplain of the Platte River, or on top of fault lines in California. It was a miracle that a man like David Cutter had lived as long as he had. He had gone to restaurants where he couldn't help but sit next to people who would do anything to gain favor with the Castiglione family. He had spent his days betting large sums of money for people, a lot of whom had gotten it in ways that must have brought them into contact with acquaintances of the Castigliones. What did this man think? When he had made his reservations for the Caribbean, didn't he wonder who might be sitting next to him on the plane?

Schaeffer had looked in drawers and closets, bookcases and backlit cabinets, thinking about human folly. All the time he was planning. If ever in his life he had to disappear, he would submerge without a ripple and never come up again. He would never allow himself to become so comfortable and mentally lazy that he forgot he wasn't the man he was pretending to be. That night he had made the decision to begin the preparations for his own disappearance. He would put money in safe-deposit boxes in towns he never visited. Often in his career he had found it prudent to use false names on credit cards and licenses. But now he would do it in earnest, start to build up a few identities and never use them, so that they would be old enough and deep enough on the day when somebody began to look for him the way he had looked for Danny Catanno.

Eddie Mastrewski had raised him to abhor mistakes. It was better to stay home than to make a mistake, better to pass up the money than to take a chance. The police could be as stupid as cattle, spend the day stumbling over their own feet, but in the evening they could go home, pop open a beer and sleep like stones. But people like Eddie and the boy got to make only one mistake. That was true of people like Danny Catanno too, only Danny didn't seem to know it. He had accepted an identity as Cutter the stockbroker, and somehow he had forgotten that he wasn't Cutter the stockbroker. The money and respectability that protected people like Cutter couldn't protect him.

Before he had satisfied his curiosity in the apartment, he had found Danny Catanno's gun. It was hidden in a little pop-out compartment in the wall beside the bed. The gun was lying under a pile of gold cuff links, a couple of watches and some hundred-dollar bills. It would have taken Danny thirty seconds in bright light to fumble around for it. It looked as though it had been placed there a long time ago and forgotten. When he examined it, he found it hadn't even been cleaned and oiled lately. But he found it worked well enough when Danny Catanno came home from the theater. The police told the reporters the next day that David Cutter was a lesson to others: an unlicensed firearm was just as likely to be used by a burglar as by its owner.

Now Schaeffer wondered how he had forgotten about Danny Catanno. He had managed to set aside enough money, and he had nurtured the identities until they had sufficient patina on them to obscure their flaws, but he hadn't done the rest of it. He had put off getting the plastic surgery, telling himself at first that he needed to get a feel for the country before he could be sure how to go about it. Surgery would involve spending a lot of time in London being photographed and examined by doctors who might wonder why a man with perfectly regular features would want something expensive and painful done to him in a foreign country. Then later, when he had learned to move around comfortably in England and was confident he could have accomplished it, he had developed other reservations. People in Bath knew him by now, and would wonder why he would suddenly do such a strange thing. He had put it off so long the dangerous time was probably past. If anybody had traced him here, they would have gotten him by now. And certainly all that time must have changed him as much as surgery would. . . .

The truth was that hiding had made him reluctant to obliterate his face, because it was the last thing left that was part of who he really was. He had already destroyed or relinquished everything else. He would never have run out of excuses to put off the plastic surgery. For the first time he understood Danny Catanno.

It was late afternoon. The southern outposts of London began to pass by the train, and brown brick buildings appeared that reminded him of the ride from Kennedy Airport through Queens. Then it struck him that the similarity wasn't the reason he had thought of it. He was going back. As the train pulled slowly into Victoria Station, he calculated: assuming the police had found all five bodies by now and were questioning everybody at the racetrack, it would still take them a couple of hours to find out that the Bentley had stopped to let out a man and a woman. They would take still longer to satisfy themselves that the man and woman were no longer in Brighton, and that the only place that made any sense if they wanted to hide was London.

Fingerprints didn't worry him. In spite of the nonsense the police put out for public consumption, not one of them in a hundred could lift a clear print from anything more textured than glass or metal. Neither he nor Meg had touched the windows, and Peter had opened the door for them. And if they had idly grasped the door handles, the killers would have touched them afterward, and probably wiped the surfaces off before they left.

His mind was already working its old, habitual, methodical way through the traps and snares. He turned to her as they stood up, careful to keep his face turned away from their companions on the train. "Keep looking out the window. You said nobody knew we were going there today?"

"That's right. I met them on the way to your house. They saw me on the street and told me when they'd pick us up."

He assessed the damage as they walked across the platform toward the gigantic enclosure of the station. It wasn't so bad, really. If the police were lazy or stupid it was nothing at all. Their professional habit of seizing upon the most easily comprehensible explanation would make them overlook things that didn't fit. They would assume a gang of thieves had murdered two wealthy citizens, then quarreled over whatever they had found on the bodies or in the Bentley. There would be no telling what that was, because somebody in the gang must have lived, and he would have carried it away with him. That part was inevitable: no matter how much they wanted to, the police would not be able to convince themselves that three men who had died of a broken skull, a knife up under the ribs and a bullet fired from five yards out had not required the services of at least one person who hadn't been found on the scene. But even that much would take them a few more hours, because before they could commit themselves, they would have to go over everything with tape measures and cameras and sketch pads. And they would bring with them the assumptions that would make their efforts a waste of time. Because all the time they would be preparing to look for the missing man among the local street thieves, not among the acquaintances of the two wealthy victims in the Bentley.

Just as he had at Brighton, he made Meg stay in the ladies' restroom while he bought the tickets. He had to get her out of here without letting more than a few people see them together. He waited at the most crowded ticket window, then all he said was, "Bath. Two," to hide his accent, and took the tickets without looking at the man inside.

They met again and stood a few yards apart on the platform just before the train was to leave, and boarded separately as though they were unaware of each other. Later, if anyone remembered seeing a pretty young woman in a yellow dress, they wouldn't remember seeing her with a man. As Margaret had walked across the huge nineteenth-century station, he had watched her. She came out of the ladies' room with several other young women in bright, stylish dresses, and stayed within a few steps of them all the way to the platform. An observer might have said she was one of them, five girls who each merited a second glance, but who all drifted across the crowded place at once, a single vision of colors, stockinged legs, clashing scents, smooth white complexions, hair up, hair hanging long. Which one was blond and which dark? Who would remember? And the women themselves were laughing and talking with animation, too interested in themselves to pay attention to each other, let alone to someone who was simply walking in the same direction. He didn't know if she had done this instinctively to fade into the herd of people who could hide her best, or had merely let the fear guide her, the terror of being alone attracting her to people as much like her friends as possible. It didn't matter; they were going to get through this.

On the train he found her again, but when he sat down beside her, he realized that she'd had time to think. "We'll stop at your place and close the house," she said. "Then you'll stay with me."

When she conducted him into the library, he was envious. She had grown up here, in huge rooms with twenty-foot walls in two tiers, all of them lined with paintings and books. It didn't matter what the books were about or who had written them. To him they were a symbol of privilege: the more ancient and eccentric they were, the greater the advantage. The room represented how many generations of people who had titles and money and manners and tutors and parents—ten?

"Do you have to go? You could stay here and call for help. Or we could drive up to Yorkshire. Even if they'd been watching you, nobody could know about that, and lots of people must have been hidden there over the years. My forebears in the time of Henry the Eighth didn't feel comfortable with the forced conversion and may have hidden a monk or two—lots of people did. I do know somebody hid from Cromwell there three generations after that. We were exactly the sort of people he was born to rid the world of—still are, to the degree we can manage it. It's a huge, rambling place with lots of rooms, but the village is small enough so nobody could come after you without being spotted."

It entered Schaeffer's mind that her ancestors really weren't from the same planet he was. Time meant nothing to her, or to any of them, really. If he chose to stay at the family estate, she would feed him and bring him the daily newspapers until one of them died, and then he would be part of the story too. He opened his suitcase and pulled out his two passports. He looked at one of them and handed it to Meg. "I've got to go to the United States. When I'm ready to come back, I may call you and ask you to mail this to me."

She looked at it, then plucked the other one from his hand and read the name aloud. "Charles Frederick Ackerman. It hadn't occurred to me that you might have another name," she said, her voice a little hollow.

"Michael Schaeffer is the real one." He put his arm around her waist. The name already sounded strange to him, like the name of someone long dead.

"What I've been trying to say is, are you going because you have to, or because you think being with me puts me in danger? Because I really don't mind." It struck her as an odd thing to have said, so she added, "Really."

"I have to find the mole." He studied her face. There was no possibility of an argument; of course he had to find the mole. Whose job was it if not his? She had read all the spy novels, then given them to him to read. He wished he had paid more attention to them, but he hadn't. Her questions might grow more astute and penetrating, so he needed to think more carefully about what he said. But he also needed to think about reality, and time was passing.

The Satterthwaites would stay on at his house indefinitely, keeping it open and clean and inhabited, and they would feed his cat. Mrs. Satterthwaite had understood that he sometimes traveled, and she would continue to pay the bills out of the household account. He had always been like a ghost in his own house, coming and going quietly without having any discernible effect on the daily business of the place. The Satterthwaites were the real occupants, living high among the rafters upstairs and showing little curiosity about anything he did. If he never came back, the will he had filed in the solicitor's office a few blocks away would be revealed to them. Mr. Satterthwaite would paint a neat, hand-lettered sign that said BED AND BREAKFAST, and they would continue to care for the place and serve the food; the only difference would be that he would be replaced by other ghosts who came and went quietly.

He closed his suitcase. "I have to get back to London tonight for the plane."

"I'll get the keys to the Jag." She moved to pull open the library door.

He watched her go. He knew that someday, if he lived to be old and alone, he would look back on this moment and grind his teeth with anguish and remorse, straining his memory for the exact color of The Honourable Meg's hair and the way her yellow dress swayed as she tugged open the big oak door.

6

Charles Frederick Ackerman walked down the long accordion tunnel past the smiling flight attendants, all poised to dart out and block the narrow aisles and offer assistance. The travelers were barely able to negotiate the cramped space with their burdens of carry-on luggage, let alone balance dwarf pillows or chemical-smelling blankets. They paid no more attention to him than to any of the others. If they'd had to describe him to a policeman, one of them might have been perceptive enough to have judged that his coat was a good piece of English tailoring but not new, and that he was no longer in his twenties but wasn't yet wearing the strangely driven look that men acquire on their fiftieth birthdays. He was, at this stop on the crew's route, invisible through protective coloration: eyes and hair a dull brown; maybe English, maybe American, maybe German, not thin enough to be French or elegant enough to be Italian. They looked at him only long enough to assure themselves that he wasn't disabled and probably spoke enough English to do what he was supposed to without exaggerated gestures on their part.

He took his seat by the window and looked out at England with regret. But all the England he could see was a patch of lighted tarmac and part of a baggage rack. The ten years were already over. Michael Schaeffer had made his final appearance before this man had gotten onto the airplane.

He settled back in his seat and meditated on the time that would come now. He knew only the name in the wallet of the man who had been carrying the pistol: Mario Talarese. That would be enough. As the rest of the passengers filled the seats around him, he tried to fathom the reasoning of the people who

46

would send a pickup team of amateurs to find and dispose of a man like him.

Somebody should have given it more consideration. If they remembered the contract, they should have remembered who he was. In all the councils that were intended to keep these men's pride and ambition and greed from interfering with the steady, predictable profits they shared, wasn't there one calm old voice left to remind them that if they killed him it would gain them nothing, and if they failed they might bring back old trouble?

He had done everything he could to convince them that he had relinquished that life. Why hadn't they just let him die? He knew the answer already: they had. There was nothing in it for the dozen old men who had the power and the right to decide things, and if they had decided, it wouldn't have been two weasels with knives and a guy with a pistol designed to fit in a lady's purse. The south of England would one day have filled up with quiet men who called themselves Mr. Brown or Mr. Williams, but each had return tickets to three American cities in other names. It couldn't have been the old men.

It had to be that an eager small-time underboss had decided to do it on his own. He even knew who it was. If the one with the gun was named Talarese, the man who had sent him had to be Antonio Talarese. That knowledge gave him one small chance to stay alive, and even that would disappear unless he took it now. If the idea had been to pull off a sudden triumph a couple of thousand miles from home and collect on a ten-year-old contract, then it had to be a secret until it was accomplished. Talarese couldn't have told anyone else that he had found the quarry, or he would have had rivals he couldn't hope to compete with.

Ackerman had no choice now but to come back, and to do it as fast as he could. Because the minute Talarese told the rest of the world what he knew, it was over. Michael Schaeffer had not made the sort of preparations that would allow him to slip into another life in time. Ackerman had to get to New York before the news that Mario Talarese was lying behind a building in Brighton.

Ackerman leaned back in the padded seat as the huge airplane lumbered down the long runway, its wheels bumping over the cracks faster and faster until its engines screamed an octave higher and lifted it into the night. Talarese had made a terrible mistake to fail in his first try. When a man's peace and confidence and the tranquility of his home were gone, there wasn't much left.

* * *

The Honourable Margaret Holroyd sat on her bed and looked at the clock on the nightstand. The clock had a red digital read-out and had been manufactured no more than a year ago of microchips shipped to Japan from a company outside San Francisco. The nightstand had been made in France in the sixteenth century out of a tree that had been young at the time when Charles Martel was gathering his troops near Tours to rid France of the baneful influence of Islam. Michael would be midway across the Atlantic by now. It was very likely that a mile from here the Filchings were awake too, sitting up thinking, trying to discern a way that they could accept the rest of their lives after what had happened to Peter and his friend Jimmy. Tomorrow the telephone would ring and one of them would tell her what they knew. She would have to feign—what?—surprise, shock, horror . . . No, the horror was real enough. She had no choice about that. What she wasn't prepared for was lying to those poor, sad people.

She put on her robe and walked along the hallway to the back stairs, then down to the library, closed the door behind her and looked around at the familiar place. She wished her father were still alive, sneaking in late at night and sitting down at the old desk to pursue some perfectly dotty arcane study. He had been completely mad, of course. Even as a child she had known it, although her mother had behaved as though it were the furthest thing from her mind until she had known she was dying. Then she had sat Meg down and told her simply, "Take care of your father, if you can." There had been no moment of doubt in either woman's mind that Meg could. He had been beatific and peaceful much of the time, the way she imagined idiot savants must be.

She remembered the day he had let her have the run of this place. She was ten, and she had been at a birthday party for Gwendolyn Ap-Witting. She had told one of her stories to Gwendolyn, a scary story with ghosts that came up out of the ancient mounds between their estates. Gwendolyn had told a duller, less-sophisticated abridged version to her aunt Clara while she was upstairs fixing her hair. The aunt had come downstairs and made a public announcement that the other children were to believe nothing that Meg said, and followed it with a lecture about Jesus sending angels to make indelible black marks in their books whenever little girls told lies. The children had been more terrified by this than by the ghosts, and they had spent the rest of the long afternoon maintaining a distance of twelve feet from Meg. Their rudimentary religious training had convinced them that God had a history of striking down sinners in groups rather than singly. The criteria were vague; usually just falling into some broadly defined category like "the wicked" seemed to be enough, so self-preservation dictated that their status be unambiguous. Whenever she came near any of them, they would recoil and move away. As Gwendolyn opened her gifts in the drawing room surrounded by all the other children, Meg had hovered in the doorway, looking at all of them from an immense distance, as though she were one of the ghosts in her story, caught alone on the earth in daytime. When the driver had pulled up in front of the big manor house at four, little Margaret had appeared suddenly from behind a thick yew tree and clambered into the back seat as though the Rolls were the last steamer out of Krakatoa.

At home she had sat alone in the garden contemplating the wreckage of her life when she had noticed her father standing nearby, staring at her. Probably he could see she had been crying, although she had taken pains to hide the signs because they were not only a consequence but also evidence of her guilt. It was unusual that he paid any attention to her, and often she suspected that he was unaware of her existence for long periods. But now he was absorbed in his study of her, looking down at her with the same benevolent curiosity that he was devoting that year to his list of medicinal herbs mentioned in ancient texts but not identifiable among modern flora.

Finally he had said, "Come with me," and walked through the French doors into the library without looking back to see if she had heard him. When they were in the secret little room behind the walls of books where nobody would ever disturb them, he had spoken to her as he probably spoke to his contemporaries. "There are times in life when it's useful to know of a place like this. Hiding places are extremely difficult to come by, so treat it with respect. You may come here whenever you please."

She missed him now as she lay on the leather couch, staring up at the vaulted ceiling and wondering if she had seen the last of Michael Schaeffer. The whole day had degenerated from a succession of bright, vivid, jarring sights and sounds into a collection of events she was too exhausted to remember very well. He was gone already, back to a place where serious people had serious things to do, and engaged in awful, deadly struggles to accomplish some ephemeral advantage. It wasn't so much his disappearance that disturbed her; it was the discovery that he really belonged to that life instead of hers. It didn't even matter that he'd told her all those lies about being a spy. That she, of all people in the world, understood. He had only wanted to make it all seem nicer and prettier for her. If he came back, she knew she would probably marry him. She already was listed in Debrett's as the last of the Holroyds, and she was a whole generation too late to do anything selfless about it. Perhaps she couldn't do anything about the fact that he was obviously some kind of criminal, but she could be his place to hide. Gwendolyn's aunt Clara would probably have said it was typical of her to fall in love with the worst person she ever met. She devoted a moment to hoping that Clara's angels had volumes of black marks on her when she had died a few years ago, and this took her mind off the present just long enough for sleep to come.

As the passengers shuffled up the aisle toward the door, Charles Ackerman reached under his seat and retrieved his small suitcase. He had brought only one. The place to trap a man like him was in an airport baggage-claim area, when he had just stepped off an international flight that required going through metal detectors at both ends and was standing mesmerized in front of a turning carousel of luggage.

He joined the agonizingly slow queue with the others. Here it was only ten in the evening, but it was three o'clock in the morning for the load of prisoners straggling into the airport. This suited him perfectly.

When the tired functionary at the Customs and Immigration barrier looked at the passport, a hint of interest almost snapped him out of his lethargy. "You haven't been home in some time, Mr. Ackerman."

"No," he said. "I live in England now." He watched with fascination as the man placed his open passport on a machine that appeared to be an optical scanner. That was new. He was glad he had used the Ackerman passport. He had obtained it fifteen years ago on the strength of a bogus birth certificate, but the State Department had issued it and he had renewed it regularly, so it was real enough. The man read something on a computer screen that didn't surprise him, then handed it back.

"Here on business?"

"No," Ackerman answered. "I just haven't been home in a long time."

"Anything to declare?"

"Nothing." It was all negatives, all denials: I'm nobody, do- ing nothing here, bringing nothing with me; forget me. The man ran his hands inside the suitcase quickly and moved on to the next person in line.

He latched the suitcase and moved into the open terminal, where rows of faces glanced hopefully at him, scrutinizing his features, and then, instantly failing to recognize the right con- figuration, discarded him and looked behind him for the brother, the father, the business associate. He passed the waiting throng and moved toward the lockers built into the far wall. He saw one with a key sticking out of it, then remembered he had no American coins. He moved on to the gift shop. There was a woman who seemed to be an Indian behind the counter, staring intently at a garish tabloid she had draped over the cash register. As he approached, she set it aside and he could read the head- line: RUSSIANS FIND WORLD WAR II BOMBER IN CRATER ON THE MOON. Meg would have said it had something for everyone she knew.

"I need to change some English money," he said.

She pointed out into the hall. "The yellow booth." Then she added confidentially, "They give you more at the bank."

"Thank you," he said, and turned to go.

"Haven't you got an ATM card?"

He had no idea what an ATM card was. There was probably another name for it in England, but he certainly didn't have one. "No."

"They'll screw you out of ten percent. I'll do it for five."

He resisted the temptation to smile. New York. It must come from the air or the water. They'll screw you, but I won't; we're in this together. Even the ward politicians got elected that way. "How much can you give me for five hundred pounds?"

"Seven-fifty."

He had read in *The New York Times* on the plane that the pound was $1.89, so her five percent was about twenty percent. He counted out five one-hundred-pound notes and accepted the money from the till. He asked for the last ten in singles and the last three in quarters and she gave them without reluctance or an attempt to palm a bill; having taken her fair usury, she wasn't interested in stealing.

He used the coins to free the locker key, left his belongings in the locker, then strolled to the ticket counter and paid more pounds for a ticket to Los Angeles leaving at seven in the morning. He looked up at the big clock on the wall and reset his watch. He still had almost nine hours.

Out in the street, the cabs were lined up, with an airport policeman flagging them forward whenever a prospect stepped up. As he presented himself, a dirty yellow Dodge shot ahead crazily and rocked to a stop on its useless shock absorbers.

The ride into Manhattan hadn't changed much in ten years. The buildings were a little older and dirtier than he remembered them, and the cars seemed a little better and cleaner. He was thinking about Antonio Talarese.

The young idiot with the gun had been Mario Talarese. There was no question that he was a relative. More than twelve years ago he had met Antonio Talarese in the back of a small gourmet-food store in lower Manhattan. There had been three men waiting when he had arrived. One had been the owner of the place, an eager shopkeeper type who was standing at a cutting board making a tray of salami and cheese and opening a bottle of wine, as though this were a little party. Talarese had said, "Leave us now," and the man had gone out to the front to wait on his customers.

He had come to the store to talk about a job with Paul Santorini. At that time Santorini was an upwardly mobile manager for Carlo Balacontano, who had been running a Ponzi scheme on the side, taking money first from a greedy New Jersey real estate agent, then from the agent's friends, telling them he was putting it out on the street at astronomical rates of interest. He had paid the man inflated interest for months, long enough to be sure he would brag to his friends about his profits. Then they were hooked too, a group of doctors and engineers, even a couple of lawyers who obviously hadn't spent any time defending criminals. Among them they had given the real estate agent about two million dollars to pass on to his underworld friend. Santorini still had about a million and a half of it in hand, and it was time to make the real estate agent disappear.

When that happened, the doctors and engineers and lawyers would remember that none of them had ever actually seen Paul Santorini, and certainly hadn't handed him any money. About half would be of the opinion that the real estate agent had taken their money to Brazil. The other half would maintain their faith in him, which meant that Paul Santorini had quietly killed him, and could very easily do the same to them. In any case, none of them would go to the police to report that they had been cheated out of their loansharking profits by their Mafioso partner. But

Santorini's clean exit from the venture required that the real estate agent be expertly plucked out of existence, not left butchered somewhere by the likes of Santorini's best soldier, whom he introduced as "Tony T," then elongated it to Antonio Talarese. At this point, a boy of about twelve had wandered in to pick up some cardboard cartons and looked surprised to see the men in the back of his father's store. He had stopped and looked at Tony T; then the store owner had rushed in, grinning and sweating, and jerked the boy out by the shoulder.

The job had been simple enough for the money. The realtor was in the habit of going out alone early on Sunday mornings to put up OPEN HOUSE signs at the places he was selling. It hadn't taken much imagination to search the New Jersey newspapers for his listings and be at one of them before he arrived. It was winter, so it was still dark when he had come upon the man taking the signs out of the trunk of his car. He shot him and pushed him into the trunk, then pulled the keys out of the lock and drove him to a woods a few miles away, where he buried him. That was the part that he remembered best. He could still see and smell the thick layer of wet, leathery maple leaves on the ground. He'd had to push at least four inches of them aside before his shovel could break ground, and then he kept hitting tree roots. They were thin, like fingers, but so tough and rubbery that he'd had to push them aside and dig around them; then, when the hole was barely three feet deep, he backed into one of them and it had startled him. At that point he decided to dump the body in and cover it. When he'd finished pushing the leaves back over the dirt, it would have been difficult even for him to find the grave. Then he had left the car in the long-term lot at the Newark airport and taken a cab from the terminal like a passenger.

The man's wife had reported his absence that night, but even she never came forward with a theory about what had happened to him. Either she hadn't known about Santorini or she had decided her husband would have wanted her to live to collect his insurance.

Ackerman thought about Antonio Talarese. He was probably a little more substantial than he had been twelve years ago, but he would probably still be in the same part of town. With all the trials that had made the London newspapers in the past couple of years, plenty of vacancies would have opened up above him in the hierarchy. By now Tony T might even be what Santorini had been in the old days, which would mean that he would have some underlings of his own.

In the old days it would have been easier in another way too. There would have been somebody he knew who could supply him with a weapon at eleven o'clock on a Saturday night in New York. This time he couldn't talk to anybody, and he couldn't wait. If Mario Talarese was a relative of Tony T, a telephone call from England announcing his death would be coming soon.

As the cab crossed the Triborough Bridge, he spoke. "Don't go down East River Drive. Take One-twenty-fifth."

The driver said, "Are you sure? It's not . . . real safe. . . ."

"I'll give you an extra twenty."

The cab coasted down the incline onto East 125th, and now he could see the distant glow of the tall buildings below Central Park. As the cab turned off the busy street to head south, he saw four young men standing under the shadow of a billboard high above them on a brick building. The building had boards nailed where windows used to be under the wrought-iron bars. He noticed that while three of them were talking to each other, the fourth never took his eyes off the cars that stopped for the red light on the corner.

There was no question what they were doing here. They were waiting for easy prey, the car that would come off the bridge with its radiator steaming or a tire flapping, or the woman alone who would stop for the light with her window open, her purse on the seat beside her and the radio turned up loud enough to cover the sound of the footsteps coming up behind her car. "I'll get out here."

The cab driver's eyes appeared in the rearview mirror. "You from around here?"

"No."

"Then let me take you a little farther down. This is Harlem. In the Fifties there are a lot of good hotels. You don't want to get out here."

"No, thanks." He handed the driver sixty dollars and climbed out. "Keep the change." The driver didn't speak. The buttons on the doors all came down automatically and the cab was already moving to catch the green light. The man had decided not to sit through another red and watch what he was sure would happen.

Ackerman glanced at the four young men beside the building. The watcher was moving his head from side to side rapidly, as he had seen one of the horses do at the post this morning at the racetrack. The life of a petty thief was mostly watching and loitering, and the thought that the waiting was over always seemed to make them twitch and flex and make unnecessary moves just to wake up their limbs.

The guns wouldn't be in their clothes. If the police surprised them on a sweep, they wouldn't want the ten-year sentence for carrying a firearm—or worse, to give a cop the excuse to open fire. The weapons would be in a trash can or behind a loose board over a window. He held the thieves in his peripheral vision as he moved up the street. It was a delicate matter to pique their interest enough to get them to reveal their hiding place, and then to induce them to reject him as prey. He knew the critical moment would be the instant when they thought he had stopped looking. Then at least one would make a move, if only to check the place where the weapons were.

He walked past their building and they held their places, but he could feel their eyes moving up and down his body. They would be looking for some sign that he was a cop acting as bait. If he was dangerous, it wasn't because he could chase down four men half his age and handcuff them; it was because attacking him might bring five or six carloads of cops screeching in from all directions with riot guns and body armor. He sensed that they were making their decision. In a moment one of them would betray the hiding place.

"Hey, man!" came a voice. It disconcerted him. That wasn't how it was done. The voice came again. "Want some crack? A little blow? Crank?"

He stopped and turned to look at them. What the hell were they doing? Of course it would be drugs these days. The watcher was the salesman. The salesman strutted out to the sidewalk, his head at a slight angle from his shoulder. He was skinny and black, with long legs in fitted jeans that ended in a pair of white high-topped sneakers with big tongues half-laced with red laces. On his left wrist he wore a Piaget watch with a band that looked as though it had been chiseled out of a two-pound gold nugget. He had misread the signs. These weren't hit-and-run thieves; they were pharmacists.

He stood thinking as the salesman approached. He had been out of the country too long. What else didn't he know? He glanced over the young man's shoulder at his three companions. Now that his eyes had adjusted to the darkness of their shadowy stand, he could discern that they were all black too. They all wore high-topped sneakers that looked as though they had been designed for players in the NBA, laced haphazardly with red laces. What was that all about—a sign to customers? A uniform? The cops would love that.

The young man smiled. "You be here buying, or looking? Don't have all night, I got shit to move. Won't do better anywhere around here." His smile was vacant, unfeeling and confident. He didn't speak quietly or look over his shoulder for the patrol car the way street dealers used to.

A line of five cars cruised up to the light, and the other three stood up, walked out into the street and leaned down to speak into the drivers' windows. Two of them made quick deals, taking money and handing the drivers tiny plastic bags from inside their jackets, then moved on to the next two cars. When one driver didn't roll down his window, the young man's expression didn't change. He just gave the door a lazy, half-hearted pat, already looking ahead at the next potential customer.

Ackerman pushed his amazement to the back of his mind. This was a distraction, and he had to work with the new circumstances, regardless of how they had come about. "I want to buy a gun."

The salesman cocked his head again and leaned closer. "Say what?" From the exaggeration he could tell that the salesman was already savoring the irony of the situation enough to want to hear it again.

"I don't want any drugs tonight, but I do want a gun. Can you help me out?"

The grin broadened. "If *I* have a gun, and *you* have money but no gun, what's to stop me from having both of them?"

"You're making too much here to fuck it up robbing people."

"Come back tomorrow. I'll see what I can do." The young man turned and sidestepped back toward his building's shadow like a base runner shortening his lead.

He followed the salesman back toward the shadow. "It's got to be now."

"Can't do that. How'm I supposed to hold my corner with no gun?"

So that was it. They weren't afraid of the police or a tapped-out, desperate customer ready to kill to get the whole hoard. There were so many dealers now that they were fighting over prime locations. "I don't want all of them. Just a pistol."

"Pistol? Shit." The salesman's professional grin returned. Behind him the light turned green and the traffic moved past again. The three vendors looked up the street, then began to drift toward the shadow of the building, so the salesman felt comfortable enough to turn his back. He removed the board from the window and reached inside with both hands. When he turned, he held a nickel-plated .357 Magnum revolver with a four-inch barrel. A gun like that weighed at least two pounds empty and was fat and squat, like a little cannon with a thick round handgrip. Ackerman could see that the salesman and his friends weren't in the concealment business. The only conceivable reason they would pick a gun like this was that it wasn't as heavy to carry around as a .44. But then, with his other hand, the salesman reached deeper into the cache and produced something bigger, black and square and utilitarian, that didn't resolve itself into a recognizable shape until he had it at chest level.

"How much for the Uzi?"

"It's not for sale. I'm not giving you a loaded piece and then standing here with nothing in my hands like a fool."

Ackerman smiled. "May I?" He took the revolver in his hand and examined it. It hadn't been fired more than a few times, but it had some kind of filmy substance on the barrel. He opened the cylinder, touched the inside of the barrel with the tip of his little finger and sniffed. It was the familiar smell of gun oil, so the kid had at least cleaned it. Then he sniffed the outside of the barrel, and detected a lemony odor.

"What are you doing? If you're going to eat the barrel, don't do it here."

"What's this got on it?"

"Pledge. I waxed it to save the finish."

Ackerman nodded sagely, as though to ratify the wisdom of spraying furniture polish on a revolver. These kids had no more idea of what they were doing than they would if they had arrived this evening from Neptune. "How much do you want for it?"

"A thousand." It was as though he had no smaller numbers in his head.

"I haven't got that much."

But now the salesman's eagerness to sell was gnawing at him. He had already spent too much time with this man. "What did you think I wanted?"

"They sell for two hundred new."

"All right. Give me five hundred and go away." He was miserable. The idea that there was a grown man walking the streets who didn't have a thousand dollars depressed him. He had spent five minutes haggling with a panhandler. He accepted the five hundred-dollar bills and jammed them into his pocket with impatience.

As Ackerman tried to conceal the big revolver under his coat, the air around him seemed to tear itself apart with a sudden roar. For the first fraction of a second he thought the salesman had let his finger stray to the trigger of the Uzi. But as he jumped to the side, he saw one of the street vendors sit down abruptly. There were muzzle flashes from the windows of a big brown Mercedes at the corner as two passengers fired wildly at the two salesmen still standing up in the street, hitting the curb, the side of the building and parked cars as though they were blind.

Cars began to squeal out of line and roar back up the one-way street. Each time one of the street vendors hid behind a car, it would move, and he would have to run to the next. Ackerman saw one of them run to the driver's side of a car, fling the door open, push the occupant over and drive off. The Mercedes now backed up to afford a better angle on the one who was left, but then it stopped abruptly as the driver saw Ackerman and the salesman in the shadows. Ackerman saw the face of a young black man, and then the barrel of the shotgun swung toward them.

As the man pumped the slide, the salesman seemed to collect his thoughts. The Uzi came up and the now-empty street became a different place. The little machine gun jerked and a brief, messy shower of sparks and flame sputtered out of the short barrel, some of the burning powder still glowing three feet out of the muzzle. It took less than two seconds to empty the thirty-round magazine into the Mercedes. Then there was a second of silence when Ackerman could hear the brass casings that had been ejected clattering onto the sidewalk. The doors of the Mercedes were punctured in at least a dozen places. The right side of the windshield was gone, and the left was an opaque fabric of powdered glass held together by the remnants of the plastic safety layer. But miraculously, there was activity in the car. The driver popped up, leaned over the wheel and began to sweep the ruined glass out of the windshield. Then the shotgun barrel swung up again, and there was a face behind it looking for a target. As Ackerman sighted the pistol, he noted with detachment that the car must have been modified. Military ammunition should have gone through the doors and done some damage to the people behind them. Probably they had put steel plates in the doors the way the old gangsters did.

Ackerman aimed with both hands and squeezed the trigger.

The big pistol jerked, and he could see that the man with the shotgun had been hit. His head lolled forward, and it appeared he had lost some hair and scalp. Now the car's tires spun and smoked. When they caught and the big Mercedes jumped forward, the shotgun fell from the dead man's hands and slid a few feet on the pavement.

The street vendor who had been sprinting for a hiding place when the Mercedes had backed up now stopped and dashed for the shotgun. He knelt beside it, brought it to his shoulder, fired, pumped and fired again at the Mercedes as it screeched around the corner.

The salesman disappeared around the building as the street vendor trotted over to his fallen companion. The wounded man was sitting in a growing pool of blood, rocking himself back and forth slowly. In a few seconds the salesman pulled up in a Jaguar that looked a lot like Meg's. The two men hauled their wounded companion to his feet and dragged him into the back seat of the car.

As Ackerman watched them, he felt something that could have been sympathy. "You know how to apply a tourniquet?"

The salesman turned on him, his eyes wild with anger and fear. "None of your business."

"He's going to bleed to death if you don't."

"No," came a frightened moan from the man sprawled on the seat. Ackerman could see that he was stiff and shivering now, going into shock. The word *no* might have referred to anything he had heard, felt, seen or remembered, but it seemed to affect the salesman, who said, "Get in with him."

Ackerman climbed into the back seat and closed the door, then squatted and leaned his back against it to stay out of the blood. He took off his necktie and tightened it around the young man's thigh as the car pulled out. He looked at his watch. It was just eleven-thirty now. In ten minutes he would have to loosen the tourniquet to keep the leg alive. "Is there a hospital we can get him to?"

The salesman sounded furious. "Okay, you popped that fucking Jamaican, but you don't know nothing."

"He's your friend. It's up to you."

The salesman leaped to adopt his point of view. "That's damned right, and that's why we're taking him to the emergency room." He was a born leader. "Don't worry, B-Man, I'll get you there."

The salesman was calming down now, driving with reasonable attention to whatever was in front of the car.

Ackerman waited and watched, counting the minutes. The wounded man was now limp and probably comatose from the loss of blood. As the car moved uptown, he wondered if the salesman had changed his mind, but the kid spoke again. "We'll take him up where they won't piss their pants if they see a black man with a hole in him. But I got to throw the Jamaicans off. If they know he's hit, they'll come right to his room and cut him up."

Ackerman used the tall buildings that floated by to orient himself. The Honourable Meg and her friends used the term "culture shock" to describe the feeling he was experiencing now. A day ago he hadn't been thinking about coming back to the United States, and now he felt as though he had been shot out of a cannon and landed here. It all looked the same, but it wasn't, and he was beginning to suspect that he wasn't either.

"What do you think?" the salesman asked Ackerman.

He held his watch up until a passing streetlight swept across it, illuminating it like a photographer's flash. There was still five minutes before he had to loosen the tourniquet. The salesman was nervous and wanted support. "Sounds okay. If you can get him there in five minutes it'll help."

The street vendor had said nothing since getting into the car. Now he was leaning back in his seat as though he were asleep. "What's wrong with your buddy?"

"Oh, shit," said the salesman. "He's hit too."

"Why doesn't he talk?"

"He doesn't know any English. The B-Man knows a little Spanish."

Ackerman looked down at the man sprawled across the seat. He was sweating and shivering and looking gray in the face. He might live, but he wasn't going to do any translating tonight. Ackerman leaned over the seat and put his head over the other man's shoulder. He could see that a bullet had hit the man's arm, and blood had soaked the front of his blue shirt. He looked closer. It was a clean hole punched through the left bicep, about the size of a double-ought buckshot pellet. But he could tell that that wasn't what had hit him; a stray round had clipped him when the salesman had hosed down the neighborhood with the Uzi. At the time he had noticed that only about half the magazine had hit the car. It was probably just as well that they hadn't called for an ambulance. The ones nearby could be filling up now with people who had been sitting in their apartments watching the late news. "It looks like only one shotgun pellet," he said. "He's not in danger, but he'll need some help, too."

The salesman didn't seem to recognize the absurdity of the theory that twelve pellets in a five-inch pattern had left only a single small puncture. "It's just down there," he said.

"Pull over," said Ackerman.

"What for?"

"Do it. We've got to go through their pockets. If they've got drugs or too much money on them they'll have to answer different questions." The salesman coasted to a stop, then executed a perfect unconscious parallel-parking job, backing right to the curb. But then he forgot to take the car out of gear and it lurched into the car in back with a crack, rocking it a little. The man in the front seat seemed to understand what was happening to him and pointed to the pockets he couldn't reach. In the back seat, Ackerman found that the unconscious man was more difficult. His limp, dead weight was enormous. There were little glass tubes of crack hidden in all his pockets, and a huge roll of bills in his jacket. The last thing Ackerman found was an automatic pistol at the small of the man's back, unfired and probably forgotten in his terrified dash to get away. He slipped it into his coat pocket.

He was aware as each second passed that he could easily raise the .357 Magnum and kill the salesman, then the man beside him, and walk away. Drug dealers had always been crazy and unpredictable, and he had stayed away from them. They always seemed to him to be driven by some horrible, aching greed that would make them feed until they burst, like ticks. He had never heard of one who had stopped because he had decided he had enough money. They just kept getting more bloated and voracious until they died in some violent explosion of overconfidence or madness, or the sheer physical principle that when a hoard of money got big enough it created its own predators to disperse it.

His reluctance to be rid of them had something to do with how young they were, and how spectacularly inexperienced. They were so alien to him, he sensed that the environment that would allow them to survive was a place he had never been. In the old days—he recognized that his urge to use that phrase trapped him in the past and made him only a visitor in the present, but he had no choice—these small entrepreneurs would have been co-opted and trained in the iron discipline of the local organization, or else swept away. The only explanation for these tiny gangs of boys in the streets was that anarchy must have descended on the world.

The salesman stared at him over the car seat, and Ackerman could see that he was sweating and frightened. He took pity on him. "Okay. Here's what we do: you pull up the driveway where the ambulances go. Get as close to the emergency-room door as you can, and keep the motor running."

The salesman drove to the blue sign that said EMERGENCY and AMBULANCES but nothing else. As he took the turn, he swung wide and had to jerk the car to the right to avoid an ambulance with its lights off gliding down the drive to return to its garage. "I'll kill that fucker," he hissed.

Ackerman knew that if he allowed the salesman to get frightened enough, his deranged mutterings might develop into a real intention, but he decided to ignore them for the moment because the Jaguar was now moving up into the bright yellow glow of the sodium lights. As soon as the car coasted to a stop, Ackerman got out, pulling the wounded man out behind him by the ankles. As he stepped back to duck under him for a fireman's carry, he stepped on the foot of a man behind him. He stopped and glanced over his shoulder.

As he turned back toward the car he still held the image of the man, a tall, barrel-chested policeman wearing a light blue shirt with little epaulets on the shoulders, and such a burden of metal and black leather around his waist that he looked a yard wide. There were a flashlight, a nightstick, a canister of mace, a pocketknife in a black leather case, ammunition and the heavy black knurled handgrips of the service revolver, all creaking and clicking as he bent to look inside the car. He heard the policeman say, "What's wrong with him?" and he answered, "I can't tell, but he's bleeding, and so is his friend. My driver found them lying in the street."

The policeman moved to the double doors, which hissed open as soon as he stepped on the black rubber mat, and grabbed an orderly who was pushing a gurney around the corner to the next hallway. He could hear the policeman's voice. "I don't give a shit who you work for. I got gunshot wounds out there." He had his hand on the orderly's back, so it looked as though he were pushing the man and his gurney out the door.

The policeman and the orderly hauled the man the rest of the way out of the back of the car and lifted him onto the gurney. As the orderly wheeled him into the building, the policeman walked over to an ambulance driver who was just putting his oxygen bottle back into its carrying case inside his parked rig. As he and the ambulance driver pulled a stretcher out of the ambulance, its legs swung down and locked. By now the second wounded man was out of the front seat and standing beside the car unsteadily, and he gladly flopped onto the stretcher for the short ride inside. The policeman muttered, "You two park the car over there and come back. I'll need you for a few minutes," then pushed the stretcher to the door.

Instantly Ackerman was in the passenger seat beside the salesman. "Drive. Get out of here," he said. The salesman had been sitting motionless, not even daring to glance at the policeman in his rearview mirror. Ackerman knew it must have taken a great act of will for him. Since childhood he had undoubtedly survived the way the thieves in the old days had, scattering at the first sign of the uniforms, each one scrambling in a different direction, down alleys and over fences, each of them alone and hoping that he wouldn't be the one they picked to chase down. Now the salesman was released from whatever had held him. His instincts, temperament and ability to calculate all urged him away, and he let them carry him. He stepped on the gas pedal and the car was in motion.

A hundred feet away, an old man was shuffling across the drive toward the emergency room, staring down at the pavement with a contemplative look on his face. He took each little step carefully, with intense concentration, satisfied with the almost invisible progress it represented. The old man was caught in the lights for a moment and looked up defiantly, squinting a little, then stopped walking as though he intended to make this young fool wait as long as possible.

"You see the old guy?" Ackerman asked.

"Sure," said the salesman, but he didn't slow down. Ackerman could see the old man judging the distance to the curb and estimating the damage he would sustain if he made a dive to the pavement. The old man's decision was conservative. He aimed himself at the curb and began to shuffle toward it, faster now than before, in a strange little dance that looked as though he were going down invisible stairs. The car shot past him, the slipstream blowing his coattails up and sending a ripple of wind to flutter his baggy pants. Then he was visible for a second in silhouette against the yellow light of the hospital entrance, still standing.

The Jaguar spun around the corner and its arc carried it into the next one, heading south again. Ackerman turned to the salesman. "Do you know where you're going?"

The salesman shrugged. "Can't stay out alone. Got to get with my friends. The Jamaicans will be hunting me."

"Let me out at the corner."

The salesman's eyes narrowed and he glanced at him quickly. "We still need to talk."

"What about?"

"I need the gun back. They're looking for me." He had obviously been thinking about the predicament he was in. He had emptied the clip in the Uzi and sold his pistol, and now he still had to make it across the city to whatever stronghold his friends maintained. He wasn't sure he would be able to do that unarmed, and even he knew he couldn't stay out in a car as memorable as a Jaguar and not be caught by the police.

Ackerman was surprised to detect in himself a certain sympathy for the salesman. "All right. Pull over up there."

The salesman steered his car to the side of the street and let a taxi go by. Then he put his hand in his pocket and pulled out the five hundred-dollar bills. Ackerman accepted them, then got out and leaned back into the car to look at the salesman.

The salesman was agitated. "Where is it? Where's my gun?"

Ackerman pulled the big nickel-plated pistol out of his coat and laid it on the floor behind the passenger seat, out of the salesman's reach. "If I were you I'd drive around the corner to a dark spot before I tried to pick that up."

The salesman looked hurt at the lack of trust, or perhaps disappointed that he wasn't going to get the five hundred dollars back. "You have another one, don't you? You took one off B-Man."

Ackerman answered, "I've been doing this a lot longer than you have. Don't try to follow me. I can still kill you any time I want." He closed the door and watched the Jaguar move off into the night.

He walked quickly down the street past a hotel, a bar and two closed stores before he ducked into the next doorway. He looked out at the street for the Jaguar, his right wrist beside his coat pocket, feeling the weight and square corners of the small automatic inside without letting his hand pat it or touch it. The Jaguar didn't reappear, even after he had watched the traffic signal change three times. The salesman had decided to forget about the money, and had gone to find whatever form of safety and shelter home could offer him.

7

Ackerman grasped the big wrought-iron handle, pulled the heavy plank door open and entered. There was a podium with a book of reservations on it, but the kitchen had been closed for hours and the hostess had been replaced by a bouncer who sat in an alcove with a pilsener glass half full of flat beer. He was a melancholy weight lifter recruited from a local gym, a thirtyish man with a cap of black, curly hair and a management-owned blue suit that had been let out to accommodate his squat, thick upper torso. He let his dark eyes stray upward to determine that the man coming through the doorway was alone, and therefore probably quiet; wearing a clean shirt and sport coat, and therefore probably not insane; and of average height and weight, and therefore manageable for the bouncer if he had been overly optimistic about either of the first two.

The bouncer took a birdlike sip of his beer and returned his eyes to a sad survey of the rest of the patrons sitting at tables ranged around the dark interior of the bar. Behind the eyes he was a small, shy little introvert who had inherited the body of generations of brawlers and laborers, then with introspective concentration had built it into a comic-book picture of a man, with muscles that he compared each day, one by one, with a series of photographs in a glossy magazine. He saw himself as a kind of lifeguard who was always in attendance at a scene of continuous and foolhardy revelry that he was never moved to join.

Ackerman walked past the bouncer to the bar, edged onto a stool and found that he had immediately intersected with the bartender's orbit. "Perrier," he said. The bartender's answer was a warning and a challenge: "That'll be three-fifty." He reached for his wallet to signal that he was aware he was going to pay that much for a glass of water, and the man moved to the cooler.

Ackerman placed a five-dollar bill on the bar, then moved toward the sign that said RESTROOMS. There was a dark little hallway, and two doors with the international symbols for the sexes, two gingerbread people so nearly alike that they signified nothing until compared for differences. He had been glad to see the bouncer because it meant that the pay telephone would still be firmly attached to the wall, and the book would be intact. The bouncer was the sort who would have considered the destruction of a telephone book an infraction that required his regretful attention.

He had no difficulty finding the home address. There were only four Talarese numbers, and only one Antonio. But then he noticed the business numbers. The first was Talarese's Bella Italia, then a number for catering, and one for reservations. The address was on Mott Street in Little Italy. It had to be the same place, the little catering store where he had met Tony T years ago. He walked back to the bar and sipped his bubbly water. The antique clock on the wall over the bar, a plain black face with glowing green numbers and a green neon ring around it, said that it was ten minutes to one.

He sat in the subway car looking at the spray-painted graffiti on the walls. The colors had gotten better, the viridian greens and new shades of orange, and the gold and silver metal-flake, but the script was now so ornate that he couldn't read any of it. When it occurred to him that it might be a different language, he decided it should still be organized into words. It looked more like the samples of Sumerian and Phoenician in the books he had found in his house in England than like any modern language. The British were always complaining that London was no longer an English city. They should see New York. It had always been a few steps closer to chaos than London was, but now no European would recognize it as having any historical relationship with anything he knew or understood. It was as though the Indians had returned to claim it after a three-hundred-year sojourn in the woods.

The train clattered to a stop, the doors opened and he stood and followed two anorectic heroin addicts onto the platform. They were probably younger than they looked, and they looked about twenty, two pockmarked young men in tight black pants that betrayed the fact that they had sat on the ground at some point, and thin almost-antique jackets of early synthetic materials—one in a silky blue-gray that he remembered seeing on someone when he was a teenager, and the other in a dirty bile-green with a texture almost like foam rubber. He could tell that they were holding, because the shorter of the two kept patting his pocket to reassure himself that he hadn't dropped the bag or his works. In England they made an effort to keep the poor bastards supplied and off the streets, so he had forgotten about them. But at least these two were holding, so he wouldn't have to watch his back when he moved out into the darkness. They would be on their way to a peaceful place where they could bring up a vein.

He ascended a set of concrete steps that smelled like a urinal, past old paint that was beginning to peel, taking with it the most recent graffiti and revealing more beneath it. When he reached the street he came around the railing and moved toward the catering shop he remembered.

He had no trouble seeing the store from a distance. It was after one on a Saturday night, and two men in suits were standing on the street like parking attendants. A big gray car pulled up in front, and one of them went to the window to talk to the driver. When the car pulled around the building, Ackerman remembered the loading dock in the back. Even in the old days, the little square of tar had been an unusual extravagance in this part of town, where trucks usually stopped on the street in front of businesses and unloaded onto the sidewalk. By now the Talareses could probably have lived off the rent on that much land. It was a place invisible from the street, where they could park a truck and bring anything in or out of the building. If the police had been both smart and honest for any extended period, they would have given themselves an education by watching that lot.

He walked up the street opposite the store, holding it in his peripheral vision. There was more to it now. There was a restaurant on one side with lights on but drawn curtains, and a big CLOSED sign in the window. The store that he remembered was dark. As he walked, the street began to take on an unreal quality, as though it were part of an old, familiar dream, the changes that time had made in it no more important than the little alterations his mind made when he invoked a landscape to contain his explorations in a dream. Once again he was walking alone on a dark street, clearing his mind and relaxing his muscles for the moment when he would need to decide and act faster than others could. This life should have been over long ago.

Disconnected bits of memory began to merge as he walked. Eddie Mastrewski must have been about forty on the winter day in Cleveland when they had sat in the car and watched the man walking through the snow toward the parking lot, and had both realized that if Eddie used his gun someone would hear. Eddie had leaned down to zip up his rubber boots over the cuffs of his pants, whispering "Aw shit, Aw shit" to himself more than to the boy. Then he had said, "It has to be now. Tomorrow he'll know, and then nobody will ever get near him." So Eddie chased the man down and killed him quietly with a tire chain. He came back red, sweating and gasping for breath, his eyes bulging as he started the car. "I'm too old for this," he had said. The boy had said nothing. Eddie hadn't been entirely serious, but from the boy's position in the front seat next to him, watching his big chest heaving under the heavy overcoat, and the bloated cheeks inflating as he blew out air, it had seemed true. Eddie had lasted a long time in the trade, and by now he had come to understand what that meant. Nobody could go on for thirty years now. It had been a generation that had something more than strength and stamina. They had some kind of animal stupidity, something that made them unaware of the pointlessness of going on. Some of the men who had dialed the telephones in the early 1950s and heard Eddie's cheerful, resonant baritone sing "Eddie the Butcher" over the wire were still at it: wizened, desiccated old skeletons, still studying the changing configurations of people and money to discern a pattern that would give them another way to steal. Eddie, younger than they were, was long dead.

Eddie had been a butcher, and the shop hadn't been a simple disguise. It was part of Eddie's homemade philosophy that a false identity was always a transparent, amateurish ruse. He had raised the boy in the butcher shop, first teaching him to sweep and wash the floors, then to care for the gleaming knives and saws, then finally to use them himself, as though Eddie had expected him to follow that trade rather than the other one. But Eddie hadn't thought things through clearly. He simply taught the boy what he knew, some of it nonsense and some of it useful. Sometimes the long days in the shop came back to him now.

"I never knew a man named Earl that you could trust. For some reason they're all thieves."

"Why?"

"I don't know why. But knowing it gives you an edge, because they don't know you know."

He had taught the boy the skills of the butcher shop, but Eddie had never imagined that in such a short time butchers would become as anachronistic as blacksmiths. Now only the rich bought their meat from a real butcher. The shops were like boutiques, and the only reason customers came was because they had the illusion that the prices they paid made the chemicals and hormones disappear from the meat. All the butchers worked for big meat-packing plants now and punched time clocks and belonged to the meat cutters' local. They couldn't accept part-time work that might take them out of town any time they got a telephone call. Eddie had lived to see the beginning of this change. He would notice that some of his old customers drove past the shop on the way to the supermarket. He would shake his head as though the small profit he made from the shop mattered to him. "You know what those bastards charge for a chicken? Two dollars a pound. When I was your age I could get laid for two dollars."

"Did you?"

"Hell, no. You think the clap is a joke?"

Ackerman turned and crossed the street two blocks down. The only way to approach the restaurant without letting anyone get behind him was to enter through the loading dock. Eddie had taught him to clear his mind and spend a few minutes in calm, dispassionate meditation before he committed himself. "You look, you wait, you think. Then, if it's doable, you think again. Do you know how you're going to get out if your first plan gets blown?"

Eddie would have taken him past the restaurant and let him look at it. "Once you're in, you're like an egg in a frying pan. You got two seconds to get in, see him and pop him. You got three seconds to get across the floor while they're wondering if you want them next. You got maybe a second to get out the door. You stand still more than a second at any step, you heat up and fry."

But this wasn't Eddie's kind of job. Eddie would not have understood why he was here. Eddie's philosophy was, above all, cautious. There were only smart and stupid; Eddie had never understood the word *audacity*. When he had heard the word applied to Napoleon on television, he had thought about it for a moment and then said it meant pressing your luck. Eddie would have told him he was a fool to come back to New York, but he'd had no choice. He had returned only because there was no practical way for him to stay alive but this. He had to kill the man who possessed the secret knowledge that he had been in England.

If Antonio Talarese had already told the others, they would have insisted on sending someone more formidable than the three hastily armed leg breakers he had seen at Brighton. Obviously Talarese had decided that the chance of a sudden coup was worth the risk. Ackerman still had a hope that he had arrived in New York before the news that Mario Talarese was dead.

As he moved down the narrow alley into the parking lot, he could see that he was much later than he had thought. The telephone call from England had already come. A hearse was parked behind the store, probably waiting to meet the body at the airport. He stood still and looked at it, but there was no sign of the driver. The funeral home must be owned by one of Antonio Talarese's friends. The driver would be a relative of the owner, a volunteer who had been invited inside with the others for a glass of grappa or anisette to help pass the time while they waited for the plane.

He was all the way back in the old life now, feeling his heart trying to beat stronger, harder, but finding he was still able to keep it slow. Eddie had taught him about noises by making him watch the cat in the butcher shop. If the cat made a sound, it would wait minutes before it moved again. The boy had learned that he could do the same. If his foot dislodged a stone or a board creaked, he rested and waited. In the early days when he had first worked alone, he had sometimes counted to an arbitrary number before moving again. It didn't matter what the number was, so long as he had waited beyond a human sense of time before he made another noise. Now, even after ten years of inactivity, he was still too good at it to have to think about it. He moved along the side of the building to the loading dock, rolled onto it, waited and listened.

He could hear low voices inside the building. They were coming from the back of the restaurant. He could see them in his imagination, sitting in the kitchen.

"Eat?" said a man's voice that he placed low and near the wall. "How am I supposed to eat? It's almost two o'clock in the morning, and I feel like this is my fault."

"Shhh. You'll give yourself *agita*." The woman was standing up, farther away.

"Nobody said it was your fault." This one was standing too; another man, and he was moving, probably pacing. "Please, Tony. Eat something. You've got to eat."

Ackerman used the aimless ritual of the conversation to crawl to the door. This was the entrance he had used when he had met Tony T. He pulled on the steel door, but it had an unbudging solidity that told him it was locked and staked down with a dead bolt in the floor. He would have to get in another way. As he moved closer to the kitchen door he could smell something cooking. It was the burning fat of meat mixed with something spicy that burned his nose and made him hungry. He didn't allow himself to smell it for long because it belonged in the category of irrelevant sensory distractions. It was other people's food, just part of what pertained to them, like their talk and clothes and names.

He stood in the darkness for a moment and tensed the muscles in his legs, feet, toes and then arms. He took a couple of deep breaths and let his heart rate speed up and the moment of dizziness turn into tension. He took the little pistol out of his coat pocket and flipped off the safety, then opened the door and slipped inside the kitchen, looking around him.

He stared into the eyes of a thin, dark woman in a black dress with a string of pearls around her neck, incongruously wearing a pair of huge, quilted oven mitts that looked like flippers. The woman froze, speechless, as he crouched and moved sideways behind the man seated at the stainless-steel table.

The man at the table saw her, twisted in his chair to see what she was looking at and scowled. In the last decade the face had gotten coarser and thicker, and the wavy black hair now had a few wiry gray strands, but it was unquestionably Tony Talarese. "What?" The mouth was thin and wide, and the pointed chin stuck out in annoyance until the eyes focused on the face that was too close. "You? Why you?"

It seemed an odd question, but Ackerman had no time now to wonder about it. He thought of Eddie's egg in the frying pan as he placed the gun against Talarese's temple and fired, then moved, not back toward the door but forward, sidestepping the woman in black, who was running to the body slumped forward on the table, flapping her arms to get rid of the oven mitts like a startled bird trying to take flight.

Nobody else in the kitchen moved as the woman flung herself on the dead man's back. Their eyes fluttered in their heads, not knowing where to look as he stepped past them: a middle-aged man in a dark suit and an apron, two girls in their twenties, one black-haired and the other blond, but like sisters, wearing short tight black dresses with a lot of stiff lace and explosions of chiffon at the hems as though they had just come from a night-club. As he reached the swinging door to the dining room, two other young women who had the flat shoes and big forearms of waitresses rushed in past him, one carrying a fire extinguisher upside down. He was prepared for the screams, but the screams didn't come from them. They came from the woman clutching the dead man to her. He slipped out the door to the dining room.

Inside the kitchen, the woman cried, "Tony!" There was a short pause, and then, "What's this?" The others flocked to her, trying to pull her away, but she didn't budge. She tapped on the dead man's back, and there was an audible electronic click. "A wire! The son of a bitch is wearing a wire!"

The woman tore at Antonio Talarese's back. The kitchen had turned into this small dark woman's personal madhouse, and confronted by the spectacle, the others all seemed to forget about the killer. The woman clawed Talarese's shirt up out of his belt to his shoulders, so that everyone could see that Tony T did have something taped to the small of his back. The woman squawked again, "See? I never would have believed my husband—" The grieving widow turned to the man in the apron. "Are these things always turned on?"

"What?" The stunned man in the apron looked as though he had been shot too. "What?"

"You know. Can they hear . . . at night? I'm his *wife*. You know what I'm asking."

The man seemed to decipher the words with great difficulty, groping toward the idea but not quite believing that anybody could be asking what he thought she was. When he arrived at it, he reacted with contempt. "For Christ's sake, Lucille! Who fucks with his coat on?"

That seemed to satisfy the wife for a moment, and her bony shoulders drooped. But what he'd said had brought understanding to one of the waitresses, a plump, fair woman about thirty-five. She seemed to remember something. "Oh, my God," she wailed, and the widow's eyes flicked toward her and narrowed. The widow's lips curled back to bare her teeth. "Whore!" she shrieked. As she hurled herself at the buxom, peach-faced waitress, she didn't notice that both of the young girls in the black dresses and the other waitress were backing toward the loading dock with identical stunned expressions on their faces. One of the young girls was compulsively jerking at the chain of a diamond pendant, trying to snap it off her neck. The widow was so alert she could see into their souls. "You too? You all let him do it wired up like a radio station?" Her voice shattered into a cackle.

Ackerman moved across the dim, empty restaurant, staying low and keeping his eyes on the door. He heard the hysterical woman exploring new octaves beyond soprano, but her screeches didn't resolve themselves into words.

Behind him in the kitchen there was a series of screams as pots and pans and then a table were knocked over. He watched the front door of the restaurant, crouching in the deep shadows below the bar. He heard the door rattle as one of the men on the street tried to open it, and then saw their shadows moving rapidly back and forth at the windows. Their voices didn't reach him over the noise in the kitchen, but he knew that eventually one would make a dash around the building to the loading dock while the other came through the front door into the dining room.

He relaxed his muscles and controlled his breathing while the minds of the two men outside lumbered toward the only possible strategy. He saw a shadow float along the front window toward the alley, and then watched the other shadow loom suddenly at the door. A moment later the glass was hammered inward, and a big arm reached through the hole and tugged at the crash bar. The door swung open and a big man pivoted around it into the restaurant, visible for only a second as his silhouette slid across the broken door into the safety of the darkness.

This man's movements were an unpleasant surprise. He was big, but he used his strength to move himself gracefully into a corner and hold himself low, silently waiting for his eyes to adjust to the darkness while he listened for the sound of an intruder. He was crouching in a spot where nobody could get behind him, and he could control both doors. With every heartbeat it became more likely that the man was cunning enough to stay where he was until his partner came in through the loading dock and flushed any intruder out the kitchen door.

In the kitchen, the widow had somehow freed herself from the man with the apron and resumed her tirade right beside the dining-room door, where the words were audible. "Whores!" she shrieked. Then there was the quavering voice of another woman, younger, frightened but steeling herself to defiance. "He was the one who wanted to." This seemed to enrage the widow even more. "Of course he was the one who wanted to.

He wanted everything, like a little boy. I hope they play this on the six o'clock news, so your grandmothers hear it and drop dead. And you with your bleached hair, twitching your ass in his face every day—"

Suddenly the big man in the corner leaped up and knocked over a table on the way to the kitchen, bellowing, "Gloria? What's she saying?"

He waited for the man to burst through the swinging door, then glided to the front of the restaurant. He pushed gently on the crash bar and opened the door only wide enough to step through it to the street. He put the gun into his pocket as he walked. In a moment he was around the corner, out of sight of the restaurant, a fortyish man in good clothes making his way toward the subway entrance two blocks down the street. As he walked, he had no concern that the two soldiers would be able to sort out what had happened in the two minutes in which they might still catch him. If they did, they would be in their cars looking for a man in a car.

As he approached the subway entrance, he reached into his pocket and felt the pistol. He was reluctant to relinquish it after all the trouble he had gone through to get it from the salesman's wounded friend, but he reminded himself that it was more dangerous to him than to anybody else now that he had used it. He moved down the steps to the shelter of the underground and used the change machine to buy a token to get him through the turnstile. It was all a sequence of simple, mechanical, logical steps.

He saw that he was alone in the big, echoing tunnel. In the silence he could hear the rails clicking somewhere, but the sound was still far off. He wondered how things had changed so much that he would be alone at a subway stop, even at two in the morning.

He jumped off the platform, ran down the track to the tunnel mouth and looked around again. There was no other human being in sight, and no sound except a train somewhere in a parallel tunnel, not even audible now, just a vibration through the bedrock. It had to be now. He took the little pistol out of his pocket, wiped it clean with his sleeve, laid it carefully across the gleaming steel rail, then turned, ran back to the platform, hauled himself up and waited. In a few minutes, even a few seconds, the New York transit system would effectively dispose of his weapon for him, turning it into something that looked more like a torn orange peel than a firearm. If the serial number miraculously survived, the nearest it would lead the most astute police force to him would be a delirious teenager lying in a hospital bed miles away.

Ackerman heard the reassuring sound of the train long before it arrived. It was rattling through the tunnel as though it had no intention of stopping. He watched the rail where he had placed his pistol. Suddenly there was a flash of light as the nose of the train swept past, and then it was just a strip of windows, most of them empty or nearly so, a few somnolent, dull-eyed faces looking out past him at the walls.

The train came to a stop beyond the boarding zone, and he had to walk quickly to reach the door of the last car as it opened automatically to receive him. He stepped through it just before it slid shut. As he moved to a seat, he took a census. Most of the cars he had seen were nearly empty, and a man alone sitting in the bright light would stand out like a stuffed animal in a diorama in a museum. In this car a dozen people sat in the sleepy boredom of the late shift, or the mildly disappointed memory of an evening out. Four big men sat in the two seats across from him, thick-necked beer swillers with pudgy fingers and bowling bags at their feet. There were two tall, studious-looking black men sitting in the seat in front of him. One of them wore wire-rimmed glasses with small, flat, round lenses that looked as though they had been issued by a Soviet medical mission to Zimbabwe. They caught the overhead lights and glinted whenever he glanced at the four white men across the aisle. His companion seemed to be a little more used to New York subways, and kept his gaze ahead to avoid meeting the eyes of any possible lunatic who might be staring at him in incomprehensible hatred.

The rest of the passengers were like him: solitary men who didn't want to be either memorable or visible in this place at this time. There were no sales to be made, contracts to be negotiated or friendships to be started on a subway after midnight, and any contact with the people surrounding them was risky. He adopted the same pose; he slouched a little, but only enough to suggest ease, not physical weakness. Like them, he cleared his mind and set his face in an ambiguous, empty expression.

He waited until the subway had stopped at Thirty-fourth and Sixth, then watched until a train decorated with a white airplane on a blue background arrived. The gradual replacement of words with colors and pictures had accelerated during his time away, and it made moving around a kind of puzzle. What could it be but an airport express? Maybe an ad for air travel? But it took him to the Howard Beach–JFK Airport station, and a bus came to shuttle him to the terminal.

Ackerman didn't see people on his route. He saw the backs of heads, collars raised and bodies bundled against the predawn chill, eyes half-closed because there could be nothing to look at until the train stopped moving. When he entered the terminal he took the precaution of finding a door with a little picture of a man on it so that he could wash any invisible traces of burned powder off his hands and forearms to fool a paraffin test. Then he went to his locker, retrieved his suitcase and returned to change his clothes in a stall.

He knew he was acting like a shopkeeper who had just killed his wife for the life insurance, but something unexpected had happened at Talarese's. He wasn't sure exactly what it was, but he knew it couldn't be good.

8

Elizabeth Waring Hart poured boiling water through the coffee filter, then set the kettle back on the burner without making any noise. She stopped and listened to the baby monitor for a second, poured the coffee into her cup and then sat in the cold predawn darkness. As soon as she raised the cup and touched it tentatively to her lips, she heard Amanda's first stirrings. There was a faint little gasp that the monitor amplified into a rattling snore, and then came the roll. The crinkle of the biodegradable diaper sounded like the crumpling of a newspaper over the thin layer of static. Then Amanda began to coo to herself in her crib, and Elizabeth listened intently. In a few minutes, she would be crying for rescue, but as long as she was experimenting happily with sounds and running the morning inventory of toys in her crib, it was better to leave her in peace.

Elizabeth took another sip of her coffee. When Jimmy was this age, Jim had been the one to do this. He had been a morning person. Sometimes, soon after he had died, Elizabeth had felt strange when she sat here, taking his place. Sometimes she had even tried to talk to him, because it seemed as though he were nearby. She would say, "You bastard. You stupid bastard. You should be doing this." The counselor from the hospital had said that anger was a normal reaction, but counselors were in the business of telling people things were normal that weren't.

When the telephone rang she snatched it off its cradle before it had finished its first jangle. "Hello?" she said, just above a whisper.

"Elizabeth." It was a statement, uninflected, and not enough to tell her who would call at this hour.

"Yes." She matched the emptiness of the tone.

"I think we've finally found something that will make you

come back to Organized Crime." So it was Richardson. When she had transferred out of the section ten years ago, Richardson had been at her level, just a data analyst with a law degree. Now he was in charge.

"What's that?" she asked without curiosity. She had been in two other sections of the Justice Department since then and taken two maternity leaves, and nobody had ever asked her to come back.

"A couple of hours ago in New York a man walked in the back door of a restaurant and put a hole in Tony Talarese's head."

"Tony T?" What surprised her was that she remembered who that was. She could be away for a hundred years, and she couldn't get the names out of her memory.

"There's only one suspect. He did it in front of Talarese's brother, his wife and three mistresses."

"Interesting. Who was it?"

"The Butcher's Boy." But she wasn't really listening, because there was no other reason why this man would call her at this hour. She was already thinking way ahead: about the kids' baby-sitter, about the problem of arranging a temporary transfer out of her section when everybody was working double shifts tracing money from Housing and Urban Development into private bank accounts and about the dress at the dry cleaner's that she wished she could wear if she had to go into that office again. Part of her was also listening to the baby monitor, because Amanda was beginning to change her tone subtly, occasionally pausing in her quiet babble to issue little bulletins of discomfort.

Richardson gave her the old desk. It was amazing that it even existed; no, not that it existed—because anything that had ever been on a government inventory stayed on it—but that it was still here in the same place, not even shifted off the little wooden wedge Elizabeth had jammed under one leg to keep it from wobbling on the uneven floor.

She played the tape recording a second time. The gun was unbelievably loud. She glanced at the report again: .32 caliber. But, of course, he was firing it two feet from the microphone, into Tony T's head. She listened to the loud scrabbling, tearing sound, and then the woman shrieking, "The son of a bitch is wearing a wire!" She punched the button.

She stood up and walked into what they had called the chief's office. In the old days she wouldn't have considered walking into that room without knocking, but Richardson was her contemporary, and, whether he knew it or not, he wasn't her boss.

He looked up from his desk. "Well?"

"And the grieving widow said it was the Butcher's Boy?"

"She said that's what her brother-in-law told her. He, of course, won't tell anybody anything."

"She happen to mention what he's been doing with himself all these years?"

"I don't get the impression she'd ever heard of him before. When we catch him you can fill each other in."

Elizabeth felt it. She couldn't help that. But she reminded herself that Richardson wasn't complicated enough to try to jab the sensitive spots. Those ten years had been her portion of a decent life, her allotment. She was a widow too. Richardson knew at least that much. She said carefully, "We're not going to catch him unless we figure things like that out. You called me down here in the middle of the night, so help me."

Richardson pushed aside his papers and looked at her evenly. "Right."

"What were they doing in a closed restaurant—a party?"

"Hardly," said Richardson. "There was an empty hearse in the back lot. They were going to the airport to pick up Tony's nephew. It's been a bad week for Clan Talarese."

"He was killed too? Where?"

"England."

She jumped up. "My God, we're wasting time. Get me the flight lists from London to New York. Every flight since the nephew died. And every flight out of New York since he killed Tony T."

"You're jumping to conclusions. We don't even know what happened to the nephew. It might have been AIDS."

"Then find out. But later. First the airline flight lists."

Elizabeth worked alone. In the old days it used to take hours of negotiations to get anything from the airlines. Now any question from the Justice Department—at least the Washington office—induced a special kind of panic. Too many planes had been dropping out of the sky. The fax machine kept buzzing, and Richardson's secretary had to keep walking back into the little cubicle to change the paper.

Elizabeth crossed off all the names of women, then all the names of travelers with Frequent Flyer credits, then all the reservations made more than a week ago, then all the passengers

with names he couldn't be expected to use—Yamaguchi, Baba-
tundi, Gupta, Hernandez and Nguyen—then looked through the
sheets again. What else? What was it that made him special?
Nothing. That had to be it. There would be nothing special at
all: no special seat, special meals, special luggage arrangements. He didn't give a damn if he rode naked in the baggage
compartment; all he wanted was to get out fast and disappear
again. She checked the notations on the printouts once more,
crossing off any passenger who had a special request.

That left an encouragingly short list. There wasn't time to
count the names, but there were still too many. She thought
about what he had done. He had walked into a kitchen, shot
Tony T in front of a lot of people and walked out. It was the
middle of the night. Of course he had known Tony T was dangerous. What he would have wanted to do was to sneak into
Talarese's bedroom while he was asleep and empty the pistol
into his head. It would have been between three and five in the
morning, the time the police always picked for a raid, when he
would be deep asleep, and the plane reservation would be based
on what he had wanted to do, not what he'd had to do. He would
expect to be finished and on the street by five-thirty at the latest,
at the airport again by six-thirty and on a plane by seven-thirty
or eight. That was the absolute outside limit.

Elizabeth pushed aside half of the flights. Would he sit around
in an airport until 10:55 waiting for a way out, when anybody
could walk in and see him? Not a chance. He would be long
gone by then. He'd be up in the air about thirty thousand feet on
his way to . . . where? Not someplace where there would be
two flights a day, eight hours apart. If he missed the first one,
there had to be another one warming its engines on the runway.
Someplace big and busy. She went through the pile of flights
again, pulling out the small cities, losing hundreds of names as
she did it, and feeling warmer now, closer to him. Once, years
ago, she had gone through the airline lists, knowing that he was
one of the names, and never gotten this close. He had already
landed somewhere before she even knew he had taken a plane.
But this time was different; these flights were still in the air.
Maybe this time.

He was running, and he wasn't going to cross his own path.
No return reservation. She obliterated all the round-trip tickets,
now finding reasons for eliminating names faster than her hand
could move to strike them out. Almost all the remaining names
had booked return flights.

Form of payment. He would certainly have credit cards, probably in a lot of different names. But if he did, he wasn't going to let them be used to trace him away from the crime scene, and he wasn't going to throw one away for an airline ticket. He would use them for hotels after he had come to earth someplace safe. He would pay cash for the ticket.

There were only five names remaining on three flight lists now, and she laid them all out on the table and stared at them. One of them looked wrong: Hagedorn, David. She was sure she had crossed that one off already. She looked quickly from sheet to sheet. Hagedorn, Mary, traveling with Hagedorn, Marissa. Parents. At one time she wouldn't have understood, but now she did. It was that awful, depressing anxiety that one of the planes was going to fall out of the sky, and some sort of magic would keep Marissa from being an orphan. She crossed off Hagedorn, David.

There was nothing to distinguish any of the other four. They had all bought tickets with cash on the day of the flight. All had chosen to leave New York on morning flights. All were males traveling alone, taking any seat they could get. Somebody undoubtedly had heard a relative was sick, another had been called for a job interview, another had a girlfriend who wanted him to join her after all. The fourth had just fired a pistol into the head of a New York caporegima, and was understandably impatient to get out.

Richardson came in behind her, but she didn't look up. "How's it going?"

"I've got it down to four," she said.

"How the hell did you do that? What are the criteria?"

"It would take an hour to show you. We don't have an hour."

"Give me the four."

She handed him the three passenger lists with four names left untouched. "I don't know how to get it down to one."

He glanced at the lists. "Dallas . . . Chicago . . . Los Angeles . . . another Chicago. What do you want to do?"

"If there's any way in the world to hold all four of them, do it," Elizabeth said. "He's running. Though he doesn't exactly run; he just sort of fades out. He won't stay put. He'll get on another flight under another name. He'll pay cash."

"How do you know that?"

"There's no time. Look at those ETAs."

"I'll get the FBI on the phone."

* * *

Elizabeth watched Richardson through the open door of his office. It was the third time he had been on the telephone with the FBI agent. He held his ballpoint pen over a yellow legal pad, at first poised to write something down, then just gripping it like a knife, clicking the button on the end of it nervously, retracting and extending the tip over and over as he listened.

She waited at her old desk and tried to avoid the bad luck by watching the first group of ambitious GS-7's and -9's coming in to work early, each expecting to be the first, seeing her and looking puzzled, then seeing Richardson's door open and looking disappointed. She had been like them once, and it mortified her now, but at the time it hadn't been ambition. She just hadn't known enough history. They had still called it the Organized Crime Task Force in those days, behaving as though they had been brought together to cope with an emergency that would go away if they worked harder than the Mafia. That was before she had learned enough to realize that criminal conspiracy was the natural state of affairs in all civilized countries. People who worked for the Justice Department had to be in it for the long haul.

But then Richardson was on his feet and out of his office, and the expression on his face was enough. "No hits," he said. "Dallas is seventy-one years old, and both Chicagos are military personnel. L.A. is already on the ground and the FBI doesn't even have its team there yet. I'm sorry."

Elizabeth shook her head. "It's not too late. He's got to be in the L.A. airport, or near it, trying to get out. He doesn't have another reservation. Don't we even have a birdwatcher in a major airport like that?"

"We don't have a picture or a description or anything else. Nobody's ever seen him. What are they supposed to do?"

"He'll be getting on another flight. Try the name. It might not be any good now; next time he can call himself Rufus T. Firefly if he feels like it. But there's got to be a way to stop him before he gets on another plane. It will be a one-way ticket bought for cash in the airport since his plane landed."

"I don't know," said Richardson. "This is getting thinner and thinner."

"Please," said Elizabeth. "This is closer than we ever got ten years ago."

Jack Hamp was sitting in the coffee shop overlooking Runway 23 with four engine mechanics from United when the crew chief happened to notice that the light on his beeper was blinking. It didn't blink often, so he didn't look at it often. He wasn't under the illusion that if there was an emergency they would think to warn him, so a month after he had gotten this assignment he had opened it up and cut the wire from the relay to the little speaker.

Jack Hamp had managed to retire from the Los Angeles Police Department after twenty years and gotten a job as what he had thought was a Justice Department field investigator. At the moment the job didn't involve much investigating. He was supposed to loiter in the L.A. airport and watch the huge amorphous, anonymous crush of people getting on and off airplanes to see if he could spot any of the fifty or so men and women that the Justice Department was giving special attention to at any given moment. Most of the time, when somebody like that was coming through, Hamp would have the reservation in advance, and all he would have to do was to pass by the gate to see him step aboard, then report what he had seen: ''Subject Vincent Toscanzio. At 13:53 subject boarded TWA flight 921 for Chicago, ETA 7:53 P.M. Was accompanied by two male Caucasians listed as Harold Carver, positive I.D. Joseph Vortici, and Paul Smith, probable I.D. Frederick Moltare.'' It all went into the hopper for some analyst to sort out in Washington.

The rest of the time he fished the crowds for Special Surprise Guests nobody had known were out and about. He had no vanity, and he was good at looking like something other than a federal cop. He was six feet three and lanky, with pale blue eyes, long blond hair and a mustache. He looked like the aging cowboy he probably would have been if he hadn't been optimistic enough to join the marines twenty-five years ago and accidentally seen a few big cities. He usually went to a gate when a crowded flight from a major departure point was unloading. He would stand a little back from the gauntlet of moms and pops scrutinizing the file of passengers to see Junior a second earlier. He would carry an object—maybe a magazine, maybe only sunglasses or a set of car keys—but never a cup of coffee, because that was what people drank when they were on duty. And like the moms and pops, Jack Hamp would stare at each face for a moment right in the eyes, because he too was hoping to recognize someone.

He managed to pick out a few interesting faces each month, and this probably made his reports worth sending, but he didn't much like the assignment. He suspected he had gotten it because the Department wanted him on the payroll, but didn't have a clear idea what to do with him on a day-to-day basis. He was young to be a retired cop—forty-six—but he was too old and uneducated to be on the Upward Trail with the rest of the Boy Scouts.

The Justice Department had put him through a refresher course in investigative techniques of the sort he had given to ten or twelve litters of rookie cops over the years, an orientation for federal employees that he had used to compile a list of whose calls he could ignore, and a little practice in shooting holes in cardboard cutouts that looked like the villains in a comic book. Then they had sent him back to L.A.

Hamp walked with a barely perceptible limp as he got up and made his way to the pay telephone at the other end of the concourse. The man who had put the hole in his left thigh eight years ago had taken a little of the femur with it, and he sometimes felt the stainless-steel pin. He dialed the number quickly. "This is Hamp," he said.

The man on the other end was somebody he had never talked to before, but Hamp knew Richardson's name. It was one of the ones he couldn't ignore.

Ackerman walked to the Hong Kong Airlines desk. The man behind the counter was Chinese, but he had an engraved nameplate on his jacket that read MR. SULLIVAN. His English accent made Ackerman homesick for Schaeffer's life. "May I help you, sir?"

"You have a flight to Hong Kong in twenty minutes," he said. "Do you have any seats left?"

Mr. Sullivan clicked some keys on his computer. "I'm sorry, sir. It's fully booked. We have another at four-seventeen."

Ackerman hesitated. Hong Kong was okay, because he could go back through British customs after a week without raising any eyebrows. If he flew back through New York, there would be watchers in the airport, and he might never make it out. He decided that waiting was the smaller risk. "I'll take it."

"May I have your passport, please?"

Ackerman plucked it from his coat pocket and handed it to Mr. Sullivan, who glanced at it and set it aside for a moment.

"How will you be paying for that, sir?"

"Cash."

"Fine," said Mr. Sullivan. "Let me just confirm that it's still available." He pressed three numbers on his telephone and began to speak in Chinese. Ackerman glanced around at the people lining up behind him and setting their luggage down. As he turned back, his eyes caught something peculiar. At the far end of the counter there was another man speaking into a telephone in Chinese. It was the cadence that caught his attention. When Mr. Sullivan talked, the other man stopped, and then Mr. Sullivan said something and the other man glanced in his direction. Ackerman watched the man until the two hung up almost simultaneously. He stood at the counter while Mr. Sullivan made out the ticket, copying his name from his passport, and then he walked away.

He knew it was possible that Mr. Sullivan was only calling his supervisor to check on that reservation. It might even be that two conversations followed approximately the same course, ended at the same time, and had nothing to do with each other. But it might also be that two men who worked for Hong Kong Airlines had just made a year's salary. He had been away a long time. Ten years ago the Balacontano family could steal the cargoes off wide-body planes in the middle of JFK and truck them out. It wasn't hard to believe that by now they could search passenger lists for the right alias.

He walked to Gate 28, where he was to board the flight for Hong Kong, then walked along the concourse until he found the right place to sit. It was two gates away, at Gate 26. The seat he wanted was occupied, but a lot of flights were going to leave before he needed it. He used the time to buy a ticket for the four-thirty plane to Albuquerque, and then sat in a coffee shop where he could watch people coming through the metal detectors that guarded the concourse, until he realized that watching was pointless. They didn't have to send faces he knew; somehow they had found out what name he was using. And they wouldn't be clumsy enough to get stopped by a metal detector. The gun would be concealed inside another steel object or, more likely, was already here.

He returned to Gate 26 and began his vigil with the idea that nothing would happen until they announced that his plane was boarding.

Jack Hamp took his old carry-on bag out of the car and walked back through the front door, up to the metal-detector station where Marlita Gibson gave him a sober nod as she looked through the fluoroscope at the outlines of his Colt .45 1911 automatic and the spare magazines in the pocket beside it. Hamp had a strong desire not to fire it. The 225-grain semiwadcutter hollowpoint ammunition was what he called the "airport load." It not only mushroomed on impact but expanded. It wasn't going through any walls if he missed. If he didn't miss, the recipient was going to find out that Jesus wanted him for a sunbeam. He snatched the bag off the conveyor and walked on. As he strode along the concourse toward Gate 28, he opened the bag and searched for a ticket folder in his collection that said Hong Kong Airlines. When he found it, he stuck it in his coat pocket where it could be seen.

At the gate, he sat down in the smoking area a few yards away from the nearest passenger and lit a cigarette. If the man spotted him first and was any kind of shot, at least he wouldn't miss Hamp and put a hole in some kid's head. And this one might be pretty good. From what Richardson had said, he sounded like a genuine badass. As Hamp inhaled the first sweet, cool smoke from his cigarette, he thought about how much worse the last puff always tasted. He kept his eyes on the passing throng, moving from face to face, first studying, then rejecting. He acknowledged that if he was already thinking about how hot and nasty this cigarette was going to get, it probably was time to quit smoking. All the pleasure of it depended on your being able to keep things from yourself.

He was going on the long odds that this Mr. Ackerman was going to be armed. It was highly unlikely that anybody could get on a plane at Kennedy and still be able to reach into his pants at LAX and come up with anything in his hand that he wasn't born with. But people who killed a lot for money got into the habit of brooding about such things in their spare time, and, more often than you would think, they found ways.

Hamp glanced at the airline desk in front of the gate and noted that Mr. Sullivan was in position. As soon as Mr. Ackerman showed his face, he was going to meet Jack Hamp.

Ackerman saw the tall, thin, melancholy blond man come into the waiting area at Gate 28 and sit down to light a cigarette, and he studied him with special care. He had a worn carry-on bag, and what looked like a Hong Kong Airlines ticket sticking out of his pocket. He was alone. He was doing pretty much what anybody would do in his position, which was to watch the people around him without letting them notice.

But then Mr. Sullivan arrived. He came up to the second floor by climbing an exterior staircase, popped through the door they never let passengers use, and posted himself at the desk near the gate, but he didn't make any attempt to do anything that could be construed as work. Ackerman wasn't going anywhere on Hong Kong Airlines today. He decided he had better try to find out exactly what kind of trouble he was in.

Ackerman moved to a seat that put the pillar at Gate 27 between him and Mr. Sullivan at Gate 28, and kept his eyes on the tall blond man. The tall guy was a possibility. He had even managed to sit in the right place, where he had a clear fire zone in front of him and nobody behind him. But how the hell could they have gotten him here so quickly? Peter Mantino would practically have to keep the guy on call in the airport in case somebody he wanted showed up.

That was unlikely. Ackerman still couldn't decide. The man had carried himself with a certain amount of confidence, as though he had some reason to be sure what was going to happen if he got into a fight, but as though he wasn't contemplating anything like that at the moment. It was the walk that came back to Ackerman. That was probably what had drawn his attention in the first place. He tried to picture it again, and when the man moved across his line of sight in his memory, he was favoring his left leg slightly. It was just the sort of unconscious change in his stride that two or three pounds of steel stuck on one side of his body might induce. No, the gun would be in the flight bag, where he could put his hand on it without attracting attention.

Then something happened that was so unexpected that Ackerman didn't admit to himself that he had caught it at first. Four men entered the waiting area at Gate 28 from different directions. They were all well over six feet tall and heavy, and they looked big and fat and white and obvious. They lurked in different parts of the waiting area, but kept glancing at each other to preserve fixed distances, like a team playing zones. Then each of them looked at the tall, thin blond man as though they had been searching for him. From time to time each of them would watch him for a second and then turn away. Even the blond man knew immediately that they were cops. Ackerman studied the man's reaction. The shooter couldn't believe it any more than Ackerman could. Whatever the shooter was carrying must have been picked up on the X-ray machine or, more likely, somebody had seen him go wherever it was hidden in the airport and stick it in his bag. Now he was going to get arrested.

Ackerman considered the possibility that he might be able to sit patiently until the cops rolled up the shooter, then stroll across to Gate 28, step onto the plane and get out of here. But then one of the cops started to walk toward the smoking area where the shooter was sitting, and the others each in his own time began to move closer. The shooter saw it too, but he didn't look frightened. He looked angry, which was a very bad sign. It meant that he was at least considering doing something with the gun in his flight bag other than letting them take it and having his lawyer claim the bag wasn't his. Ackerman couldn't take the chance of sitting here while the tall guy opened fire. No matter what happened, this wasn't the way out of Los Angeles. He stood up and turned away, adopting the same purposeful, self-important gait as the men and women nearest to him on the concourse. They all seemed comfortable in the knowledge that airports weren't about space, but about time. Like them, he didn't pause anywhere or slow his pace, and he didn't look back.

Elizabeth dialed her own number and waited four rings before the answering machine kicked in. "Maria," she said, "it's me. Please pick up the phone." After a few seconds, she heard the baby-sitter's voice.

"Waring residence," said Maria. If she knew who it was, why did she say that? Elizabeth reluctantly accepted that she would have to explain it again, along with the part about the phone numbers. The line in the office at home was Waring; the one in the bedroom was Hart. Maria had easily understood that Jim's name was Hart, and that Elizabeth's name was Hart. But then Elizabeth had gotten overconfident and told her she used the name Waring at work. At first Maria had been suspicious. Did that mean that what Elizabeth did for a living was illegal? No, she was a government lawyer, and Waring had been her name before she was married. What did being married have to do with being a lawyer? Nothing. Then, was being a government lawyer dangerous, like in Colombia? No, not usually.

Then Elizabeth had been subjected to a lengthy cross-examination on precise gradations of risk. When Maria had satisfied herself that nobody was doing anything illegal that would put her in jeopardy of deportation, or anything dangerous that would harm the children, she had clearly decided that there was something disreputable going on. Her questions indicated that she suspected that Elizabeth had never been married, and that Hart was a fiction adopted to protect the illegitimate children.

Since she loved the children, she could live with this. So where did "Waring residence" come from?

"Maria," Elizabeth said, "how are the kids?"

"No good."

"Not good? What's wrong?" Her heart stopped beating and began to quiver.

"Jimmy wore dirty old sneakers to school."

"That's okay. I told him it was all right." This was a lie, but it was the only way to close the issue. Maria had been educated by nuns who really appeared to have believed that cleanliness was next to godliness, and she was convinced that going to school every day was a privilege to be celebrated in shined shoes, immaculate shirts and pressed trousers. "What about Amanda?"

"She spit up."

"How much—a little spit-up, like a burp, or a big one? Should I come home?"

"Not too big. Little bit, but then she happy and go to sleep."

"Did you take her temperature?"

"Yes, normal."

"Well, thanks, Maria. I'll call again later. You have the number here, right?"

"I have it."

"Do you need anything?"

"No. Good-bye."

"Good-bye."

Elizabeth stared at the telephone. This was a special taste of hell that somebody had thought up for her. She had wanted children, and from the moment Jimmy had been conceived, she had understood that the term "blessed with children" wasn't an ironic way of saying it, because it really was how you felt. But there they were, and here she was. She was living the life she had said she would never live. Her children were growing up without seeing her for ten or twelve hours a day while she was out chasing a career she didn't want. Another woman played with them, dressed them, took Amanda out in the stroller and said the word *tree* or *squirrel* to her for the first time.

She heard the phone in Richardson's office ring and watched him snatch it off the hook. At first he looked elated, which meant that it was the FBI calling him from Los Angeles and not a file clerk letting him know that she was going to be late. But now he looked concerned, then frustrated. He leaned his head on his fist and let his shoulders slump from the tense shrug that had held them for the past five minutes, and she knew it was over. She drifted to the doorway and looked at him, lifting an eyebrow. "They lost him," he said.

"Why?" Her throat was dry, and it was just a sound to make anyway. It didn't matter.

"They don't know. He paid cash for a ticket to Hong Kong, then never showed up. Our birdwatcher at the airport says it's because the FBI sent four identical G-man types who proceeded to walk up to him and ask him to point out the suspect. Who, incidentally, was still calling himself Charles F. Ackerman."

"Today."

He nodded. "Today."

"Did the birdwatcher say anything else?"

"He's a little annoyed. He said if this guy's so important, how come nobody told the FBI to send the first team."

"Good question."

"I thought it was implied in what I told them, but he said they acted like we were after an eight-o-niner."

"What's that?"

"I was afraid I was the only one who didn't know. It's what he calls a person carrying money out of the country for illegal purposes. They're not usually dangerous."

"What's eight-o-nine, an IRS regulation?"

"No. It's a telephone area code. Cayman Islands, Dutch Antilles . . ."

"I'll remember that. It's probably where all the HUD money went." She turned and walked over to her old desk to get her purse. As she picked it up, she tried to remember whether she had left anything in the conference room. No. She could feel her pen, wallet, keys and glasses through the soft glove leather. It was going to be all right. She could be in her office in the other building in time for work, and none of this would have to take up space in her mind. Then she realized that Richardson had followed her out. In a way it was an appropriate gesture. She had given up several hours of her time to a division she didn't work for, and somehow the fiction had been allowed to grow between them that they had been friends in the old days, so for the moment it was good to maintain the pretense long enough for her to get out of here gracefully. The truth was that when she had left the section ten years ago, she had officially gone on vacation and then never come back. She'd had no impulse to say good-bye to anyone at the time, and when it had occurred to her that she should have, it was too late. Nobody in the office had called her, either.

"Elizabeth," Richardson said. He was going to thank her for the favor. Fine, she thought. She'd say it was nothing, and then she would be out of here.

But he said, "I've got a favor to ask."

Carlo Balacontano had been playing gin rummy since he was twelve, and he was very good at it. In October he would be sixty-six, and it was one of the things he could still do as well as he ever had, because even though his arms were no longer heavily muscled and his knees were sometimes a little stiff, his mind was still able to determine and remember the locations of all fifty-two cards, if a game came down to that. Usually he needed to hold only about thirty in his head at once, and he could do that, talk and think about business at the same time. But today he wasn't doing any of that, because he was sitting across the weight-lifting table from José-Luc Ospina.

Every day Carl Bala came to sit under the overhanging roof of the weight-training area. When he approached in his slow, leisurely stroll, four young men would step up and begin to haul the barbells off the leather-bound table so that he could sit down, take his deck of cards out of the breast pocket of his blue-denim shirt and rip open the package. This ritual had gone on since his second month at Lompoc Federal Correctional Facility eight years ago.

He would have begun to play gin right away, but for the first four weeks he had been out of his mind. His lawyers had assured him right up until the last day that his case would be retried in the Court of Appeals. But the judge had read the trial transcript in one afternoon, then ruled that there were no grounds for appeal. This had somehow stuck with him during the next few weeks, tormenting him, awake or asleep. Carl Bala was not a no-neck whose reading speed was determined by how fast he could move his lips, but he simply did not believe that anyone could read twelve hundred pages of testimony in one afternoon. He suspected that the pompous little bastard was one of those people who had gone to a class where they learned to read by moving their index fingers down the center of the page. The fact that after all these years he had finally been convicted on a bogus charge had not struck him as outrageous. With few exceptions, the people he knew who had gone to jail had been guilty, but not necessarily guilty of the particular crimes discussed at their trials. The system knew its enemies. If he'd had the choice of either accepting the simple murder of Arthur Fieldston or confessing to all the things he had actually done, he would have chosen Fieldston.

These days, the irritant that made Carlo angry most frequently was the existence of José Ospina. Four years ago on a summer afternoon Balacontano had arrived at the weight table to see the usual gaggle of prisoners wearing the thick leather belts cinched around their middles to keep their guts from popping out, straining to raise the heavy weights above their heads and curling the small barbells to make their already-bulging forearms look like ham hocks. He had sat down at the table, pulled the little red string to open the cellophane on his new deck of cards, removed the jokers and begun to shuffle. Then he had looked up to see a tall, dark young man with curly black hair and eyes like a cat sit down across from him. The man had his shirt cut off at the sleeves to reveal bony arms decorated with strange greenish tattoos. They were pictures of some sort of vegetation. They didn't look like natural plants; they seemed almost architectural. Most maddening of all, they looked familiar. Carlo Balacontano didn't recognize the tattoos until José Ospina had set his cards down on the table and whispered, ''Gin.'' Then he had taken off his shirt and Bala had found himself staring at the face of Benjamin Franklin. The tattoos were the flourishes and scrollwork engraved on a hundred-dollar bill.

From that day onward, José Ospina proceeded to ruin Carl Bala's life. Carl Bala was rich: even now in New York there were large, quiet men who spent all their time driving big, heavy cars to various places of commerce to collect his rake-offs, percentages and tributes. He was also famous, in the way that mattered. Even here, three thousand miles and eight years away from the scenes of his triumphs, he could have walked into a hotel on the shore of the Pacific and taken the best suite in the place on the strength of his name. But that was in the outside world, and Carl Bala wasn't living in the world. He was in a small, sun-bleached federal prison twenty miles into the dry yellow countryside of central California, hedged between jagged, impassable stone mountains that rose abruptly from the valley floor to the east and broad, open lowlands that stretched to the sea on the west; twenty miles of sparse, ankle-high weeds with every mile or so a crabbed, tortured live oak tree no more than eight feet tall to provide the only shade.

In this place, meeting José Ospina was like watching a cockroach scurrying off his dinner plate. At first he had been a shock, but Carl Bala had tried to reconcile himself to it. Then, day after day, he had sat and felt the sting as the young man, looking a little bored, had set his cards on the weight table before him and said in his soft voice, "Gin." Even worse, there were times when José Ospina would watch Balacontano discard once, then pick up his cards, fan them out, close the fan and say, "I'll knock with ten." Or eight or three. And Carlo would be frantically leafing through his brand-new hand, staring at the face cards, aces and tens he hadn't had time to count up, let alone unload.

Stacked decks Carl Bala could have understood, but these things happened when José Ospina hadn't so much as cut the cards. Palming and substituting a whole hand was not unheard of on the planet Earth, but José Ospina always played with the sleeves cut off his shirt, the flourishes of scrollwork copied from the currency of the United States visible running up his bare arms. He had no place to hide extra cards, no way of cheating at all. José Ospina was lucky. Admittedly he was a pitiless, competitive, supernaturally alert gin player, but the immutable forces of probability and chance simply kissed him on the forehead and passed by him each day to settle with their customary ferocity on the shoulders of Carl Bala. Bala found himself living in this little penal outpost where the only pleasure permitted him was winning at gin, something that happened so seldom now that when it did it felt like mockery.

Carlo had used his status in the prison underground to find out what he could about José Ospina, and had obtained a copy of Ospina's official file. He had learned that José Ospina had been transferred to Lompoc after two years of good behavior at Marion, Illinois, where he had been serving five to ten on a conviction for possession of counterfeit money and an arsenal of automatic weapons, including an M-60 machine gun. Under "Distinguishing Marks and Scars" was a description of the greenish tattoos, which the prison rumor establishment later told Balacontano had been done in Marion by Ospina's partner, a talented engraver named Cardero. Under "Place of Birth" was the entry "**Lexington, Kentucky**," suspicious since Ospina had a thick Spanish accent. But when he double-checked "Eye Color," the form said "hazel," the category in which the United States government placed all colors other than brown or blue. Ospina's eyes were certainly not blue or brown; they were bright golden yellow, which was to say "hazel." There was no sign that he was a card mechanic or a gambler or even intimate with gamblers. So Carlo had concluded that Ospina was merely riding a streak of luck like the vein of gold under Sutter's mill, long and deep, but still finite, and he had decided to wait it out.

He had been waiting it out for three and a half years of frustration and simmering anger, having run up a tab of $344,000 in the process. In that time he had stepped up his purchases of decks of cards, sometimes bringing out a fresh one twice in a single day. He had also been treated by the prison doctor for an incipient ulcer and given a rubber mouthpiece to keep him from grinding his teeth while he slept. In 1958, when all of the East was at war over territory and dominance, and every three days somebody was found mutilated in the trunk of his car or broke loose from his anchor and popped to the surface of a river, Carl Bala had been able to eat heaping plates of hot sausage and peppers, then sleep like a hibernating bear. But not now; the effort of containing the anger had begun to threaten his robust constitution. The only release he had for his hatred was to send messages to his employees, subordinates, relatives and colleagues who lived in the outer world, demanding that they find the man who had framed him and get him out. Lately his demands had become more urgent, the implied rewards more princely and the veiled threats more dire. There were already those who believed that, like others before him, Carlo had gone mad in prison. But a madman with untold millions of dollars might overspend to reward those who humored him, and nobody doubted that, mad or not, Carlo Balacontano would be capable of finding strong hands to carry out any form of revenge that stayed in his agitated imagination long enough to turn it into words.

These threats had become particularly worrisome to some of the lieutenants who were now serving as stewards and trustees of his empire: Giovanni "John the Baptist" Bautista, Antonio "Tony T" Talarese, Salvatore Callistro, Peter Mantino. These men had covered themselves in advance by mentioning Carl Bala's mad desires with exaggerated seriousness to their soldiers at more frequent intervals as the years passed and Balacontano's parole was becoming more easy to imagine. Bautista and Mantino had also quietly discussed the possibility that if the culprit didn't turn up before the old man's first parole-board hearing, it might be inconvenient or even suicidal to let him walk out of prison alive. Talarese had come to the same conclusion independently, spurred by the possibility that the old man might figure out that Talarese had been stealing some of the profits.

Carlo Balacontano had intuited much of this, and informers had kept him abreast of the rest. He could easily have taken his revenge from the prison yard, but he needed these men for now. Thinking that they were working to fill their own pockets, they were amassing a greater hoard that he would come back and reclaim later. But he needed their memories more than their greed. They were all old enough to have seen the man he wanted. The young wise guys, the little weasels who were so eager to sell their bosses to the imprisoned chieftain and take over their fiefs, were too young. The Butcher's Boy hadn't been seen by anyone in ten years.

Carlo Balacontano knew how the system worked. In order to get out, he would have to supply the system with someone to take his place. The replacement could be dead, as long as something linking him to the murder of Arthur Fieldston was found with him: a forged suicide note with a confession, the cigarette lighter that Bala had pocketed at Fieldston's office in the old days, when he had been there to discuss a deal—anything. A reasonable doubt might be enough excuse for someone to sell him a pardon, and would almost certainly be enough to get him a parole after eight years. Then he could get away from this place and from José Ospina, the man who was driving him mad.

Elizabeth Waring sat in the small cinder-block building just inside the gate of the prison, watching the other visitors go through the formalities with the prison guards. There were a pair of lawyers who seemed to know each other, one tall, thin and bespectacled and the other a squat little blond man with a brown suit that looked as though he had bought it cheap in a store that had a fat boys' department. They kept calling each other ''counselor'' and ''learned colleague,'' as though it were a long-standing joke.

Fidgeting nervously on a bench across from her were three women who bore the same dazed, sickly expression on their faces, but had nothing else in common. One was a young, coffee-colored girl who seemed no more than nineteen. She wore a

shapeless brown-and-black outfit that seemed to include a kind
of sweatshirt and something below that could have been a pair
of pants from an Israeli paratrooper's uniform, but in sizes so
large that her shy, cringing posture allowed her to hide in the
material. Beside her was a tall, thin blond woman who might
have been fifty but had such tight skin on her cheeks and forehead that she might as easily have been thirty-five. Her nose had
likewise felt the surgeon's scalpel, and seemed rightfully to belong to the sort of teenage girl who waited on tables in a short
skirt and luminous panty hose. She wore no jewelry except a
gold wedding band and an engagement ring with a diamond that
might have been two carats. The third woman was about thirty,
and Elizabeth had grouped her with the lawyers until she sat
down with the other women and her face assumed the same
fixed, humiliated expression. She wore a business suit and a
white silk blouse with a bow at the neck that wasn't a good idea.
She even carried a briefcase. When the guard called, "Henley,"
she stood up, walked to the desk and handed the briefcase to
the guard, who opened it and removed a black lace negligee.
The guard left the garment on the desk while he went through the
briefcase for contraband, and Elizabeth could see that the woman's ashen face was aimed downward, her eyes not on the guard
but on the negligee, as though she were willing it to disappear.
The two lawyers stopped talking and stared frankly at the proceedings, then listened while the guard repeated a short orientation speech on the rules of conjugal visits. The young black
woman seemed to shrink still deeper into her clothes, but the
older woman turned to wood, staring straight ahead like the
figurehead on the prow of a sailing ship.

"Miss Waring." The voice was behind her. She stood up and
turned to see a man in a suit waiting for her. He looked like a
dentist, serene and well scrubbed, with a shiny bald head. He
held the door open and Elizabeth went through it to the concrete
steps outside, then shook the man's hand. "I'm Assistant
Warden Bateson," the man said. "I was told to expect you.
Anything special you need?"

Elizabeth would have preferred to hear a list of standard procedures for this kind of meeting. "I'd like to see him alone, and
I suppose it would be better if the other prisoners didn't know
about it."

Bateson smiled. "No problem there. We only have three conjugal visits, so we've got a couple of bungalows vacant. He's
been assigned to clean one of them."

She sighted along Bateson's pointing finger to a small, low cinder-block building just inside the fence. It looked like a communal bathroom in a trailer campground near a national park. "Can I be of any help?" asked Bateson.

"No," Elizabeth said.

At the door of the little building, Elizabeth stopped and listened. There was a slow, rhythmic, scraping sound, then a splash and clank, then silence. She opened the door slowly, which set off another clank. She took the scene in at a glance. The mop had been set in the bucket and leaned against the door, so that it would warn Balacontano in time to get up off the bed.

When he saw her, the old man was swinging his feet to the floor, not looking toward the door at all, but reaching for his shoe and pretending to tie the lace. She hadn't seen even a picture of him in ten years, but he looked about the way she remembered him. He was short and stocky, and wore his hair combed straight back, but close at the neck so that it didn't touch the collar of his blue work shirt. The prison jeans looked odd and baggy on him, as jeans always do on old men, the unaccustomed informality of them evoking a businessman who had bought them to wear on vacation and never broken them in. Balacontano's face was pinched and the nose hawklike, his little eyes glaring back at Elizabeth from behind a pair of glasses with a slight brownish tint. He finished tying his shoelace, then put the other foot up on his knee to tighten its lace to show he hadn't been caught at anything.

"Keep your clothes on," he said. "Your old man will be out here when I finish."

"Mr. Balacontano?" Elizabeth began.

"That's right."

"My name is Elizabeth Waring."

"Good for you." The old man stood up, walked to the bucket, placed the mop in the wringer and prepared to go back to work on the floor.

Elizabeth reached into the inner pocket of her purse, pulled out a little leather wallet and held it out toward Balacontano. "U.S. Justice Department." He glanced at it, but showed no interest. "I have a couple of questions for you if you've got time."

Balacontano leaned on his mop, and the cold eyes turned on Elizabeth as though he had just noticed her presence and found it peculiar. "Is that some lame witticism?"

"No," said Elizabeth. "Not at all."

"Save your questions," said the old man. He didn't sound bitter or angry. "I don't answer questions."

Elizabeth had prepared herself for this. "These aren't hard ones. They're about an enemy of yours."

"Just out of curiosity, what are you offering me?"

Elizabeth sighed. "I don't usually have much to do with the people who run these places." She looked around the sparsely furnished room with mild distaste. It looked like motels built fifty or sixty years ago, when they had consisted of six little shacks arranged around a gravel drive. "I plan to tell Warden Bateson that you cooperated. I don't know if that buys you time off for good behavior or just two desserts at dinner."

Carl Bala looked at her shrewdly. "Come back when you can tell me which."

Elizabeth met his gaze. "Last night Antonio Talarese was murdered. The killer was somebody named the Butcher's Boy. Do you know him?"

Balacontano considered his options in a new way. "You're from the Justice Department?"

She nodded.

"What do you do there?"

She decided that telling part of the truth would give the right impression. "I'm an agent on temporary duty with the Organized Crime section. I'm here because I think there's something unusual going on. I didn't bring my résumé with me."

"What makes you think I know anything about this Tony Talarese or this other guy?"

Elizabeth took a deep breath. This man must be better at detecting lies than any prosecutor. The fact that he was alive and in his sixties proved it. She would have to work into it slowly. "The charts in Organized Crime show an arrow going up from Antonio Talarese to you. That means you're his boss. If that's not true, let me know and we'll change the chart. It's no trouble. We have to change it anyway because he's dead."

"This isn't how it works, you know. I'm supposed to have my lawyers with me, and then we sit down and talk over your offer. If we can cut a reasonable deal, I tell you something. They can't just send some special agent in here to flash a badge and ask me questions."

"Okay," she said. "I understand. I assure you that you won't be bothered again for the rest of your sentence."

Bala looked into her eyes, and the thought occurred to him

that maybe she wasn't lying. This was it, the first time in eight years that they had even bothered to come here. It was one thing to bargain hard, but it was another to see the only buyer on earth walking out the door. "Wait a minute. At least let's talk for a minute."

"All right." She sat down on the chair across from the bed.

"Here's what it amounts to from my point of view. You want me to do something that's risky. I have a right to something in return."

"Here's what it amounts to from my point of view," she said. "At the moment the Justice Department is interested in finding the man who killed Tony Talarese. I believe you are too. The difference is that you're in jail and I'm not. Oh, and there's another difference. You know who he is and I don't."

"You're not offering me a pardon or an early release or anything?"

Elizabeth shook her head. "I'm not at the level to make that kind of offer, and nobody would approve it. Those things have happened, but much more seldom than you'd think from the amount of publicity they get. And what nobody mentions is that they always involve special conditions."

"What kind of special conditions?"

It was time for the lie, and she gave it apologetically so that she could look down and avoid his sharp little eyes. "Look, I don't know an awful lot about your case." She knew everything about his case. "But I don't want to lie to you. As I understand it, you're not a likely candidate. In addition to being cooperative, the person provides some evidence that what he did was minor, or that there were extenuating circumstances."

"I was innocent. Is that extenuating enough?"

She ignored his protest. "I just thought that since this man murdered a friend of yours last night, you might at least know who he is."

Carl Bala considered. If he said nothing, that would be the end of his pardon. If he said something, what would this woman do to him? He could tell the story in a way that wouldn't incriminate anyone but himself for what had happened in the old days. If he did, what were the police going to do to him? Throw him in jail for longer than life? There was *omertà* to be considered, but if he didn't mention anybody else's name, the cops couldn't go after them, so how would they know he had talked? Besides, from what he had heard, *omertà* didn't mean shit to anybody these days. This was just the same as it had been all his life: a simple question of consequences. If he told her what he knew, maybe she could begin a process that would someday get him out. But even if he was making a mistake, there was nothing she could do to him. The one thing he was sure of was that it was his last chance. "Yeah, you bet I know him," he shouted. He knew that he had spoken too loud, but it had taken such an effort to break the words free that he had forgotten to modulate his voice.

Elizabeth kept her face slack to hide her surprise. "Who is he?"

"He's the crazy little bastard who framed me for murder." Balacontano let go of his mop and let the handle topple to the floor, then sat on the bed. Elizabeth watched the discarded glasses bounce once on the tight blanket; Balacontano noticed them too, and went through the ritual of putting them back on. "You want to close out your file on him. I want to close out my file on him too. But not just yet. First he's got to give me my life back.

"Ten years ago, I made a mistake. I was an important man, *capo di tutti capos*. I had a lot on my mind in those days. You probably think it's like the movies: an old guy with a face like a prune and a shiny suit sits behind a table in a room so dark you can't hardly see him and sends big zombies out to machine-gun a mom-and-pop grocery store because they didn't pay their nut that week."

Looking at Balacontano, Elizabeth decided this was probably accurate. All the old man needed was the suit.

"Well," said Bala, "it's not. It's like any other business. It's the shifting of capital to where it's going to do the most good. At the time I came here, at least ninety-five percent of my business was perfectly legal. I had interests in corporations, T-bills, oil leases, franchises, bonds, real estate, stocks. That's what made the money. Why do you think the people who really own this country put their money in those things? Because they've got no balls? Let me tell you, if Citibank or Salomon Brothers thought they could make more money stealing cars, you wouldn't be able to get a ride from here to the bathroom. Once in a while, when things got rough, I'd cut a corner."

"Was that your mistake?" asked Elizabeth. She couldn't believe it. Carlo Balacontano was talking to the Justice Department. "Cutting corners?"

Bala's left eyebrow formed an arc. "Please, don't make me think you're stupid now."

Elizabeth had allowed herself to get too excited to think clearly. She had to concentrate on what he said and keep him talking. "How did this man fit in? Did he work for you?"

Balacontano thought about it, then shook his head. "Even the people who worked for me weren't like that—employees with a lunch bucket. But he was something else. He was a specialist. One day, with no warning, I suddenly developed a tax problem, and I want you to know I wasn't the only one. Some of the biggest corporations in the country developed the same problem on the same day."

As Bala remembered it, he could still feel the shock and outrage as though he were hearing it for the first time instead of telling it. A United States senator who had been obsessed with the unfairness of the income-tax laws for twenty years had begun to assemble a list of profitable corporations. They were doing nothing illegal, which was why they made such an effective set of public examples. All they were doing was plowing profits back into the business on capital improvements, acquisitions, new markets, new equipment. But in the computer search the senator's staff had uncovered, along with the corporate giants, a company called FGE. They had left it on the preliminary list because it sounded big. The G and E might have stood for "Gas and Electric."

But FGE had been a low, dirty beige building beside a shopping mall on the edge of Las Vegas. Half the building consisted of rented post-office boxes, and the rest was devoted to a small office with secondhand furniture and paneling on the walls that looked like wood but wasn't. In it a man named Arthur Fieldston did business as Fieldston Growth Enterprises. His entire trade consisted of receiving large amounts of cash from the quiet men Carl Bala sent to him and paying it out to accounts that Carl Bala designated, as payment for imaginary investments and services.

The day Carl Bala learned that FGE was about to become famous, he had experienced a shock that felt as though he had taken a sucker punch from a small, weak opponent. He summoned Harry Orloff, the fat, disreputable lawyer who had invented FGE, to his farm in Saratoga, and ordered him to dismantle his invention. Orloff had whined that it would take weeks, and in the meantime Arthur Fieldston, the last remaining member of a well-known western landowning family, would receive a subpoena to testify before the Senate Finance Committee. At that moment, Carlo Balacontano had experienced a fit of something he would later describe to himself as "mad caution." He had exaggerated the importance of the problem in his own mind. Then he had told Harry Orloff it was worth his life to be sure Fieldston didn't testify.

To Elizabeth he said, "My attorney, Harry Orloff, decides that he needs time to get the papers in order. He tells himself the only way is to get to the senator who's causing the problem. That was Senator Claremont of Colorado."

Elizabeth was listening to something she had waited ten years to hear. It was what had brought her into the case. At first everyone had thought the senator had committed suicide, but then the lab people had discovered that the poison had been in the glass he'd used to soak his false teeth.

But Carlo Balacontano was still talking. "I didn't know what Orloff was doing to take care of things until it was too late. I'm sitting in a restaurant in New York one night, a nice family place owned by the son of a friend of mine, and I get the word. This United States senator didn't die in his sleep in Colorado. Or he did, but the reason he happened to do that was that Harry Orloff had managed to hire a specialist to come in and do him. I'm shocked. I'm knocked on my ass. I'm furious. On the one hand, the hearings are held off, and Arthur Fieldston is hiding so he can't be dragged in to answer questions. On the other, my little tax problem with Arthur Fieldston is nothing compared to assassinating a fucking senator. I figure my only hope is that the rest of the world is going to look at the list of corporations getting subpoenas and figure that one of the oil companies or the car companies had decided that they might save a couple billion dollars by not answering too many questions. The problem is that when a big public figure dies, everybody in the country with a badge, gun or law degree, or even a typewriter, comes out to beat the bushes.

"And that's where I made my second mistake. I'm sitting there at the table in the restaurant, and there's a candle burning on the table. My man tells me that Harry Orloff needs two hundred thousand dollars to pay off the specialist, because he's done his job and he's just shown up in Las Vegas to collect. I'm already so pissed off I can barely see. I'm looking at my guy, and it's like his face is at the end of a red tunnel. My head is pounding, and I notice I'm breathing so hard that the candle flame is flapping like a flag. When I hear the part about the two hundred thousand and the specialist showing up and registering at Caesars, I go absolutely berserk. I tell the people at the table with me that I want out of this. I want it to be like it never happened. And that was it.''

''What do you mean?'' asked Elizabeth. ''That was what?''

Balacontano shrugged. ''That's what put me in here. What I'm guilty of is understating my income to the IRS. I figure two years is enough time on that, so I ought to be out six years ago.''

Elizabeth's face showed no expression. ''Except they tell me you weren't convicted of tax evasion.''

Balacontano waved his hand in frustration. ''You've got to understand what we're talking about here. I don't know how to make you see it. There's a lot of talk about hit men and all that, so it sounds like going to an exterminator or something. What people don't think about is that getting somebody killed isn't all that hard. I saw a couple of days ago in the paper that some woman in Phoenix hired two teenagers to strangle her husband for a hundred bucks apiece. With competition like that, how does anybody make a living? I'll tell you how. There are only maybe five or six genuine specialists that I know about, so there can't be more than two dozen, tops. And they're an odd bunch. You hear about movie stars and famous heart surgeons and these morons with the guitars, and somebody says they're prima donnas. They don't know what the hell a prima donna is.

''These specialists I'm talking about are very hard to deal with. A movie star does it for the money, sure, but he likes the applause too—the glamour, the admiration. Not these people. They honestly and sincerely don't give a shit what you think, whether you like them or hate them; if people flock around them or avoid them, it's all the same. A friend of mine once told me it was because their egos were so big that they didn't think anybody else was even real. I don't know if that's true, but it's not out of the question. If you hear about some piece of ass who decides she's a great actress and throws tantrums at the director, people say she's impossible. You want to see impossible? Try sitting across a table from a guy who wouldn't notice it if he had to tear your heart out of your chest on the way out, because he's done it a hundred times before and he's so good at it he can do it without having to wash his hands. Well, that was the kind of man Harry Orloff hired to delay the Senate hearings: one of the fifteen or twenty serious specialists. After that, when I said I wanted everything to be as though the whole Fieldston fiasco never happened, I was talking in general terms, and I was misunderstood.''

''What did they do?''

Balacontano sighed. "They arranged a meeting to pay him, but it was really a setup to lure him out on the Las Vegas Strip and blow his head off."

"I take it this was without your knowledge."

"Damned right. They only had it half figured out. They knew he could be terrible trouble and had to be out of the picture as soon as possible. They also knew that nobody strolls up to a professional killer and says, 'Sorry, pal. It was all a mistake. The man who hired you had no right, so we're not going to pay you.' But what didn't occur to them is that there's a reason why these characters keep going into dark places with people where you know only one of them is going to come out, and it's always the same one. I'm not saying my people should have known what the reason was, because I sure don't. I'm saying they should have known that there *was* a reason, and accepted it, and given the son of a bitch his lousy two hundred thousand and prayed to God they never saw him again. It's like watching the same dog go down a hundred rabbit holes and always come out with a belly full of rabbit. When you come to the hundred-and-first hole, do you bet on the rabbit?"

Elizabeth could see the frustration and anger growing in the old man as the story began to move closer to his own defeat. What he didn't know was that it was hers too, seen from the other side as though through one-way glass. "What happened?"

Carl Bala smiled a sad little half-smile, and snorted as he thought about it. "You probably wonder why I can tell you all this, don't you?"

"The question did occur to me," Elizabeth conceded.

"Because they're dead. Harry Orloff, all of the people I'm talking about. He killed six or eight people that night. I think he didn't get Orloff until the next morning." Carlo felt a little twinge at the mention of Orloff because he had ordered his death personally, but it was the same thing. He wouldn't have had to if it hadn't been for the Butcher's Boy, by that time running amok: a man who had shown that he could and would do anything, who had no allegiance to anybody, no discernible fear and nothing to protect. Balacontano had simply reasoned that if Orloff were gone, the hired killer might not be able to figure out who he had been working for. That had turned out to be his third mistake. "But he didn't stop there. He went across town to Castiglione's house."

"I thought the Castigliones were a Chicago family?"

Balacontano looked at her, distracted, then seemed to collect himself. He spoke patiently. "This is old Paolo I'm talking about. He was retired. Don't get me wrong, though; Castiglione was still a very important man. In the old days he used to run Chicago. I don't know how old he was ten years ago, but he had to be in his late eighties. He lived in a big brick house at the edge of Las Vegas because it was supposed to be good for his emphysema. Vegas was under a truce. All the families had business there, and anybody could go there. Castiglione was one of the old ones—strong, didn't know what pity was. When he retired, he had generations of enemies. You should have seen the place he had there. From the street all you could see was a big wall. When you got through the gate it looked like the Maginot line. There were floodlights and windows like slits in a pillbox. I wouldn't be able to swear he didn't have the place booby-trapped too. Somebody new bought it a few years ago, and I wouldn't be surprised if someday they flipped a switch in the den and half the lawn blew up.

"Anyway, it's late at night, and this character has just finished turning my friends' little ambush into what looked like a busy day on the Eastern front. But he doesn't go away. Instead he takes a little drive over to Castiglione's. The rest of it nobody knows much about, because everybody there is, as usual, dead. This includes old Castiglione, his four bodyguards and—get this—a special agent of the FBI who just happened to be there because his job was to sit in a car down the street and take pictures of everybody who came to the old man's house.

"So when I wake up the next morning, not only is Senator Claremont still dead, but so are five or six men who worked for me, and the lawyer who set up some corporations for me and who hid Arthur Fieldston so he couldn't accept a subpoena. So I've got millions of dollars in accounts that only Arthur Fieldston can sign on, and no living people on the spot to find him, and my little tax problem has turned into a multiple-murder case involving a federal officer. Then around noon things got ugly. I didn't get any phone calls; I got visitors. All day and most of the night, lots of very important men pulled into my driveway and came into my parlor and sat in my chairs and asked me what the hell I was doing breaking a truce that had kept Las Vegas open for forty years. Some of them thought I'd killed Castiglione, some of them didn't know what to think, but all of them knew that when the sun came up in Vegas there were about a dozen corpses lying around out there, and that maybe half of them belonged to me and the others were Castiglione's." Balacontano seemed to be out of breath, but he added quickly, "Except for the federal cop, who was going to attract such an army of federal undercover types that even the pay phones would be tapped for the next hundred years."

"Why did he go to Castiglione's? Did he think Orloff was working for Castiglione?"

"Hell, no," said Balacontano. "He did it because he knew it was going to create confusion. And it worked. To tell you the truth, I don't think he had any idea who those guys were working for. But he was sure that as soon as the newspapers printed their names, there'd be people a whole lot scarier than he was who would know. The thing that scared me wasn't who showed up at my house; it was who *didn't*. I spent the next few days kissing powerful asses because I was going to need them on my side if things blew up. Even after I did, it was a near thing."

Elizabeth prompted him. "What did you do about the killer?"

Balacontano studied the little woman who sat across from him and had a thought, but then dismissed it. She was a bureaucrat. "I did what anybody would do. I hunted him with everything I had."

He stared at her for a reaction, but she waited in silence. Balacontano shrugged. "He found Arthur Fieldston before I did. I don't know how far he was thinking ahead. Maybe he knew that I couldn't get my money back if Fieldston was dead, and then he thought of the rest of it after he'd killed him. He buried Fieldston's head and hands behind the stable at my farm, then made a phone call to the Justice Department. Nobody ever saw him again until now." He looked at Elizabeth. "You've got to help me."

"I'll do my best to find him."

"I'm not talking about *him*; I'm talking about *me*. He's just the way to get me out of here."

"I'm not your attorney, but if you do get an appeal, I wouldn't tell the judge everything," said Elizabeth.

"I shouldn't have to tell the bastard anything," Balacontano said. "I'm not . . . wasn't some errand boy. Does anybody seriously think I went out and shot Arthur Fieldston, then sawed off his head and hands in Arizona and brought them across the country to bury them in my yard? The only two parts you can use to prove who it was? What do you think I am, Edgar Allan Poe? Well?"

"I'm wondering who you think Edgar Allan Poe was," said Elizabeth.

"You know what I mean. I was an important man. When they have those cars with power surges that kill people, do they go to the president of the company and dig up his back yard to see if he's buried some suspicious carburetors? No. Does anybody even wonder who made the anonymous phone call to the Justice Department?"

Elizabeth had asked the same question in as many words ten years ago, but her superiors had been too eager to convict Balacontano to listen. She had asked it so many times that they had sent her on a vacation and deleted her name from the record of the investigation so that the defense couldn't call her to testify. "Can you tell me where to find him?"

The old man's anger and frustration were barely controllable now. "If I knew that, do you think I'd be sitting here talking to you? You're the one who's got to hunt him down."

Elizabeth stood up and glanced at her watch. "Just for the record, do you want to tell me his name?"

"No," said Balacontano. "I don't know his name. What the hell does he need a name for?"

10

He hated to throw away the name Charles Ackerman. It had been a comfort since Eddie Mastrewski had given it to him as a child, and it was his oldest possession. Eddie the Butcher had always assumed that someday a lapse of professionalism would put an end to him, and the young boy he had taken in would be alone and running. The first thing he would need was money, and the second was a plausible identity, and Eddie knew how to provide him with both. The money Eddie wrapped in a package that looked exactly like the ones he kept in the freezer for the cat. Like them, it was marked "Giblets and Gizzards for Cat."

The identity had been almost as easy in those days. Eddie took the boy for a walk in the sprawling forty-acre Catholic cemetery at the edge of town one sunny Memorial Day when hundreds of other families were wandering over the grass and looking uncertain about exactly where Grandpa was buried. He'd had the foresight to buy a small bouquet of forget-me-nots on the way, which he carried with just the right degree of discomfort. They had taken a pleasant walk in the sunshine to look for the gravestone of a child born in 1950, '51, or '52 who had died after the age of five but before the age of twelve. They had found six of them, and Eddie had dutifully copied down the names, the dates and his estimate of the cost of the stones.

Then they went to look at a couple of graves of men they had encountered professionally, and Eddie had explained his theory of reasonable fees. It was his hypothesis that the cost of a man's gravestone should be proportionate to the fee Eddie had received for killing him. Important men left lots of money, had lots of admirers—or, at least, associates—and had heirs who would not miss this final chance to remind people that they had been relations of powerful men. Killing these men was potentially more difficult and dangerous than killing the ones with small domestic granite plaques that bore only a name and two dates. Eddie had appeared satisfied, even though two of the men had eight-foot-high Italian marble structures the size of toolsheds, with carved birds, flowers, statues of angels holding trumpets and lengthy passages of verse that might have been copied verbatim from Hallmark Mother's Day cards.

The next day Eddie had taken him to the county hall. There Eddie had paid three dollars for a duplicate birth certificate for his nephew, Charles F. Ackerman. He had eliminated the other five possibilities because two had names that didn't seem likely—he remembered that one of them was Wung Cho Fo; two had graves in the middle of huge empty plots, which meant that they still had lots of living family members the boy might someday meet; and one had a gravestone of such massive proportions and extravagant opulence that it must have been a sign of either conspicuous wealth or a memorable death. Thereafter, Charles Frederick Ackerman used his birth certificate to obtain a social security card, used both to apply for a driver's license, then opened a bank account in a city a hundred miles away, where he also obtained a library card and a post-office box. Then he began to get on mailing lists, and Charles F. Ackerman took on a kind of life, with credit cards, club memberships and finally even a pistol permit.

In later years, he had built a dozen other identities that he had used and discarded, but he had never done much as Charles F. Ackerman. After Eddie had died, the name had begun to seem precious, and he couldn't think of it without remembering the sunny Memorial Day when he and Eddie had strolled together on the unnaturally lush green grass, playing the game of finding dead children with approximately the right dates of birth.

Charles Ackerman's existence wasn't as well documented as Michael Schaeffer's, but it was older and deeper, started before the age of computers and well established before a policeman would imagine he'd had the need or the capacity for adopting it. The methods he had used to create the identity were now out of date and impossible, because the trick had been done so many times for so many reasons that the police had put a stop to it years ago. He hated to say good-bye to Charlie Ackerman, but he had to. He had rented the car in Albuquerque under the name, and that had to be the end of it.

The gun had been easier. He had found an advertisement for

a firearms show in the Albuquerque newspaper, clipped it, then gone into a gun shop and looked around for something that would inspire the right amount of greed in the heart of an aficionado. He settled on an antique Italian shotgun with ornate scrollwork carved into the stock. It even had a carrying case that looked like a briefcase. He had taken it to the show and walked past the booths run by dealers, but lingered at the card tables manned by private collectors until he had found the right one. The man was in his fifties and had a pot belly that he kept in check with a wide belt with a silver buckle that had a bird dog on it with turquoise eyes. He had five handguns to sell, three of them nickel-plated modern replicas of Colt .45 single-action revolvers with white plastic handgrips like the ones the good guys used in cowboy movies—and two shotguns, one of them a double-barreled ten-gauge that his grandfather might have used for hunting ducks. The man had eyed his gun case and said, "What'd you buy?" He had opened it, and the man's eyes had widened, then narrowed. "I brought it with me," Ackerman said. "I'm trying to see if anybody wants to trade." The man asked, "What would you take?" Ackerman indicated that the Ruger .38 police special on the table in front of him looked pretty good, but he didn't feel like hanging around all day filling out papers for a handgun. The man thought for a long time, then set his jacket over the pistol and said, "Meet me in the parking lot."

The transaction was quick and simple, but as he was getting into the car, Ackerman was quietly accosted by a skinny young man who looked like an out-of-work car mechanic. "Didn't you see anything in there you liked?" His mind compared the two possibilities, cop and thief, and neither won. He just shook his head. "No. Same old stuff," he said, and prepared to start the car. The man said, "Looking for something in particular?" He decided on thief. "Why? You got something?"

"A few things. I'm a gunsmith. I do modifications, custom work, make a few accessories." The word *accessories* interested him enough to get him out of the car. In the trunk of the man's old Chevy was an oily bath towel, and laid out on it were a few homemade sears for converting M-16's to full auto, a couple of forty-round banana clips made of two standard twenties welded end-to-end and various devices designed to hold handguns under dashboards and car seats. He took a chance. "I can see why you aren't at a table inside." The man grinned sheepishly and then compulsively glanced around to see if anyone was watching. "See anything you like?" He shook his head. "Sorry." The man looked disappointed. "This ain't all I got. Give me a hint." He said, "Ever made a silencer?" The man had.

William Wolf was watching the effect of the sun coming up, hitting the distant face of the low mesa on his left and giving it a pink glow beneath the deep purple of the predawn sky. Driving felt like a novelty. He loved the feeling of enclosure in the small box hurtling down the smooth highway at sixty-five as the sights around him changed. It wasn't just one object being replaced by another like it, but a change in the possibilities. He had been in New Mexico several times before, but now it looked new to him. There were low, rolling hills that flattened into unexpected places where the level plains dropped abruptly to reveal that they had been plateaus. All of it was covered with dry, knee-high sage that was almost gray, with dark piñons growing out of it like plants at the bottom of a vast ocean. And along the impossibly distant horizon, here and there a mountain would rise, not a range of mountains but a single one, or a saw-toothed ridge of three, tilted a little as though something big had swept over it to push it aside.

He had spent a few hours becoming William Wolf in a motel in Albuquerque, and now the name had displaced the others in his mind. He had repeated it to himself a thousand times, rehearsed introducing himself to imaginary strangers and even planned the signature. It would be two big, fast *W*'s, each followed by low, cramped scrawls that looked so cursory that some letters might appear to be missing.

The name William Wolf had presented no problem to him. Names were the first accidental training that Eddie had given him as a child. Eddie had never actually taken any legal steps to adopt him, for fear that some public agency would be called upon to visit the home and create a file. Instead he had sometimes referred to the boy as his son, sometimes as his nephew, or even as the child of a friend, as convenience seemed to dictate, and had made up names for him on these occasions. But as soon as he was old enough to learn a trade, the boy had been taught to select his own aliases. Circumstances had never allowed him to attach any interior significance to names. He might be Bob or Ronald at one moment, or "the Butcher's Boy," or even "the third one from the end of the line." It made no difference to him; in a heartbeat he would be the second from the end of the line without experiencing any interior alteration. Names were for other people's convenience, and their convenience was seldom of any interest to him. For a decade he had found it useful to be Michael Schaeffer; for a day he had resurrected Charles Ackerman; now it was easiest to be Wolf.

Wolf thought about Santa Fe. It was too small to have a serious airport, but it was always full of tourists. The only reasonable choice was to fade into the amorphous, shifting group that came and went each day. He would arrive the way they did and dress the way they did, and that was as near to invisibility as he could get. People in tourist towns let their eyes acknowledge new people only long enough to be sure they wouldn't bump into them. There was no reason to remember faces because they would never appear again.

Wolf felt the early-morning cold as he got out of the car in the parking structure beneath La Fonda. It was a strange, calm and airless chill that seemed to have been stored in the dark enclosure for a long time. La Fonda was the only hotel he remembered from the old days, a seventy-year-old five-story sprawling adobe building on the corner of the ancient city square beside the palace the conquistadors had built for their governors in 1610. There were already three cars exactly like his that he could see as he walked to the swinging door that led into the hall to the lobby. As he turned the first corner he could see into the big dining room, with its uneven ceramic tile floor and the fifty-foot canopy of painted glass that let in just enough light for the potted trees. There were only a few people sitting under the trees and eating breakfast; he knew that these were probably the ones who had come here from the East, where it was already late morning. There were two young couples who wore ski sweaters, jeans and hiking shoes, and a table of five elderly people, three women and two men, who had the manner of a permanent traveling committee. They each spoke to the whole group and then winked and nudged some particular ally, while the others felt comfortable ignoring what was said.

Wolf could also see a table where four dark-suited businessmen held a serious discussion, looking as though their plane from New York had been hijacked and they had been released, unharmed and unchanged, in the center of this small western town and were now waiting for the answer to their inquiries about whom to buy it from. He glanced around the lobby, first at the registration desk, where a dark-haired woman in her forties made quick, proprietary movements, arranging registration cards and keys to prepare for the morning check-ins. He avoided that side of the room and walked past two ancient Pueblo Indians, a wrinkled, leathery little man and a woman who undoubtedly was his wife, both of them busy opening modern, black sample cases full of silver and turquoise jewelry for display on the bench by the wall.

He drifted past a wooden rack of free tourist pamphlets, selected a Santa Fe street map and walked out the front door of the building to the street. There were a few little patches of the early autumn's first crisp, hard snow in the square, and the air was clear and thin. He would have been tempted to ask for a room in the hotel, but he knew that Santa Fe was too small. He looked up and down the streets that led into the square. There were the stores he remembered, their windows full of intricately painted Indian pots, handwoven blankets of wool dyed with bright vegetable colors and antique pounded-and-burnished silver bought, by tradition, so cheaply from the once-credulous Indians that it was still called "pawn." But among the stores was a coffee shop with outdoor tables turned upside down as a concession to the first taste of cold weather. He found it by following a couple in their thirties who were tourists but looked purposeful in their gait, reasoning that nothing else could be open yet.

Inside the door there was a steamy warmth to the air, a comforting heaviness to the dark wooden tables and a glow of hanging antique copper implements that he doubted the employees could even identify, let alone use. Wolf sat at a table and studied his map, while the waitress, a plump blond girl of the type he could imagine leaving college to study astrology, poured him a cup of coffee and left a menu beside him.

Andalusia was one of the narrow, cramped streets that ran parallel to Canyon Road, where he remembered that the galleries were. He had never felt an impulse to own paintings, and in the days when he had lived in the United States it would have been foolish, but he had walked down Canyon Road once, years ago, to pass the time, and he remembered the neighborhood. He judged from the map that he would have to leave the car blocks away and find Peter Mantino on foot.

When the waitress came to stand beside him and said, "Ready?" he answered, "Huevos rancheros," because he hadn't had time to read the menu, and it was the only thing he remembered that places like this would have. When she left, he studied the map again, letting it suggest the way things would happen. If things were as they should have been, a man like Peter Mantino would put some obstacles between himself and the world. But six or seven years ago, Mantino had been convicted of a bunch of charges that Wolf couldn't even remember now, all of the bribery-and-suborning variety. Now he was on parole, supposedly living in voluntary seclusion hundreds of miles from the centers of power in Los Angeles and Las Vegas. All of this had been in the newspapers years ago, and even the reporters clearly hadn't believed a word of it. But the important part was true: if he was on parole, he couldn't have the sort of protection he was about to begin needing.

Wolf still had not gotten over the shock of seeing the shooter at the airport, but he had never for a second doubted what had happened. The truth was, there was no way even Carl Bala could send a specialist to kill somebody in the Los Angeles airport. The airport lay unambiguously in the center of Peter Mantino's empire, and any consequences would fall exclusively on his head: the text of every letter to the editor would mention his name, the resulting crackdown would cut into his profits and the token arrests would make his people cautious and unproductive. He had to have been the one who made the decision, and the man must belong to him.

Mantino had started out running a crew for Balacontano in New York in the sixties, and then gotten to run the family's interests in the West, supposedly as a reward for faithful service. At the time, people had said there was more to it than that. They said Mantino had begun to attract a lot of loyalty in the family, and Balacontano had just wanted him out there and away from the soldiers. The world was full of little men who knew what big men were really thinking.

It didn't matter why Mantino had reacted so quickly. Maybe he was still loyal to the Balacontano family, and maybe he was making a safe, easy bid for respect while the old man was in prison and Talarese was out of the way. The only thing that was certain was that Mantino was taking enough of an interest to send shooters into public places. That changed Wolf's problem into figuring out how Wolf was going to stay alive.

He needed to get out of the country, but nobody was going to let him step onto a plane to London without a passport. He knew of only one place where he might be able to get one after all these years, and that was in Buffalo, over fifteen hundred miles away. It would take time to get there, and time to make the contact, and time for the passport. And every second that passed, he was heating up. He needed to buy some time.

The only thing that gave him hope was that word of his return couldn't have traveled faster than an airplane unless it was passed by telephone from somebody in New York to Mantino. And Mantino wouldn't have told a lot of people in his organization that he was going to have somebody killed. That was the sort of thing nobody talked about until after it was accomplished. And it hadn't been accomplished. The shooter had gotten himself busted in the airport. Wolf had to take advantage of that mistake. The only way was to do the unexpected: Mantino takes a swat at a fly, and the fly goes right up his nose.

Twice in his life he had seen what happened when a capo unexpectedly died. People reacted in different ways. A few would check in at out-of-town hotels and start making phone calls. But a lot of them would stay home and wait for somebody to get in touch with them. Usually it would be some acquaintance—a guy they had been introduced to at the races, or somebody's cousin they had met at a wedding. The guy would say, "Peter's dead. You have a problem with that?" or just, "What are you going to do now? If you want to go with us, I can talk to some people." But until they heard from somebody, they were going to be watching a lot of television with the blinds drawn. Sometimes nobody got in touch, and the trouble just got worse. There had even been one famous time when a boss died, and forty of his friends across the country died the same day. That was what they would be afraid of—not that somebody Carlo Balacontano had put a contract on ten years ago had come for Peter Mantino.

The low brown stucco wall around the yard would present no problem unless it had some electronic component that Wolf couldn't see from the street. He couldn't see or hear a dog, and the sign on the gate that said NORTH AMERICAN WATCH—ARMED RESPONSE was comforting. It made it unlikely that Mantino had anything more sophisticated than a conventional alarm system that would summon untrained night watchmen. The house was a single-story adobe-colored building. Like all the others in this part of town, it was required by the building code to look as though the Spaniards had never left, although he suspected that any Spaniards that had made it this far north and east must have been a forlorn, raggedy-assed bunch.

He maintained an even, leisurely tourist's pace, and studied all the houses on the street with equal attention. At the corner he turned, walked to the street behind Andalusia and examined the houses there. There appeared to be nothing of any consequence to protect any of them, but the situation was still troublesome. There were no cars parked on the narrow one-way street, and he had passed only a few pedestrians during his walk, none of them within blocks of Andalusia. Even if he could get in, getting out would be difficult.

It was dark now, and the cold air was still and crisp. The patches of dirty snow that had melted in the sunlight were now furrows and tumuli of iron-hard ice, and Wolf watched for them so that he could step around them on the sidewalk. In his left hand he carried a paper sack from the store where he had bought the gloves and channel-lock pliers a few hours ago, but now it also contained the Ruger .38 and its silencer. If necessary, he could drop the bag surreptitiously, but for anyone who might see him, the bag was an indicator that he had gone out on foot for a purpose and was on his way home.

He moved along the storefronts on Galisteo Street, keeping under the roof and away from the thick pillars, where he could remain only a shadow. Santa Fe was still a sunlit town for most of the year, even now. The inhabitants were out and in evidence when the bright sunlight warmed the ground, reaching it unimpeded by the extra mile of clouds, smog and dust that covered other cities, and without being blocked anywhere by tall buildings. But when the sun set, they disappeared behind the stone and clay walls, the oldest ones a yard thick. Even the restaurants that catered to the small, quiet night trade were hidden in mazes of courtyards and passageways.

The office of North American Watch was even more difficult to find. It had an entrance to the street, but that had been closed for hours. Behind the dusty venetian blinds he could see a thin slice of the light from the dispatcher's desk. He walked around the building to look for the cars. These people were in the peace-of-mind business. They provided louts to drive by every four hours with flashlights, and since this was a state where anyone could wear a gun in a holster unless the weight of it pulled down his pants, they were armed louts. He didn't know the current procedures, but if they hadn't changed radically, on a cold night when there were few people on the streets, the management would save a few dollars by keeping some cars in the lot. If a call came in or an alarm lit up the board, they would call the police and then send one of the men in the office on a slow stroll to a car so that he would arrive about the time the cops were composing their theft reports.

It was better than he had imagined. There were three blue-and-white imitation police cruisers parked behind the building, and a fourth at the curb. Wolf walked to it and put his hand on the hood. It wasn't even warm. He ducked down beside it, opened the door and slipped into the driver's seat. He felt the ignition for the key, but he wasn't that lucky. They must have a hook inside the office with the keys hanging on it. He took the heavy pliers out of his bag, pried the bar away from the steering column, wrenched the ignition switch out of its hole and tugged the wires out of the back of it. He pumped the gas pedal to the floor once, touched the two wires together and started the car. He let the engine idle for a moment while he watched the back door of North American. There was no sign that anyone had heard, so he pulled away from the curb. Just as he was passing the building, another set of headlights came up the street behind him. As he turned the corner, he saw the car pull into the space he had vacated. It pleased him. If one of the louts happened to glance out the window, he would see a car where he was looking for it.

Wolf kept the car at a crawl as he moved down the quiet, empty street toward Andalusia. He knew that when he had hot-wired the engine, he had started an invisible timer, but the danger would increase if he deviated from the pace people expected of this car. He made the turn onto Andalusia and allowed himself a little more speed. At 1500 Andalusia he applied the brakes and let the rear end of the car swing out a little, so that he could stop at an urgent-looking angle to the wall. He glanced up at the house to be sure the car was visible through the iron gate, left the motor running and ran up the walk to the door, his pistol in his hand.

He rapped on the thick wooden door, then rang the bell. Inside, he could hear feet pounding down a hallway. He turned to the side so that whoever was looking out through the fish-eye lens of the peephole could see the car. As he forced his eyes to scan the yard like a man looking for something, he felt his heartbeat quicken. It was these few seconds that would decide everything. Then he heard the dead bolt slip out of its receptacle and watched the big door open a couple of inches.

A voice said, "What is it?" and Wolf turned to look into the man's eyes. He was in his thirties and wore his wavy hair long, cut in a style that seemed out of date until Wolf remembered that it might have come back.

He forced his voice into a tone that would carry it. There had to be enough urgency to make the man forget his natural suspicion and want to find out what was going on, but enough confidence to assure him that Wolf was going to take care of it. "North American Watch," he said. "You Mr. Mantino?"

The man moved away from the door, and Wolf stepped beside him into the warm chiaroscuro of a dimly lit space. There was a fire burning in the big whitewashed adobe fireplace at the other end of the room. He was startled when he saw a man in his fifties, lean and limber in the way that men were who spent a lot of time playing tennis, moving to a big cabinet on the far wall. "What is it? I'm Mr. Mantino."

"You got an intrusion," Wolf said. Almost instantly he regretted it. He had expected to have time to attach the silencer before he fired. But now there were two of them, and they moved in different directions with surprising decisiveness. Mantino turned a key in the lock on the cabinet and reached inside. His hand came back holding a short-barreled shotgun, and he didn't swing it around like a man gripped by panic, but held it pointed upward. He pumped it and moved into the hallway. "Where is he? Have you seen him?"

Wolf had no time to answer, because now the younger man was beside him, and cradled in his arms was a thirty-ought-six hunting rifle with a large clip in it. "Holy shit," said Wolf, trying to infuse some incredulity into his voice. "He's probably just trying to boost your hubcaps or something."

The young man snapped, "Then he made a mistake," and stepped toward the rear of the house.

Wolf reminded himself that speed was really a matter of deliberate, economical movement. He fell into step with the younger man, pulling Mantino with him. He took two steps, raised the pistol, shot the younger man in the back of the head, stepped back and swung an elbow into Mantino's face. He was surprised at how fast Mantino's movements were—he was already moving away, trying to swing the shotgun around in time. The elbow struck Mantino on the shoulder, and Wolf barely had time to jab the pistol against the man's chest and fire.

Mantino toppled backward, and Wolf fired three more times as he fell. Each time he fired, there was an instant when he wasn't sure the shotgun wasn't coming the rest of the way around. The man's body made a spasmodic jerk backward each time he was hit, and Wolf had the sense that he was pushing a man toward a cliff by jabbing him with his finger. When Mantino finally hit the floor, Wolf kicked the shotgun away and fired the last round into his forehead.

Wolf stood still for a moment and listened. He'd made a mess of it, and he still had to get out. The security-service car might buy him the most time left where it was, parked in front and still running. The neighbors would assume that someone whose job it was to respond to gunshots had arrived to take charge, and the police, who knew better, would be cautious about barging in without warning the armed and frightened rent-a-cop they would expect to find inside. He began to wipe his prints from the pistol.

He went to the gun cabinet and opened it. There were five rifles of varying makes and calibers, and a whole section devoted to handguns, all fastened to a blue velvet display board. He spotted a Ruger .38 police special, pulled it off the board and replaced it with the gun he had used to kill the two men, then hurried to the back door of the house.

He stepped out the back door, climbed over the fence into the neighbors' back yard and kept walking toward the next street. As he moved along beside the house, he heard the first of the sirens. Things were happening too quickly, coming now like punches from an opponent he had underestimated. He listened for the route of the police cars. The electronic blips went on long enough for him to hear them on both sides of him before they stopped. He moved to the wall beside the house, knelt among the garbage cans, swung out the cylinder of the pistol he had stolen and pushed in six rounds. Then he remembered the silencer he had brought with him. It had been machined to fit a weapon of the same make and model. Even if it didn't silence the report of the new pistol, it would suppress the flash a little. In the darkness this edge might keep him alive.

Carefully he raised himself above the level of the garbage cans and sighted between the houses. He saw the police car on Andalusia pull up behind the North American Watch car, and two uniformed policemen get out. After a moment one of them returned to pull the shotgun out of its mount in his squad car. Wolf turned to look at the street behind him and saw two more police cars glide silently to a stop. They seemed to have practiced a drill to cut off the escape of an intruder in these quiet streets.

He ducked down and concentrated on what he had seen of

the neighborhood as he fitted the silencer to the revolver. There
were no crowds of pedestrians to lose himself in, and not even
a passing car to distract the police. He had to break their cho-
reographed plan, and the only way to do it was to add some
element that they hadn't imagined. He considered starting a fire,
but he would have to be nearby when the first flames flickered
to life, and would be caught in the light. Then another squad
car passed slowly up Andalusia. A spotlight mounted on its
window strut swept along the thin trunks of the trim shrubbery,
sliced down the spaces between the houses, then shot upward
to the roofs. Just before it came abreast of his hiding place, Wolf
crouched to let it pass, but as he disappeared into the darkness,
he retained an image: the spotlight moving along the fronts of
the houses illuminated, one after another, bright reflecting signs
that read NORTH AMERICAN WATCH—ARMED RESPONSE.

As soon as the car passed, he came up again. He aimed his
pistol at the front window of the house across the street and
squeezed off a round. There was a faint spitting noise, and he
could see that a spiderweb network of cracks had appeared.
Pivoting, he shot the back windows of the next four houses, then
ducked down to reload. He was satisfied for the moment. No
matter how crude an alarm system was, if it was triggered by
sound, motion or simply the dislocation of a conductive tape, it
would go off when a window broke.

He resisted the impulse to move his wristwatch up to his face
in the darkness to time the "armed response." Now was his
time of greatest danger, while the police were still free to run
their prearranged tactic unimpeded. He had to hope it would
take them a few minutes to analyze the scene at Peter Mantino's
house before they started to sweep the neighborhood on foot.
He listened for footsteps or radio voices to reach him, and then
heard more engines. There was the squeal of tires at the end of
the street in front of him as the North American Watch cars
started to arrive.

A voice on a police bullhorn said, "Pull back out of here.
This is a crime scene." But there was no diminution of the
sound of engines or dimming of the glare of headlights. "Yeah,
you. Get out of here."

Wolf decided it was essential to see how the competition was
faring, so he moved to the gate that led to the front lawn and
looked through the crack by the hinges. There were two cars
like the one he had stolen, and they had pulled into the driveways
of two of the houses whose windows he had shot out. Men in

jeans, flannel shirts and sweatshirts were outside the cars now, carrying an odd assortment of handguns and flashlights.

Two of them stood on the lawn across the street, looking skeptically at a policeman who was walking toward them; a third was already at the side of the house, looking over the fence and aiming his flashlight into the back yard.

As Wolf waited for the mix to get as volatile as it needed to be, he glanced behind him toward the Mantino house. In front of it, he could see another North American Watch car pull up in the middle of Andalusia. A large man got out of it, leaving the door open. He already held a heavy, long-barreled revolver in his hand, as though he had driven with it lying on the seat beside him.

Wolf took three deep breaths to ensure that he had expelled all the carbon dioxide he could. It was carbon dioxide in the blood that made the hands shake. He eased his body upward, rested his arm on the top of the fence and fired a single shot.

The policeman on the lawn jerked in pain, let out his breath in a grunt, then crumpled to the ground clutching his calf. The three security guards looked at him in disbelief, then at each other. Finally it seemed to occur to them that the shot had come from somewhere else. They crouched and swept the horizon around them over their gunsights, looking for a target. But the policeman's partner was still at the microphone in his car. In his panic he left the external amplifier on, and as he shouted into the radio, his message echoed through the empty streets. "Officer down! This is One X ray Twenty-two. Officer down! Need assistance. Officer down!"

Wolf could see the three security guards now, but he couldn't see the other policeman in the car. He decided to take a chance. He stood up at the fence and shouted at the frightened guards, "Police officer! Drop those guns!" then ducked and ran along the adobe wall across the front of the house. He knew he must be abreast of the police car now, but he stopped and crouched in the corner of the front yard and listened. "You heard the man," said the lone policeman. "Drop them!"

Wolf decided he had to increase the sense of danger a little more, or they were going to obey and let the solitary cop get control of the situation. He looked back along the house toward Andalusia Street. He could see that the policemen there had heard either the bullhorn or the radio and were moving toward him through the back yards.

He rolled over the wall to the next yard, then aimed a round over their heads and ducked down. They had seen the muzzle flash aimed in their direction and heard the crack of the bullet breaking the sound barrier as it passed over them, and they responded as he had hoped. There was the blast of a shotgun, followed by eight pistol shots slamming into the corner of the wall. Then he heard three rapid shots fired from the house across the street and judged it was time.

He sprinted to the front of the next house and moved along the façade, then rolled over the next fence and kept moving. There were other sirens in the distance now, all converging on the quiet neighborhood.

Wolf didn't dare slow down or look back. He trotted unerringly from one fence to the next, each time hoisting himself up and over the identical adobe enclosures, thankful that the sudden, unseasonable start of fall had made it too cold to leave a dog outside all night. At the end of the block he waited and listened for approaching sirens, but it seemed they had all arrived by then, screeching past him on the other side of the wall as he ran from their destination. He pulled himself over the last fence and walked across the street to the far side of Galisteo.

As he walked northward toward the ancient plaza, he crossed a little bridge over the captive river with concrete banks that sliced across the town. As he did, he noticed that it had the strange quality of magnifying sounds. Far in the distance, he could hear a voice shouting into an electronic amplifier. The voice echoed and broke up, but he knew it was another police bullhorn. He also knew, from the rapid reports of guns, that the untrained North American Watch guards had been too frightened to relinquish their weapons. The heavy firing was the sound of the police reluctantly concluding that the guards, either for this reason or because they had killed Mantino or wounded the policeman, represented a danger to the community.

He hurried on toward La Fonda. Right now there would be crackling, fragrant fires of mesquite and piñon in all the big stone fireplaces, heating the bright, intricately glazed Spanish tiles along the mantels. Lots of Santa Fe natives would pass through for a drink on an evening like this, but some of them would have heard that the police were gathering on Andalusia Street. He would pass by the lighted windows and into the subterranean parking garage without crossing the threshold. By the time he had driven the few blocks to Highway 25, the heater of the little Ford would have warmed his hands as much as a fire.

* * *

"I think this is the second one," said Elizabeth. "If he wanted Peter Mantino, this is the way he'd do it. I think it's not over."

"You're making a hell of an assumption," said Richardson. "You've got to act as your own censor on this kind of case."

"I know that," she answered, her voice close enough to a monotone to serve her purpose.

"You're feeling frustrated and disappointed that we didn't get him at the L.A. airport, right?"

"I admit it," said Elizabeth. "I volunteer it, and waive all right to a jury trial, but—"

"All I'm asking," Richardson interrupted, "is that you think about it. Is it possible—not certain, but possible—that you see another gunshot homicide of another important man and say it's the same perpetrator because you want it to be? You want another shot at him."

Elizabeth's jaw clenched. "You brought me in here to analyze raw data. My preliminary hypothesis when there are two murders of ranking members of the Balacontano family within two days is that a pure coincidence is unlikely. There. I've done my job. Your job as section chief is to decide now, this minute, whether to send an investigator out to Santa Fe to find out what actually happened to Peter Mantino."

"Are you volunteering?"

Elizabeth's eyes narrowed. "You're not calling my bluff, you know; I'd love to. But I just went to California, and I have two children who are expecting me to feed them dinner tonight and still be there when they wake up tomorrow. Have things gotten so bad since I left here that you don't have any real field men for a case like this?"

Richardson shook his head. "No. I just figured out who to send. Give me a minute on the phone with him, and then I'll transfer him to you."

"Who is he?"

"His name's Jack Hamp."

Elizabeth turned and walked out of Richardson's office. She had heard the name before. He could be somebody she had met on another case. No, she had read it at the bottom of some report recently. But the button on her phone was already blinking. She punched it.

"Hello," said Elizabeth. "This is Elizabeth Waring. Is this Mr. Hamp?"

"What can I do for you, ma'am?"

Her expectations oscillated between two extremes. It was the

unimaginative-sounding western official voice that California
highway patrolmen used when they wrote you a ticket. But she
was going to need him in the West, after all, and Richardson
had picked him for a difficult situation. If Richardson knew the
man's name, he must at least be competent, and maybe a lot
better than that. "I understand you've agreed to work with us
on this case?"

"Yes, ma'am." It was the "ma'am." The last time she had
heard it was from one of the prison guards at Lompoc.

"When can you be ready to leave for Santa Fe?"

There was a significant pause; then the voice said, "I'm at an
airport now." Then Elizabeth remembered where she had seen
the name: it had been at the bottom of the report on the mess at
LAX. Jack Hamp was the birdwatcher.

Hamp walked up Andalusia Street, then down Galisteo to the
street behind it. He liked the feel of the sun heating the sidewalks
without affecting the thin, cold air. He thought about Elizabeth
Waring again. At the time he'd had to pay too much attention to
what she was telling him to give her voice the sort of analysis
he considered necessary. All he really had on her for sure was
that she was in her mid-thirties. She had mentioned that she had
young children, but she was old enough to call herself Elizabeth
and not have to tone it down by a couple of syllables to Liz or
Betty or Bess or whatever. She was not a large woman because
there wasn't the kind of lasting tone that came from the big-
boned ones with pink hands that were all knuckles. It wasn't a
question of high or low, because women varied only from alto
to soprano anyway, but something about how much real force
and staying power was behind the voice. He judged that she was
between five feet five and five feet eight, and probably a straw-
berry blonde or a redhead.

It was a brave guess, even for an expert like Hamp, because
not many real redheads went through law school. A lot of the
bright ones were like Hamp's second wife, Donna, who was
sort of a career redhead. She was a trained painter, but apparently she had spent her college years exploring the shades of
green, blue and purple she could wear to set off her hair. The
marriage had been made in heaven during what must have been
a celestial holiday, when everybody up there was blind drunk
and frisky. Donna had cried when she had found out he was a
cop, but by then it was too late, because he had already verified
her credentials as a bona-fide redhead, and she was a committed

woman. At the time, his pants were hanging on the rail of her bed with the butt end of his pistol showing, but that hadn't bothered her. Later he decided he hadn't given her reaction as much thought as it had deserved. Not that she wasn't a law-abiding citizen, within certain limits, but she was not a cautious person, or a docile one. They'd had a lively time of it for nearly five years, but it had ended by her going after him with the claw hammer she had been using to attach a canvas to its stretcher bars. Donna's problem was symbolized in his mind by the fact that she had gone after him with the claw end of the hammer. It was uglier and more spiteful that way, but the bludgeon-death victims he came across professionally almost always got it with the blunt end; it was just more practical.

Maybe Elizabeth Waring had brown hair, the sort that had very tight little curls in it that made it stick out. There was a certain intensity in those women too, and a lot of them went to law school.

Hamp spotted the police sticker on the door of Mantino's house, and took in the rest of it. The killer had seen it all the way he was seeing it now. The houses were all too close together, the streets too narrow and quiet for an easy shot and a quick retreat. Since the police had found a North American Watch car in the street, he had probably chosen to impersonate a security guard, but something had gone wrong. At that moment the ordinary man would have defeated himself. He would have tried to do something to save his skin—hide in an empty house or look for an escape route the police knew better than he did. But this man had done something else. All policemen were drilled in hesitation, firing warning shots into the air and trying to keep innocent bystanders away. If they'd had a plan, it would have been to contain his movements and assume that his desire to stay alive would make him behave rationally, and therefore predictably. But this one was an aggressor. Any victim was as good as another. Anything that caused confusion or added to the escalating violence was an advantage. His best tactic would have been to give the impression that what he was trying to do was not to run but to kill them.

Hamp looked around. There were lots of long, straight firing lines he could use: adobe walls around the houses to hide his movements, tall trees and thick hedges to complicate their view but not his. In the dark the police had to distinguish which, among the twenty or thirty silhouettes they could discern, belonged to their comrades and which to another man they didn't

even have a description of. By the time there were fifty policemen and armed civilians on the scene, any shot fired had a two
percent chance of hitting a murderer and a ninety-eight percent
chance of creating one.

This was what the old gangster in the California prison had
been trying to describe to Elizabeth Waring. The tape-recorder
team in New York had managed to stumble on a man who had
never done anything for a living except kill people. He had been
doing it for, say, twenty years, and he had gotten pretty good
at it.

There was only one stop left to make, and that would have to
wait a few hours. Evening was the time for visiting policemen,
when you could talk to them in their homes.

Hamp walked to the door of the freshly painted one-story gray
house and rang the bell. He could hear a dog barking somewhere
in the back, then the loud scratching noise of its toenails as it
ran across an uncarpeted floor to sniff under the door. He sensed
that it was big, probably a shepherd or a Doberman, and he felt
better when he heard a deep male voice cajole it away from the
door. "Go on," it said. "Into the kitchen." Then, "Kitchen.
Stay." The toenail sound receded into the distance.

A dead bolt gave a metallic clank as the man slipped it. Hamp
conceded that the precautions were understandable. Lorenz was
an ordinary policeman. He'd have spent enough of his career
looking at the work of intruders to develop a desire and talent
for home security. His house wasn't impregnable, by any means,
but a burglar would find it discouraging enough to make him
move on to the next one. The door opened, and Hamp looked
the man in the eye and held out his hand. "Jack Hamp," he
said. "FBI." Now he rapidly revised his expectations. Lorenz
was in his early thirties, over six feet tall and athletic, his black
hair cut by a good barber.

The voice was quiet and the eyes were intelligent. "Fernando
Lorenz. Pleased to meet you."

Hamp regretted the lie, but Elizabeth Waring had spent an
hour telling him what she knew and what she wanted, and the
quickest way to get it was to lie. She hadn't told him to; he had
figured it out on his own. He had been a cop for a long time,
and he knew how it felt to wear the uniform. When a cop heard
"FBI," he had a pretty clear idea of what to expect, and of who
he was talking to. He might like it or he might not, but he was
going to answer questions because he didn't think he needed to

ask them. If you said you were a special investigator for the Justice Department, he was going to spend a lot of time looking at your ID and asking you what you did for a living, and maybe after you left he would make a couple of calls, and maybe find out through his own connections that you had spent the last two years sitting in an airport, or even that you were just doing legwork for a woman lawyer you had never met and he didn't need to care about. The image that would come to mind was that of a young female assistant DA, and the fact that the office where she did her nails was in Washington instead of at the county courthouse didn't make any difference. She wasn't the one whose hands shook while she was strapping on the bullet-proof vest to go in after the barricaded suspect; she was the one who let the suspect go the next day because the paperwork didn't look to her like it was going to add to her won-lost record—or else on the second day, after the charges didn't get filed in time because she was at lunch with the councilman from the seventy-fifth district. It was simpler not to have to get past all that.

He followed Lorenz into a small living room furnished with a few large leather chairs and a long couch that had a half-folded army blanket on it. On the wall hung a dark-red Indian weaving that Hamp recognized as a good nineteenth-century pattern.

"Sorry to bother you at home, Lieutenant," said Hamp, "but I'm sure you understand that we'd like to handle this as quietly as possible. The press seems to take a particular joy in letting the public know when we're on a case, and this time it might lead to some wrong conclusions." He had brushed across the sensitive spot without poking it. The police here would be smarting now, defensive because they sensed people were wondering how fifty men had lost a gunfight with one, and disoriented because they didn't know the answer either. The press would imply that the FBI was wondering too.

Lorenz said only, "Sure. You mind dogs?"

Hamp hesitated, relinquishing the relief that he had felt at having this behind him. "No," he said. "I used to have one." If it was a working police dog, he knew from experience that when Lorenz told it to leave him alone he would have to say it in German. Every department in the country figured that the average fleeing suspect didn't remember enough of what he had learned in high school to get a job, let alone call off a dog.

Lorenz said, "Martha," in a normal voice, and Hamp heard the toenails again, tapping lightly toward him from the back of the house. He turned and saw a gray-brown standard German

shepherd, at least three feet tall, with a chest like a barrel and a
huge gaping mouth, emerge from a hallway. She walked past
Hamp, gave him a look and then sat down in front of Lorenz's
chair. When he pointed at the couch, the dog leaped up and lay
down on the army blanket. "She gets lonely," said Lorenz.
"She and I were Air Police."

Hamp nodded. "How old is she?"

"Nine."

"You made lieutenant fast." Hamp stopped trying to remember his German. It wouldn't do any good. Lorenz had been one
of the men Hamp had seen when he was in the marines guarding
the most sensitive installations: Strategic Air Command bases,
air force communication centers and listening posts, walking
the perimeters with guard dogs. The sight of them had always
struck him as vaguely poignant. The dogs were given to the men
as soon as they were weaned, and man and dog trained together,
sleeping together in the same barracks, never more than a hundred feet apart for at least the length of an enlistment, and more
often for the life of the dog. If the man was married and lived
off the base with his wife, the dog lived with them, and the two
would report for duty together. The attachment between them
grew so strong that they were like two men, or sometimes two
dogs, the one who walked upright representing to the other one
mother, father and head of the wolf pack. The loyalty was so
blind and unbreakable that when the AP's enlistment ended, the
dog had to be discharged with him because it couldn't live without him. Hamp had seen them in Thailand, Vietnam and other
places, the strange solitary pairs the embodiment of a primal
nightmare, the big vulpine creature perfectly capable and even
eager to hurl its ninety pounds of muscle and fang into a man's
throat if it would bring a whispered word and a gentle pat from
its master, who had trained it to attack even more efficiently
than its ferocious instincts would have prompted.

Hamp stared at Martha. The dog lay quietly on the old army
blanket and stared unblinking into his eyes, her head resting on
her paws. He turned back to Lorenz, who seemed to be looking
at him with the same expression. "In your investigation of the
break-in at Mr. Mantino's house . . ."

There was something about the term *break-in* that jarred
Hamp's mind. Whatever had happened, the entry was the least
of it. But Lorenz's eyes moved to the dog, and Hamp's followed.
The dog's ears were up, and its head was turned toward him
attentively. Hamp felt a sudden alarm. The dog had sensed that

he was feeling uncomfortable, maybe by smell, or by a sound in his voice, and it was already beginning to show little signs of agitation. He had to do something before the animal began to suspect that he wished Lorenz harm. He had to stay on solid, neutral ground and get the master to talk. "Tell me anything you found that the FBI might need to know." He knew better than to try to talk to the dog or make a friend of her. She had been brought up to feel no interest whatever in any human being but Lorenz. He tried to formulate something that he could say for the dog's benefit, something scrupulously true and sincere. "I know that's a tall order. I'm asking you for information without being able to reciprocate." The dog set her head down again. "Anytime someone like Mantino dies violently, there are possible consequences and implications, and I don't know yet what they might be. The report says it appeared to be a simple B and E for purposes of robbery." The dog seemed to be satisfied, so he sat back in his chair.

Lorenz hesitated, then began. "You have to understand that this is the biggest disaster for our department in the last hundred years."

Hamp answered, "I understand. We can . . ." he sensed that he was in danger again. "I can assure you that I haven't any intention of letting what you tell me go into wide dissemination, and I'm not interested in the details of what went wrong. I'm interested in the murderer." The tension seemed to go out of the big dog. She kept her eyes on him for another moment, then looked at her master without lifting her head.

"He hot-wired a car from North American Watch and drove it to the front of the house so the occupants would see it and open the door to him. After that we don't know the exact order of events—no witnesses, no prints—but here's what I think. He got them to believe there was some danger, and Mantino and Sobell picked up guns from the gun cabinet in the living room. When Sobell headed for the back of the house with a thirty-ought-six, he shot him in the back of the head. Sobell had to be the first, because it's pretty hard to do that to a man carrying a loaded weapon if he knows you're coming. Then he shot Mantino five times in the chest and the front of the head before Mantino could get a shot off."

"What next?"

"He kept his head, created confusion and got out. He behaved like a real soldier."

Hamp held Martha in the corner of his eye as he spoke. "I'm

interested in this man." Martha cocked an ear, but there was no agitation. It was just like trying to beat a lie detector, he realized, and pushed on. "Is there anything in this to indicate where he came from, or where he'll go next?"

"Nothing," said Lorenz. "In the early fall there are about a thousand hotel rooms available, and about forty percent are rented. We're pretty close to having all of them accounted for. We're working on the planes and trains and buses. I'd say he drove in, did his job, then drove out without attracting any attention. He's got nothing to worry about from anybody around here."

"Who was Sobell?"

"Male Caucasian, six-one, one-eighty-five, good build, broken nose, lots of his prints on the guns in the cabinet. He was licensed as a private detective, but I can't find any indication he worked at it much. I think he was a bodyguard." Lorenz and his dog watched Hamp closely.

Hamp leaned forward. "Do you have any idea why Mantino hired a bodyguard instead of a member of his own organization? Was he afraid of something?"

"I was hoping you could tell me. It got him, though, didn't it?"

Hamp thought about it. If Mantino was afraid of a paid assassin who used to work for the Mafia, it made a lot of sense. The one who gains the most is the one standing closest when the body falls. But he couldn't allow Lorenz to start asking him questions. Even if he managed to compose answers, the dog would smell his tension and premeditation and turn on him. "What was missing from the house?"

Lorenz gave Hamp a wry look. "Nothing. Kind of odd, isn't it? The theory is that he didn't have time, or made more noise than he'd expected to."

Hamp recognized that Lorenz was better than he looked—not as an investigator, because anybody could see it wasn't a botched robbery, but as a cop. He had been pondering the murder, stewing about it for two days, and using the time to look, listen and evaluate. He had found the discrepancies between the official story he was paid to help concoct to keep publicity down and what his common sense told him was true. Now he was working on his own theory. If he was working on it alone, then all he could do was get in the way. But if he was good, there was some small chance that it might lead him, not to the predator who had made a brief and relatively harmless stop in this little community, but to Mantino's associates. This good man could have no more idea than his dog did what it would mean to bring himself to the attention of those people right now. Hamp eyed the dog and determined to discourage him.

"He wasn't trying to rob him," said Hamp. "Washington is sure of that much." Elizabeth was, at least. The dog sensed Hamp's discomfort and turned its head to face him. In a moment, he knew, it would slowly align its body with its head, aimed toward him. "It was a hit."

Lorenz nodded. "Okay. So what?"

"So his death doesn't fit the standard motivation of an ordinary murder. I don't know why he was killed, and we might not know for years, but it wasn't a local matter. Do you understand?"

Lorenz reserved judgment. "Tell me."

"I'm asking you not to go out and pursue any leads on your own. If something comes up, turn it over to the FBI." Hamp was tempted to try to frighten him, but he could tell this was not a man who allowed himself to be frightened; to threaten him would just ensure that he would never drop the case.

Lorenz sighed in frustration, and the dog looked confused. Was her master angry at this stranger? She decided not to take any chances. Hamp watched as her big, muscular body sidestepped into line with the head, so that she was hunched on the couch, ready to spring at him if her master triggered the impulse. "Fair enough," said Lorenz.

"Do I have your word?" asked Hamp. The dog smelled the tension and her master's uncertainty. She hunched lower and her upper lip twitched, as though she could already imagine the taste.

"Yes," Lorenz said finally.

Hamp smiled. "Good," he said, and he meant it. He felt the tension begin to go out of him. "I appreciate it." He stood up and took a step toward the door, then stopped and patted Martha's shoulder hard. He could feel the muscle and bone under the fur, like a man's upper arm. A tongue like a wet slice of ham slipped out between the lower teeth, and the thick tail whipped back and forth.

As Hamp walked to the door, Lorenz shook his hand. "Now, that's something," he said. "She doesn't like people much, but she sure likes you."

* * *

Hamp sat on the bed and looked above him at the big, crude wooden lintel beam over the door that led to the bathroom. There were lots of Spanish touches in La Fonda, little colored designs hand-painted in unlikely places on the white walls, and even the walls themselves, a foot and a half thick on the outside. It was the sort of building that conveyed a sense of security.

Hamp had seen curiosity take some strange forms in his time, and if a man like Peter Mantino was dead, it was conceivable that some of the people who felt close to him were in town. If they were, none of them would be above bugging the room of a Justice Department field man just to see if his leads were any better than theirs. He decided that all he could do was to turn on the television set to mask some of what he was going to say.

When Elizabeth Waring answered, her voice was almost a whisper. "Hello," said Hamp. "I hope I didn't wake you."

"Jack?"

"That's right. I just finished up with the local police here. They don't have much to go on, but the best guess is a lone man who probably didn't have anything in mind except to kill Mantino. The second best guess is what's going in the papers."

"What's that?"

"A robber impersonated a security guard to gain entry, found the victims armed and had to kill them to get out."

"Do you think it's the same man?"

"I don't know that two crimes are enough to establish a reliable pattern."

She sighed deeply enough so he could hear it. "Jack, yesterday I used up a favor in Personnel to look into who you are. I know you probably don't expect much from me, but please don't let that keep you from telling me what you think—not what you *know*, because nobody really knows anything yet. Because I found out I can expect a lot from you, and I'm going to need it."

Hamp ran this through a second time, and it surprised him. She was manipulating him with flattery. It was exactly what he would have done if he were the one stuck in Washington. She could easily be one of those blondes with long, straight, shiny hair and light, empty eyes who could look at you without blinking and dazzle you with bullshit. "Ninety-nine to one it's him."

"Why?"

"There aren't a whole lot of people who would do it this way. It takes a certain kind of person to walk into the other fellow's home ground, look him in the eye, drop the hammer on him and walk away. See, Talarese and Mantino were both people he knew probably weren't alone. If he knew who they were, then he'd know they were as likely to be armed as he was. It's not like the sort of thing a psycho does, where he wants to watch some defenseless victim get scared and suffer and all that so he can feel powerful. It's the opposite. He knows he's outnumbered and probably being hunted, and he has to be sure because he can't hang around and try again. He does it this way because he knows that the other fellow is going to take a second or two stuttering and fumbling, and he knows he isn't. You hear what I'm saying, right? He *knows* he isn't."

There was a pause on Elizabeth's end of the line that sounded as though she were thinking hard. "What's he doing now?"

"I think he's already done it. He wouldn't have booked a Hong Kong flight if he wasn't trying to get away. I think the reason he went after Mantino has something to do with that. Maybe it was a payoff to somebody to get him out: Mantino had an outsider for a bodyguard, which to me means that he didn't trust somebody in his own organization. But it's just as likely that our boy simply wanted to get everybody in an uproar so they'd be too busy putting in bulletproof glass to go out and look for him."

"Welcome aboard, Jack."

"What?"

"You just figured out as much about the way he thinks as anybody else knows after ten years."

"Save the congratulations."

"Why?"

"Because if I get too good at this, sometime I just might get a look at him."

"What's wrong with that?"

"I might waste a second or two making up my mind."

11

The New Mexico experience had been a disaster. He couldn't keep putting himself in positions where some scared cop could pop him in the dark.

Eddie Mastrewski had been the world's greatest advocate of caution. Wolf could see Eddie again, fat and sweating, his eyes bulging and the veins in his forehead visible as he drove the car onto the highway outside St. Louis. "That wasn't right, kid," he had said, glancing up at the rearview mirror, then down at the boy, then into the mirror, then into the other mirror so often that the road in front of him seemed only an afterthought. It was at this moment that the boy had begun to worry. Eddie looked as though he were about to explode. The boy had seen piles of internal organs in the butcher shop, but had only a cloudy notion of how they worked. He thought that the pumping of Eddie's heart was increasing the pressure in his body, and that if it didn't stop, he would have a heart attack, which in the boy's mind meant an explosion of the pump.

"We do this for a living," said Eddie. "It's not some kind of contest. We can't go around getting into gunfights." The boy had nodded sagely for Eddie's benefit, and watched him start to settle down slowly.

The boy's part of it had gone as Eddie had planned. He had sat in the back of the movie theater next to some boys his age, and Mancuso hadn't even noticed him. To all the adults, he had just seemed to be one of a gang of kids who had come together from the neighborhood to see the movie. When Mancuso got up in the middle of the movie to go to the upstairs bathroom, the boy had followed.

He hadn't wanted to follow because he was getting interested in the images on the huge screen at the front. The movie was

La Dolce Vita, and he could still remember the moment when he'd had to walk out. It was dawn somewhere outside Rome after a night of incomprehensible carousing, and Marcello Mastroianni had climbed onto some woman's back and was riding her like a horse on the grass. The boy had no clear notion of what was going on, or if indeed it really was going on or was just some foreign way of conveying decadence. It was the only image he now retained of the film thirty years later, because it was what had been on the screen as he had glanced over his shoulder when he reached the aisle. He had longed to stay at least until the scene changed, because although it had never happened in any movie he had ever seen, he had some forlorn hope that somebody was about to have sexual intercourse, or at least that the woman was about to become naked through some happy act of negligence. Even he could see that the rules were different for foreign movies—he had never seen Doris Day and Rock Hudson behave like this—and he hated to leave without knowing.

Because of this he was annoyed with Mancuso when he followed him into the men's room in the loge. But when he had opened the door, he had forgotten about the movie. Mancuso hadn't gone in to relieve himself; he had gone in to meet two other men. When the boy walked in, all three had turned to face him, jerking their heads in quick unison like a flock of birds. The boy had looked away from them and gone straight to the urinal because he couldn't imagine any other act that would explain his presence. He had stood there, straining to coax some urine out of himself. Could they tell he wasn't pissing? The three had moved away to the end of the room. He could hear their leather soles on the hard white tiles. Mancuso gave the two men crinkly envelopes, and then the men left, swinging the door against the squeaky spring that was supposed to hold it closed.

As Mancuso went to wash his hands at the sink, the boy had wondered why. But Mancuso was using it as an excuse for standing in front of the mirror and admiring his thick brown hair. Then he had run his wet hands through the hair and taken out a black plastic comb. The boy had tried to stop time, to hold everything the way it was while he decided, but it didn't work.

Mancuso put the comb in the breast pocket of his suit and turned to dry his hands on the filthy rolling towel. The boy turned with him, took the revolver out of his jacket and aimed at the base of his skull. When he fired, the noise was terrible and bright and hollow in the little room. Then he dashed out,

as much to escape the ringing in his ears as the corpse. But in
the dim light of the small, orange, flame-shaped bulbs mounted
on the walls of the mezzanine, he saw his mistake.

The two men hadn't left at all. They had been waiting just
outside the door for Mancuso to join them, and now they pulled
guns out of their suit coats and aimed them at the boy. He remembered the puzzled face of one of them, a tall, thin man with
a long nose. He looked at the boy, then past him as though he
expected someone else to come out of the men's room. The boy
ran.

Years later he understood that it was probably the only thing
that had saved him. To pull out the gun again, even to stand in
one place long enough to allow the two men to think, would
have doomed him. But he ran down the stairs to the lobby, where
Eddie was just coming out of the swinging double doors with
some scared ushers and three other middle-aged men in hats
and long overcoats. At first the boy thought that Eddie had been
caught, because they looked like plainclothes cops. But when
the two men with guns had appeared behind him on the stairway,
everybody but Eddie ran back into the theater. Only the boy and
Eddie fired. Both of them aimed at the same man and hit him,
and left the other to get off two or three shots over the railing.
He was too cunning, because he fired at the big glass door to
the street, where Eddie and the boy should have been, instead
of into the lobby, where they were. The boy aimed again, but
then the railing was a blur because he was being snatched off
his feet and hustled through the pile of broken glass into the
street.

Eddie had been right to do it. Eddie was a born foot soldier.
He always kept in the front of his brain the certainty that anyone
who thought he had a valid reason to put his head up when the
air was full of flying metal was an idiot. And now it was time
for Wolf to put his head down.

It had taken him two days of driving to reach Buffalo, and he
felt a kind of empty-headed euphoria to be able to stand and
walk. His right foot was cramped and stiff, and the tendon behind his right knee felt stretched and rubbery. He walked along
Grant Street and studied the buildings. They hadn't changed in
the ten years since he had seen them except for the signs, so
there was some hope. When he had arrived in Buffalo he had
found it gripped by some kind of madness. The center of the
downtown section had been bulldozed and sandblasted, and now

lived a strange, mummified, decorative existence, with a set of trolley tracks running down Main Street and a lot of lights to verify the first impression that there was nobody on the sidewalks. They had hosed the dirty, dangerous occupants out of Chippewa Street and turned the buildings into the core of some imaginary theater district.

The whole business alarmed him. What could have become of the old man if there was some urban-renewal craziness going on? But the juggernaut had obviously run its course before it reached Grant Street. The respectable blue-collar sections obviously hadn't struck anybody in city hall as a priority, and they retained their ancient gritty integrity.

When he had been here on business with Eddie when he was sixteen, they had driven by the house slowly, but didn't stop. "What is it?" he had asked. Eddie had answered, "There's a man in there who makes people disappear. He's black—sort of brown and leathery like my shoes, and he's about a thousand years old. Remember where it is. Never write it down, just remember."

Years later he had made his way to Buffalo with a contract on him so huge that it wasn't expressed in numbers. The word had gone out that the man who got him would never have to do anything again for the rest of his life. So he had found himself one winter night in the musty, dark parlor talking to the quiet old man, with the big clock ticking on the mantel and the old furnace in the basement pumping warm air up through the register at their feet.

"I know who you are," the old man had said. "It'll be expensive."

Ten years later, here he was in the parlor again. This time the old man said, "I remember you. It'll be expensive."

"I know," Wolf said. He considered himself lucky that the old man was still above ground with ten years added on to the unknowable number he had already lived.

The old man seemed to be thinking about how long ten years was too. "How hard are they looking after all these years? Don't lie to me."

"They found me," he said. "They must be trying hard."

"Why?"

"You know why."

"No. Why *now*?"

"I've been living far away all this time. I wasn't stupid enough to even think about coming back, but Tony Talarese found me."

"So you killed him, which makes four. Peter Mantino makes six, because you had to shoot a man to get to him."

"So everybody knows."

"People talk. This time I listened."

"Why?"

"I knew you'd been away. That meant you don't have anybody you didn't know ten years ago."

"So you waited for me to come."

"I waited."

"Are you going to help me?"

"When you were in trouble before, you didn't want to run away from it until you hurt them. You killed about twenty of them before you let it go."

"It wasn't twenty."

The old man shrugged. "It don't matter. I want to know if you're going to do that again."

"No," Wolf said. "It was worth trying to get Talarese before he told anybody where I was. I thought he was too greedy to let anybody else collect. Then there was a shooter waiting for me at the L.A. airport. Unless things have changed a lot, there's nobody who could have arranged that except Mantino."

"Who else do you want? Did you come to town to get Angelo Fratelli?"

"No. All I want is a passport and a way out. I want to go under again."

"Then I'll go see a man." The old man pushed himself up out of the chair with his arms, and stayed bent over for a second before straightening. As he dressed for his errand, he looked frail and antique. He put on a sleeveless sweater, wrapped a scarf around his neck, put on a dark brown overcoat and then snapped a pair of rubbers over his sturdy leather shoes to keep his feet dry, as though it were midwinter. He walked carefully to the door. "Lock it behind me. Anybody comes who don't have a key, shoot him."

"I didn't bring a gun."

The old man had to turn the whole upper part of his body around to look at him. "There's a shotgun in the closet." He closed the door, and Wolf could hear him slowly and carefully moving over the elastic boards of the porch toward the steps, and then silence returned.

The house was still fiercely neat. The knives hanging from hooks in the kitchen had been sharpened so many times that they all had fillet blades, but they were hung in unbroken descending order of length. The old man's collection of boots was lined up in ranks in the front of the closet. The shotgun was a Remington that might have been acquired any time after the turn of the century, and it rested in a stand that the old man had made, with a block at the floor cut with a jigsaw to fit the butt, and a pair of bent clamps on the barrel to keep it from toppling over. The plastic cap of an aspirin bottle had been fitted over the muzzle to keep out the dust. Wolf lifted it out of its stand and sniffed it: linseed oil on the stock and gun oil on the barrel. He pumped the slide and felt the smooth, easy clicks as he ejected a shell onto the carpet. He glanced at it before he slipped it back in: double-ought buckshot. The old man didn't want to have to shoot anybody twice.

He had been awake most of the time for seventy-two hours now, and his mind was beginning to feel the wear. He had to force himself to stay alert for a few more minutes. He found the box of shotgun shells on the floor behind the boots, filled his coat pockets with them and took the shotgun with him.

He was beginning to feel an exhaustion almost like dizziness, so that when he turned his head he had to take a moment to focus on the new sight. He knew he was probably reacting to this more than to the danger of sleeping alone in the old man's house, but he felt a nervous restlessness that made him afraid to close his eyes.

Eddie had given him advice on that too. "Before you go to sleep, always be goddamned sure you're going to be alive when you wake up." He used to keep the boy up watching the cars behind them while he drove, or sometimes just looking for a likely place to drop a weapon or change a license plate. Once he had even made him check off landmarks to be sure the road map didn't have any mistakes on it. Sometime in the last few years Wolf had admitted to himself that he had always known it was because Eddie hated to be alone when he was scared. Eddie would have said, "I'm not scared. I'm just alert." It still made him sad to remember that Eddie had been alone when he had died.

He walked through the house to the pantry, opened the door and turned on the light. The shelves were lined with cans and bottles to last for years, all arranged in rows, front to back like the displays in a tiny supermarket. He found a twenty-five-pound sack of rice, placed it on the floor as a pillow, laid the shotgun on the floor next to it and turned out the light. For a moment he lay there in the dark, opening and closing his eyes and not detecting a difference. He wondered if he would have to try something else. It had been ten years since he had slept on a floor, and the tile squares were harder and colder than they looked. But the idea of getting up again seemed an immense labor at the moment, and then he forgot what he had been thinking, and had to remind himself. He decided he had better move, but later, when he felt more uncomfortable, and then he was asleep.

He didn't dream. Instead, his mind roamed the house, running hands along the walls, feeling the faint vibration of the old man's oil furnace, like the sound of an engine pushing it somewhere with glacial slowness. Deep in the timbers there was the almost-inaudible creak of the house standing up to the wind off the river, and outside, tiny particles of grit blowing against the impervious shell of brittle paint on the clapboards. It was like being deep in the hold of a ship at anchor. His mind kept patrolling the surfaces, reassuring itself that the shell was tight and unbroken, and that his sleeping body was secreted in the center, where he had hidden it.

When he awoke, his first sensation was that he had missed something on his rounds, made a mistake. But then his mind tripped on the contradiction: he couldn't have been both asleep and awake. But he knew there were people in the house. The floor amplified the impacts of their steps, and he could feel them in his body. The old man would have come in alone and warned him if he was bringing somebody back with him.

He picked up the shotgun and slowly crawled to the pantry door. He pushed the door open an eighth of an inch and looked out into the kitchen. It was still dark. He listened for a moment, until he was sure they were no longer in the room. He heard the creak of a door in the hallway being pulled open quickly, then a long silence. If there were people sneaking around the house in the dark, then the old man wasn't one of them. He would have known it was the best way to get his head blown off. Could the old man have sold him? Not after giving him a loaded shotgun. Somebody was looking for Wolf.

At first the search would be quick and cursory. They would duck across doorways and step aside to swing doors open. When they had been through the whole building once without any resistance, they would go through again looking for hiding places. He had to get out before they got to that stage. He held the shotgun level with the floor as he slipped out of the pantry into the open kitchen. He set his feet down softly, moving to the kitchen door. Now he could hear voices in the parlor, quick and urgent and soft.

He slowly turned the doorknob and pulled the door open before he let the spring turn it back. He took a step over the threshold, then another to take the weight of his body, then another and another until he was down the steps. He took a deep breath of the cool, damp air and blew it out to let it merge with the wind. As his head cleared, he admitted to himself that the old man must be dead.

He walked around to the back of the house, looked in the window and saw them. There were two of them, both carrying pistols in their right hands. One was tall and fat, with bristly gray hair brushed back like porcupine quills. He kept his pistol pointed down at the floor, while the other, a twenty-five-year-old with a pitted complexion and a sharp, chiseled face, danced around opening closet doors and jumping out of the way as though he weren't sure when his partner might decide to shoot.

As he watched them, he studied the eager, predatory expression on the face of the young one. He looked as though he had just watched the old black man die, and the sight had agreed with him. He was in a state of excitement, thrilled that he was going to get to do it again. It took no more than a second for the impulse his look ignited in Wolf to travel its course. He knew Eddie Mastrewski would have said, "What do you get for it?" But by now the impulse was traveling too fast, gaining strength and getting hotter, and it made him raise the shotgun to his shoulder and hug it tight. He fired through the window, pumped it and fired again. After the second shot, as the barrel leveled from the kick and he pumped it again, there was an instant, like the wink of a camera shutter, when he saw pieces of glittering window glass turn end over end and sprinkle the two bodies sprawled on the floor.

He lowered the shotgun, pressed the disconnector and quickly pumped out the last three shells. Then he released the magazine, gave the barrel a quarter-turn and removed it from the receiver. He held both halves under his coat and walked down the driveway to the street. He had told the old man he hadn't come to town to get Angelo Fratelli, but a lot had changed since then.

Angelo Fratelli hated white wine. It was his belief that it was a weak, sour version of the rich, blood-red Paisano that he had been drinking since he was a child. He had heard the sister say in school that when Jesus was on the cross, the Romans had given him vinegar and water with a sponge, and he had assumed they were talking about something that just tasted like vinegar, maybe cheap Spanish sauterne. That was what Angelo was drinking now. Every year, between Ash Wednesday and Easter, he drank white wine only. It was a legacy from the days when people ate fish on Friday, and although religion had said nothing about what went with it, the Fratellis had always assumed that the Scriptures implied white wine. The drop of cognac or grappa that he liked after dinner was out too, because those concoctions were clearly on the side of luxury. He was still drinking white wine this late in the year because of a promise he had made to Saint Giovanni in return for a favor, and from time to time he wondered if the favor was sufficient to merit the sacrifice.

But he always lost weight during Lent, and on the whole he was satisfied with the return he got on this last vestige of his religion. He weighed two hundred thirty pounds on Easter morning each year. By the time Ash Wednesday came again he weighed two forty-five, and over twenty years that was an extra three hundred pounds. So he calculated that if he hadn't switched to white wine every Lent and spoiled his appetite, he would weigh about five hundred fifty pounds. He was fifty-three now, and it would have been a real problem; he wouldn't even have been able to slide into his reserved booth at the Vesuvio Restaurant.

This would have been more than a humiliation, because the booth where he now sat was his place of business. It was under a stained-glass window with a picture of Mount Vesuvius trailing a huge cloud of white smoke across the blue sky. It allowed him to sit with his back to the wall without seeming to, because behind the window were six inches of whitewashed brick with light bulbs cunningly placed to simulate the light of the Italian sun and the glow of the volcano. The booth wasn't reserved in a crude way; it was simply that the waiters never seated anyone else there. If an outsider asked for it, they would smile and nod and conduct him to another part of the restaurant.

Angelo Fratelli was an important man. In a way, he was the restaurant's biggest attraction. Every night at six he would drive into the lot at the rear of the building, walk around to the front, come in, smile at the older waiters and go through the dining room to his booth. When he sat down, Lorraine, the fiftyish blond waitress he seemed to prefer, would bring him his wine. She would set the carafe on the table roughly, nearly spilling it, and clank down his glass. If he said, ''Nice day today,'' she would snap, "Can't prove it by me. I've got to be on my feet in this dark hole all day." If he said she looked good, she'd say, "Don't even think about it." For reasons nobody had ever fathomed, Mr. Fratelli found Lorraine amusing, and when he left each night, he would give her a large tip. Since all the employees in the Vesuvio divided their tips equally, Lorraine's rudeness to Mr. Fratelli was considered a form of heroism. From a certain point of view, she was risking her life for the good of all. Angelo Fratelli was the reigning leader of what in Buffalo was called "The Arm."

Nobody presumed to guess why Angelo tolerated Lorraine, but it was for a combination of reasons. One was that he thought it made him seem affable and approachable. In reality he was anything but affable. In the wars of the fifties he had filled his share of car trunks, and since then had cultivated a reputation for savagery by ensuring that the kills he wanted attributed to his wrath were found naked and mutilated in fields south of the city. Everything he did was calculated and premeditated. Although he had no interest in spending time with other people, he had found that a good portion of his business was brought to him by people who would never have dared speak to him if it weren't for his supposed accessibility. His demeanor had been practiced since the forties, when he had been given as a franchise a stable of shopworn and unprepossessing prostitutes by Francisco Del Pecchio, the potentate of that era. Angelo's natural temper was gloomy and dyspeptic, and at first he found that the prostitution business was tough going. Potential customers were instinctively frightened when they saw him, and often left before they saw the merchandise he was offering because they suspected that the young two-hundred-thirty-pound entrepreneur might have conducted them to his lair in the Albemarle Hotel to garrote them for their wallets and watches. This in fact, was one of the business practices he was reduced to considering, when one day a prospective client, a gypsum buyer from Ohio, enlightened him. "You think I'm crazy enough to go out in the dark in a strange town with you?"

Thereafter Angelo had concentrated his considerable will on changing his image. He had spent some money on decorating the upper floor of the Albemarle, more money on some respectable suits for himself and still more money on presents and clothes for his sullen and underworked talent. He made it a policy never to enter a room without smiling at everyone he saw and, if possible, calling them by name. He developed a comical way of talking to his girls, patterned after the way he and his male colleagues in The Arm talked to each other, a tone that was simultaneously conspiratorial and derisive. He even gave them nicknames like mobsters. One, a girl who had been born with a blond, bovine beauty in a part of Alabama that hadn't seen fit to reward it suitably, he called "Slowly-butt Shirley." Another, a tall, bony woman who might have been a fashion model if she had had a pretty face, he called "Olive Oyl," and a younger girl of similar charms and handicaps, "Extra-Virgin Olive Oyl." His star, an intense young woman named Gloria Monday, was so inventive in what she did to, on, under and with her clients that she achieved a clientele that wasn't either blind drunk or lost, but actually knew the way to the Albemarle. Angelo had never heard Latin outside of church, but he could read an inscription, and when he saw "Sic Transit Gloria Mundi" on a tombstone, he started calling her "Sick Transit Gloria."

That had been a long time ago. Now the girls were old or dead, and Angelo's hearty, expansive manner had become so habitual that he had often displayed it at the most inappropriate times, such as the night when he had executed a young Canadian named Boromier for being found in close proximity to a truck-load of cigarettes that unofficially belonged to Angelo, and again when he had attended the funeral of a close friend. Because it bore no relation to his feelings, this bogus jocularity could surface at any time when he wasn't concentrating. It added to his stature and reputation in his later years, because when it appeared it was chilling.

Angelo was alone in his booth tonight; it was a brief vacation for him. Usually he was encumbered by Capella and Salvatore, two young retainers sworn to die to protect him. The problem with young men sworn to die to protect their patrons was that they didn't actually want to die, so large portions of their mental capacities were devoted to vigilance and suspicion. This left so little for ordinary human commerce that it made them dull and preoccupied companions. But tonight Angelo was to meet with a man who wasn't willing to speak in the presence of third parties and hadn't the experience to appreciate the fact that at any given time Capella and Salvatore were only half conscious of anything that was said, and in any case had no interest in it.

Angelo sipped the terrible white wine and rolled it around his mouth so that he could detest it. Then he set the glass down, filled it again, stood up and went to the men's room. As he walked across the dining room, he felt the eyes of a dozen people on him, all establishing his presence to the satisfaction of a hundred grand juries. He had seldom done what he was about to do. The Vesuvio was his sanctuary, and to use it as an alibi in any illegal activity would have been a violation of trust. But the man he was going to meet was a banker, a solid citizen who had, to Angelo's knowledge, never done anything that wouldn't put a grand jury to sleep.

Angelo passed the men's room door, went out the fire exit in the hallway near the storeroom and emerged beside the dumpster in the lot behind the restaurant. He was so overwhelmed by the sweet, nauseating smell of fermenting vegetables that he stopped to peer over the edge to see what they were. He was dispirited when he saw that the smell was from a collection of empty quart cans of tomato paste, all opened and dumped hastily without being scraped. These days everybody was in a hurry; in the old days they had made the sauce from fresh plum tomatoes.

He looked for the car Salvatore had left for him, and saw it immediately. It was a small gray Toyota registered to someone named O'Reilly who ran a gas station and used it as a loaner for regular customers. O'Reilly had no idea who would be driving the car, or that it had anything to do with the way Salvatore made his living. It was a favor of no consequence to O'Reilly, but the fact that he had done it had, without his knowledge, made him eligible for dividends in the future. He would probably find that over time he would gain a few customers who would mention that Salvatore had recommended him. But he might also find that when he was worried about his property taxes they had already been paid, or that his daughter had miraculously moved up the waiting list for admission to the most desirable girls' school. In the most extreme case, he might find that when his enemies were about to triumph over him, forces that had nothing to do with him would destroy them, suddenly and utterly. The world worked on goodwill, favors and reciprocities, but the system was too crude to keep the exchanges in proportion.

Angelo drove out of the lot without even glancing in the direction of the space where his own Cadillac was parked. In ten or twenty minutes he would be back at his table. He drove carefully. The car was probably like a fingerprint collection by now, having been loaned to half the city without being cleaned, but if he hit something there wouldn't be much question as to who had been driving it.

* * *

Wolf heard the sound of the Toyota leaving the lot. As soon as its lights had passed, he knew the driver's eyes would be turned to look up the street, and he sat up in the back seat of Fratelli's Cadillac. What he saw seemed impossible. The driver of the little car that was going past Angelo Fratelli's new Caddy was Angelo Fratelli. He ducked back down, opened the door a little and kept the light switch in the door frame depressed with his keys while he opened it wide enough to slip out into the darkness. He reached inside to the floor to haul the shotgun out after him, then hurried to his own car.

Angelo wasn't sure why he was going to the trouble of meeting McCarron in secret and alone, but he was intrigued by the request. McCarron was the president of a small bank that operated only in Erie County. Banks had always titillated Angelo, and they had titillated him even more since he had begun to read the stories about savings and loans being closed by the government. It amazed him that so much crude bad-boy thievery had gone on behind the substantial institutional columns of those places. There had been clowns who had imagined they could practically stuff their briefcases with their depositors' money and walk out the door free and clear the day they had declared bankruptcy. But oddly enough, it seemed that the clowns were right. The government was picking up the tab, and those former savings-and-loan officers were sitting on their yachts drinking champagne. Obviously Mr. McCarron had been reading the same newspapers Angelo had. He would be thinking that right now, as the army of sweaty little federal bookkeepers were busy breaking their pencils and gnashing their teeth while they worked their second year of double shifts to figure out what had happened to all the money in the savings and loans, they would be letting the banks alone.

McCarron obviously had a scheme. Those guys must all know each other too, just the way Angelo and his colleagues did. They weren't exactly competitors, because there was plenty to go around, but they kept an eye on each other because nobody ever knew the future, and if one of them got too big he would be dangerous. McCarron would be sitting in his big old Victorian mansion on Delaware Park Lake, and he would read about how the dumbest bastard he had known at Harvard Business School had just gone under. He would say to himself, "It makes sense." Then he would read on to learn that two hundred million dollars had somehow disappeared on bad loans, and he would know. For an hour or a day he might pretend he didn't but he would know. The dumb bastard had somehow ended up with the money. The federal regulators wouldn't be able to figure out how, but McCarron would because he was in the same business.

So now McCarron had done something that not even the most cynical and suspicious of investigators could have anticipated: he had set up a meeting with Angelo Fratelli. This bank president, whose social life was reported in the *Buffalo News* and seemed always to involve his being in a tuxedo at an odd location like a hospital or the art museum with others like him, needed Angelo. All that remained now was for Angelo to hear what his part in the scheme was, and what he was going to get out of it. It might be that one of Angelo's companies would be the one to default on a big loan, or even that McCarron had somehow found a way to get the money in cash and needed someone with connections to haul it to offshore banks. Angelo didn't waste much time speculating on the specifics because he wasn't dealing with a little teller with a drug habit. This was a bank president, and if he had a scheme, it was probably so complicated and devious that nobody else could even follow it.

Fratelli drove to the park, and along the curving drive around the lake. Across the water he could see the fronts of the art museum and the Buffalo Historical Museum on a little hillside, gleaming white in the moonlight. Then his view was blocked by trees again, and he passed the first brick walls of the zoo. Now he saw McCarron. He was standing on the first of the asphalt basketball courts in the park, and he had a big tan dog on a leash. Angelo was a little unnerved. When McCarron had said he walked his dog at night, Fratelli had imagined a hairy little yapper, not a big slavering monster. But he pulled over anyway, extricated his large body from the little Toyota and stepped onto the lawn.

"What kind of dog is that?" he asked. He leaned against the fence instead of going through the gate onto the court.

"It's a golden retriever," said McCarron. He reached down and pounded the dog. To Fratelli it seemed he had hammered it pretty hard, but the dog appeared to love it, so he ventured closer. "Don't worry," said McCarron. "He doesn't bite."

"Then what good is he?"

McCarron seemed to think about this for a long time. "My wife bought him," he said finally.

"Come on," said Angelo, "Get in and we'll go for a ride. If

we stand around here, it's only a matter of time before kids come to hit us over the head or cops come to save us.''

McCarron and the dog moved out of the basketball court and to the side of the car. As the banker opened the door, Fratelli stopped him. ''Has he taken a leak lately?''

McCarron smiled. ''He won't foul the car.''

As Angelo went back to the driver's side, he thought about that one: ''foul the car.'' Whatever this McCarron was going to be worth, he was a real dog-and-horse, riding-boots-and-driving-gloves asshole.

As Angelo started the car, he felt it lurch and rock, once as the dog bounded into the back seat, and once as McCarron seated himself in the front. He pulled out onto the drive. He wasn't surprised that in the enclosed space of the little car he could smell the dog, but he could also smell something fainter. McCarron was wearing some kind of perfumed after-shave or cologne. He had always heard that it was déclassé to slap that stuff on. It seemed to Angelo that as you moved up the social strata, at each step all the rules were reversed. It was like clothes. At a certain level, not wearing nice clothes meant you didn't have a job. Two levels up from there, it meant you didn't need one.

Wolf was driving past the park that abutted the zoo when he saw a man and a dog come out of one of the basketball courts. At first he couldn't be sure what was going on, but in the rearview mirror he saw the man join somebody who could have been Angelo Fratelli. When the dog and the two men got into the little gray Toyota, he knew. At the first turn Wolf pulled over, stopped and lay down on the front seat. When he saw the head-lights flash on the ceiling of his car and then vanish, he sat up and prepared to follow.

Angelo drove to Delaware Avenue and turned left to go out of the city. He had begun to feel that he needed to bring this one up into the light and take a look at him. Driving around in the dark wasn't going to tell him who he was dealing with. He turned the next corner and then turned again at Elmwood toward the state university. The traffic was consistent and still heavy, but most of it was going away from Buffalo State at dinnertime. On an impulse, he turned on Forest Avenue and went up a short driveway to a parking lot at the edge of the campus. Ahead of him was a carload of young men. They took a ticket from a dispenser, and a wooden beam raised itself to let them in.

"What's this?" asked McCarron. "Why are we stopping?"

"The university. There's plenty of people. It's a good place to talk."

"Is this safe?"

"Who do you think those kids are going to recognize—you or me?" Angelo waited for a stupid answer, but when it didn't come, he drove into the lot, stopped the car in the middle of a row, then turned toward his passenger. "Okay, Mr. McCarron. What do you want from me?"

The banker took a deep breath and spoke carefully. "I have a problem. I was going to say 'I have reason to believe,' but that's not strong enough. I *know* I have a problem. I've been borrowing funds from certain accounts. They were secret, set up with false names. I knew that the owners wouldn't go to the authorities if they discovered a problem, but now they know, and I think someone will come for me at some point."

Angelo didn't conceal his disappointment. "Shit," he said. "What do you want? Protection?"

McCarron said, "I don't think that if they really want me, bodyguards would be of much use. I'd like to get out of the country. Maybe you could arrange whatever you do for your own people in this situation—plastic surgery, papers and so on."

Angelo moved his head from side to side and let out a little snort that was partly a laugh. It was absurd, but maybe if he did this man a favor he wouldn't regret it. After all, McCarron was still the president of a perfectly good bank. "That kind of thing mostly happens in the movies. But if you'll tell me who's pissed off at you, I might be able to get him off your back." He began to calculate how it would work. He could tell McCarron his enemy was demanding a million dollars. Then, with a hundred thousand or so and a slight expenditure of bluster, Angelo could probably convince any reasonably small-time wiseguy that he had saved his honor and had settled his dispute.

"It's not like that," said McCarron. "I can't tell you much. I thought they were drug dealers, but now I believe it's the . . . uh, CIA."

Angelo's hands gripped the steering wheel, and he could see that his knuckles were turning white and feel that rage was gripping his chest and throat. All of his visions of access to a bank were laughable; this man was insane. He had heard of this kind of thing happening. Sometimes they saw religious visions, or heard voices telling them to do things like drop their pants in some public place. Sometimes they decided the CIA was bombarding their feeble brains with radio waves and listening to what they were thinking. He wasn't going to get inside the bank, and clearly within a short time McCarron wasn't going to either. He held his temper. "Gee," he said. "I don't know what to tell you."

McCarron was alarmed. "You won't do it?"

"The C fucking IA . . . I just don't know." Angelo avoided McCarron's wide-eyed, gaping face, letting his eyes wander to the nearest lighted building. At the corner of the building were two glass doors, so the whole corner was glass. Beyond the door, in the hallway, he could see a few students, but there was also a man in his late thirties or early forties with sandy hair. The man was looking at something on a bulletin board; no, he seemed to be reading *everything* on the bulletin board. He looked odd to Angelo. What was it? There was something about the way he carried himself, a slight slouch, as though he were keeping most of his weight on one foot, his coat open and his arms down at his sides. Then Angelo realized that the man was looking at him in the reflection on the dark glass of the door beside him.

Angelo studied the face in the window and then began to sweat. "My God," he said, and realized he had said it aloud in front of this lunatic, but then decided he didn't care.

"What's wrong?" asked McCarron. "What is it? Your heart?" He grabbed Angelo's arm.

"No! Get your hands off me." Angelo started the car and backed out of the space, then guided the little car around to the exit. He made it down the narrow drive about forty feet, then had to stop to wait for the cars ahead of him to pay the man at the kiosk and drive off.

The station wagon at the head of the line settled its accounts with the man and pulled forward under the raised barrier, but then something very noisy happened to it. At first Angelo didn't see the bus coming any more than the driver of the wagon did, but just as its nose moved a couple of feet into the street, the bus arrived to occupy the same space. It was on its approach to the bus stop, so it was only inches from the curb when it hit the station wagon. It popped the front bumper off, took the grille and smeared the front end of the station wagon sideways as it came to a stop across the driveway.

Angelo looked for a way out. The curb on both sides of the

car was at least a foot high, and if he tried to bump over it he would probably get stuck halfway. His Caddy might have made it, but this little Toyota's doughnut tires didn't have a chance. He was stuck in a track like a go-cart in an amusement park. There were two cars and something that looked like the end of the world ahead of him, and at least four or five behind him. Curious people were now beginning to come out of the nearby campus buildings, some of them looking amused, some worried. The man he had seen would wait just long enough for the confusion to peak, and then he would be here. Angelo couldn't defend himself; he didn't even have a gun. If he had been in the Cadillac, he could at least have used the phone to call for help. He looked around him. Far down the street to his left was the lighted yellow sign of a bar called The Canal.

He turned to McCarron. "We've got a little problem, and here's what we're going to do."

"Problem?" said McCarron. "They'll have that cleared up in a few minutes."

Angelo was afraid he was going to break the steering wheel with his bare hands, so he carefully put them in his lap. "I'm going to get out of the car and walk down to that bar with the yellow sign. You slide over, take the wheel—"

"I can't slide over in this car."

"You come around, wait for them to clear the exit, drive down to the bar and meet me."

Angelo's slow, clear, quiet voice had frightened McCarron more than it would have if he had been screaming and shrieking. He held on to Angelo's arm with a grip that slowed the circulation. "No. No, you don't. Tell me first."

Angelo glared at him. This was when he would have killed him if they hadn't been stuck here surrounded by people. This was a man who, if left alone, would shortly begin to line his hats with tinfoil to protect his brain from the CIA's microwaves. But he tried anyway. "There's a man in that building. Don't look. *I said don't look.* He kills people for a living. He shouldn't be here. I haven't seen him for years, and now here he is."

"See?" said McCarron. "He's after me."

Angelo sighed. "He's not after you, for Christ's sake. He's after me."

McCarron wasn't to be dissuaded. "I came to you tonight to tell you they want me dead, a hit man shows up and you say he's not after me?"

"Please," said Angelo. "Just do it. Come around and take the wheel."

"No," said McCarron. "Not a chance."

Now Angelo grabbed McCarron's wrist and freed himself of the lunatic's grip. It was much more difficult than he had anticipated; McCarron was as big as he was. "This is not the kind of man the CIA would send—give him a membership card and security clearance and all that shit. He's a fucking animal."

"That's very reassuring. Look, my life depends on you now. Get us out of here."

Angelo nearly said, "No, *my* life depends on *you*," but the thought was too distasteful. "This guy doesn't know you from shit. You're nothing. The people he works for could take out six of you a day and he still wouldn't make enough to pay for gas. This is my town. If he's in my town and nobody told me he was coming, he's looking for me. Now I've got to get to a phone." He gave McCarron's wrist a little twist as he threw it back in his lap, and got out of the car.

He walked fast, stepping over the high curb and striking out across the shrubbery to the sidewalk. But then he heard a car door slam, and he listened for the other door to slam and let him know that McCarron had gotten into the driver's seat. Instead, he heard the loud blare of a car horn. Then there were running footsteps, and an unfamiliar voice yelled, "Hey! Get back in the car! Fight it out at home, you old faggots." He was mortified more deeply than he had been since he was a child. He felt chills in his spine, inside the very bones, but when he touched his face it was hot.

When McCarron caught up with him, Angelo was so angry that patches and bursts of color were floating across his field of vision. "You couldn't listen, huh?" The man was dead. He might still be walking around, but now the only gratification that Angelo could promise himself was that McCarron was going to know why he was dying while he died.

"You expect me to sit there and let him kill me? My only chance is if I stick with you."

McCarron obviously didn't know that he was beyond having chances. His chance had been the chance to do what Angelo had told him to do. "Shut up," said Angelo. There was no possibility the Butcher's Boy hadn't been looking at him, but why would he be looking for him in a university parking lot? If he wanted Angelo, he would look for the Cadillac in the parking lot at the Vesuvio. Of course he had, but he had seen Angelo come out and get into this little Toyota, and had followed him. Tonight, of all nights of the year, he was away from his soldiers, unarmed and alone.

"Where are we going? Shouldn't we get off the street?" McCarron asked.

Now it occurred to Angelo that the reason he was in this situation was the call from this lunatic who was dogging his steps, practically stepping on his heels. He glanced at McCarron again, but the suspicion dissolved into simple anger. McCarron was too crazy to have knowingly betrayed anyone. He really was frightened. "No," said Angelo. "We go to the bar and call for help. If that one gets us into the darkness off the street, we don't come out again."

Behind them a horn honked again. This time it was a long, loud bleat that ended with what sounded like someone beating his fist on the horn six times.

Wolf drifted out of the building with a crowd of curious students. The bus driver and the owner of the station wagon were out of their vehicles and standing on the street, so the onlookers began to lose interest. There was no tragedy to participate in, or even carnage to see. The event had already been diminished to the dull haggling in which the drivers served only as temporary representatives of the insurance companies and lawyers who were the real principals. The horns started again, the two drivers in the accident climbed back into their vehicles, the bus driver pulled away from the wrecked car and stopped at the bus stop, and then a few young men pushed the station wagon away from the exit and around the corner to the curb.

Now the horns began in earnest, and Wolf looked at the source of the commotion. There was the little Toyota stalled in the narrow drive to the exit, and behind it there were now eight or ten cars, all honking their horns. Two of the young men who had pushed the station wagon were looking into the gray car and shaking their heads at someone inside. When the someone lunged over the back seat into the front and began to bark at the horns, he understood their problem; they wanted to get in and move the car out of the way, but they were afraid of the big dog.

As Wolf stepped to the street, he could see two men walking quickly up the sidewalk toward a lighted yellow sign. The big man with Fratelli, whose face he hadn't been able to see, was probably a bodyguard. He obviously had the knack. There had been no way for the bodyguard to sense that Fratelli was in danger—as in fact he wasn't, at least for the moment. Wolf had already decided not to make an attempt tonight. There were too many witnesses. When the gray car had entered the university visitors' lot, he had followed it on a whim. He regretted it now as he walked back toward his car amid the sound of horns. Somehow he had frightened the bodyguard and a whole series of responses had been triggered, each placing additional obstacles in his path. Now Fratelli would dig in, the bodyguard would marshal reinforcements and in an hour Fratelli would be a very difficult man to kill.

Wolf climbed into his car and started the engine. He backed out of his parking space and joined the line of cars waiting to get past the toll gate to the street. He could see that the two men were just coming under the big yellow sign down the sidewalk. Then something odd happened. The two of them tried to squeeze through the front door at once, and got stuck for a second. Then Fratelli stopped and let the other man go in front. It was puzzling behavior for a bodyguard.

Once inside the Canal, Angelo could see that the place was disgusting. It was full of the kind of people he had seen on television buying cars like the one he had just abandoned or talking about tax-sheltered annuities, and every one of them was drinking white wine. The place was dim but full of living plants with little spotlights on them, and the bartender was dressed up like a neutered poodle, with a high collar that had a little black bow around it.

He could see the telephone in the little alcove just this side of the bathrooms, so he rushed across the room, fishing in his pockets for change. He was almost at the telephone before he admitted to himself that he didn't have any, so he came back to grab McCarron, who had been headed off by a woman in a little blue suit like a man's. "I'm afraid we're all booked up," she was saying.

Angelo said to McCarron, "Give me your change."

The woman looked at him doubtfully. "I was just telling your friend—"

"Fine," said Angelo. "I just want to use your phone." McCarron placed a little pile of coins in his palm. As an afterthought, Angelo added, "And we'd like a drink. White wine."

Angelo returned to the telephone to find a young woman dropping a coin into the slot. He leaned close and said, "Are you going to be long?"

As she turned to look at him, he could see that she was about twenty-five years old and the sort of young woman he hated most. She smirked at him. "Probably, but it's none of your business." She had light brown, almost blond hair, a big pair of glasses with red frames and lenses that glittered in the light of the little spot on the nearest philodendron. The enormity of the situation engulfed Angelo as the young woman took off her earring on the side where she was going to clamp the phone. She was actually going to prolong this just to piss him off. She had no idea of what the planet she lived on was really like. She was probably a clerk in the women's clothes section of a department store, or, with that arrogance, probably the senior clerk who decided which clothes to buy from the distributor. She was very much like that young woman two years ago who had come up behind him on the street on the day when the computerized timing device on that year's new Cadillac had malfunctioned. He had been coughing along on about four mistimed cylinders, spewing black smoke and going twenty miles an hour, just trying to make it to the nearest gas station. She had pulled up behind, leaned on the horn for a full minute, then passed him. As she went by, she turned, that same smirk on her face, held out her upturned fist and raised a carefully manicured middle finger at him.

Angelo had gone mad. He let the Cadillac glide to a stop by the side of the road, ran out into the street to flag down a cab and followed her. She went to the parking lot of a real-estate broker, got out and entered. He waited long enough to see her sit down at a desk and put her purse in a drawer. She was so overconfident that it never occurred to her to look behind to see what might be breathing down her neck. That night, when she walked out the door of the realtor's office to drive home in her bright red Ford Tempo, she had a surprise. The surprise was embodied in two men who had made the trip over the bridge from Fort Erie in Canada for no purpose other than to demonstrate to this young woman that the world was a much darker and more dangerous place than she or anyone she knew had ever imagined.

Angelo couldn't believe it. This night was the worst experience he'd had in five years, even before the girl. Now he was stuck in this fern bar with a man so crazy that he might change his mind about his persecutors at any moment and start screaming that they were from Jupiter instead of Langley, Virginia. But even that was nothing. Angelo had seen the Butcher's Boy. Everything else was a mere distraction in comparison. He had to get on that phone. He waited while the young woman dialed, then watched while she counted the rings. When there was no answer and she hung up, he felt as though a weight had been lifted from his chest, but when she snatched the quarter out of the coin tray and put it into the slot again, he started to have trouble breathing. It was at this moment that the woman's boyfriend appeared. He stepped up beside her, glanced at Angelo and said, "Everything okay?"

The young woman frowned and said, "Sally's not answering. Not that I could talk to her without any privacy."

The young man turned to Angelo and seemed to puff up like a male grouse. "Can I help you?"

Angelo's eyes burned with a heat that made him feel as though they were sweating into his head. His right forearm came forward and his hand went to the man's groin and clutched his testicles. The man's eyes bulged with something beyond surprise. What was happening was so unheard of that it couldn't be real. The pain told him it was, but it also told him not to attempt to do anything about it. To push this insane demon away from him meant that when the hand came away it would still be holding on to his testicles.

Angelo said, "I need to use the phone. Tell her."

The man said, "He needs to use the phone." His back was to his girlfriend, so she couldn't see anything except that the two men were face to face.

"I know he does," she said. "Tough."

Angelo gave a little squeeze. The man said in a very different voice, "Tracy, get off the fucking telephone. Now. He's got me by the balls."

"What?" said the young woman.

"I mean literally. It's not a figure of speech. If you don't, I'm going to kill you myself."

She slammed the phone onto its hook, stomped out into the dining room, grabbed her coat and was out the door before Angelo loosened his grip a little.

"I'm going to let you go," said Angelo, "but before I do, I want you to know that my name is Angelo Fratelli. You don't know that name, but you can probably find out who I am. You can tell your girlfriend that if I ever see her again—it doesn't matter where or how: on the street, in a store, *anywhere*—she's going to die."

He let the man go, and the man walked stiffly to the table,

pulled several bills from his wallet, left them on his empty plate and then continued out the door. Angelo put his quarter into the telephone and dialed the number of the Vesuvio.

12

Driving up Delaware Avenue, Wolf concentrated on the moves he had made in the past few days. He'd never bothered the bastards in ten years, but they had found him and sent three badly chosen messengers to kill him. He was still convinced he had done the only sensible thing. As fast as he could he had followed the trouble to its origin, Tony Talarese. Then he had taken the most direct route out of their way, trying to fly out of the country through Los Angeles, but they had managed to have a shooter in the airport waiting for him. They should have known he would go for the only man who could have sent a specialist, Peter Mantino. But he still had to get out of the country, which required that he go see the old man for a fresh passport. Then soldiers who could only belong to Angelo Fratelli had killed the old man. Of course he would go after Fratelli now. Why didn't they know that? Or had the ten years made each of them so fat and powerful and overconfident that they all thought he would just lie down and die?

Angelo sat across the table from McCarron, nodding and smiling. The table was the one that had been occupied by the young couple he had met at the telephone. While he was talking to Salvatore on the phone, the hostess had come up to McCarron and told him that a table had unexpectedly become available. Angelo was preoccupied, and his practiced jovial demeanor returned unannounced, like a facial tic. Now he knew the cause of his problem, and it was giving him a tight stomach. Some forger had thought he could pick up some extra money by mentioning to Angelo's stringers that he had a passport request that sounded a whole lot like somebody who wanted to get out of the country instead of into it. But Angelo's men had not risen to

the occasion. They could have had the forger tell the old black
man that the customer needed to come in person to get his picture taken. When he got there, if he was who they thought he
was, they could blow his head off; instead, they had killed the
fucking middleman. Angelo wasn't known as an eminent strat-
egist, but at least he knew that when a hornet flies into your
house you don't slam the door shut and consider the problem
solved.

"Sure, we can still do the deal," said Angelo. "If you want
to spend the money, I can handle things for you."

McCarron said, "Thanks. You don't know how much better
that makes me feel."

Angelo saw the door of the restaurant swing open and Salvatore walk in. Behind him, standing out on the sidewalk, Angelo could see two other men looking the other way at the passing
cars. The sheer bulk of Salvatore in his dark gray overcoat reassured Angelo because part of the bulk was the little Uzi submachine gun in a sling inside the coat. Angelo stood up. "Our
ride is here. I hope you weren't hungry."

"No," said McCarron. He stood up too and, like the young
man before him, set some money on the plate before he followed.

Wolf was getting tired. He knew that what he was doing wasn't
certain to work. But Fratelli had picked the man up here in
Delaware Park, and there was a small chance that he might come
back and drop him off on his way into hiding. Wolf had already
decided that there was no way he could hope to get into the
mansion Fratelli had built in the hills overlooking the Niagara
escarpment in Lewiston. Fifteen or twenty years ago there had
been stories about people who had tried, and now Fratelli knew
he was in danger. The only hope was to catch him in a place
like this, where dark and emptiness would help.

It was taking a long time. He had no choice except to wait,
but now he began to study the area for signs that someone else
was waiting too. He watched the cars going by on the distant
road around the park. They looked the way cars look from an
airplane, not unreal like toys, but separated from him so completely by the unfamiliar distance and lack of sound that they
were part of an alternative world. As long as none of them
stopped, he was safe. Then he saw the gray Toyota. As it pulled
up in front of a big brick house, a door opened.

He watched the car, but he couldn't see how many people

were in it. Nobody got out, but then it slowly pulled away. Something had happened that made no sense. The big dog was standing on the front lawn; then it stopped looking after the car and trotted happily around to the back of the house.

Wolf decided it was time to move. He wasn't sure why they had stopped to let the dog out, but he knew he had to ignore it. He had to keep his eye on the car. He moved out of the woods quickly, glancing to his right from time to time to be sure he was keeping the trunks of the tall trees behind him. He could see the little gray Toyota move along the road toward the zoo, past the basketball courts and then past Wolf's car. He stopped and watched it go. He could discern a couple of heads in the car, but it was too dark to see the faces.

When the Toyota stopped by the curb, he broke into a run for a spot from which he hoped he could get a clear view. But at this distance the trees seemed to leap into his field of vision, so he went on, finally slipping from the grove of trees to a big oil drum full of trash. As he dropped behind it, he heard a door open and ventured to peer around the can at the car.

Two big men got out of the car and moved around to the trunk. One of them was Fratelli, but he couldn't be sure the other was the man he had seen with him earlier. This man was wearing a bulky gray overcoat that Wolf hadn't seen before. Now Fratelli bent over and opened the trunk. Both men leaned in and seemed to be dragging at something inside. Then they both bent their knees and hauled something out.

Wolf moved closer. They were carrying the man who had been with Fratelli in the Toyota. His head lolled to the side at nearly a right angle to his shoulders, and swung a little as the two men staggered into the park carrying him. Wolf had seen too many corpses to have much doubt that this was another. What the hell was going on? He kept moving from tree to tree, closer and closer, as the two men carried the body into the park. He had never seen the man in the overcoat before, but there was no doubt about the other; he was Fratelli.

Angelo wheezed at each step as he backed into the park, his leather soles slipping a little on the wet leaves. McCarron's legs were heavy, but Angelo was feeling better now. All evening he had been waiting for a chance to get this asshole into a dark place. Every second with the man, his rage had grown and sharpened. Finally, when he had gotten him out of the restaurant, he had made Salvatore take them to the building on Allen

Street. Angelo owned the whole block of old brick buildings, and they were all fenced and boarded. He was remodeling them to accommodate restaurants and shops, but for now they were empty. He had told McCarron that this was the ultimate hiding place; but as soon as the man was in the door, he swung his right forearm around McCarron's neck and gripped his own wrist with his left hand. It had taken only a couple of seconds, so it didn't last quite as long as he had hoped, but he had felt the neck crack and the muscles tighten spasmodically, then go limp, so he supposed he had gotten as much out of it as possible. He had also been able to tell him a little bit about being a self-important crazy asshole who didn't do what he was told, hissing it into McCarron's ear as he broke his neck. Probably he hadn't heard all of it, but enough. Angelo had caught a glimpse of Salvatore's face while he was doing it, and it was a mask of dumb surprise and horror. It was kind of funny to remember it, and now he couldn't stifle a little laugh, but as his breath huffed out of him, he never got to draw it back in because at that moment there was the blast of a shotgun.

Salvatore had never seen anything like it. Mr. Fratelli's head just seemed to fly apart as though a bomb had gone off in his brain. When Salvatore started to run, his mind hadn't yet settled on exactly what he was running from. It didn't matter, because he managed only one step before the next blast found him.

Wolf trotted toward the woods, wiping off the shotgun with his handkerchief. He was systematic about it, moving from the barrel to the stock and back again, then taking another pass and ending up holding the shotgun with the handkerchief near the muzzle. He dropped the shotgun in some bushes, then turned to run through the woods toward his car. He had owed the old man a debt he couldn't pay off with money, but now it was over. They could never be even, but he had done all that had been left to do, and now he had to get out.

He was still feeling dazed from the loud roar of the shotgun and the tremendous kick it had delivered; he hadn't fired anything like it in years. The shots he had taken outside the old man's house had somehow been muted by anger and outrage, so he had not been prepared for the way the shotgun had torn up the cool, quiet air of the park.

As he moved through the woods, he thought he heard something. It was a faint, steady rustling like the sound of a wind blowing through the wet leaves on the ground, but he could feel no breeze on his face. He stopped, stood beside a tree trunk and waited for the sound to resolve itself into something he could identify. He stared through the trees in the direction of the sound. Beyond them he could see the silvery gleam of the tiny lake, the white front of the museum on the other side and then a car's headlights on the distant road. It was moving along at about thirty, and as it made a turn its headlights swept across the little woods. Then he saw the men. There were three of them about twenty feet apart, shuffling along slowly through the trees. The car turned again and the light disappeared just as the one in the middle fired. The bullet thumped into the tree above his head, and stung his cheek with a spatter of bark and dirt.

He knew that ducking or diving to the ground wouldn't save him. He had to run, and hope that the trees and the darkness, distance and difficulty they would have in planting their feet for a steady shot would give him a chance. Of course a man like Angelo Fratelli wouldn't be out here in the dark with one man and a corpse. It was ridiculous.

He considered going back to look in the bushes for the shotgun, but he knew he would never make it. The gun was hidden badly enough so that the police would have no difficulty finding it in the morning, but they wouldn't have people shooting at them, and this wasn't morning. He concentrated on his immediate problem, which was that in a moment he was going to run out of trees. He would have to dash across what looked like a picnic area under a few stately old maples, and when he did it he was going to be a hard target to miss.

He kept running. He could tell from the sounds that he was putting some ground between himself and two of his pursuers, but the one directly behind him was having an easier time of it because he could run exactly where his quarry did without stepping into a hole or crashing into a tree trunk. Wolf broke into a sprint to give the man a chance to get ahead of the others. At the edge of the grove he saw something that gave him hope. To his right was the old brick wall of the zoo, covered with ivy and skirted by uncut brush. The top of the wall was protected by old-fashioned foot-long steel claws that curved inward, looking as though they had been put there to keep a lion from jumping out, but probably designed to keep morons from climbing in.

Wolf stopped, made a quick pivot to the right and reached into his pocket. The only heavy objects he had were the extra shotgun shells. He listened for the approach of the pursuer, then threw four of the shells as high into the air as he could. Their trajectory carried them up and over the wall before they began to fall. They came down to the right of the first man, and on the other side of the wall.

Wolf waited behind a tree for the sound of the shells hitting. When it came, he was pleased. The first one hit with a heavy thump on a surface that sounded like concrete. Then the others came down in a group, and there was a dull, grating noise as they rolled down some kind of incline. It was as though he had set off a weird perpetual-motion machine.

When the first man appeared, Wolf could see he had heard the sounds. He was small and wiry, and from his silhouette and speed, Wolf judged that he was young. The man stuck his pistol into his coat pocket, jumped up and grabbed the curving bars at the top of the wall. But just as he pulled himself up to peer over the wall, something big on the other side made a decision. The something big was a male polar bear named Caesar. He had been born in the zoo, so he had no idea that the reason he was half crazy was that polar bears hadn't evolved to occupy small concrete pens with tepid swimming pools painted aquamarine. First there had been the two loud blasts, then a smaller one. When the pieces of metal and plastic had fallen from the sky into his enclosure, he had stopped cowering in the dank concrete pillbox he used for a den and come out looking for something to maul. When he reached the edge of his pool, he saw that the intruder was only a bunch of cylindrical shiny objects rolling off his patio into the deep moat that kept him at home.

When Caesar saw the ridiculous sight of a man hoisting himself up on the bars above the wall, it made him angry. He stood up on his hind legs, spread his forelegs and, with a tottering, staggering gait, trotted quickly toward him, baring his fangs and uttering a loud, deep, groaning noise from somewhere inside him. The sound was part joy at finding something close enough to take a swipe at with his powerful forepaws, part anger because he knew that usually when he did this they raised a little black one-eyed box and flashed something bright in his eyes and part frustration because even if he killed it, he would probably never get to eat it. Caesar was just going through the motions; still, as his huge form waddled forward out of the darkness, it was nearly nine feet tall, glowing white in the moonlight, and appeared to be composed mainly of claws and teeth.

The man on the wall bared his teeth too, but it was only because he needed to open his mouth wide to let out a scream.

Instead of simply letting go of the curved steel rods, his arms
gave a reflexive push to get him as far away as possible from the
charging apparition, and his legs pushed off the wall too. He
took the weight of the fall on his shoulder blades and lay there
for a second with the wind knocked out of him, unable to move.
He had forgotten about Wolf for the moment, but when he remembered and drew the conclusion that lying on his back across
the protruding roots of a maple tree was a good way to commit
suicide, Wolf was already looming at the edge of his vision. The
kick in the head didn't kill him, but it brought the same sudden
explosion of pain and an approximation of the same darkness to
shut down his brain.

Wolf reached into the man's coat pocket and extracted the
pistol, then stepped back behind the tree to scan the woods for
the next pursuer as the bear let out an anguished cry of disappointment behind his protective wall. Wolf had no idea what
kind of animal made that kind of noise, but it had to be huge
and it wasn't happy. The sound brought the other two men closer.
He could see them slipping from tree to tree, waving and nodding at each other in turn to provide cover for each movement.

Wolf waited for a clear view to present itself. He ran his hand
over the fallen man's revolver to identify it, but could tell only
that it was probably a .38. He tried to remember how many
shots its owner had taken at him, but he wasn't sure. Then the
man on the ground began to come to life. First there was a gasp,
then a groan, just his body making a sound to celebrate having
some air it could take in and let out again. Then the man's brain
began to struggle to reassert itself. He said loudly, "Oooooh,"
then, "Oh, boy." Wolf glanced at the man. There still was no
movement, but he wouldn't shut up because he still hadn't re-
gained enough of his consciousness to remember where he was.
"Oh, damn," the man muttered.

Lurking in disappointment behind his brick wall, Caesar the
bear heard the voice. When the sound of his fallen enemy groaning helplessly reached his keen ears, he began to salivate and
stagger toward the wall again. He couldn't get over the inward-
curving steel rods, so he placed his paws on top of the wall and
bounced up and down on his hind legs, trying to see. When this
didn't work, he let out a cry of rage. This noise set off a reaction
deep in the half-conscious man's brain. A tiny pulse of electro-
chemical energy crackled across a recently altered synapse and
indicated to the brain that it was now or never. Wolf saw the
man's head jerk up off the ground and keep rising. As though

the motion of his head had begun an involuntary reflex, the rest of his body moved after it. When the impulse reached the man's legs, he stood up so fast that his feet actually left the ground, and when they came down again he was already running. He sprinted back the way he had come, into the trees where his partners were hiding.

Wolf listened, hoping for a pistol shot, but instead he heard the sound of a struggle. One of the runner's companions had the presence of mind to grab him, but the frightened man wasn't ready to be grabbed. "It's me," said someone in an urgent, hushed voice. "Hey, it's only me."

Wolf judged that his moment had come. He pushed off the tree with his foot as though it were a starting block, and then he was out in the open park, running hard. But immediately he heard other footsteps and realized that the two remaining pursuers had not been as distracted by their partner's plight as he had hoped. He knew that he probably wasn't going to make it across the open-grass picnic area in time. He was going to die. It made him angry. He felt a wave of contempt building in his chest. Who the hell were these three anyway—the Greater Buffalo Pistol Team? They were three losers who spent their lives walking stiff-legged into little bars and scaring the shit out of people with their bent noses and scars. Probably none of them had ever fired a gun at anybody before, and if he did he pushed it down the guy's throat and pulled the trigger. Only two of them even had guns now, but if they could hit anything, it would be the back of a running man.

Wolf didn't stop running. He just let his feet outrun his torso, and went into a kind of baseball slide. When his side hit the ground, he rolled over onto his belly and aimed the pistol at the path out of the grove he had just left.

The first man out of the grove didn't see Wolf at once. He took three steps onto the grass, then stopped, lifted his weapon and stared at Wolf's prone form as though he were trying to decide whether it was a man or not. Wolf fired twice, and he could tell within a second that both shots had caught the man in the chest. The man went to his knees, then toppled over and gave a loud grunt and then Wolf was up again and running. Over the sound of his own breathing, he heard the second man say, idiotically, "Are you all right?"

Wolf kept running. He probably had one round left in the cylinder of the revolver, but he knew that his best chance lay in what the one remaining man was thinking; by now he would

have noticed that for all practical purposes he was alone. He
would also be aware that he had an acceptable excuse for not
continuing to chase an armed man into a series of dark places;
he had a colleague who was seriously wounded, and was lying
there bleeding to death. There was only one thing left that the
man needed to do before he officially gave up the pursuit.

Wolf made it to the first tree on the other side of the open
space and ducked down while the survivor fulfilled that need,
firing his weapon six or seven times into the darkness in Wolf's
general direction. Now he could show the underboss who was
in charge of punishing the weak that he had been in the battle
with the rest of the soldiers.

Gripping the telephone receiver, Richardson tried to calculate
how much of his life was spent pressing one of these damned
things against his ear. "What the hell is Jack Hamp doing?" he
asked.

"Jack is still in Santa Fe," said Elizabeth. "He's trying to
find out how our friend is getting around. Santa Fe is a small
place, so he has a hope of getting a credit-card number, a rental-
car license or the Butcher's Boy's latest alias. He's also at least
eight hours from Buffalo, because he'll have to change planes
at least once."

"What are you going to do with the kids?"

"Please don't make this harder. I'm paying Maria a sum I
can't afford to stay all night, and probably let them watch old
horror movies in Spanish and teach them to love potato chips.
But I can't pull Jack away from the only place this man has been
where he might not have been hidden in the crowd because there
is no crowd. I've got to go myself, and my plane is getting ready
to leave."

Richardson shrugged and stared at the telephone. She hadn't
changed much in ten years; this was how it had started the last
time.

Lieutenant Delamo of the Buffalo Police Department stood beside his plain-wrap Dodge and watched the long line of uniforms
make their sweep of the park. He could see their flashlights
moving back and forth on the grass in little circles. This was the
sort of case that had lots of cracks and potholes to fall into.
There were three bodies in a row in the middle of the park, and
they hadn't even died in the same way. One of them looked like
he had been hanged, and the other two were shot with some-

thing, most likely double-ought buckshot at close range, judging from the mess it had made of them. One of them had about two thirds of a head left, and that was the one that occupied Delamo's thoughts now. It had been a disgusting sight, and he could close his eyes and still see it. That was the test for him; it meant that at some point, maybe not tonight, but soon, it would come back to him in his dreams. It wouldn't be accompanied by the sympathy and sadness that he usually felt when he had to look at human bodies that had run into something made of metal. This time he felt something different, and he would probably pay the price for it in guilt. The partial head that remained was perfectly recognizable as the property of Angelo Fratelli.

There had been several times in his career when Delamo had caught himself wishing that somebody would blow Angelo Fratelli's head off, but he had always pushed the thought aside into a compartment of his mind that he never visited. Now somebody had done it, and Delamo had learned enough to realize that it wasn't time to celebrate. It had already occurred to him that this midnight outing in Delaware Park might be only the first of many trips to look at bodies in the more deserted parts of Erie County. There had been no warning of any kind from any of the agencies that kept an eye on these people, which didn't surprise him; it simply showed that things hadn't changed as much as a lot of people had thought.

Delamo didn't pride himself on his knowledge or expertise. The only claim he made for himself was that he was not a fool. In keeping with this modesty, he had not ignored the old-timers who had been around the last time this had happened, in the fifties. If he listened carefully, the frustration and anger were still evident in their voices. In those days, police intelligence on organized crime had been so sparse and unreliable that they'd had no idea of who was at war with whom, or for what stakes. All they had known at first was that kids started to find mutilated bodies lying in empty lots.

It had gone on for years, and the cops had been able to do little beyond carting away the corpses and writing down their names. Eventually it had turned out to have no local cause at all, having been started by a bungled murder attempt at a restaurant in New York City, and it had ended at a small meeting a year or so after the famous interrupted conference about two hundred miles from here in Apalachin. But nobody had even known that much until the late sixties, ten years afterward.

"Lieutenant," said a voice behind him. Delamo turned and saw a young patrolman named McElroy coming toward him with a woman. He had sent McElroy around the neighborhood to knock on doors and ask the neighbors the usual "Was it two shots or ten shots?" questions, but he had done so principally to give the kid a chance to pick up his second wind. McElroy had been held over for this mess after working a twelve-hour shift which had, according to his sergeant, included a twenty-minute wrestling match with a particularly nasty pair of drunks, followed by a gruesome car accident on the Father Baker Bridge in which a family of four had been roasted in their station wagon, and he was beginning to get that peculiar look where he was forgetting to blink his eyes regularly.

"Lieutenant? There's someone here," said McElroy. "This is Miss Elizabeth Waring of the Justice Department."

"Thank you, McElroy," Delamo said. He looked at the woman. She was very young, he decided, then changed his mind and revised his estimate to the middle thirties. "We haven't met, have we?"

The question took Elizabeth by surprise. Then she realized he must be assuming she had come from the Buffalo office. "No," she said. "I don't think so. I just flew in from Washington."

Now Delamo was surprised. "How did you get here? How did you know?"

"I was expecting something like this, so I was waiting for the right sort of report to come over the wire." She couldn't wait any longer. She tried to keep the eagerness out of her voice, but she had to know. "Have you confirmed that it's Angelo Fratelli?"

"I don't have to confirm it. I've seen him before."

She could hear the annoyance in his voice, but she couldn't allow herself to think about him yet. "Then it's the third."

"The third?" Delamo asked. His face was flattening into an exaggerated expression of incredulity, so there could be no question that she would interpret it correctly.

Of course, she thought. How could he know? "A week ago a man named Antonio Talarese was killed in New York. He was an underboss watching things there for Carlo Balacontano while he's in jail in California. Two nights later, Peter Mantino was killed in Santa Fe. He was the family's western regional boss. I haven't had time to find out what he was doing in Santa Fe. And now Fratelli.''

"Miss uh—Waring. I'm a simple honest-to-God policeman. I've got to confess that I don't know what the hell you're talking about. I assume you do. I know who Carl Bala was—or is—but that's about it. If you people knew that there was a war on, why the hell didn't you say something?''

It was starting to feel to Elizabeth like one of those moments when cops made suspects admit things they hadn't known they were accused of. "I still don't know anything about a war. I think this is somebody we heard about from an informant ten years ago, and I think he's alone. He's a killer for hire that people call the Butcher's Boy—no real name, no record, not even a description. One of the witnesses says that's who killed Tony Talarese in New York. We know he was somewhere in the West when Mantino was killed.''

"So who hired him?''

"I don't know if anybody hired him, and I don't know what it's about. The others were from the Balacontano family, and Fratelli wasn't.''

"So what am I supposed to expect—a couple of hundred new faces from Chicago or New York moving in and carving up Fratelli's estate?''

"I don't know. I don't think that's what it's about.''

Delamo took a deep breath, let it out slowly and then said it anyway. "You people don't have a whole lot of useful information, do you?''

Elizabeth wondered if he would have said that to Jack Hamp. It wasn't that another man would have punched him, but there was something about her being a woman that made it easier for them to behave like this. If she answered the same way, she would be a bitch. She explained patiently, "There are too many things happening at once. Some of them are contradictory, others are meaningless and some are probably fake. In any case these people don't always make long-term plans and stick to them. When they feel threatened, they lash out at somebody, and when they see an opportunity, they take it.''

Delamo sighed. "Come on. You might as well see what we've got.''

He walked her over to the grove of trees and stopped where the yellow police tape was stretched from tree to tree. He pointed to the three body bags. "This one is Fratelli. Shotgun

blast to the head, took off the top of the skull. Ditto this one.
He was a bodyguard named Salvatore Gamuchio, age thirty-
eight, twenty years of rap sheets for strong-arm robbery, ex-
tortion, assault, et cetera. He was carrying a submachine gun
in his coat and a pistol in an ankle holster, neither one fired.
This one over here is a puzzle. He seems to have a broken
neck. The coroner will have to tell us how that happened. No
identification. One of the guys said he looks familiar, but so
far we can't place him.''

"All this happened here? In the park?''

"Yeah. Lots of calls from people living around here—loud
gunshots, yelling, the whole bit. Units in the area responded,
but this is a big park, and by the time they could sweep it with
lights nobody was standing up anymore, so the patrolmen didn't
find them until they walked the area on foot.''

"Have you figured out . . . how?''

"I think some people over there in the trees shot them with
shotguns. With the exception of this one. How he died I can't
imagine.''

Another voice came out of the darkness behind them. "Lieutenant . . .''

He turned toward it in a leisurely way. "Yeah?''

"We found a shotgun over there in the bushes.''

"Anything interesting about it?''

"No, sir. Twelve-gauge Remington pump. Not sawed-off or
anything.''

"I know I don't need to say this, but be careful with it. I'd
sure like to get a print off it.'' As the patrolman walked away,
Delamo turned to Elizabeth. "I guess that eliminates looking
for a man with a shotgun.''

"Lieutenant?''

As Delamo turned in the other direction, Elizabeth had a
sense of what a Homicide lieutenant's life must be like.
They would bring him items one after another, and he would
evaluate them and sort of put them into his pockets.
"Yeah?''

"They just called in with the IDs on the other ones.''

"And?''

"The two on Grant Street were Fratelli's too. The house was
owned by the old man they found in the river.''

"Thanks,'' Delamo said, then turned to Elizabeth. "I think
your theory's starting to look a little weak.''

"Why?''

"Well, there's an old black man we found in the river about suppertime with a thirty-eight bullet in his head. It seems that two other guys got killed in his house. With one or more shotguns. Then you got Fratelli and Salvatore Gamuchio, and this other guy who got his neck broken. All in the space of about three or four hours. It's a lot of work."

"Lieutenant," came another voice. "We got some more blood way over there."

"Get a bunch of it on slides," Delamo said, "and then look for some more bodies. I think we're going to have to drag the damned lake as soon as the sun comes up."

"I think there may be some way to drain it," said the voice.

"Find out. Call the Parks Department."

"Right."

Delamo turned back to Elizabeth. "I guess that once again the 'lone gunman' theory doesn't hold up."

"How can you be sure?"

"Because I don't care who this no-name-no-description guy is. It's pretty unlikely that he came in all by himself and wasted six-plus men in at least three locations in three different ways in one night. And if he came here because he hated Angelo Fratelli, he would have killed Angelo Fratelli. He wouldn't have killed three men who worked for Fratelli first. Do you disagree with that?"

"I'd have to know what he was thinking to answer that." Oh, God, she thought. I'm only a few hours behind him, and this man is sending the police to look for a gang while he wastes time convincing me.

"How do you think one man could do all that?"

"I'm not sure how," said Elizabeth, "but I know that ten years ago a man in Las Vegas who had never laid eyes on him came to me for protection because he was afraid to go to sleep. I couldn't blame him, because that morning we'd found nine bodies around town. The man who killed them is the one I'm looking for now."

It wasn't long after Ms. Waring left that McElroy appeared at Delamo's elbow again. "We just got a radio call from downtown, Lieutenant. They said another fed will be here in a few minutes. We're supposed to extend him every courtesy."

Delamo turned to look at him. "What the hell is that about? Why wouldn't we?"

"I'm just repeating what they said. The guy wants to examine the body. Fingerprints, pictures, the whole thing."

"Didn't you tell them we already did that? We've got a positive ID. It's Fratelli."

"Not that body. The other one—the one with the broken neck."

13

Eddie Mastrewski had shown him what to do in a variety of situations that arose in their business. He remembered Eddie waking him up in the middle of the night in a hotel in Milwaukee. At first the boy had been terrified because he thought the only reason to get up in the dark was that the police had somehow found out about the man Eddie had killed by the lake. His name had been "Good Eye" Fraser. Eddie had told him it was because Fraser had lost an eye in a fight years before, and it had been replaced by a very expensive and well-crafted glass sphere. That was the good eye. The other was small, red and piercing, and Fraser moved his head like an enraged turkey to bring it to bear on his enemies, a group that seemed to include everyone it looked at. The boy had assumed the police were now moving up the two stairways quietly because only a few hours before the satisfied customers had paid Eddie in a room behind an old pool hall a mile from there. They had scarcely been able to contain their joy at Good Eye's demise. There could be no question of Good Eye's friends seeking vengeance, because his friends had been the customers. They had literally stopped a game of rotation on the back pool table and passed a hat around to collect the money.

The boy had leaped out of the bed, snatched his revolver out of the drawer of the nightstand and groped for his pants. At this point he had seen Eddie's grin. "Don't get excited. Everything's fine," he had said. "It's just time to go home." The boy had been puzzled, but Eddie was busy packing his suitcase. "We did the job and we got paid for it, but if we're still around after a day, those guys in the pool hall are going to start wondering why. We're dangerous now. The police might find us, and that's bad enough, but we also showed them we could take out a man they were afraid of, and that's even worse. They might get scared that we'll take over and bully them the way Good Eye did, and then they'd be even worse off. Or they might get to feeling ashamed that they had to hire us, and that we did it so easy. They'll think, If it was that easy, we should have done it ourselves, so we wasted our money. No matter what they think, it's bad for us, so we won't give them time to think. Anyway, it's part of the contract. If you hang around after a job and get the customers into an uproar, you're denying them the peace of mind they paid for, and you deserve to die. It's only fair.''

"Fair?" The boy was still groggy from sleep, and Eddie's reasoning was hard to follow even in broad daylight. "To kill us for that?''

"Sure," Eddie had answered. "In this life you always get a little bit worse than you deserve, so you have to take that into account.''

He had been a child then, and some of it was vague in his memory, but as he thought about it now, the rest of it began to come to him. It had been easy, as Eddie had said, and he realized that Eddie had probably just approached Fraser from his glass-eye side. But the part that seemed different now was the payoff in the pool hall. It hadn't taken place in the back room, really. That was where they had made him wait while Eddie had accepted the money. His memory of it was the loud laughter and hooting coming from the men around the pool table in the front. For the first time, he remembered it as though he had seen it. Eddie sends the boy into the back room and closes the door, then walks up to the pool table and reaches into his pocket. When his hand comes out, the glass eye rolls the length of the table, looking as though it's winking at the men gathered there. What other proof would they have asked for?

He knew what Eddie would have said about his situation at this moment: it was his own fault, so he deserved it. It was the result of what Eddie would have called a lapse of professionalism, and he would have said that it had started with The Honourable Meg. Eddie had been the ultimate pragmatist, with little time for sentiment. He had never married because it would have been foolish to imagine he could keep his second profession a secret from anyone who lived with him. He had had a series of liaisons with married women in the neighborhood whom he referred to as his "home-delivery customers." He would go to their houses on slow afternoons, bringing some lamb chops or a roast for their husbands' dinners, then return in a couple of hours and go back to work behind the counter. He would not have approved of The Honourable Meg.

But as Wolf searched through his memories of Eddie, he could recall nothing that would help him out of this mess. Eddie had never worked in the league where the customers were more dangerous than the jobs; he had known his limits.

Wolf realized that everything he did now would take on huge proportions in the future. There could be no more mistakes. It was time to lose the rented car. If he turned it in, he faced the risk that somebody would have had it traced through the credit card.

Just outside Cleveland, in the fringes where car lots, carpet stores and furniture warehouses marked the farthest reaches of the city, he found a huge new apartment complex. He parked the car on the street in front of it, then walked two miles down the road to a big motel and called a taxi to take him to the airport. Eventually, the people in the complex would realize that the car did not belong to somebody visiting their neighbors, or the cops would notice that it hadn't been moved and would tow it. But that process would probably take a week. If he wasn't out of the country by then, he would probably be dead. It was time to go see Little Norman.

Little Norman was the longest-running lounge act in Las Vegas. Each day at four o'clock in the afternoon for eighteen years, he would eat his breakfast in the back bar at the Sands, then place a two hundred percent tip on the table, stand up to his full six feet six and stroll out in a pair of cowboy boots that added two inches to his height. Today's boots were hand-sewn iguana with carved silver toe caps and little silver imitation spurs at the heels, selected because the iguana hide went well with the Armani suit he was wearing.

As Little Norman stepped out of the bar and across the casino toward the door, the throngs of gamblers looked only at the clicking, buzzing, jingling displays on slot machines, or the brightly colored playthings on green felt tables. The only people who really watched Little Norman were some men on the walkways above the mirrors in the ceiling because they were paid to see everything, and a couple of women in the cashier's window because they were bored. Their eyes settled on him for only a second and moved on. Little Norman was a regular, part of the garish sameness that they looked at every day.

There are places in the world where a man nearly seven feet

tall, blacker than the king of the Zulus and weighing two hundred eighty pounds might well cause eyes to linger, but Las Vegas isn't one of them. Little Norman was a familiar sight, and he never caused any trouble. If he had, it would have been very quiet and ended very quickly, because there were not many people who could have offered more than negligible resistance.

Little Norman had discovered Las Vegas in 1958, when he arrived there as the bodyguard of a boxer named Walt "The Animal" Homer. A convincing bodyguard for a celebrity who made his living beating other celebrities senseless had to be big, ugly and mean. Anyone could see that Little Norman was big and ugly enough, and the rest of his credentials came to the Las Vegas Police Department by way of his parole officer in Kansas City. Walt Homer turned out to be a bad ticket. He had his nose moved half an inch to the right in a match in Florida later that year, and the promoters decided not to invest any more in his doubtful future, so it was left in doubt no longer.

But in those days Little Norman was a warm, comforting presence for people in certain professions to have around. He met some friends of the promoters, made himself agreeable, did some favors and eventually built a place for himself in the world. By the time he returned to Las Vegas fifteen years later, it was in the position of responsibility and trust he now held.

After breakfast Little Norman always promenaded along the Strip, stopping in each of the casino lounges he passed. He would spend a few minutes in each bar, conferring with various consultants he kept on retainer—waitresses and dealers who worked in the casinos, chambermaids who worked above them and people who simply made it their business to be there because Little Norman had told them to. Whenever he had heard enough, he would reach into the pocket of the tailored suit, pull out a wad of twenty-dollar bills and strip off one note or several, depending upon the freshness and weight of what he had been told.

What Little Norman was doing was checking the weather in Las Vegas. For a number of years now—ten, to be precise—the weather had been fine. The money he paid for the recitations he heard each day came to him indirectly from fourteen old men, none of whom lived within five hundred miles of the city, who had gotten into the habit of depending on Little Norman. His job was to ensure that nothing ever happened to disturb the tranquility that had prevailed with few interruptions since their predecessors had formally agreed to it forty years ago.

Today, as Little Norman sampled the weather, he stared particularly intently at his observers and listened for mistakes. It wasn't that any of them would be so foolish as to tell him a lie, but after so many days of clear weather, they might have missed something. As usual, he asked them who had checked in that they recognized, and who had played with a lot more money than his clothes indicated he should have. But today he also asked if there was a man of average height and build, with sand-brown hair, who seemed to be looking for someone. He would have sat watching at a remote table in the bar, or passed through the casino slowly, never gambling or talking to anybody. None of Little Norman's people had seen such a man, so by the time he had finished his rounds at eight, he was satisfied that the weather was still fine.

At nine P.M. Little Norman's long strides took him into Caesars Palace, where he had a light lunch with a girl named Yolanda. She claimed to be nineteen but provided him with evidence that was ambiguous. When he went to the men's room, she tried to steal some of the money he had left under the check for the waiter. This meant that she was old enough to be squeezing each opportunity to put something away for the future, so she might have seen a sag or a wrinkle already, which argued twenty-five. But doing this also meant that she was young enough not to realize how bad that sort of behavior was for her future, because until the waiter picked it up, that money still belonged to Little Norman. He explained the distinction to her patiently, with a reassuring smile on his face, and she listened with the alertness of a rabbit. For her benefit he added that Las Vegas was going to be a cold, hard place for her if she didn't value the goodwill of people like waiters and doormen. She demonstrated her native intelligence by openly taking the money out of her sleeve and putting it back on the table—not on the check, but under her own plate. Little Norman liked her for that.

By eleven P.M. Little Norman was making his second circuit of the casinos. He couldn't be everywhere, but he could seem to be. He made eye contact with everybody he saw whom he knew, so that if they had seen anything he might like to hear, they wouldn't need to wonder where to find him.

Little Norman returned to his car in the lot at the Sands at six in the morning. It was a bright red Corvette with an engine that could do a hundred fifty if he had been reckless enough to try it. He had bought the first one he could afford in 1960, and kept trading them in ever since, always bright red, because that was the color of the first one he had seen in Kansas City; it was the color Corvettes *were*. He always had experienced a comfort in having more car than anybody he was likely to have to chase down.

Little Norman had lived in some of the big hotels downtown when he had first come to preserve the good weather. The fact that he could afford this luxury had appealed to him then. Now he lived in a three-bedroom house on the edge of town near an entrance to the Interstate. The fourteen old men were deeply conservative in their souls, and they didn't trust a man who lived as though he didn't intend to stay.

The traffic was sparse, and Little Norman drove home with only a couple of almost-stops at corners where he had mistimed the lights. He unlocked the door of his house and entered, punched the buttons on the panel in the wall to let his security system know who he was. Then he locked the door and walked into his bedroom.

Outside the window at the back of the living room that looked out on the empty swimming pool and the cactus plants, Wolf ducked into the darkness. "One-five-two-four: fifteen twenty-four." He waited, then moved to the bedroom window, stooping to look through the crack in the blinds at Little Norman's bedtime ritual. The big man carefully took off his clothes and boots and put them in the closet, then opened the drawer on the nightstand, pulled out a .45 ACP pistol that Wolf judged was a Beretta and slipped it under the pillow beside him. He disappeared into the bathroom for a few minutes, then returned, climbed into bed and turned off the light with a remote control on the nightstand.

Wolf waited for a half hour, lying on the still-warm weeds beside the house, then stood up and began the walk to his motel. It was a couple of miles away, and he was tired.

The next day, Little Norman was pleased to learn that the weather in Las Vegas was still fine. He made his rounds wearing boots of crocodile and ostrich hide, and celebrated with an evening meeting with Yolanda in a room he had rented for her at the Frontier. It was after five A.M. when he compressed himself into his Corvette and drove back to his house. It wasn't until he reached his bedroom that he learned the weather had changed. "Hello, Norman." He didn't have to turn his head to know who it was, but he did it anyway. He wasn't going to go into the darkness without being man enough to look.

"Hello, kid."

"You're not surprised to see me."

"I'm surprised you let me see you." Little Norman stared at him. He looked almost the same. He wasn't that much older—no big gut, no less hair, maybe a few wrinkles. Little Norman's mind was full of irrelevant impressions now, each setting off thoughts that would have been distractions if it had mattered what he thought. The Butcher's Boy would kill him, and they both knew that he wasn't going to stand around and wait for it to happen. He would make an attempt to get to a weapon because he was Little Norman. But he wouldn't make it in time because the man sitting in his chair holding a .45 on him was who he was. Little Norman also knew that the gun wouldn't jam or misfire because it was the one he kept under his pillow.

The Butcher's Boy had fooled the alarm system and sat here in the dark waiting for him. This didn't surprise him either. Alarm systems weren't for people like them; they were to keep out some junkie who needed your stereo. He let his eyes dart to the nightstand for the remote control, but it wasn't there. He could have turned out the lights and taken his chances in the dark, but of course this man knew that. So it had to be the lamp itself, quick and low and hard.

"I'd like to talk to you for a minute," said the Butcher's Boy.

"About ten years ago? I know why you're here. I'd be here too."

"Okay, let's start with ten years ago."

"I didn't think I was setting you up. I thought they really were going to pay you. If I'd known they were going to take you out on the Strip and kill you . . ." He stopped and shrugged. "You know me."

The Butcher's Boy nodded. "You would have made sure they didn't fuck it up."

"I was the best. Maybe not ten years ago, but before that."

"You were the best once. Not a lot of people can say that, especially the ones who were."

Little Norman nodded. "I might have been able to talk them out of it, too. I always liked you. You were the only one in the trade that seemed to really be alive. Besides me." Little Norman kept the lamp in his peripheral vision. He was too far away to grab it; he would have to bat it at the Boy. "I'm curious, kid. I know you're not going to tell me where you've been."

"No."

"But tell me this: did you have any fun?"

This seemed to take the Boy by surprise. "Fun?"

"Yeah. I mean, was it worth it? Ten years is a hell of a lot of time to be hiding in a hole somewhere. Did you put together any kind of a life while you were gone?"

"I liked it. It was a hell of a lot better than I thought it would be. I'd have stayed forever. It doesn't make me any happier to be here, but at least I didn't waste the time I had."

"I'm glad. At least old Eddie taught you something that did you some good. Don't tell me when you're going to do it. Just make it in the head."

"I'm not here for that. I'm not taking you this time, unless you can't stand good luck and go for the lamp or something. I want you to talk to the old men."

There was no question of who the old men were. "What for? What do you want to say to them?"

"Remind them of what happened ten years ago. I behaved like a professional. I did the job, I came here to get paid and the customer tried to chew me up."

"They don't give a shit about any of that. They didn't then. They cared because of what you did after that. You buried a lot of people. It took them years to clean everything up."

"I want them to remember that too. You understand what I'm saying."

"You want to scare the old men? Has it been that long? You don't remember who they are?"

"If they kill me, they get nothing. If they leave me alone, they can forget about me. I'm not working anymore."

"You did Talarese and Mantino and Fratelli. Three medium-big fish in one week."

"Talarese is the one who found me. Mantino had a specialist waiting for me when I tried to get out on a plane. Fratelli had people looking for me. I guess he was doing Balacontano a favor."

"That ain't the story they're telling."

Little Norman could tell that this wasn't what the Butcher's Boy had expected to hear. "What are they saying?"

"Talarese was wearing a police wire when you got him."

"Talarese? Bullshit."

"You wanted to know what they're saying. That's it. A lot of people think somebody who had problems with what was on the recording hired you to get all three of them. Some people think you just went crazy from hiding: you figured it wasn't enough to put Carl Bala in jail. You had to cut down the ones he left in charge, so his family would fall apart.''

"I did them because it was the only way they left me to stay alive.''

Little Norman watched him for a reaction. "Then you made a mistake. If Talarese was wired, Mantino would be on the recordings. He'd be glad Talarese was dead.''

"I didn't imagine that guy at the airport. When I left the cops were moving in on him.''

"Did you know his face?''

"No. A tall guy with blond hair and a mustache.''

"Did you ever let anybody take your picture?''

"No.''

"Couldn't Mantino have found somebody who saw you in the old days? Think about it. You sure he wasn't one of the cops?''

Wolf didn't have to think. "Who did the wire belong to?''

"I won't know unless they arrest somebody. Maybe they won't. Maybe you killed everybody worth jail space.''

"I'm leaving now,'' said the Butcher's Boy. He stood up, the gun still trained on Little Norman. "Tell the old men what I said. Make sure they know what they're doing if they decide to come after me.''

"You think Carl Bala's going to leave you alone?''

"Carl Bala can't do anything unless they let him.''

"What about the police?''

"I'm worried about the old men.''

"How do I give you their answer?''

Wolf shook his head. "This is the last conversation anybody's going to have with me. If somebody is looking for me, watching me or waiting for me, I'll know where they came from.''

"All you're offering is that if they leave you alone, you'll leave them alone?''

The Butcher's Boy gave a little shrug. "It's not a bad deal.'' He stepped backward out the door and closed it behind him. Little Norman strained to hear his footsteps, then listened for the squeaking hinge on the front door, then waited for the rattle of a car's starter. He heard none of them.

"No,'' he said aloud. "Not a bad deal at all.''

Elizabeth cradled the baby in her arms. Amanda was asleep, but every time Elizabeth tried to ease the bottle out of her mouth, she would suck on it a few times to reassure herself that it was still there. Elizabeth stared across the baby's room at the wall.

It had occurred to her a few seconds ago that if she were the Butcher's Boy, right about now she would be on her way to Boston to get Giovanni Bautista. It would have to be done right, though, a virtuoso performance, because Bautista would be expecting him. He was the last of Balacontano's old stalwarts, and if the Butcher's Boy killed him now it would accomplish two things: it would cut off, at least for the moment, Carl Bala's most potent remaining means of finding him; and it would scare the hell out of everybody outside the family who might consider hunting him. This was the part that nobody else had ever understood about the Butcher's Boy ten years ago: in order to survive, he'd had to remind people of their mortality. That would be what was on his mind now—surviving by convincing people that if they didn't leave him alone he would kill them. What else did he have?

Now she slipped the bottle out of Amanda's lips, jammed it upright beside her in the padding of the chair, then carefully eased her weight forward and straightened her legs to stand. So far, so good; Amanda was still limp and sleeping, a little gurgle in the back of her throat coming in slow, regular intervals, like a snore. Elizabeth stepped carefully on the boards of the hardwood floor that she remembered didn't creak much, and made her way to the crib in her stockings. She leaned over the bars with Amanda in her arms, setting first the little heels, then the bottom, then the back, and only then, very slowly, the head on the mattress. She pulled the soft blanket up to the baby's armpits, and was turning to sneak out of the room when she heard the telephone down the hall ring. She froze and looked at Amanda, then tried to step toward the doorway more quickly, each step now landing unerringly on a board that cracked like a rifle shot, and the phone growing unaccountably louder.

She slipped out, quickly closed the door and skated on her stocking feet to the telephone in the office. "Yes?" she said into it. She knew her voice sounded angry, and how could they know?

Richardson's voice had a stupid cheerfulness. "Hi, Elizabeth. Hope I didn't get you up."

"No," she said. "You know, I never asked you. Do you have any kids?"

"Sure." She could hear him beaming, probably looking at a picture that he kept somewhere out of sight. "Dan's twenty-two and Brenda's nineteen. She just transferred to Northwestern." Of course the question had been a mistake. She had wanted to know whether he had any idea what time one-year-olds get up, or whether he had simply forgotten, but the instant she had asked she realized that Richardson wouldn't have been the one to get up with a baby.

"Actually, I was going to call you before work anyway. I'd like to have the Boston office watch Giovanni Bautista as closely as possible, starting now—I know it's expensive—and also get the people who watch airports and borders to step up security on the major routes from Boston into Canada."

"Why Canada?"

"That's in case the ones who are watching Bautista make a mistake. The Butcher's Boy is ready to leave. I can feel it. He'll do something to get them off his back so he can disappear. Killing Bautista is one possibility. There are others, of course, but that one just struck me. Can you do it?"

"I'm not sure what we can do. We're going to have a meeting. The deputy assistant wants to talk about the case."

"Which one?"

"Hillman's in charge of us. How soon can you get here?"

"I'm not sure. I've got to get Jimmy up and give him his breakfast; then I'll call the baby-sitter and ask her to come early. I'll be there as soon as I can."

As soon as she let the receiver's weight press down on the button it rang again, as though it were alive. She snatched it up. "Yes?"

It was Hamp. "Hi, Elizabeth. I'm sorry to call you before work, when the baby's probably getting ready to nod off."

"How did you know? Do you have kids?"

"I just have a knack for waking people up. Can you talk?"

"Yes. Where are you?"

"Cleveland. They found the car he was using. I can see it from where I'm standing. He abandoned it in the parking lot of a big project. He left it clean."

"I hope you're not waiting for me to sound surprised. Did you get anything out of it?"

"Dead end," Hamp said. "He rented it on the Ackerman credit card. As far as I can tell, he hasn't let anybody run the card through a machine since then."

Elizabeth sighed. "Great. Jack, I think the place he's going might be Boston. He could be after Giovanni Bautista."

There was a long silence on the other end, and she could hear the sounds of traffic. Finally he said, "I don't think so."

"Why not? Maximum trouble, maximum confusion. Bautista's the logical one to hit."

"That's right. It's practically a straight line. L.A., Santa Fe, drop off the car in Cleveland, then Buffalo. There's not much left in that direction but Boston."

"I see your point: too obvious for him. What's your theory?"

"I think he's someplace in the Midwest. I think he's laying low and looking for a way out."

"What are you going to do?"

"The best place to wait for him to poke his head up is Chicago. I can get just about anyplace from there in an hour or two."

"Jack, there's something I just found out that I ought to tell you about. My boss has called a meeting. The deputy assistant is going to be there, so it's got to be about money or resources or whatever you want to call it, so—"

"Don't worry about it. I'm independently wealthy. I have a pension from the LAPD. I'll call you with my new number when I get to Chicago."

The conference room looked different, even though it was another dark, rainy dawn. It was because the last time she had been here she was alone, laying out printouts on the big table and sitting in one chair, then another, and looking at each corner of the room without knowing she was seeing it, because the front of her mind was thinking about the way he would be traveling. People in the room changed it, and even though it was their place, it wasn't an improvement.

Hillman, the deputy assistant, was already seated at the head of the table. It was typical of Richardson to relinquish his space to a visiting potentate. In a subtle way, this made it the deputy assistant's meeting, and he obviously knew it. He sat back and watched her enter and look around at the others, then take a seat at the opposite end of the table. If it was going to be that kind of meeting, then she would take a place where she could face him. Elizabeth studied him without letting her eyes rest on him. He had thick brown hair that had begun to recede, and he had allowed some hairdresser to convince him to comb it forward in the front, so that at first it appeared to be a hairpiece. When she had come in, she had assumed he was tall because he had wide shoulders. But now he lifted his arms and rested them on the table, and they were so short that she thought that she must be taller than he was, and that he had probably arrived early enough to be seated before anyone saw him. He was going to interfere, just as his predecessors had ten years ago. Simply by being here and asking questions for an hour or two, he would cost them half a day. In half a day the Butcher's Boy could put them another ten years behind him.

The deputy assistant looked down at his watch, then at her. "Miss Waring?"

"Hello, Mr. Hillman," she said. There were three other women in the room, and all of them were in their twenties and wore designer glasses that had been chosen as accessories to outfits of the sort that nobody in this office used to wear except in court. From the looks of their hair, all of them had gotten the call hours before she had.

"It's nice to see you again." She could tell that Hillman wasn't sure if he had seen her before, but if she had been in the Justice Department for more than ten years, she had a right to expect that the upper echelon at least knew her by sight. "I understand you've been transferred from Fraud. What's your first impression?"

"I'm not exactly new," she said. "This is where I started. And I'm not transferring back; I'm just on loan for this case."

Hillman nodded sagely. "That's right." It was as though he had been testing her hold on her sanity. "The reason we're having this little get-together is that this case came as a surprise upstairs. I'd sort of like to get up to speed. I understand that this Butcher fellow assassinated one of our informants in New York so that the wire was discovered; then the theory is that he flew to Santa Fe and killed a boss named Peter Mantino, and then went to Buffalo and killed the boss there."

Elizabeth nodded. "That's one possibility."

Richardson looked alarmed. "Just a day ago you were sure of it." He glanced at the deputy assistant as though he were checking to see if he was on fire. "Has something changed?"

Elizabeth answered him but looked at the deputy assistant. "The Buffalo police pointed out to me that it's a lot of work for one person, no matter who he is. It meant he had to kill several other people in Buffalo—at least three—in different ways in a few hours. Not that he couldn't do it, but it leaves the question of why."

"Why?" This time it was the deputy assistant. "I understood that this is what he does."

"It's easy to think of reasons why a boss is murdered. Somebody hires the killer, or he has a personal grudge to settle. It's not as easy to imagine why one man would come in and shoot two or three soldiers in one part of town, then go shoot the boss

and three more soldiers afterward. Nobody would hire one man
to do that, and the only reason anyone would want that sort of
massacre is an unfriendly takeover. The Butcher's Boy isn't eligible for management.''

Richardson smirked. ''I don't think we really need the advice
of the Buffalo police on this sort of thing, do we?''

''I didn't ask for it, but it makes a certain amount of sense.''

Richardson prompted her. ''But you aren't buying it, are
you?''

''Some of it.''

The others waited, but she didn't go on. Finally Richardson
prodded her. ''Which parts?''

''The last time we heard of the Butcher's Boy, ten years ago,
he did something very similar, only we didn't know what was
happening until later. I think that something went wrong that
made his clients turn on him, so he was on the run and did it to
churn up the water so he could get away. I can't be sure why
he's doing it this time, but I don't think it's for money.''

''All right, Elizabeth,'' said the deputy assistant. She noted
the change to her first name. ''You've just come from Fraud, so
you know something about revenue-center budgeting. That's
what I'm here about. We have limited resources to work with.
This is one case, one man. What do we get if we catch him, and
what does it cost?''

Elizabeth thought for a moment, then decided. She was going
to have to defeat Hillman by tunneling under whatever position
he took so that she got there before he did. ''In Fraud that wasn't
hard to answer. We were recovering money stolen from the Department of Housing and Urban Development. We just figured
out who took the most who was likely to still have it, and we
went after him. This is different. I don't have the slightest idea
what it would cost to catch him, and I don't know what we get.''

The deputy assistant nodded again, and this time he was smiling in contemplation of the triumph he was about to savor. ''You
have to look at this from the Malthusian point of view. I have to
go upstairs and tell *our* bosses what I think we should do with
our finite resources that will result in the greatest good. Or the
maximum damage to evil, if you will. The range of options is
staggering, and we'd like to do it all. But you have to be hard-
nosed about this. Is this something we should pursue on a federal level?'' He smiled as though he knew the answer, then
added, ''Of course, you could tell me that this is the kind of
decision I get the big bucks for making.'' He looked around,

and the people at the table chuckled on cue. He seemed pleased. "But I've got nothing to go on unless you help me."

"All right," said Elizabeth. What a loathsome little man. She would have to argue his position for him, and let him see what was wrong with it. "As I said, I believe that the Butcher's Boy fell out with his employers ten years ago, and as a result killed a number of organized-crime figures—some important, some not—in order to create the maximum chaos so that he'd have time to get away. I think that he's an evil man, and in a perfect society would be forced to suffer some punishment. But if you're asking if you should take, say, two million dollars from enforcing civil rights laws to spend on getting him, I don't know. I doubt it." The current administration had spent virtually nothing on enforcing civil rights laws, and everyone at the table knew it.

Richardson looked faint, but the deputy assistant seemed to relish the conversation. "Give me your reasoning, Elizabeth."

"The reason we wanted him ten years ago was that we believed he knew a great deal about the men who ran organized crime and their activities. He'd have to. He was a sort of contract exterminator for people at a very high level. But I think he's been in hiding for ten years. If that's true, what he knows is mostly old news, which might make it hard to get convictions. There's also the problem that his knowledge is pretty much limited to capital crimes. If we find him, we may not take him alive. If we do, he probably won't tell us anything. I can't assume many judges would grant him immunity to testify, or that immunity would be worth much without protection from the Mafia. Which would get us into the area of the Witness Protection Program. If he's stayed alive while they were looking for him for ten years, he can do better on his own. And, of course, it would put the Department in the position of setting a man free who has probably killed dozens of people."

"Dozens? Literally?" Hillman raised his eyebrows.

"That's if the stories are true. It's hard to tell."

"And we won't know unless we go out and catch him?"

Elizabeth didn't take the bait. "I can't guarantee we'll ever know more than we do right now. I'm not qualified to tell you whether taking him off the streets will be of political value to the Department. I do know it probably won't contribute much to the safety of the average citizen in his home; in fact, what he's been doing all week is killing off some of the very people we'd most like to take out of the game. That includes the informant you mentioned. Tony T was a bad man.''

"I'm impressed, Elizabeth," said the deputy assistant. "I asked for hard-nosed, and that's exactly what I got. What's your conclusion?''

"I think the opposition is more likely to get him than we are.''

"You do?''

"Sure. They would consider him a more serious problem than we do because his memory can put a lot of them away for life. They know more about him than we do, and they have an unlimited budget.'' She hesitated for a second, not because she was considering not saying it, but to be sure he got it. "And they operate on utilitarian principles too.''

Richardson came out of the elevator and stalked directly to Elizabeth's desk. "He likes you.''

"He does?''

"He thinks you're the best thing that could happen.''

She shook her head. "I could see it from the minute I walked in there. We were made for each other. The electricity in the air, the—''

"Jesus, Elizabeth, you handled him brilliantly. You won. Now, be gracious in victory and stop fighting. He wants us to go for it.''

14

Wolf stood in the shower and let the heavy flow of water pour over him. He needed to be soothed. When he moved, he could feel a small hitch in his back where he had taken the jolts of the bus ride across Arizona. He had been awakened a few times during the night, not by the sounds of cars, the motel ice machine or the voices in other rooms, but by his mind running through its accumulated clutter. Each time, when consciousness came, he would find himself in midthought, sometimes in midsentence, fully aware of the specious train of logic he had been following in his sleep.

The last time, he had been thinking about Meg. He hated to think about her now when he was awake, because she was gone forever. He never had any trouble recalling the sight of her, or even the scent of her perfume. He had been constructing a dream about her; in it he would live, and then he would go back and look at her. It wouldn't be easy to accomplish, because women of her class ventured off the enclosed, protected parks their husbands inherited less and less often as they grew older. They were occupied with their children until they sent them away to some awful boarding school, and after that they saw a select group of friends who were, after so many generations, so closely related that they looked like sisters. When he reached this part of the dream, the sense of loss and disappointment woke him up, and he began to scheme in the darkness for some way to go home. At some point in the night he had let go of it, and awakened to the one thing the darkness and isolation had let him forget. He had been doing his feeling and thinking on the premise that he was a constant, unchanging being, that the continuity of his memories and consciousness somehow guaranteed that he was the same. But now, as he became more alert to the physical world that chilled his bones, put pressure on his joints and reflected his body in mirrors, he remembered. When he was asleep, or when nothing reminded him of it, he felt exactly the same as he had the first time he had put on his Little League baseball uniform. He could even remember the incredible whiteness of the flannel, and feel the softness of it against his legs. That was the ridiculous part of memory, or one of the ridiculous parts. It was only his body that wasn't still ten years old.

Wolf dried himself with two of the big rough white towels and walked into the bedroom. There were really two problems now, and the way to get through this was to look at them separately. The old men were the big problem. He had done the right thing by going to Las Vegas. Little Norman might be able to convince them that the best thing they could do was to let Carl Bala stay in his cage and forget about helping him with his revenge.

The other problem was new to him. He knew that Little Norman must have been telling the truth. Tony Talarese had been wearing a wire. It was the only thing that explained the commotion in the kitchen when he had popped the bastard. It had been so obvious; why hadn't he figured it out? Because it was such an outrageous idea that his mind had somehow blocked it. But now the New York police knew something about him. Hell, they must know a lot about him if they could have five cops waiting for him in the Los Angeles airport a few hours later. Because that's what it had been; he had seen the whole thing wrong. It wasn't four cops looking for a shooter; it was five cops looking for him.

He sat down on the bed and thought about this, and it was still wrong. The New York police couldn't have gotten on a plane and caught up with him like that. They would have needed to take practically the next flight out of New York, and what could they expect to do in Los Angeles? They wouldn't have jurisdiction. Now it fell into place inevitably. It wasn't the New York police; it was federal cops—the FBI. It fit better anyway. They were the ones who were always bugging telephones and taping microphones to people, and they wouldn't have to put anybody on a plane; they would simply make a phone call to the Los Angeles office to have their agent bring four bozos across town to scoop him up.

Wolf dressed quickly and walked across the street to the pay phone outside a small diner. He had twenty dollars in quarters, two ten-dollar rolls that he had bought from the sleepy change

girl posted near the slot machines in the lobby of his motel in
Las Vegas. He had picked up the habit from Little Norman in
the old days, and it had come back to him. Little Norman had
always told him that his hands were too small to use by themselves. A fist wrapped around a roll of quarters might lose a few
hundredths of a second getting there, but when it did it would
make an impression.

He put a quarter into the telephone and dialed the number.
The operator came on the line and said, "Please deposit three
thirty-five." He laboriously pumped fourteen quarters into the
slot, and after the fourteenth, the operator wouldn't go away
until she had said, "You have fifteen cents' credit." Then it
sounded as though she were climbing into a jar and then screw-
ing the lid on after her. And finally he heard the ring. It sounded
different from the ones here, sort of bubbly and quick, and it
made him feel as though he were home. It was maddening. He
was listening to her phone, and he could see the room in his
memory.

"Hello?"

"Hi," he said. "I'm going to have to talk fast."

"After leaving me alone this long, I should say you are." He
tried to remember how long it had been since he had heard
anyone talk with a smile in her voice.

"Not to make excuses. It's the connection. Wiring problems,
I think." She would understand that. It was from one of those
silly books she had made him read. The British spy had detected
a couple of ohms of extra resistance on the line to his reading
lamp, and concluded it must be a bug. An American would have
gone through the place with a bug detector. You could buy one
for twenty-five bucks.

"Oh," she said. Then, *"Oh."*

It was the FBI that worried him. In another book she had
forced on him he had read that the National Security Agency
had the capability of recording every transatlantic telephone call.
The book hadn't said whether they did it, or what use they made
of all those tapes, but if they didn't share them with the FBI,
they were stupid. He had heard a lot about American intelligence services, but he hadn't heard that they weren't devious
enough.

"I'm going to have to stay longer than I thought," he said.

"Why? Can you—"

"It's because I made a mistake. I'd like to say it was something else, but it wasn't."

"Is there anything I can do?"

This was the hard part. If they were listening, it had to be plausible nonsense. "Yeah. It's funny I should be thinking about this right now, but I can't get it out of my mind. The best thing you could do is spend today rearranging things. Maybe move your clothes and stuff. A good place might be at the north end, where the bed used to be." He spent a second hoping she had gotten it, and knowing she couldn't have. He thought of Yorkshire pudding, and there was an archbishop, but if he got that crude, they would have it before she did.

But she said, "Oh. The present arrangement isn't good?"

Her voice had the sort of concern he was listening for, but he needed to be sure. "I've done a lot of this kind of decorating," he said. "If you take my advice, I think it will brighten things up a lot."

"Is it . . . that dark now?"

He was satisfied. She knew. "It just struck me as a good idea. I'd love to look the place over myself, but I just can't get away right now. I'm hoping I'll be able to soon."

"I'd be very sad if you couldn't."

"I would too."

There was a long silence on the other end, and he thought he could hear her breathing. It began to bring her back as a physical presence: the barely detectable scent on her hair, the incredibly soft skin just in front of her ear, and then, "I wanted to say," Margaret said, "just in case we don't get to speak again soon, that I . . ." She paused and then said the next two words softly: "love you." He drew in his breath to answer, but she went on rapidly. "Please don't answer, because it wouldn't mean anything if you did right now. I wouldn't have said it today either, but I thought I'd better, given the circumstances. These things often don't get said, and then you regret it and all that. I know this is being unfair to you in case you wanted to say it for the same reasons, but that's the way it is."

"I love you."

"After all that? It makes me feel worse than I thought, because it's so typical of you."

"I've got to go now. Don't forget what I said."

"Michael, wait!"

"What?"

"That was stupid of me. I'm sorry. I just—you know. I hope it's not long. But if it is, I'll—"

"Don't."

He hung up the telephone and heard a loud jangle as the machine dumped the load of quarters into its collection box. As he watched for a break in the traffic so that he could get back across the street to his motel, he felt worse. He hadn't made her understand. He should have told her something closer to the truth. He wasn't delayed; he was probably dead. The dons might sit back and wait while he disappeared and then tell Carl Bala in his prison cell that it was just one of those things, but if he didn't disappear, then he was in trouble. After allowing him a decent interval, they would change their minds. And already the people who worked for Carl Bala would be out in force, hanging in all the places where he had ever been seen, watching for him. He might be able to avoid them for a time, but not forever.

He had never worried much about the authorities before. He still didn't think they could catch him, except by some gigantic stroke of blundering good luck, but what if they could actually keep him from leaving the country? He had just used up the only passport he had that would get him past the computerized scanners they had installed in the airports since he had left, and there was no way he could try again to buy one. What had happened in Buffalo had closed that down for all time.

He had to get out before Bala had time to replace Talarese and Mantino and Fratelli and the new men got things organized enough to come after him. What could it take, two or three days? A week at the outside. What the hell else did the old son of a bitch have to do?

Wolf was starting to feel a kind of claustrophobia. Somehow the country had shrunk. Ten years ago it had been a place full of possibilities. He could disappear simply by fading into a crowd, or take a quick jump that put him five hundred miles away so they would have to start looking for him all over again. Now everything seemed to be a lot closer to everything else. He had to find out something about this FBI business.

Sergeant Bob Lempert had spent most of his career under suspicion. In 1965 he and an older cop named Mulroy had been assigned to stay in a hotel to be sure nothing happened to a bookmaker named Ricky Hinks before he could testify in the conspiracy trial of Paul Cambria. Ricky Hinks was later found to have slipped into the bathroom, cut the shower curtain into strips with a razor and tied them together to make a rope. He had then used it to lower himself from the bathroom window to the alley below, where he had been shot to death by persons unknown. It was considered to be bad luck all around—certainly for Ricky Hinks, who must have lowered himself into the gunsights of some obstructors of justice; but also for officers Mulroy and Lempert, because he had died without revealing how he had managed to slice up the curtain with an electric razor, or lower himself sixty feet on a twenty-foot rope. The internal inquiry was not released in detail, the Gary police chief was quoted as saying, because it was inextricably intertwined with an ongoing investigation. The two officers involved had done their duty.

But from that moment on, Bob Lempert's career took a detour into limbo. He was considered to be a competent cop at a time when cops who were eager to respond to those two A.M. "domestic disturbance" calls from sparsely patrolled neighborhoods, or to venture into the very asshole of the city to check out "shots fired" reports were at a premium. Jobs were plentiful in Gary, Indiana, for healthy white veterans who could read, and not many of them paid less than a cop made, so there was no point in throwing away a good body. Lempert remained a trusted member of the force, the kind you wanted behind you when you kicked in a door. But this trust went only so far. You didn't want him behind you if you kicked in certain very expensive doors, and you didn't want him in plainclothes, where he could get too used to the availability of payoffs. But for your B and E's, your Aggravated Assaults, your "Shut Up and Go Back in Your House Because I'm the Law" situations, you couldn't do much better than Bob Lempert.

Lempert had made sergeant when he was pushing fifty. In his case, it was a sort of honorary title because nobody wanted him put in charge of anything. This was not because the aroma of the 1965 incident had lingered in the nostrils of the powerful for so many years; it was because from time to time the odor returned. In the mid-seventies, when Eddie Parnell, the challenger for the presidency of the laundry union, was killed with his two brothers on the eve of the election, people pointed out that Eddie and his family were not completely ignorant that some such thing might happen. All three of them wore pistols in shoulder holsters twenty-four hours a day, and would not have opened the door to just anybody who took the trouble to rap his knuckles on it. It would have had to be somebody they had no reason to suspect, somebody who could walk in armed without being frisked, somebody they couldn't have simply told to come back tomorrow after the ballots had been counted. It would have had to be a cop.

In the eighties there had been a number of puzzling incidents, notably the strange death of a known cocaine dealer named Milo "Mucho Más" Figueroa. He had been shot down at his heavily fortified house after firing several ineffective shots with an AK-47 into trees near two officers. In the inquiry it was learned that the two officers had no search warrant because they had not intended to enter the dwelling; in fact, they were off duty and had simply been fired upon as they were passing by. Odder still were Mr. Figueroa's garb, consisting of a sleeveless T-shirt and silk boxer shorts; the hour he had chosen to go berserk, which was four A.M.; and the fact that he had chosen to defend his fortress from outside its walls. None of this would have merited a page in the annals of cocaine-induced paranoia except that when the premises were thoroughly searched, not a milligram of cocaine was found, nor any currency. One of the off-duty officers who assisted at Mr. Figueroa's suicide was Bob Lempert.

Lempert could not be considered a bitter man, in spite of all this coincidence and bad luck. He was, in fact, cheerful most of the time. He had stayed on the force long after he had done his twenty years, and showed up for work each day ready with either a joke of his own or a laugh at someone else's. Today he was in a worse mood than he had been in since the Internal Affairs Division had called him in to ask about the death of Miriam Purnaski, the jeweler. That time he hadn't really been prepared since it had been such a rush job. Miriam Purnaski was one of the modern practitioners of the ancient process of changing money into gold, then changing it back again in another country. At some point in her career she had lost her appreciation for simplicity and begun performing the same kind of alchemy simultaneously for several local dealers in recreational chemicals. Then she had made the mistake that attorneys and accountants sometimes do, which was to merge the accounts of several clients. Having made this first step into unsound bookkeeping, she had gradually betrayed her fiduciary responsibility for the funds of the Cambria family entirely, and begun feeding what she received into the big end of the funnel, paying out what she needed to at the small end, and paying herself whatever profit she could make in between. When mutual-fund managers did this, it was called an administration fee; when money laundresses did it, it was called skimming. At the moment when Lempert had learned about this, he was told

that she was already on her way to the airport and that he had
an hour to stop her.

Afterward, when the shooting team had grilled Lempert, he
had been able to explain her unfortunate accident adequately.
The woman had sideswiped a police car because she was in such
a rush to get to the hospital, having been shot in the abdomen
by persons unknown, probably in a robbery attempt. But what
had put him in a bad mood was learning what was in her suitcases only *after* the ambulance had arrived. It was more than a
million in cash, and bank deposit books with numbers in them
that were so big they didn't have any meaning.

Lempert was in the same kind of mood today. Paul Cambria
had told his man Puccio to get the word out: the Butcher's Boy
had come back. If he were the sort of man who had a lot of luck
going for him, he might have managed to drop the hammer on
the bastard, because Lempert was one of a small, select group
of people who had seen the Butcher's Boy up close in the old
days and was still alive. About fifteen years ago, Lempert had
worked with him. At least that was the way he would have put
it to Paul Cambria if he had been important enough to talk to
Cambria personally. Actually, he had been the driver—or he
would have been, if necessary. It was the night when the Butcher's Boy was supposed to walk through the back door of the
Garibaldi Social Club and quietly rid the city of the menace of
Andy Ugolino. The idea was that afterward, if things weren't
quiet, Lempert would pull up in a squad car, everybody else
would run the other way, and the Butcher's Boy would slip into
the back seat and get a ride across town. As it happened, things
had gone very quietly, and the police escort hadn't been necessary, but Lempert had seen him twice—once before, and once
while he was walking out of the social club.

The problem was that the Butcher's Boy had also seen Lempert. At the time Lempert had believed that it was likely to be
useful in the future to get to know all the important people he
could. Important people knew other important people, and op-
portunities could come from anywhere. He even had the odd
notion that they might get to be friends. Lempert was an ordinary guy, after all, and he had never heard anything about the
man that said he wasn't one too. When he said it to himself, he
had a picture in his mind. He didn't analyze it, but the essential
elements were that the guy would be somebody you might drink
a beer with in a neighborhood bar, and that he should have some
passing interest in sports, maybe enough interest to place a small

bet now and then. There was a subtle bond between men whose lives were contested, who could keep living only as long as they won. That wasn't exactly Lempert, but he had been in some tight spots.

So he had contrived to meet the bastard. Puccio had told Lempert he was going to see the guy the day before and give him the money. It was supposed to be in a restaurant called The Golden Cock, and Puccio had wanted to be sure there wasn't some plan to raid the place that day because the cops knew there were slot machines in the room upstairs. Puccio didn't want to be sitting in the place holding a hundred thousand in cash when some idiot rookie with a fire ax in his hand burst in through the back door to arrest illegal gamblers. But even more fervently, he didn't want to be sitting across the table from that particular man when the cops came in. Lempert assured him that the place was not due to come up on the list until August, and maybe not even then, but it gave Lempert an excuse to show up and meet the Butcher's Boy.

It was a mistake. He wasn't an ordinary guy. Lempert walked up to the booth in the corner just as Puccio was saying something in a low voice about whacking Ugolino. The man was a disappointment at first glance. He didn't look like much—no big shoulders or bull neck, and he was wearing a herringbone tweed sport coat with no tie. He had thin, sandy brown hair and brown eyes, and his fingers were long and thin, like a musician's. One hand was sort of playing with his napkin on the table as though he were preoccupied, and his eyes seemed almost dull as they passed across Lempert. Then he looked up. "Sit down."

Lempert had grinned and pulled out a chair, but then he noticed that Puccio was scared shitless. "What the fuck?" he whispered. "Get out of here."

Lempert's grin lingered on his face because he didn't know what to do with it. The man repeated, "Sit down." This time he let the napkin slip a little, and Lempert's grin disappeared. Under the hem of the napkin he could see the black muzzle of a silencer aimed at his belly, and the hand was preparing to pull the trigger of the pistol through the napkin. He sat down.

The man turned his expressionless face on Puccio. "Keep your money."

"But he's—"

"I know who he is. He's your cop."

"Look," said Puccio. "He just made a mistake. Please. Don't kill him."

Lempert had never heard these terms applied to himself before. Even after he had seen the gun, it had not occurred to him that he had done anything that could conceivably raise the stakes to that level. On reflection, he realized that he should have known before the gun, as soon as he had seen the eyes. They were not the eyes of a man who was afraid or angry. They weren't even eager, like the eyes of a cat or a dog about to tear something up; those eyes had a kind of excitement or anticipation. This was not an ordinary guy. Lempert had been a cop for a long time by then, and he had seen something like this before. He didn't know a lot about what he was looking at, but he knew that if this man started to smile, Lempert was going to dive for the floor and try to get his gun out in time.

The Butcher's Boy said, "I won't. I'm going to get up in a minute. You're both going to sit where you are until I'm gone. Don't send for me again."

Puccio looked at Lempert, a quick glance that was intended to communicate a lot of things at once. It said something like, "See what you did?" But it also said, "If you speak or move or even change your expression, we're going to die. And if I die here like this, I'll hound you through hell for all eternity." Puccio was like that. He never forgot or forgave or made allowances. He was a brilliant man, and it was his tragedy that the Cambria businesses had grown so large that he couldn't handle all the details himself. Lempert let all the life go out of him and sat there, barely breathing. "Look, kid . . ." said Puccio. "I apologize. I'm embarrassed. The money just doubled. I'll throw in another hundred thousand out of my own pocket."

"The job's not worth that." It was a strange thing for a man to say. "The price isn't the issue."

Puccio nodded, but slowly, and he didn't talk with his hands the way he usually did. "I know. I'm sincere. I'm trying to make up for this and show you I'm a serious man."

The Butcher's Boy looked at Puccio for a minute, then said, "All right."

Lempert wasn't sure he had heard correctly at first because he was busy remembering the sight of the Goschia brothers. Puccio had actually had them hung on meat hooks in the freezer of the Ritzmar Quality Packing Company, like some don in a movie. Only he had taped the button on the electrical track so that they were still going around and around when the rest of the employees came to work on Monday morning. Lempert had arrived just after the Homicide guys, and they were still up there.

The rumor was that they had run their own football pool in the plant and had cost Puccio about ten thousand dollars in receipts.

Puccio was already saying, "I know you'll get out, but just in case . . ."

The Butcher's Boy let his eyes settle on Lempert and said, "I want him. No sense having everybody in town see my face."

Afterward, Puccio didn't kill Lempert, but he did everything he could to make him think he was going to. As soon as the Butcher's Boy had gone, he shrugged his shoulders, chuckled and patted Lempert on the back. "We dodged it that time," he said. The only reason Lempert could think of why Puccio would behave that way was if he didn't expect to see Lempert again.

When Lempert had tried to stammer out, "I'm sorry, I didn't know," Puccio had said, "It's forgotten. Just don't do it again."

It was only after Ugolino was dead and Lempert was still alive that he started to take breaths that actually kept enough oxygen going to his brain. At that point he understood what was going on. By the time he had arrived in his squad car to watch the Butcher's Boy come out of the social club, Ugolino had been dead almost an hour. That was what the coroner's report had said. Lempert read it three times to be sure. But what gave him such chills that the skin on his jowls tightened and made his whiskers actually rise to the touch was that the death was listed as "natural causes." The best he could figure it was that the bastard had somehow gotten to Ugolino in the crowd and injected him with something that made his heart stop, and then let him slip down under the table at the booth in the back before anybody saw him. Who the hell would try to kill somebody like Ugolino that way? But whatever he had done, he had hung around for an hour inside the building before leaving.

Paul Cambria had gone to Ugolino's funeral, with his foreman, Puccio, in attendance. In the surveillance photographs, the two of them had looked dignified and mournful as they accepted the homage of Ugolino's family and friends. Two hundred thousand was a bargain. They didn't just get to see Ugolino dead, they got to eat him afterward, like cannibals.

Now the Butcher's Boy was supposed to be back. It made Lempert's jaw ache to think about it. He could get rich in the fraction of a second it took to exert four ounces of pressure with his right forefinger. But it wasn't just money; the invisible men who quietly owned the planet would be so pleased that they would give him a charmed existence. Nothing could ever touch him again. The secret agony he had felt and lived with since the first time he had been passed over for promotion twenty-odd years ago would be transformed in an instant into a cosmic joke. Sergeant? Hell, governors didn't live the life he would live if he were just lucky enough to be standing there when the bastard showed his face. It was exactly like winning the lottery.

But there were problems. Puccio had called him to give him the news, and he wasn't looking at it like an early payday. That meant Paul Cambria wasn't either. Paul Cambria was one of the men who ran things in the world, and that put him just below the old men themselves, the ones you saw only in blurry photographs. If Paul Cambria had something to worry about, then the rest of the human race was in trouble.

But at work two days later, he learned why a thinking man like Puccio wasn't seeing this development as an opportunity, but as an occasion that might cause his name to be left out of next year's phone book. The FBI was in an uproar because suddenly, for no known reason, Antonio Talarese, Angelo Fratelli and Peter Mantino had stopped being suspected organized-crime figures and become homicide victims. The FBI wasn't just sending circulars, but was making urgent inquiries to learn if anyone in any big-city police station had ever heard of anyone aka "Butcher's Boy." Lempert could almost feel the velvety texture of the first cushion-soft stack of hundred-dollar bills. The bastard wasn't out depopulating the civilized world. He was on some kind of a batch job, slicing off a few of the heads that stuck up above the crowd. Lempert didn't have to ask himself who was likely to be the next of the heads; Puccio had told him. Lempert was going to get rich.

Lempert sat in the back of the van he had taken from Impound and watched the line of people inching slowly toward the front door of the Cinema Marrakesh. Over the door the giant 1930s marquee had actually been washed, and a couple of thousand burned-out light bulbs had been replaced. Some of the plaster carvings on the lintel had actually had a little gold paint slapped on them too. The green, foot-high letters on the marquee said only BELLADONNA. The movie had so many big stars in it that there wouldn't have been room for them, and maybe it didn't make any difference, because everybody knew what it was and who was in it, and the star was supposed to be the director, anyway.

In a way, it was ridiculous for Paul Cambria to take his wife to a movie like that, even if it was an opening. It had to be comical to him. The idea was supposed to be that this beautiful young girl, the daughter of some Mafia guy—not a local boy, but an old Sicilian with a mustache—takes over after his untimely death and gets very rich. To the real thing, someone like Paul Cambria, it had to be pretty strange. Those guys didn't even tell their wives what the hell they did for a living. It was also odd that Cambria would sit in the dark with a thousand people for two hours. Maybe he thought his guys needed to know that he wasn't going to pull in his horns just because there was somebody looking for him.

Anyway, it was a one-shot deal. They were having an opening in Gary only because the writer or director or somebody was from here, and because some of it had been filmed in town. One day there were a couple of trucks here, some guys with lights they turned on in the daytime, and a lot of confusion, because this was roughly the place where Punch Mayall had been blown away in the thirties, but that was about it. There hadn't been any movie stars within a thousand miles of here. The real opening was going to be in Hollywood tomorrow, and that was where you would see the stars, not just these schmucks in corduroy coats with patches on the elbows and big thick glasses.

Lempert judged that his chances might be good tonight. If Cambria was in the theater, his guys would be there too. They would be all around, stuck to him like shit to a blanket. The Butcher's Boy would know that too. Still, he might just be crazy enough to want to go inside anyway and cut Cambria's throat while they were all sitting around with their thumbs up their asses, but you couldn't bet your future on how crazy somebody was. You had to assume that he knew what he was doing. He would get Cambria *afterward*. All Lempert had to do was sit in the warm van on the swivel chair and wait and watch for the muzzle flash. It was like a duck hunt. When he had parked the van here this afternoon, he had taken the precaution of writing himself a ticket and sticking it under the wiper so that nobody else would decide to do it.

He had thought this through very carefully, and he was ready. He had a Ruger Mini-14 next to him, all sighted in on the front of the theater with a four-power night scope. It would take about half a second to put his shoulder to it, pop the window and draw a bead on the bastard as soon as he saw him. A beginner wouldn't have thought of the Ruger. The barrel was short enough to swing around in a van without banging it on something. Lempert was a good target shooter. He knew that if he could just get a clear view for the first shot, so the target would stay put, he could punch four or five holes in him within two seconds after that.

When the ushers in their brand-new, old-fashioned bellboy suits came out and shut the doors, Lempert studied what was left outside. There were eight uniformed patrolmen that he could see, picking up a little overtime pretending to control the crowds that were already inside the building watching the movie. He looked through the scope at each of their faces in turn. There was Jimmy Clinton and his partner, Bucklin—looking like the Pillsbury Doughboy with all the fat he had put on in the last few months. And—oh, shit—Olney and Winks. They were the ones to watch for. They had managed to wangle this assignment, of course. It was probably easier than just signing in and cooping in their car in the cul de sac off Breckinridge. He didn't like seeing veterans out here. One or two of them might be calm enough to realize what was happening in time to put a round or two into the van. The other four he didn't know. All of them were young, and one was a woman, so at least it wasn't the Butcher's Boy in a uniform. He was certainly capable of thinking of that one.

Lempert turned in his swivel chair to study the upper windows on the street again. If you assumed the bastard wasn't out-and-out berserk, you had to imagine that he might find his way into one of those buildings with a rifle. Lempert saw no changes from the last time he had looked. There were no glows from dim lights on the ceilings, no shades raised a little, no objects visible. He ducked his head, made his way on his knees to the front of the van and peeked out the windshield. There was nothing up the street that could be construed as a problem. The traffic was moving at the usual rate. He crawled to the back window and moved the curtain half an inch. There were no new vehicles parked along the street, no knots of people the Butcher's Boy could join to get a closer look at the place.

There was one more thing that Lempert had to check. He opened the back door of the van, swung his legs to the street and quietly closed the door. There wasn't any point in locking it with eight uniforms loitering around across the street, and unlocking it made noise, so he left it. He walked away from the theater and turned the corner on Fourth before venturing to look over his shoulder. His colleagues were standing around now talking to each other instead of watching the place. Probably not one of them had any idea that Paul Cambria was even here. He wondered if that would have made a difference. Probably not; you had to know the rest of it before it meant anything.

Lempert turned again at the alley behind Chautauqua Avenue, put his head down, pulled his collar up and jammed his right hand into his jacket pocket so that he could grasp his service revolver before he took the first step down the alley. If the Butcher's Boy was in one of the buildings, he would have a car waiting in back of it, or, at most, one street over. Whatever happened with Paul Cambria, he would need to have a reliable, invisible way of getting in and then getting out. The one thing Lempert remembered about his experience with the bastard ten years ago was that he thought things through. He would probably have a couple of ways out.

Lempert made his way up the alley, trying to look like a schlemiel who was watching the ground to keep from stepping into a puddle, but every few yards he scanned the old brick buildings, fire escapes and the dumpsters, looking for a change. He wasn't afraid he would miss a parked car, but he might miss something else—a broken window, or a garbage can moved a couple of feet so it could be used to climb in through a vent. It wasn't that he had any intention of going into an empty building after him: not this one. But if he just knew where the bastard was, he was pretty sure he had him. All he had to do was wait. The waiting reminded him that it was time to take a leak. He looked up and down the alley, then stepped into the shadows behind the shoe store and urinated against the wall. It was a delicious feeling because of the danger and the darkness.

Lempert continued up the alley another block before turning onto Sixth and crossing the street to the other side. The cops standing out on the sidewalk would be cutting the amenities short about now and getting into their squad cars to rest their feet, which meant they would have nothing to do for about two hours but stare up the street and watch the lights change. He made it across while they were still gathered in a gaggle in front of the theater, then made a circuit of Atlantic Avenue behind the theater and back to Fourth. If tonight was the night the bastard was going after Cambria, then he hadn't done anything much to get ready.

Lempert made his way back to the van on Chautauqua, still walking along with his head down and his collar turned up. As soon as he had passed the last parked car, he stepped into the gutter and followed it to the rear of the van. He had swung the door open and was all the way inside when he felt it. He stopped

moving, but just to be sure, the son of a bitch slid it up his back
and let the cold muzzle touch the nape of his neck. It was the
kind of thing any of them would do because Puccio had taught
them to be sadists. He was angry, but he supposed he would
have to go through the whole idiotic cross-examination before
he reminded this one that Puccio had called him and that he was
doing no more than what Puccio wanted everyone to do.

"What do you want?" said Lempert.

"I want you."

Holy shit, it wasn't them; it was *him*. Lempert started to
shiver. He was on his hands and knees, and his damned elbows
wouldn't stop shaking and giving out on him; what if the bastard
thought all this twitching was some kind of a lame attempt to
struggle? Suddenly he was overcome by a clear vision of his
stupidity, and it brought a sort of repentance. What the hell
could he have been thinking, coming out here to try and ambush
a man like this? The money wasn't even real anymore.

"I think you remember me."

Lempert started thinking about a move a burglary suspect had
tried on him once. He had told him to lie facedown and kiss the
pavement, but when the guy got on his hands and knees he
sprang forward like a damned gazelle, so all Lempert could do
was trip the guy and then put the boots to him. The Butcher's
Boy could open fire and blast his spine. Then, as if he were a
damned mind reader, the voice said, "Don't do anything. I'm
going to take the gun because I want to talk."

As the invisible hand reached into his jacket pocket and took
the service revolver, Lempert felt a secret joy. But then the hand
went directly to his right ankle and took the other one too, the
.32. "What do you want to talk about?"

"First I want you to crawl up to the driver's seat and pull out
of here."

"Why should I?"

"Because I won't need to kill you if you do."

The answer mesmerized Lempert. Need to? But of course he
would say anything to get Lempert to drive out of here. If he
burned Lempert here, he wasn't going to be able to walk away
whistling. Eight cops—even *those* eight cops—were not going
to let him do that. But need to? It gave him a tiny bit of hope
that he might get out of this. If the Butcher's Boy didn't want to
kill him, maybe he still had a chance. And even if Lempert
somehow reversed things and managed to kill the bastard instead
of having the bastard kill him, what was he going to say to the

eight cops himself? What was the dead suspect doing in the van? He crawled to the seat, pulled himself up, started the engine and tried to look in the mirror to back up.

"Turn the lights on," said the Butcher's Boy.

"Oh, yeah," said Lempert. He could barely get his hand to stop shaking so that he could turn the switch. Oh, God. He really had forgotten them, and now the bastard thought he was playing some trick.

As he started to turn out onto the street, the Butcher's Boy said, "Go straight while we talk."

Lempert obeyed, and he decided the bastard had made a mistake. There was something about driving—the thing he had spent eight hours a day doing for more than twenty years—that revived him. He was in control of all this power, so he couldn't be powerless. "So why didn't you kill Paul Cambria?"

"I don't have anything against Paul Cambria. I came to see you."

Lempert's bravado disappeared. He had to talk to him, to say something that wasn't in the groove of the bastard's logic. "How do you even remember me?"

"Things come back to me. I figured you'd be hanging around Cambria, so I found him. You're still a cop, right?"

"Yeah." Oh, sweet Jesus. What could this be about? The bastard didn't say another word for three blocks. Then he got it. Carlo Balacontano. Ten years ago. The bastard had some wacko idea that because Lempert was a cop he could get to Carl Bala in a federal prison. What happens when he finds out Lempert can't?

Finally, "I want you to get something for me. I'll pay you."

It was coming. Maybe he could convince the bastard with some bullshit story: if you come to the prison with me, all I have to do is flash my badge and they'll let us in armed. Bang. "What do you want?"

"Pull over up here."

Lempert looked around as he slowed down. He made a guess; this man wouldn't shoot him in front of a copying store that was still open, and next door to a bar that had barely begun its prime hours, and across the street from a pizza place. He stopped the van by the curb, but didn't turn off the engine until the man said, "Come on. We're going in there."

The bar? He must mean the bar. Lempert turned off the engine. "Drop the keys on the floor and come out after me." He dropped the keys on the floor, then waited until the bastard got out. He looked for an opportunity, but there was none. Then they were both on the street, and he could see the bastard in the light. He hadn't changed much. It was almost eerie. He was six feet away, and had the service revolver in his hand, and his hand in his coat, and Lempert had no doubt that if he moved wrong or tripped on something and stumbled, he would have a hole in him before he hit the ground.

They walked into the copying store. There were typewriters and computers for rent, and lots of envelopes and colored paper for sale, and about a dozen Xerox machines in two rows. When Lempert saw the kid behind the counter, with his long, greasy ponytail and dark, bushy eyebrows that showed over the tops of his dark glasses, he decided there was a God. He remembered pulling this kid out of a 280Z after following him for ten blocks. It was the end of the month, and Lempert needed to write a few more tickets, so he had decided that this kid was going too fast. The kid had smirked at him, so he had whirled him around, slammed him against the car and frisked him, then put the cuffs on him and made him lie on the ground while he searched the car for drugs. If only he had found some, or planted some. Then this kid wouldn't be the one to lean on the counter and smirk at him while he got his brains blown out.

"Here's what I want," said the Butcher's Boy. "I want a copy of whatever the FBI is sending out to the police computers about me."

"The NCIC file? How am I supposed to do that?"

"Maybe somebody will fax it here from the station, or Washington, or whatever. Maybe you can get one of these computers onto a phone line and call it up. Anyway, do it."

"Give me a minute to think."

"If you do it, I'll pay you. If there's some trick or something, I"—and then he paused for what seemed like a long time—"won't."

Lempert went to the kid at the counter. "I want to use a phone."

The kid recognized him. He hesitated, and Lempert had the impression that he was scared, but it gave him no pleasure. "Here's the phone."

Lempert only briefly considered saying something on the phone that made no sense. Who could say what this man knew? He dialed the squad room and heard McNulty's voice say, "Police Department Metro Division." Of course it had to be McNulty working tonight, somebody who not only didn't like

Lempert but was also so stupid that his partners wouldn't ride in a car with him unless they had personally checked the shotgun to be sure there wasn't a shell in the chamber when he stuck it in the rack.

"It's me, McNulty. Lempert," he said. "I need a favor."

"Don't we all," said McNulty.

Lempert thought for a moment. What was in his desk? Nothing that would get him into this much trouble. "I want you to look in the lower left-hand drawer of my desk, and fax the stuff in the file folder on top to me."

"So where are you, Paris?"

"This is serious."

"Where you at?"

Lempert turned to the kid, who was pretending to be dusting a shelf with a cloth. "Give me the fax number here."

As the sheets rolled out of the machine, the Butcher's Boy barely looked at them. He just took them out of the tray, glanced at them, folded them with one hand and stuffed them into his coat pocket. Most of the time he watched Lempert. What kept driving Lempert crazy was that the kid at the counter knew him. He was watching the proceedings out of the corner of his eye, and unless he was retarded, all this must have struck him as strange. He could probably see the lump in the Butcher's Boy's coat where he held Lempert's service revolver. But he also knew that Lempert was a cop, and naturally would assume that the Butcher's Boy was a cop too, and since cops carry guns, there was nothing strange going on at all. Anybody else would slip out the back door and dial 911. Even this kid would if it was anybody else but Lempert. Now the bastard was probably going to kill them both, walk out of here and drive away in the van. The keys were on the floor.

Finally the machine stopped grinding out pages. The Butcher's Boy said, "That's good enough. How do you usually get your money?"

Lempert knew he didn't mean his police pay. "A post-office box."

"Write it down and give it to me."

Lempert couldn't believe it. "You're really going to pay me?"

As the Butcher's Boy looked at him, Lempert could tell that he was being evaluated, and that somehow the assessment wasn't good. "I said it."

Lempert smirked. "Yeah. I heard you."

"People lie to you a lot?"

"About money? Just about everybody."

The Butcher's Boy looked at him with a mixture of pity and distaste. "Then it's your fault. You should have killed the first one."

The man was absolutely serious: *he* had killed the first one. Lempert could tell, and it had a strange effect on him. For a few minutes he had been gaining strength. He had begun to look at the hand that gripped his revolver and feel a certainty that his hand was bigger and more powerful, and just a minute ago he had begun to wonder if maybe it wasn't faster too. He had begun to visualize how he would grab it while it was still in the pocket and break it at the elbow, and his blood had started to warm in preparation for the moment. But now the other feeling had returned, the one he had felt when he had first met this man years ago. Not this time, not this man. He simply was not somebody you could do that to and have any real expectation of succeeding, because you couldn't surprise him. A dozen people must have already tried whatever he had just thought of, and all of them were dead.

Lempert wrote the post-office-box number on a piece of paper that was meant to refill the fax machine and watched the free hand pick it up and put it in the pocket with the other sheets. But then Lempert was distracted. The back door of the copying store, the one that opened onto the parking lot of the plaza, sent a glint of light in his direction. It had moved, and the reflection of the overhead fluorescents had flashed too. As he watched, he could see the reflection swinging a little, back and forth. Somebody he couldn't see had touched it. A sick feeling came over him; it was somebody testing to see if the back door was locked.

Apparently the Butcher's Boy hadn't seen it. He said, "You'll get some money in the mail in a couple of weeks. Let's go." He tossed a twenty-dollar bill on the counter where the kid could see it and moved toward the front door. Then he stopped. "Coming?"

Lempert was sweating again. Whatever happened next, he was going to be in the middle of it, standing here without a weapon or a place to hide. If it was cops, he could give a yell and dive to the floor, and they would know enough to fire. He hoped it was cops. But how the hell could it be? It must be either the wind or Puccio's men. God, he hoped it was Puccio's men. Even if they were the ones who actually got him, Lempert would share in the credit. It was only fair.

* * *

As Albert Salcone stood outside the back door, he saw Ficcio across the door from him, reaching out his hand. Salcone gasped, then realized there was no way to keep Ficcio from touching the door. He pressed himself against the back wall of the building, blew the air out of his lungs and waited. As he watched the door swing back and forth a little, he forced the hatred he felt for Ficcio to drain out of his mind. Ficcio was a kid by today's standards. In Salcone's day, by the time you were nineteen, either you were in some jungle wearing camouflage fatigues or you were in jail. Now a kid that was nineteen might not have been in a real fight in his life.

Salcone turned to Ficcio and shook his head disapprovingly. Maybe Ficcio understood. At least he looked crestfallen. Salcone hoped he was devastated, but there was no way to explain to him now why he should be. Either the door was unlocked, in which case it would offer no resistance when they moved in, or it was locked. If it was locked, then when one of them tried to get in for real, it wouldn't budge and he would have to fire through it. Either way, there was nothing lost. The one thing you didn't want to do was test it and let the occupants know you were coming.

Salcone had been planning to have Ficcio go in through the back door alone while he waited in the street at the front of the store. But that wasn't going to happen now. So much for all the cunning that had gotten them this far—Puccio's and his own.

Puccio had come up to him in the theater and told him to find out what he could about the van that had been parked in the street across from the building. He had said there was something peculiar about it, and Salcone had known Puccio long enough to forget about asking questions and get out there. When he had sneaked to the rear corner of the van a while ago, he had peered inside and seen something every bit as peculiar as Puccio had suspected, but not as ominous. It was Bob Lempert, sitting in a swivel chair like the ones bass fishermen installed in their boats so that their butts wouldn't get sore.

He had gone back inside and told Puccio that it was only Lempert, but Puccio had not been reassured; he had been puzzled. He had said in Italian, "He can't be doing that for the police department. The only reason he might is if he was pretty sure the Butcher's Boy was coming to get Paul. I told him to keep his eyes open like everybody else, but he's too lazy to sit out there all night without getting paid." He thought about it

for a moment. "You know, he's just stupid enough to have seen
something in the police reports and kept it to himself so he could
collect on the contract. Do me a favor. Go out and find a place
to keep an eye on him, where he can't see you. And take Ficcio
with you."

Salcone had responded to that with a raised eyebrow, and
Puccio had read it instantly. "I know. But you might need somebody to come in and get me, and he won't attract attention."
Then they could hear the movie starting, and it was time to
move.

Salcone had led Ficcio out the back of the theater and up the
alley to Salcone's car. He had thought about the situation for a
moment and then gone around to the trunk and pulled out the
two MAC-10's. He had shown the kid how to flip off the safety
and put it on automatic, then handed him the gun and told him
to keep it on the floor by his feet, where he wouldn't make a
mistake and take off the roof of the car with it.

Then they had driven around the block and come up the street
looking for a vantage point from which they could see whatever
it was that Lempert was watching for. But at that moment, the
van was pulling out of its parking space and moving up the
street. Salcone had followed it nearly a mile, to this store. It
wasn't until the van's doors opened that he had seen that Lempert hadn't been alone in the van. The truth was much more
startling than anything Puccio had imagined. Lempert had hired
himself out to the Butcher's Boy. He was driving the getaway
car.

Salcone had forced himself to take a moment to think about
what he had seen. It made sense for the Butcher's Boy to hire
Lempert. Lempert knew enough about Paul Cambria to know
where he would be tonight, and how to get close enough for a
shot, and probably how to get past the police afterward. Salcone
didn't have time to send the Ficcio kid back in the car to the
theater for help, and anyway, that would leave Salcone stranded
here if Lempert and the Butcher's Boy decided to leave. He
would have to kill the two of them right here.

He had brought Ficcio up to the back door of the copying
store and told him the plan. What he had neglected to tell the
boy was that when Ficcio stepped through the back door and
opened up with the MAC-10, it didn't much matter what he hit.
Salcone would be at the front of the building. By the time Salcone stepped in, either the Butcher's Boy would be dead, or he
would be busy killing Ficcio. But then, without warning, Ficcio

reached out and pushed on the door. If they had seen it, they hadn't opened fire. That meant that either they hadn't seen it, or they were on their way out the front door. Either way, Salcone couldn't afford the luxury of going around to the front. He had to move.

"All right, kid," said Salcone. "Go through the door fast as you can, stop and open fire."

"You mean now?"

"Now."

To Lempert, everything seemed to happen at once. First, he was surprised to see that the Butcher's Boy hadn't waited and made him go ahead. He pushed the front door open, and then he seemed to disappear for a second. Lempert whirled to look over his shoulder just as the back door swung inward hard, so that it banged against the wall. He recognized the two guys. One was Salcone, the guy Puccio always talked to in Italian because they came up together in some shithole in Pittsburgh that didn't even sound like it was in America; and the other was a kid they called something that sounded like Fish, who wasn't much older than the one who must have ducked behind the counter. They both held little assault weapons that looked sort of like Ingrams, although he had never seen an Ingram from this angle. In fact, from here the angle looked a little off.

Lempert's body jerked, partly in surprise because even the body feels noise somewhere in the diaphragm when two .45-caliber automatic weapons roar in an enclosed space, and partly because the .45-caliber bullets were punching through his chest, arms, neck and head.

Wolf crouched beside the door with his back to the bricks and covered his face while the machine guns blew the glass out of the front window beside his head. He knew they would be approaching the front of the building fast, to get a shot at him as he sprinted down the street.

The first one was the older man, who walked directly to the empty window frame and leaned out to see which way the prey had run. Wolf looked up at the underside of his chin and fired the revolver through it. When the man toppled forward, he still held his little MAC-10. As Wolf snatched it out of his grip, he realized he had seen the man somewhere in the old days. He leaned inside the ruined window and opened fire on the second man, who was approximately where anyone would be, squatting low beside the front door that he didn't have the guts to open.

Then Wolf dropped the MAC-10 on the body and looked at the face again. He remembered where he had seen the man; he was the one who used to keep the security people busy while Puccio stole suits off the loading docks of clothing stores in Pittsburgh. In the old days he'd had more meat on him, and looked like a longshoreman or a trucker. Now he had flecks of gray in his hair, and wore photogray glasses—sort of distinguished, like a professor. Seeing him here like this was not a pleasure. Little Norman must have failed.

As he walked to the van he kept his pace leisurely. He got into the driver's seat, picked up the keys, started the van and, as he pulled away from the curb, glanced into the copying store. From this height he could see that the kid at the cash register still was not ready to peek up over the counter. It was hard to blame him.

Wolf could feel his heart beating faster than he liked it to. What the hell was wrong with these people? They must have seen Lempert and followed the van, and then the older one had seen Wolf. Coming through the back door together like that was the tactic of losers; it was the way addicts robbed grocery stores. Then somebody had panicked or made a mistake and opened up on Lempert. Or was it even a mistake? It was as if the whole world had lost all sense of the way things were done and the way men behaved, so you couldn't even figure out what they thought they were trying to accomplish.

The words "the slaughter of the innocents" came into Wolf's mind. That had been Eddie's term for it. Presumably it was something that had happened in the Bible, but he had never looked it up. He remembered Eddie arguing with a man who was trying to collect on the same contract. It was one of the few times Eddie had ever let the boy work with colleagues, because he considered them to be competitors by nature and acquaintances only through some regrettable coincidence of geography. But this time Eddie and the boy had found a major prize. A man named Frank Basset had run a small-time burglary ring based on restaurant reservations. He had placed confederates as waiters and busboys in the best establishments, and each night they would go over the lists to see who would be at the restaurants, leaving their houses empty. If it were particularly tempting, Basset would hit the house. If a woman came in wearing diamonds, for instance, they would know that her house was worth the trouble. Eddie had sniffed as soon as he had heard this. "Well, for Christ's sake, if she's wearing them, then they're not going

to be in the house, are they?'' But that had not been the only
flaw. Wolf couldn't remember the details, except that there had
been a child and a baby-sitter in one house, and that the owner
had been a lawyer with friends who had connections. Eddie had
heard about the large, open contract at a time when he had been
feeling vulnerable.

Eddie had found Basset in a small town north of Syracuse
along Lake Ontario. It was winter, and most of the cottages near
the lake were closed. Apparently there had been some plan in
Basset's mind to go to Canada, because Wolf remembered a big
boat frozen in the ice along the shore where it had been tied up.
But when Eddie and the boy surveyed the house, Eddie had a
nasty surprise; he discovered that he and the boy were not the
only ones who had found Basset.

A man named Cathead Maloney drove past in a two-tone
Pontiac just as Eddie was peering at the target through binocu-
lars. Eddie had dragged the boy to his car, and followed. Eddie
had been so angry when he had caught up with the Pontiac on
the lake road that he had rushed to its side and flung open the
door. Then he calmed down rapidly; Cathead Maloney had three
other men with him.

Eddie had proposed that they share the danger and rewards,
and Cathead had agreed in theory to the proposal. Their arguments had come over the execution. Cathead had decided that
the way to get Basset was to wait until dark and approach the
house from the lake side, walking on the ice to surprise him.
Eddie pointed out that if a light went on, there would be six of
them standing in the middle of a featureless white backdrop that
stretched behind them at least forty miles, too empty to hide on,
too slippery to run on, and probably too thin to hold their weight
since Lake Ontario was too deep to freeze with any solidity.

Cathead responded that if the ice was thick enough to strand
a twenty-five-foot boat with a car engine in it, then it would hold
five men and a boy, and implied that anyone who passed up six-
to-one odds against a mere sneak thief, with the advantages of
darkness and surprise, didn't really want to work very much.

Eddie held his temper, although the last part had nettled him.
He countered that Frank Basset never worked alone; he'd had
three men in the restaurants and four working the houses, and
if he were alone now, he wouldn't need a twenty-five-foot boat
in the first place. From this point the discussion deteriorated,
until finally Eddie uttered his benediction. "I give up. It's all

yours, Cathead. Have a ball. It's going to be the slaughter of the innocents.''

Eddie had been right. There had been at least six very tense, alert, heavily armed men in the cottage, and Cathead Maloney and his partners had received the full benefit of their ability to find a light switch in the dark and aim a rifle afterward.

Wolf drove along Route 90, across the state line into Chicago, then pulled off the interstate. He went past a gas station, and noticed a set of three pay phones near the men's room. He glanced at his watch, then patiently wheeled around the block and pulled in beside them. He walked into the office, asked the tired young man sitting on the high stool for the key to the men's room and opened the other roll of quarters he had bought in Las Vegas. It was four-thirty in the afternoon in Las Vegas, and unless things had changed for no reason in two days, Little Norman would be in the Sands having breakfast. The efficient machine voice told him to put in more money, and he did. He asked the hotel operator to page Norman.

Seventy-five cents later, he heard the voice. ''Yeah.''

''Norman.''

''I thought I wasn't going to hear your voice again.''

''I ran into trouble. Did you do what I asked?''

''You know what that is, kid. It takes time. I started.''

''How does it look?''

''How can it look? Carl Bala lives to eat your eyeballs. The Castigliones know that if they forget that you did the old man ten years ago, they lose respect. The New York families aren't sure they can pretend that Tony T wasn't right in their back yard when you came to see him.''

''Are you giving up?''

''No, but it's a fantasy. The old men aren't like that. You chose this life. You knew what it was.''

''Norman?''

''What?''

''Tonight some people came for me. I'm going to assume that the man they worked for didn't get the message yet. It's a gesture of good faith.''

''Oh, shit, kid. They don't care about your good faith. Just run.''

''I'm running, Norman. Tell them.''

''Right. Just remember, I don't work for you. I work for them.''

Wolf hung up the phone and walked back to the van. It was

time to get out of the area. The simplest thing to do was to try to drive another twenty miles to O'Hare Airport and find a room in a small motel in the neighborhood, where there were miles of them. It was already beginning to feel like a long night.

At the cashier's counter in the Sands coffee shop, Little Norman was preoccupied. He paused for a moment before placing the telephone back on its cradle. He was watching the liquid-crystal display on the little screen that stuck up over the back of the telephone. It still held the number: (312) 555-8521. Illinois. Chicago area.

15

Wolf awoke in the big, hard bed and stared in the direction of the window. He wondered what had awakened him. The thick, opaque curtains were still drawn over the glass, so the room was dark, but at the side there was the tiny muted glow of a ray of light bouncing off the white lining of the curtain and onto the wall. It was daytime. He reached to the bedside table and held his watch close to his eyes. It was only seven-thirty A.M. It couldn't be a maid who hadn't seen the DO NOT DISTURB sign. He listened, then swallowed to clear his ears and listened again. There was no sound at all. It was almost eerie. He resigned himself to the fact that he wasn't going to sleep again. He threw off the heavy covers and felt a kind of relief at the sound of the starched sheets sliding over one another. At least he wasn't deaf.

He walked across the thick carpet to the window, pushed his index finger to the edge of the curtain and squinted to see what Rosemont, Illinois, looked like in the daytime. He started to breathe deeply in order to wake up and stop the shock before it made him slow and stupid. He stepped to the other side of the window and slowly moved the curtain a quarter of an inch. But when he looked out at the parking lot from the new angle, it was still the same. There were no cars in the lot. Last night there had been at least twenty, all in a row outside his window; now all he could see was black macadam, with the spaces marked in faded white paint. Somehow they had come in and evacuated everybody from the little motel without waking him, and now they were getting ready to move in.

Wolf dressed quickly and threw everything he had brought with him into the little suitcase. It must be the FBI. They had come in with pass keys or even called every room on the telephone to tell them to get out quietly, and in a minute they would be coming through the only door with shotguns. There would be something like a SWAT team watching the only window. He had been lucky they hadn't seen the curtain move, or there would be holes in it already.

He looked around him. There was the closet door, but there was also a sliding door on the side wall. It had to be a door to the next room, put there in case somebody wanted to turn both of them into a suite. He put his ear to it and listened. There was no sound of movement in the next room. If they were planning to come in that way, they would have it unlocked. He exerted a soft pressure on the door to see if it would budge, but it didn't.

Wolf concentrated on dismantling the standing lamp. He cut the plug and jerked the cord through the long steel pole, pocketed it, and unscrewed the bulb and receptacle. Then he forced the motel's bottle opener between the door and the jamb. Now he fitted the hollow steel pipe over the opener to extend the handle by six feet. When he pried with the long lever, the door lock gave a little groan, then popped. He slid the door open and saw an identical door on the opposite wall. Closing the one he had just come through, he headed for it.

Inside the third room, he decided it was time to try another way. He picked up a chair, tied the lamp cord around the back of it and carried it into the bathroom. Setting it in the center of the floor, he stood on it, then reached up to push the plywood hatch off the access hole to the attic. After shoving his little suitcase into the crawlspace, he reached up, grasped both sides of the cubbyhole and pulled himself up. Inside the crawlspace it was dark and dusty, and the sloping roof was only a yard above the floor of bare two-by-fours with layers of insulation between them. Here and there were wires for the light fixtures below. As soon as he had turned around on his hands and knees to face the hole again, he pulled the chair up with the lamp cord, set it aside and put the cover back on the access hole.

Wolf crawled carefully from one two-by-four to the next, at each advance setting his suitcase down ahead of him, quietly making his way down the long empty space. He could see the small louvered vent at the end of the building, and he used it as a goal.

In the hallway Cabell whispered to Sota, "Remember, anything that's alive in there is no friend of yours."

Sota grinned at the door and clicked the slide on his new

MAC-10. "Lock and load," he whispered. Sota's dumb cheerfulness was beginning to wear on Cabell. The fact that the last time he'd had a weapon in his hand he had fired point-blank into a pane of bulletproof glass at a man selling lottery tickets didn't inspire confidence.

Cabell and Sota were thieves. The difference was that Cabell knew it, and had been nervous about going along on something like this to begin with. But Sota seemed to think he was a bad-ass. Puccio had decided it was some kind of weird Mafia justice that somebody should shoot this guy with the gun that Salcone had carried when he got killed. To Cabell it was just asking for trouble, so he had given the gun to Sota, who hadn't figured out that if you found blood on a gun, it wasn't from the guy it was fired at.

Puccio was calling in lots of markers today. Landsberg was only another thief like Cabell, but he had his own crew working out of a travel agency Puccio owned. Once in a while, when a whole family sailed for Fiji or someplace, Landsberg's crew would come in with a moving van and take out everything but the plumbing. Everybody owed Paul Cambria the right to work in town, but Puccio was the guy who kept track. There were at least ten or fifteen guys around the motel right now, all of them called in the middle of the night.

Cabell kicked in the door, and when he brought his foot back to the floor he let his momentum carry him to his right and into the room, as Sota slipped in low and to the left. For a second, Sota's mind didn't allow the possibility that the room was empty. He fired a short burst into the couch, which seemed to be the only thing that wasn't where it was supposed to be. Then he rushed into the bathroom, where there was nothing to point his weapon at but a couple of wet towels draped over the shower curtain. Cabell said, "You didn't happen to slip out for a smoke while you were supposed to be watching the hall?"

"No way," Sota protested, but Cabell hadn't said it seriously. He was already checking to see if the window had been opened. He did it cautiously, without moving the curtain, so that Landsberg wouldn't get a glimpse of him from outside and put a hole in him. He looked around the room, and then saw it. "You said there wasn't but one door." He walked to the sliding door that led to the next room and studied it. There was a deep indentation beside the lock, and the wood around it had been compressed and cracked. He silently pointed to it, stepped to the side, and abruptly slid it open to allow Sota a clear shot, but Sota just stood and stared.

Cabell cautiously craned his neck to peer into the next room. It was identical to this one, and he could already see that some damage had been done to the lock on the sliding door that connected it to the third. He turned to Sota. "You go out in the hall. When I flush him, that's the way he'll go."

At the end of the attic, Wolf lifted the plywood square just enough to fit the muzzle of Little Norman's pistol. The roar of the automatic weapon a minute ago was a sure sign that somebody down there was getting jumpy. It also seemed like a reliable indication that the people down there were not from the FBI. As he looked down through the crack, he saw something he had not expected. There were a man and a woman, both about fifty, lying on the floor in the motel office. They were both on their backs, so he could recognize them as the owners, but they'd both had their throats cut. He could see that the counter drawers and cash register had been rifled.

Wolf lifted the hatch a few more inches. It was stupid. All they'd had to do was flash a badge they could have bought in any toy store and tell everybody there was a gas leak. For a moment he considered staying in the attic and waiting for his pursuers to leave, but something about the scene below made it seem foolish. They weren't going to leave. He ran a mental inventory of the contents of his small suitcase and decided there was nothing in it that would tell anyone anything about him, so he left it in the attic, then lowered himself to the top of a filing cabinet, went to the counter and began to look in the drawers.

There was no sign that the couple lived here, so there had to be a car. Finally he found the woman's purse, a large bag made out of something that looked like carpet, with wooden handles. Her key chain had a little flashlight and a whistle on it. It was sad that she would have imagined that those things would keep somebody from hurting her.

He moved toward the back door of the office. The car had to be in the back, because the lot was empty. There were only a couple of things in his favor now. One was that the only men he knew about for sure were still somewhere behind him firing automatic weapons into empty rooms, so nobody would expect him to emerge from the office. Another was that there couldn't be many people still around who knew him by sight after all these years. He glanced back at the two bodies, already half drained of blood. Of course, those people outside didn't seem much worried about killing the odd bystander. If any one of them had a functioning brain, at least some soldiers would be positioned around the motel waiting for him to break cover. He had to get them to show themselves.

He searched the other counter cabinets. What he was looking for wasn't hard to find. It was a big cardboard carton full of boxes of matchbooks printed with an idealized drawing of the motel with imaginary trees around it and the words ''Hanniver House Motel.'' He had seen the matches in all the ashtrays in his room, and the supply had to come from somewhere. He opened a box and took a couple of books out of it, then tossed half the boxes up the access hatch to the attic and poured the rest against the wall of the office that joined it to the rest of the motel. He lit the pile of boxes in the attic first, then climbed down and waited a minute until he heard a crackling noise that told him the old, dry two-by-fours were beginning to burn. Now he tossed a burning match on the pile of boxes against the wall. After a few seconds the first matchbooks ignited with a bright, sputtering, sulfurous flare. Then the whole pile seemed to go up at once in a big flame, like the afterburner on a jet, licking up the wall, peeling the paint off it and covering the upper parts with a poisonous black smoke. He backed away, keeping himself within arm's reach of the door because he wasn't sure just how fast this place was going to burn.

Cabell was preparing to kick in the door of the fifth room when a familiar sound reached his ears from a distance. It sounded like an electric smoke detector. At first he felt the special sort of anger that he reserved for people like Sota. It would be right out of Sota's repertoire to toss a burning cigarette somewhere just because there was nobody to make him pay for the damage to the carpet, and therefore no reason not to. Right now he hoped Sota was listening to the reason not to, but then a second thought occurred to him. What if the ten or twelve impatient geniuses stationed around the place had heard the gunfire a while ago, and then expected Sota and Cabell to come out? They hadn't, so those guys might have assumed that it meant they couldn't, that what they had heard was the sound of the Butcher's Boy shooting him and Sota. He thought about the ones he had known before this excursion. Some of them were thieves like him, a couple had something to do with the gambling business and three were apparently pimps. The only ones he was sure had any experience at all with this sort of thing were Puccio's own men, and where the hell they were right now was anybody's guess. The others would react to the sound of an automatic weapon the way he would—with a resolution not to enter the building hastily. But whose idea was it to burn the guy out? Well, if that was the plan, it was time he got with the program. He went to the door of the room, opened it and peered into the hallway. Sota whirled and aimed the little submachine gun in his direction, but he didn't fire.

"Jesus," said Sota. "You scared me."

"It's about time," said Cabell. "Let's get out of here."

As he glanced down the hallway to look for the most likely exit, he saw two things he didn't like. One was that black smoke started to pour out of the crack under the door of one of the rooms down the hall. It wasn't seeping out; it looked as though it were being blown out with a fan. The second thing he saw didn't look as ominous at first. On the ceiling of the hallway thirty feet from Cabell's head, a little red disk popped and fell to the carpet. Then the little brass pinwheel it had held in place started to spin. It gave a hissing, gurgling noise, and then began to spew a thick spray of muddy, rust-colored water onto the carpet. A second later the next spigot did the same. Cabell started to run, but it was too late. All along the pipeline, the spigots of the sprinkler system popped and vomited red-brown, icy water down on the hallway. The first eruption was so cold that Cabell's heart stopped and he gasped, but in an instant he and Sota were drenched. As he sloshed toward the exit, he could taste the metallic, gritty stuff, and he kept waiting for the pipe to clear itself and maybe blow the sediment off his head and out of his eyes. But he made the exit without knowing if it ever got any clearer.

As they dashed out of the main entrance and slopped onto the pavement, Cabell could see two or three other men moving away. He looked to see if any of them were running, but they all moved with the same chagrined strides that he was taking. The son of a bitch they were supposed to kill must be long gone. If he had still been here, they would have heard him laughing.

Wolf finished ripping the woman's dress off her bloody, lifeless body. He slipped the wet rag over his clothes and cinched it together with her dead companion's belt, rolled his pant legs up over his knees, then pulled a little tablecloth that had "Chicago" embroidered on it off the counter, folded it, threw it over his head and tied it under his chin like a scarf. The torn, blood-stained dress covered his clothes, and if nobody got too close, he might make it the five yards to the car.

The only one out there who would be positive the woman couldn't be dragging herself out of the burning building to drive herself to the emergency room was the one who had brought the knife across her throat. If any of the others were still around the motel, with all the noise and smoke attracting police and fire-men and gawkers, they weren't likely to open up on anything wearing a bloody dress. He just had to hope the one with the knife was gone.

As he slipped the bolt on the back door of the office, he had a brief attack of irrational reluctance. There was something hor-rible about the possibility of dying in this bizarre costume. But he reminded himself that he didn't know any way of dying that wasn't horrible, and if they got him, it wouldn't much matter what he looked like. He swung the door open and bent over to cross the open space as quickly as possible.

Wolf slipped into the old Ford station wagon, started it and pulled away from the back of the motel slowly. There was a car parked across the drive, but nobody seemed to be in it, so he pulled around it and bumped across the lawn and onto the high-way. When he saw the fire engines coming toward him, he pulled over to let them pass, but after that, he felt it was probably safe to get into the left lane and give the car its last hard ride. It was probably only good for about a half-hour drive, and after he abandoned it, the heirs would undoubtedly junk it.

"I love you," said Elizabeth.

"I know," said Jimmy. He was cheerful about it, and he seemed to mean it, but she wanted him to say, "I love you too," and he didn't seem to think this response was appropriate from somebody who was already four and on his way out the door to catch his ride.

"Be good."

"Okay," he said, then stepped out the door and ran down the steps toward the van. She watched him climb up the big step and pivot to sit down hard on the bench seat in the back. They grew up so fast. No, it wasn't growing up; it was growing away—becoming a separate person.

Elizabeth spotted Amanda crawling across the floor toward the pole lamp. As she approached it, she was like a soldier in a movie scrambling up the last few yards of a beach under fire.

Her little legs pumped so fast that her knees slipped out from under her and she made a premature grab for the pole. Elizabeth closed the front door and got there in time to hold the lamp upright as Amanda lifted her body, hand over hand, up to a standing position. She looked pleased and proud as she stared up at the bulb, her little face containing a hint of the explorer planting a flag on a peak, as well as a hint of the escaped felon. She had made it in time to keep her mother from stopping her. "Up, up, up so tall," said Elizabeth helplessly.

It was a simple matter to hold the pole firmly while Amanda bent her knees and bobbed up and down in an attempt to dislodge it and topple it over. "Careful, baby girl. That's not a good game." Elizabeth acknowledged that she should have stored it in the garage with the glass coffee table months ago. Maybe tonight, when she had gotten into her jeans and sweatshirt, she could face that corner of the garage. Jim used to do that sort of thing. A lot of the stuff in there was just where he had put it a year ago, and it would probably stay there forever. She wasn't very good at getting rid of things.

Elizabeth heard Maria open the door behind her and then hang her purse on the doorknob. "Hello, Maria," she said. "Say hello to Maria, Amanda. Say, 'Hi, Maria! How's it going?' "

Maria moved into the living room. "I'm here, little Amanda," she said. "I missed you so much. I wanted to come back just as soon as the sun came up. I said, 'Where's my little Amanda? I better get dressed quick and run to the car.' " This was to tell Elizabeth that she knew she was late, and that nothing was wrong. "Now we better say bye-bye to Mama." This was to tell Elizabeth that she was dismissed.

Maria snatched up Amanda and carried her to the door for the ceremony. Elizabeth kissed the baby's incredibly smooth little cheek, and Amanda's fat little chin started to quiver, her eyes filled with tears and she began to cry the lament of the forsaken. Elizabeth said, "I'll be back before you know it. I love you," and the tiny, uncomprehending victim held her arms out in a final plea as her mother slipped out the door. For some stupid reason, this morning she could feel tears forming in her own eyes as she hurried down the steps toward the garage. She knew that the stupid reason was that her period was going to start, and that a lot of unnecessary hormones were coursing through her and making her feel weepy. But at the same time she also didn't know it, because even though it always happened, and had since she was thirteen, each time it was as though such a reaction had never occurred before. Because what she was feeling was as real as any other feeling at any other time, and maybe it was, after all, the true reaction. Maybe the difference was that at other times she had the strength to keep herself from seeing things clearly.

As she started the car, she thought again that it was probably going to begin giving her trouble unless she found time to get it into the shop for maintenance this week. Maybe Thursday, so it would be okay again by Friday and they wouldn't have any excuse to keep it over the weekend. This morning everything seemed to be overdue and about to fall apart.

As Elizabeth drove into the city, she made a point of looking at the trees. She had read in a doctor's column in a magazine that looking at trees was a cure for stress. It had something to do with focusing one's eyes on faraway objects, and something to do with the color of the leaves. But the same column had said that a cure for depression was looking at the light in the sky just before the sun came up. She hadn't missed a day at that in one year and two weeks.

Elizabeth found herself in the Organized Crime office earlier than expected. Maybe looking at trees was a cure for slow driving. She sat down at her desk and saw with sadness that someone had taken the time to provide her with an "In" box. She didn't want an "In" box, so now she would have to spend some time trying to find out who had done such a thoughtful thing and then try to keep from hurting her feelings.

Elizabeth had learned years ago that analysis had to do with taking the flow of information that moved through the bureaucracy and preventing it from moving in its normal way through the old channels. Sometimes she collected tidbits and left them lying around for weeks until they made sense, and sometimes she merely scanned the printouts and knew that there was nothing in them but distractions. If you had an "In" box and an "Out" box, you were treating information the way it was meant to be treated, which was the wrong way. The system put you here to process paper, but you had to resist the system in order to make it work.

She put her purse in the "In" box so that nobody would deliver anything there, and walked to the communication room to look at the night's reports. As she entered, she saw a copy of the NCIC entry lying on the desk. Something had been added to the bottom of it: "Information concerning the suspect: Attention E. V. Waring, Department of Justice, Washington, D.C., as Agent in Charge.''

Wolf sat by himself in the back of the diner in the Chicago railroad station and looked at the pile of folded papers. If they had not been about him, he wouldn't have had any idea what they said. As he had thought, Charles Ackerman had been burned for all time: the paper referred to him as ''AKA Charles Ackerman, AKA the Butcher's Boy, real name UNK.'' They had tagged him with Tony Talarese for sure, but said they also wanted him for questioning about Peter Mantino and Angelo Fratelli. So Little Norman had been right about the wire on Talarese. That had brought the FBI in right away, and then somebody there had told them who he was.

Still, the physical-description part didn't seem to fit this theory. Hair color, eye color, height, weight: all UNK. If somebody had recognized him, what the hell had they used—smell? What it sounded like was that they had heard about his identity from somebody who didn't know he was telling them. They must have picked it up from the wiretap. If they had put a wire on Talarese, they would have tapped his phones too.

In one way it was reassuring; they didn't seem to know anything about him at all—where he was, what he looked like, what he was doing. In about four other ways, it was starting to scare the hell out of him. The reason he was stuck in the United States in the first place was that somehow they had managed to figure out he was using the Charles Ackerman passport, then had shut down an airport three thousand miles away in time to keep him from using it again. Maybe they had shut down every airport in the country with one phone call. He had no way of knowing how they did things, or whether there was any practical limit to what they could do.

In the old days he hadn't spent much time worrying about the police. He had thought about them only when he was actually doing a job. If he managed to get through it without making too much noise, leaving fingerprints or getting himself hurt, he stopped thinking about them at all. It didn't take much thought to stay out of their way; once you got out of the water, you could probably stop worrying about getting bitten by a fish.

He wanted to stop worrying about the FBI. He thought about going to Mexico. He could certainly get across the border, but what then? He didn't know anybody in Mexico, and the Mafia must have lots of people there to keep an eye on its drug interests. It was a fairly obvious place for him to go into hiding, so they would be looking for him, with fewer chances of missing him. Even if he could buy a passport there that would get him into England, it wouldn't do him much good. The British customs man would ask him a question in Spanish, and he wouldn't understand it.

He could get into Canada with even less strain. A Canadian passport would be perfect, but the setup there had always been worse than in Mexico. The Mafia had established footholds all along the border during Prohibition in order to bring in liquor. Even before that, a lot of the old Mustache Petes had gotten into the United States by signing up for a wheat harvest in Manitoba or someplace and walking across the invisible line. It was hard to know what the Mob controlled there, but one thing they were sure to have a corner on was forged passports. He kept remembering the computer scanner that Immigration had used on his passport at Kennedy. He needed a real passport or he was going to be stopped. And unless he got out of the country soon, there was no question that he was going to die. The way he had survived in the past was by quick retaliation. The hand would move in his direction, and he'd sting it, and it would hesitate long enough to let him disappear. It still worked, too, except for the part about disappearing.

It wasn't the Mafia that was keeping him in the fire; it was the damned FBI. But he was overlooking something. Organizations didn't *do* anything; it was some person in charge, some human intelligence that was working on him. He looked at the sheets of paper again. On the last one was "Attention E. V. Waring, Department of Justice, Washington, D.C., as Agent in Charge."

Wolf finished his coffee and walked out into the cavernous train station. The place was not just wide but vertically immense, in a way that buildings constructed now could never be unless they were designed to shield some sport from the weather. The ceiling must have been seventy or eighty feet above him, and they could have held a cattle drive through the waiting area without taking up more than a third of the marble floor. These places had seemed archaic to him when he was a child, remnants of some richer time when there was more stone and wood and leather in the world, and more time to think about what things looked like. In the old days these places were always noisy with the echoes of feet, luggage carts, yelling and amplified announcements, but for some reason he couldn't remember ever hearing a train. Now the station still echoed, but the sound of his shoes on the marble was all he heard as he walked to the one ticket window that wasn't boarded up and bought a ticket to Washington, D.C.

Elizabeth looked at the list she had made before falling asleep last night. The way to keep the cost down was to get in touch with the people who already were paid to watch things and give them something specific to look for. If she was right about what was happening, he was running; that meant small motels, cars fraudulently rented or stolen, bogus identification and credit cards and paying cash for merchandise anybody else would buy with a check. These were details that gave him a chance to make a mistake. If he did, he might come to the attention of a police department somewhere. All she could do was to send out circulars to introduce the possibility that the next time it could be him.

It was essential to keep the Butcher's Boy from getting out of the country as long as she could. If he had survived for ten years with Carlo Balacontano screaming for his head, then he must have lived someplace where Carlo Balacontano's voice wasn't very loud. She had made a formal request to the State Department to examine new passport applications for male Caucasians aged thirty to forty-five with extreme care, checking independently at least two of the statements or supporting documents supplied. It might not turn him up, but it would delay the processing, which might keep him here a little longer. This had brought a strange inquiry from the CIA, but the questions they had asked had been about McCarron, the man who had been found dead with Fratelli in Buffalo. Maybe he was a former agent or something. Whatever their interest was, it couldn't hurt.

The main thing was to keep trying. If every policeman in every department asked his informants about the Butcher's Boy, and every person who watched airports and steamships and provided passports and rented cars kept alert, somebody just might notice him. The most depressing thing about it was that the only way she was going to recognize him was if he did something, and what he would have to do to identify himself was to kill someone else.

Elizabeth started to move her eyes down the list again, but now Richardson was standing over her desk. "You know what I think is going on?" he asked. "I think this is a cleansing ritual."

"What are you talking about?"

"Who was Tony Talarese? He was about forty-five years old, a capo at the time of his life when he should have been out there scrambling. But what was he doing? He wore fancy clothes, spent lots of money, had a house that Al Capone would have thought was too ostentatious. But the main thing was, he was corrupt. He'd been schtupping the waitresses in his brother's restaurant, the wives of at least two of his soldiers and his brother's wife's niece, which in those old-time families is incest. But most of all, he'd been robbing his boss while he was in prison, and he was wearing a wire for the FBI. Think about it."

Elizabeth rested her head on her fist. "Okay, I'm thinking about it. What conclusion am I supposed to be reaching?"

Richardson frowned and churned his hand in the air to conjure the next example. "Peter Mantino. He was about the same age. He'd been in charge of the western operations for a while. Was he in Las Vegas robbing the suckers? No. Was he in L.A. cutting into the drug trade? No. Was he in Portland or Seattle trying to organize the ports? No. He lived in Santa Fe like a retired homosexual art dealer. He did nothing to increase his family's stake in the richest, fastest-growing region in the country. He was lazy and corrupt."

Elizabeth squinted her eyes and tilted her head to look up at Richardson. "It's been a long time since you actually prosecuted a case, hasn't it? I mean in front of a jury."

"Angelo Fratelli." Richardson stopped for a moment. "You're not buying this, are you?"

"Go on, Angelo Fratelli," she prompted. "Corrupt."

"What I'm getting at is this. We suddenly get three killings, at least two of them done by a very special professional exterminator. Forget everything else we think we know about him. In fact, forget him completely. One correspondence that we seem to have overlooked is that these three people were lousy specimens, and that raises the possibility that their deaths were purchased by reformers."

"What sort of reformers were you thinking of?"

"Two kinds come to mind. One is the old men at the top—the last generation, who came to power before World War Two. They see that the next generation has grown up into a bunch of slobs, and they don't like it. They decide, in effect, to replace all of middle management."

"Okay," said Elizabeth. "That's possible. But you said two kinds."

"The other one is conservatives."

"Somebody out there who's older than the old men?"

"In a way. An ultra-neoconservative movement."

"This is something you know about, or are you making it up?"

"A little of each. You've got the generation that's coming up now, in their twenties and thirties. All over the world—in the Middle East, in Europe, in this country—you have a big stampede toward the past. Every last one of them is dirt-ignorant, and more conservative than their great-grandmothers. Why should the Mafia be immune?"

"No reason that I know of. So what would these people be after?"

"Power. They're old enough now to have seen a little action and done some dirty work. When they see the degenerate jerks who are in charge they become instant reformers."

"Okay, then what?"

"They get in touch with a hit man."

Elizabeth thought about this for a moment. "No, I don't think so. That's not the way it works."

"What do you mean?"

"Reformers have to pull the trigger themselves. If they think the generation that's in power is fat and lazy, they have to prove that they themselves are not by killing them personally. I can see the old dons hiring some messenger to go out and clean house, but I can't see a revolution by proxy."

Richardson paused. "No," he said. "I guess I can't either. What are the other alternatives?"

"I don't know," said Elizabeth. "I can't prove that the lieutenant in Buffalo was wrong. It makes perfect sense that with Carl Bala in jail, somebody might kill his caretakers and take over his holdings. And what you were saying about the three victims makes it seem more likely. If you have a business with terrific potential but inefficient management, you have unfriendly takeovers, right?"

"Okay, let's start with what we know. Tony T was killed by the Butcher's Boy. He waltzed in there alone and flew out on the next flight. Is that how you'd do an unfriendly takeover?"

Elizabeth shrugged. "It wouldn't be a bad start. You hire somebody who's supposed to be the most efficient and reliable at that kind of work but who has no known connection with you. He spends a couple of days decapitating the hierarchy and disappears again. That leaves the field clear, with Carlo Balacontano locked in jail, his lieutenants dead and his troops presumably in disarray.''

''Is that what's happened?''

''I don't think so, but if the information we've been treating as factual is accurate, then it's possible.''

''You mean we still haven't started at zero? We have to go back further?''

''I'm just saying that we shouldn't get too attached to our facts. We both listened to the tape recording of Tony T getting killed. He says, 'You?' Big bang, lots of screaming and scuffling. Then Mrs. T says, 'He's wearing a wire!' Nobody says, 'Hey, wasn't that the Butcher's Boy?' or words to that effect. Not on the tape, when they were alone. Only Mrs. T says it later, and what she says is that her brother-in-law told her, but she'd never seen the man before in her life.''

''Why would either of them lie?''

''I don't think they did. But do you remember what it was like ten years ago? When Dominic Palermo came to me in the middle of the night looking for protection, he told me all this stuff about a hired killer. He'd never seen him, just heard about him. The people who were talking about him just referred to him as the Butcher's Boy. What if there is no such person? What if it's just a name for a whole lot of men who have done murders for money? Nobody knows who it was, so it all gets attributed to somebody whose exploits are, by this time, mostly imaginary like Buffalo Bill's, or maybe even attributed to a completely imaginary person, like Paul Bunyan.''

''You're leaving out the best evidence we have—Carlo Balacontano. He told you about him.''

''He told me that the Butcher's Boy was the man who really committed the crime he's spending his life in prison for. I mentioned him first.''

''But you believed him.''

''I still do. I think Carlo Balacontano was framed for the murder of Arthur Fieldston, and I think this department was so eager to put him away that people forgot to ask a lot of questions they were being paid to ask.''

''Did you say anything at the time?''

''You mean you didn't hear? I said it until everybody got tired of listening, and then I said it again until they decided I wasn't a team player. That's what got me my vacation in Europe.''

''No . . .'' Richardson looked genuinely shocked. Elizabeth couldn't tell whether he was lying, but how could he not be? He had been here in those days. "I thought . . . They said you'd just sort of burned out, because of the killings . . ."

She wondered if he was figuring out the rest of it, and hoped he wasn't. He had at least the right to assume that he had his job because he had earned it, and not because all the competition had turned it down. "It's not as bad as it sounds," she said. "I did all right. Jim came over and joined me there, and that's how I got him to marry me."

Richardson accepted the escape route gratefully. "Really? That sounds romantic."

"Oh, Jim was a romantic guy." She smiled.

But she could already see Richardson's youngest analyst hurrying toward them with the morning's list of disasters. He followed her eyes and saw her too. "Lana," he said. "What have you got?"

"I'm not sure," she said. She glanced at Elizabeth, and seemed to wonder if she should acknowledge that she knew the older woman was somehow above her in the department, so she said, "I wondered if one of you had time to look at this." She laid the printout on Elizabeth's desk, and hovered while Elizabeth and Richardson read it.

Elizabeth saw the inconsistency almost instantly. "Salcone, Albert, 42. Ficcio, Daniel, 19. Lempert, Robert, 53." *Sergeant* Lempert, Robert. A police officer. Lempert and Ficcio both shot numerous times with an Ingram MAC-10. Salcone shot with Sergeant Lempert's service revolver. But a witness says Salcone and Ficcio both had MAC-10's, and they came in together and killed Lempert and another man.

"What is this?" asked Richardson. "Where is this?"

"Gary, Indiana," said Lana.

"We've got one too many dead people," said Elizabeth. "Or one too few."

Jack Hamp stepped up to the yellow cordon of police tape and waited for one of the patrolmen to meet his steady gaze. Ducking under the tape to enter the area and then flashing an ID only after somebody stopped him wasn't a good idea at this particular crime scene. Somebody *would* stop him, and it might be a more vivid experience than he was in the mood for right now. Policemen didn't much like letting strangers in when a fellow officer was shot down. They protected each other from having a photographer come in and put the picture in the newspapers. When an officer was shot, they made sure all the papers got to run was a formal portrait of the man in his uniform, usually taken about the time he graduated from the academy.

The man Hamp had been staring at seemed to feel the heat on the back of his neck, turned and strolled toward Hamp, who held out his identification wallet so that the policeman could take it into his hand. "Jack Hamp, Justice Department," he said. "I'd like to come in and look around."

The policeman handed it back to him and said, "Suit yourself." Hamp let this reverberate in his mind as he slipped under the tape and walked to the front of the store. It wasn't right. It didn't tell him what was going on, but it wasn't right. If they were eager to accept federal help, the policeman would have taken him to the ranking officer on the scene and introduced him. If they were still shaken by having one of their own killed and were operating on the herd instinct, he would have brought the head man out to the tape to talk to Hamp. But this man had done neither.

Before Hamp reached the broken window he could see the destruction inside. Automatic weapons at close range made more hits than misses and spread a lot of blood around. The floor and walls of the store made a horrible first impression.

Hamp didn't have any trouble spotting the captain; he was the only one around who didn't look as though he'd had to pay attention to the fitness regulations. He approached the man warily. "Jack Hamp, Justice Department." The captain saw his hand but didn't shake it, so he added, "Sorry about Sergeant Lempert."

The captain looked at him, then looked away. He didn't say, "Yeah, he was a good man," or, "We'll get the bastard who did it." All he did say was, "What can I do for you?"

This told Hamp that what he could see right now was about all he was going to see. But that was all right, because looking at dead men didn't tell you as much as looking at the ones who were still alive.

16

Wolf was only a little surprised after he had looked through every telephone book the Washington public library had and still couldn't find a listing for anybody named E. V. Waring. There were lots of Warings in the books, but no E.V. He supposed it wasn't unusual for somebody who worked for the Justice Department on cases like this not to want his address printed out where everybody could read it. But it was the Department of Motor Vehicles that really surprised him. He paid his ten bucks, filled out the department's form at the long, stand-up writing table, waited for three hours and finally was told that E. V. Waring didn't have a vehicle registered to him. This was more peculiar, but Waring was listed on the NCIC printout as "Agent in Charge," so maybe he had a government car. Still, this was starting to feel like somebody who actually went to some trouble to keep out of sight after the office closed at night.

Wolf was experiencing a sense of increasing uneasiness. Waring had to be the one who was making it hard for him to get out of the country; Waring had figured out his escape route and blocked it within hours. He was also careful enough to keep himself from being found easily, and this was the part that was worrisome. Wolf could find anyone. If he wanted to, he could start going through lists at the county clerk's office to find the house Waring undoubtedly owned, or pay the credit bureau for a credit report, or use any of a hundred other lists that solid citizens couldn't help getting their names on. But all of these took time.

On his second day in Washington, he took a bus to Georgetown University. He walked around the fringes of the campus until he found a stationery store that looked as though the owner had been around long enough to be trustworthy, and was prosperous enough to stay. He picked out a folding leather notebook cover of the sort that he had seen people who worked in law offices use for notes. He ordered the engraving on the leather, then picked out the paper for it and selected a serious, businesslike typeface for the printing.

By afternoon Elizabeth had decided that she liked Lana. It was such an odd name for a woman her age. It was a relic of the fifties, and she had to admit that Lana must have been born in the late sixties. But Lana had found another anomaly, so Elizabeth forced herself to think about it.

This time it had happened right inside Cook County. It was a small motel, and the couple who owned it had been murdered. But either before that or afterward, several heavily armed men claiming to be police officers had gone from room to room just before dawn, telling everyone to leave because they had cornered a fugitive in the building. Then they had gone through the place breaking in all the doors, and ended by burning it down. Or maybe they had opened the doors to make the fire move faster. The police had already declared the fire an arson to cover up the murder of the proprietors when they got a call from one of the motel guests who was in a phone booth in Springfield and was curious to know if they had caught the fugitive. A second call came from Carbondale, and that guest wanted to know if the police were going to refund part of his room rental, since he had been forced to leave a full eight hours before checkout time.

Elizabeth picked up the telephone and dialed the number of Jack Hamp's motel room in Chicago for the third time, listened to six rings and then set it down again. It was infuriating to know that he was practically on the scene, and she couldn't even tell him it had happened. Finally she took the report and started to walk toward Richardson's office, then realized that she was walking alone. She stopped and turned. "Come on, Lana."

Lana hesitated, then caught up with her. "I don't usually just pop in," she said, and then gave a nervous, apologetic laugh.

"He's not doing anything more important than this," said Elizabeth.

"What have you got?" Richardson asked as they entered.

"We're not sure," said Elizabeth. "What I think we've got is several men trying to burn him out of a motel near O'Hare. I'm not sure who that would be. It's Castiglione territory."

"Maybe Paul Cambria's men," said Richardson. "I've been

trying to sort out the one from yesterday. The night the cop and the two guys with machine guns got killed, Paul Cambria was at a public function in Gary, maybe a mile from the spot. The local cops think he might have been trying to establish an alibi.''

"A mile from the place where his men were going to shoot someone? An alibi should have some distance . . ."

"More likely, our friend was trying to get Paul Cambria. I'm not sure where the cop fits in."

But Elizabeth was racing ahead. "And he missed. Or somebody saw him. Anyway, something went wrong, and they followed him to Chicago, or knew where he was going to stay, and . . ." she stopped.

"What's wrong?" asked Richardson.

"The cop. You're right. Sergeant Lempert. He doesn't fit in, does he? Maybe he's what went wrong."

Richardson was getting excited now. "Maybe he's the reason the Butcher's Boy couldn't get Cambria. Lempert saw him near Cambria doing something suspicious, and chased him."

"For a mile? Alone?" asked Elizabeth.

"Followed him, then. Kept him under surveillance. Only he wasn't the only one. But wait. The only reason the two soldiers with machine guns would kill Lempert is if he were with the Butcher's Boy, and they couldn't just wait until he left. Which means he must have actually arrested the Butcher's Boy."

Lana said, "I don't follow—"

Elizabeth said, "I do, but I don't buy it."

Richardson spoke faster now as his scenario became clearer and more obvious. "The cop and the Butcher's Boy are in the same store. A Xerox copying business, which probably means the Butcher's Boy ducked in there to evade capture because there's nothing else he could conceivably want in a place like that. The other two wouldn't shoot a cop unless they had to. The only reason they would is if he was going to take the Butcher's Boy away to someplace where they couldn't reach him. And where's that, except the police station?"

"But, then, how . . ." said Lana, and stopped.

"How what?"

"Well," Elizabeth said quietly, "they usually handcuff a person with his hands behind his back. But what you're saying is that the Butcher's Boy got out of the handcuffs, took the policeman's gun and shot somebody who couldn't hit him first with a machine gun."

"You're right," said Richardson. "I got carried away."

Elizabeth nodded. "He can do that to you."

"And we're not even sure he was the one," said Lana.

"But if he was," Richardson said, "then you've got to take my hypothesis seriously. There's no vendetta against Balacontano that could include Fratelli in Buffalo and Cambria in Gary."

"I already take it seriously," said Elizabeth.

"You do?"

"Sure. I was making a mistake. What I was doing was putting myself in his body, saying, 'What would I do if—?' and that's the wrong approach. In the first place, we don't have enough information that we can be sure is true, and so we can't build a theory that's based on it. In the second place, he *wouldn't* do what I'd do. Or rather I wouldn't do what he does: that's a better way of saying it because it's a proposition I can prove, and it means the same thing in the end. We don't know what he feels, or if he has any sensations that we would recognize as feelings, so we can't build a theory on that. All we can do is try to figure out what would be the smartest thing for him to do, because that's pure logic, and catch him while he's trying to do it."

Elizabeth saw that Lana had slipped away, and turned to see where she had gone. She was outside in the hallway talking to a deliveryman.

"Is she any good?" asked Richardson.

"Didn't you hire her?"

"Not really. The system hired her. She was in the pool of applicants and had the best school record. When she came in for an interview she was wearing clean clothes and showed no symptom of mental illness, so I would have had to make a written argument to hire anybody else."

"Nicely put," said Elizabeth. "I think she's smart. Eventually she's probably going to figure out that she's wasting her time here and do a lateral transfer."

Lana signed the man's clipboard and came back with a wrapped package. "It's for you, Elizabeth."

"Thanks." She put the package under her arm.

"Aren't you going to open it?" asked Richardson.

"Weren't we in the middle of something?"

"Open it."

The other two watched while Elizabeth looked for a return address, then tore the brown paper off and opened the plain white box. Inside was a leather folder with gold leaf that said "E. V. Waring." When she opened it, she saw the stationery with the heading "E. V. Waring" on it. "I didn't order this," she said.

"Maybe it's a present," said Lana.

"Is there a card?" asked Richardson.

"There's an envelope for one, but nothing inside. See?"

"What a shame," said Lana. "It's beautiful."

Richardson said his version of the same thing. "It cost a lot of money. English glove leather, engraved vellum. It adds up quick."

"What am I going to do?" asked Elizabeth.

"What do you mean?"

"Somebody sends you an expensive present for no reason at all, and you don't have any idea who did it . . ."

She noticed that Lana was at her desk talking into the telephone. Of course. The messenger. He would know who had paid for the delivery, or at least the name of the store. There must be paperwork because Lana had signed for it. At least her brain was working, even if Elizabeth's wasn't.

The phone on her desk rang and she snatched it up. "Waring."

"Hi, Elizabeth."

"Jack, I've been trying to call you about—"

"About the fire in the motel. I just heard all about it on the police radio."

"Police radio? Where are you?"

"Gary. I've been talking to the cops at the copying store. I figured you might be looking for me and thought I'd better call you."

Elizabeth's mind strained in two directions at once. First things first. Find out what Jack knows. "Good. We've been trying to work it out. There's something missing, so it still doesn't make sense. This Sergeant Lempert—"

"He's what I'm calling about," said Hamp. "What I'm about to tell you doesn't get written down on paper. It's an impression, a kind of instinct. I don't want to have to fly to Washington and try to prove it, okay?"

"If you say so."

"Lempert was dirty. Watching the cops going over the scene a little while ago, I got the feeling they didn't think much of him. It's just a feeling, and I don't have time to go into it real deep, but he was dirty."

Elizabeth groaned.

"What?"

"Nothing. It's just that it so obviously fits, and it's the one thing that never crossed my mind. I mean it did, but I kept pushing it out because it didn't lead anywhere. It didn't take me to the next step. Except that what I was doing was assuming I was the one who got to say what the next step was. That's stupid." There was a pause, and now her voice betrayed annoyance. "If the police knew, why didn't they tell anybody?"

"It's hard to say what they knew or when they found out. But they're ashamed, which means that they're sure. No matter how you look at it, they don't get anything out of telling somebody like me."

Elizabeth was already exploring this new terrain. "If the sergeant was taking money from somebody, it wouldn't have been our friend. There's nothing we know about him that would lead us to the conclusion that he'd have a corrupt policeman on the payroll. So who would? The local Mafia. And that explains why we have three bodies lying in a copying store: They were all on the same side. The only one that's missing is the winner. Though I'd love to know what he won."

"Another wake-up, and that's about all. The next morning he's in a motel outside Chicago and they tried to kill him there too."

"So what did he want in Gary in the first place?"

"I know what I'd want if I were in his place. I'd want a way out. Maybe he thought Lempert could do it for him. People who can be bought once can be bought again, and cops meet a lot of people who can do a lot of things."

"And Lempert arranged an ambush?"

"That sounds about right."

"Where are you going next, back to Chicago?"

"Yeah, he's long gone but I thought I'd go rake through the ashes like everybody else. If we're lucky, I might be able to talk to somebody who knows something."

"Jack?"

"What?"

"This is kind of . . . embarrassing, but did you send anything to me at the office?"

"No. What's embarrassing about that?"

"Well, it's a present. It just came, and the card got lost, and . . . you see what I mean."

"You didn't open it, did you?"

"Sure, why?"

"Forget it. I was going to tell you to call the bomb squad, but if it hasn't exploded yet, I guess it must be from a secret admirer.''

"I guess so."

"It ain't me, though. I've never laid eyes on you. You might be ugly."

"Good-bye, Jack."

It was after six when Elizabeth finished going through the supplemental reports from the Gary police, the Cook County sheriff and the Chicago Fire Department, and then pulling the files on Salcone and Ficcio. There was no question from the rap sheets that Salcone had worked for the Cambria family most of his life, and if Ficcio was carrying an identical weapon and entered the shop with him, then he must have too. But no matter how she put it all together, it still didn't tell her exactly what had happened. She put away the papers and prepared to go home.

Now that she was alone in the office, without the unnerving sensation that somebody could overhear her thoughts by looking at her, she allowed herself to admit the truth. If she set aside the ugliness of what had happened, and thought of it as an event in the Butcher's Boy's personal history, the last two reports were promising. Whatever he was trying to do, he was getting himself into deeper trouble. Now he was being hunted by the Mob in Gary, and more ominously in Chicago, the territory of the huge, powerful Castiglione syndicate. He would understand better than she did what this meant. He was still alive, but the chance of his seeing the end of the month was virtually nonexistent. As long as he survived, each day it became more difficult for him to move freely, and eventually he would realize that he couldn't do it anymore. Years ago she had spent months looking at windows he might have touched, or carpets he might have walked on, talking to people who might have seen him, always arriving after he had left, never getting closer than a few hours behind him. But pretty soon now he was going to have to walk into a police station somewhere. He would have to come to her, if only he could stay alive long enough to realize it.

She almost forgot to take the leather folder with her when she left the office. At home she was going to hold the paper up to the light and try to read the water mark to see if she could find some store that sold that kind of paper. Lana's inquiry to the delivery service had yielded an order number that helped them to locate a copy of a receipt that said only "Cash" and Elizabeth's name and office address.

It wasn't as though she had a lot of friends who might suddenly send her an expensive present. She corrected herself. When she had begun making tactful inquiries this afternoon, she had run through six of them. Then she had forced herself to call Don Yeter, who had been one of Jim's friends in the old days. Since a few weeks after Jim had died, Don had shown an interest in her that made her nervous and a little queasy, and she was relieved when she realized that he had no idea what she was talking about.

She had left the present in the white box and even retrieved the paper wrapping from the wastebasket, because either might help. Ten minutes after it arrived she had begun wishing the gift hadn't found its way to her, and now she was beginning to resent the giver. She spent enough of her life trying to decipher puzzles, and the best she could hope for at the end of this one was to get an address for a thank-you note.

When she reached her car it was already looking lonely in this part of the lot. As she unlocked the door, she remembered that it was Thursday and that she still hadn't taken it to the garage for its rejuvenation treatment. She felt guilty, and as she settled herself in the driver's seat the feeling escalated to regret. But when the engine started she forgot about it; all that was important now was to get home to the kids.

Wolf watched the woman pull the little green car out of the parking lot and into position for a right turn onto the street. Even though there was nobody behind her, and nobody across from her, and anyone coming down the road could see that her only choices were to turn right or rise into the air like a dirigible, she had her turn signal blinking. She was E. V. Waring, without a doubt. There was no particular reason to switch the signal on, but no particular reason not to, and it made more sense to use up one ten-thousandth of the life of a forty-cent bulb than to surprise a pedestrian she hadn't seen. The engraving should have said, "E. V. Waring, No Fool."

As he pulled out after her, he wondered if she had fallen for the stationery after all. It could be a trap. She could lead him out into some spot in rural Maryland where forty FBI agents were waiting to drop on him like an avalanche. He had made sure the gift was something engraved with the name so that E. V. Waring couldn't give it to his secretary, but he hadn't considered the sophistication of logic that E. V. Waring might command; suppose she had figured out why he had sent it. But

Waring—Miss or Mrs. Waring—was careful and methodical. If it was a setup, there would be at least one car behind him. He kept glancing in the rearview mirror as he drove, but no car stayed long enough to worry him. He concentrated on keeping one vehicle between her car and his so that she couldn't get a clear view of him for long.

He followed her to a quiet street in Alexandria. There were tall trees and a lot of two-story houses built in the fifties by upscale couples with identical taste. He could have called hers the white one, except that he could have said the same about most of the houses on the street. All of them had some form of brick facing. When she pulled into the driveway, he considered lingering to get a closer look at her. But a glance up the street revealed cars in all the driveways and lights on in the front windows, so there was too much chance of being noticed. He drifted past.

Wolf turned at the next corner and cruised up the street behind hers. The houses there were almost the same. He tried to assess what he had gained from the time he had spent locating E. V. Waring. Well, for one thing, he had stayed out of sight and given the old men some time to think about the value of peace of mind. For another, he had probably forced the FBI to use up a lot of the money it was allocating to pay its grunts overtime to watch airport departure gates. But E. V. Waring herself was going to take more thought. Miss Waring wouldn't pay the freight to live in a neighborhood like this, in one of these four-bedroom houses, but Mrs. Something would. Also, the car she had been driving had been Japanese, so it couldn't have been issued by the United States government without starting a riot in Detroit. That meant it was registered in another name, probably her husband's. Suddenly it occurred to him that he had fallen about as far as he was likely to go. He was probably going to be reduced to popping a suburban housewife with a deer rifle some morning when she opened the front door to pick up her paper in a pair of fuzzy slippers and a housecoat. The Sport of Kings.

Two days later Elizabeth gave up on the stationery. The paper was made by one of the largest manufacturers in the country, and the engraving, the manager of one of the stores told her, could have been done by anybody in the business, on the premises, in about an hour. The leather folder was impressive to his professional eye, but since it was stamped with a famous French trademark, it could hardly be traced without a great deal of difficulty. Elizabeth felt guilty using the folder, but since she had gone to so much trouble, she decided she had earned it.

On that same day she learned that she had a new neighbor. There was something annoying about having Maria be the one to tell her because a few months earlier she had told Elizabeth that the Bakers were having loud arguments. "They're going to get the divorce," she had pronounced with the air of a gypsy fortune-teller. Elizabeth had said she didn't think so. Then, when the divorce was still in the stage where the opposing lawyers were bluffing each other about assets, Maria had said, "She's going to take the house." Elizabeth was more wary this time, and merely asked, "How do you know?" and Maria had answered, "The house is important to a woman," as though her employer had just arrived from Jupiter. Sure enough, a few weeks later Brad Baker's car was gone and Ellen was planting tulips in the front yard. Then, only a few days ago, Maria had announced that Ellen Baker would move out soon. "She was a fool and took the house," she said. "The money was what she needed. Money doesn't make you weep when you see it."

Elizabeth never saw the rental sign go up, and never saw it go down. All she saw was the man. He wasn't anybody she would have noticed except that he was living across the street from her, and therefore couldn't be ignored. He was of average height and build, about five feet ten or eleven, in his late thirties or early forties, and he had light brown hair that she decided had probably been blond when he was a child. When she looked at him across the distance provided by the width of the street and their two little front lawns, she had to admit that he seemed unremarkable enough to share the general characteristics of a whole physical subgroup of men she'd known, including—there was no way to keep this thought from emerging—her own dead husband, Jim. He wore sport coats that seemed to fit him and ties with subdued patterns, didn't carry his keys on his belt, have a wallet with a chain attached to it or wear shoes with noticeable heels, so he was probably all right. She was secretly pleased that he left for work every morning when she did because it meant that she didn't have to rely on Maria for a description. She waited a few days for Maria to tell her he was taking drugs or bringing prostitutes into Ellen Baker's house during his lunch hour, but he hadn't stimulated Maria's interest, and Elizabeth forgot about him.

* * *

Alexandria wasn't a bad place to be while he waited for things to sort themselves out. It was important to stay away from the parts of the Washington area that were likely to be full of people who worked for Jerry Vico. Unless things had changed in ten years, they would be out in force looking for just about anybody who was alone, just in case they could take something from him or sell him something. But Alexandria didn't seem to be that kind of place. He slept in a quiet residential neighborhood, then put on respectable clothes and left each morning at the time when the people who lived there left for work. He timed his departure to coincide with E. V. Waring's. It was a risk, but he decided that it was more of a risk to be invisible and therefore inexplicable.

Eddie had taught him this method when he was a kid. He had called it turkey hunting. "Everybody thinks turkeys are stupid, because all they ever see is the fat-ass domesticated Butterball kind. But the wild ones are scrawny, tough and smart. They live in the woods and only come out into clearings they know to peck around, and then they go back into the woods. If they see anything that's different, they don't come out at all. So what you do is this. Wait until maybe midsummer. Then you take a broomstick and saw it off to about forty-eight inches. You paint it black and go out in the woods to a good clearing. You prop it against a log at a thirty- or forty-degree angle and then go away for a couple of months. The first day of the season you get up in the middle of the night, go out to the clearing and lay your shotgun right where the broom handle was. When the sun comes up, the turkeys peek into the clearing, see your gun, think it's the broom handle and walk right in front of it. It's the only way to get them."

Eddie had bagged Otto Corrigan that way. He had closed the butcher shop for a month and moved into a house in Cincinnati right next door to Corrigan's with the boy. The month that followed stuck in Wolf's memory as one endless sunny afternoon with the smell of grass and trees and the buzz of seventeen-year locusts. Eddie had him working on the lawn, and trimming the shrubs and planting flowers, tomatoes and radishes all day long while he himself performed less strenuous chores that Wolf could no longer remember in detail. It didn't matter what either of them did as long as they were visible in the yard. Corrigan was supposed to be a lawyer, but he had only one client, and instead of a secretary or a clerk, he had four big guys in his house who looked like defensive linemen. He almost never went out, and the four guys made sure no one ever came close. By the end of the month, Corrigan and his four bodyguards were so accustomed to the sight of their next-door neighbors that on the last afternoon, when Eddie and the boy came for them, they appeared not to notice.

But Wolf had not needed to rent the house across the street from E. V. Waring to kill her. There was nobody protecting her, and unless she was carrying a firearm in her briefcase, she didn't appear to be capable of protecting herself. He had taken the risk because he wasn't sure that what he wanted was to kill E. V. Waring. Now that he had found her, he wanted to stay close enough to watch her. Once he had gotten past the first moments, when his instinct for self-preservation had prompted him to get rid of her as simply and quickly as possible, he had begun to let his imagination work on her. The only thing he wanted now was to get past whatever barriers she had erected to keep him from disappearing, and killing her probably wouldn't help. But it was just conceivable that there was some way of finding out what those barriers were: who was looking where, and what they were looking for. The solution to his problem might be as simple as reading some papers in her briefcase, but probably it wasn't.

There were a couple of things about E. V. Waring that gave Wolf something to think about. She had kids. One was a little boy who got picked up in a van that had the name of a private school written on it. The other was a baby who was walked around the block every day in a stroller by a baby-sitter who went home at night. He never saw a husband, although he spent all of one day and night watching for him to show himself. A couple of days later the mailman arrived just after the maid and the baby went out, so he went across the street and pretended to knock on the door, but used the gesture to cover his other hand's movement into the mailbox to pluck out the letters. He scanned the envelopes, and saw that about a third were addressed to Elizabeth Waring, and that the others were for Mrs. E. Hart, Elizabeth Hart or Occupant. Since a couple of them were utility bills, he decided that there was no husband to worry about.

He began to wonder if the easiness of it was making him complacent. The more he studied her and thought about her, the less impatient he was to do anything about her. He could take her off anytime he wanted to, but as long as he didn't need to make a move, there was nothing for E. V. Waring, Department of Justice, to interpret. She couldn't do him any harm unless he made some ripples on the surface. The time for her to die was the day he was ready to leave.

Carlo Balacontano was playing gin with the Mexican counterfeiter. As he laid down the nine of clubs he watched the man's left arm and saw the tattooed scrollwork on his bicep move a little. He wondered if this was the sign. For years Bala had been studying parts of the hundred-dollar bill the maniac had tattooed on himself to see if he could discover a nervous twitch. But the nine of clubs didn't attract Ospina. He moved his left arm to scratch an itch on his face, then drew a card from the pile.

Carl Bala hated losing more than he hated death. He was an old man now, sixty-six, but life in the prison had allowed him no vices. He ate plain, nutritious food, breathed clean, dry air and was forced into the moderate exercise of cleaning one of the outbuildings each day. He knew he was living a life that was much like his grandfather's in the mountains of Sicily, and would probably last the same 104 years. Death was still a remote prospect, but losing was a daily experience.

The tattooed Mexican grinned at him, laid down his hand in a fan and said, ''Gin.'' Balacontano looked at the ten cards with distaste. The wily little bastard hadn't even been collecting clubs; he had picked up the eight just to make four eights. Bala forced a smile and wrote down the thirty-six still in his hand. The horror of it was that he didn't see a way for it to end. Ospina would probably leave here in a few years, but he was so crazy that he would be rolling out hundreds in a basement in L.A. as soon as he'd had a decent meal. How hard was it to catch a counterfeiter with a green Benjamin Franklin on his belly and ''Federal Reserve Note'' on his chest? So he would be back, this time with a longer sentence.

For some time Bala had been quietly nourishing a hope. The visit from that woman had raised a distinct possibility. He wouldn't be the first one to have secretly cut a deal with the authorities and been rewarded for it. He had attained a high position in life by developing a shrewdness about people, and he was sure that Elizabeth Waring had believed him. She hadn't believed Bala's necessary disclaimers, but she *had* believed the part that was true. There really *was* a Butcher's Boy, and he really *had* set up Carlo Balacontano for a killing he himself had committed, and that sure as hell ought to be enough for an appeal or a pardon.

In a little while Bala was going to have another visitor. This

one was a second surprise. He was coming as an emissary from
the old men. This pleased Bala enormously. To the outside world,
he was one of the old men, but not to the old men; to them he
had always been a kind of younger brother. He was powerful
and controlled a lot of bodies and a lot of territory, but when he
had started having his troubles he was only in his fifties. He had
never had time to get white hair and sit on the Commission
demonstrating his wisdom. Now they were sending somebody
to consult him about an important matter. Maybe he had spent
so much time in prison that people had begun to think of him
as older and more important than he was, like that guy Nelson
Mandela in Africa. But he doubted it; it was more likely that
something was going on out there. They had heard something
about his pardon coming up and wanted to make the effort now
to keep on his good side. Maybe they would even imply that
they had done something to bring about his release, although he
knew different.

He saw the guard coming for him from a hundred feet away.
They always looked around at other people as they made their
way across the yard, but the man's eyes kept coming back to
him. Bala stopped shuffling the cards and stood up. He noticed
that Ospina didn't seem disappointed. He was confident that
Carl Bala would be back, that the endless gin game would continue and that by the time he took his next vacation in the world
he would be another million points ahead. But Carlo Balacontano just might have a surprise for him.

Bala held his arms up and submitted to the pat-down. The
guards had never been particularly thorough with him because
they knew that a man like Bala didn't need to carry a homemade
knife for protection, and that if he felt a sudden urge to harm
somebody, he wouldn't do it himself in a waiting room. They
only did what the prison regulations required them to do, then
guided him out the door and turned him loose in the pen.

He looked along the fence and saw his visitor immediately. It
was Little Norman. He was disappointed and insulted. What the
hell were they doing sending that giant black Mau Mau son of
a bitch? What kind of emissary was that? Then it occurred to
him that although Little Norman might not be an important
person, he wouldn't be a bad choice if you wanted somebody
killed without a struggle. His head spun first to the right, over
his shoulder, and then to the left. If the guards had suddenly
disappeared, he was going to try to make it to the fence. They
were there, though, still looking bored, but alert enough to look

up. He stood where he was and let Little Norman take a couple of long strides to him.

"Mr. Balacontano," said Little Norman. "I don't know if you remember me."

"How the hell could anybody forget you?" said Carl Bala. "You lose five pounds or something?"

Little Norman chuckled deep inside his chest. "I guess I do have that kind of face."

"Why did they send you?"

"A few days ago the Butcher's Boy came to see me."

"What for?"

"He wanted me to talk to the old men for him. I talked to some of them, and they said I had to come and tell you."

"What did he want from them?"

"He says the only reason he did Tony T was because Talarese sent people after him. Then he did Mantino and Fratelli because they were trying to keep him from getting out afterward."

"Good. I thought they were worthless, but now I'm sorry they're dead—Mantino and Fratelli, anyway." He looked up at Little Norman with his hard little eyes. "At least they didn't come around and try to cut a deal for him."

Little Norman shook his head. "You can play that on me if you want to. By the time I knew he was around, the most I could have done about it was make him kill me. And I did what he asked because I wasn't going to be the one who decided on his own not to deliver a message to the old men."

Carl Bala shrugged. "You could live a long time. So they sent you to me."

"They want to know what you think about it after all these years. He says he'll disappear forever if you all leave him alone. If you don't he seems to think he can make some trouble."

Carlo Balacontano straightened to his full five feet eight inches and began to walk. His face was cold and impassive. It was a feeling he had not experienced since 1951, when he had been hit a glancing blow with a baseball bat in a bar in upstate New York. The man who had hit him had been one of his own soldiers, a big guy named Copella, who was smashing a jukebox, and the bat had bounced off the metal top and into the forehead of Carl Bala. This had been the occasion of a profusion of apologies, and Bala had felt the same terrible frustration. He couldn't kill Copella for the clumsy accident or his other soldiers would have turned on him, and he couldn't betray how much it hurt or how angry he was because he would have looked weak. But he

had never liked Copella after that, and the man had been forced
to seek advancement in Portland, where there was more room
to swing a bat.

What Carl Bala wanted to say was that if any of the old men
ordered their soldiers to leave this psycho alone, what was it but
giving aid and comfort to his enemy? If anybody held back now,
they wouldn't have to worry about some lone maniac slipping
arsenic into their milk of magnesia. He would send an army to
batter down the walls of their houses, drag them into the street
and hack their heads off with hatchets. But he couldn't say this.
In the first place, saying it to Little Norman was about as satis-
fying as telling the mailman that you were going to write a nasty
letter. In the second place, if he said it, they would kill him in
jail. Still, it did make something he'd had floating around in the
back of his mind push its way to the front of it. He was going
to get out of here, and when he did there was going to be a war.
Apparently the old men had gotten so old that their balls had
shriveled up like dried figs. He was going to get out of here and
roll them up one by one.

What Carl Bala said was, "I'm trying to be reasonable about
this. I've been in here for eight years because of this man. I
asked before the trial that my friends and associates do their best
to help me. I got no help. I asked that they make this man pay
for what he did to me. I was told that nobody could find him.
Now he's back, and he's killed Mantino and Talarese because
they were mine, and Fratelli because he helped me. What am I
supposed to say—that it's all right?"

Little Norman towered silently above Balacontano as he
walked along, a half-step behind and to his left.

"Tell them I repeat my respectful request that this man be
found and his body turned over to my people in New York."

"Yes, sir," said Little Norman. "I'll tell them that. Anything
else I should say?" It was common knowledge that somewhere
in New York there was a safe-deposit box full of things that
Balacontano's men had lifted from the house of the man he was
convicted of killing. The key was going to be planted on the
body of the Butcher's Boy.

Balacontano wasn't really listening. He was thinking about
how soft and weak the old men must have gotten. It would be
easy. With a little probing he could find two or three at the
beginning who would probably let him take over just for leaving

them alive. Then he would be that much stronger when he was ready to face the ones who still had a little blood in their veins.

He realized that Little Norman was waiting for him to say something. "You can go now. I'm in the middle of a gin game."

17

Wolf watched the small green Mazda back out of the driveway across the street, and then walked out his front door
in time to be seen. He didn't want to let her see his face too
often, just to be somewhere near the edges of her peripheral
vision and consciousness as the man who lived across the street.

He would have preferred to rent a car, but he didn't have the
kind of identification that companies felt comfortable with, and
so he had bought this one for cash at a used-car lot in Virginia
Beach. It was about as far from Washington as he could conve-
niently get and still have Virginia plates. These transactions were
always delicate. If you walked into a Mercedes showroom and
handed them eighty thousand in cash, you had better be able to
convince somebody that you were a lovable millionaire. The car
had to be a beater, so the amount wasn't huge. The best way to
do it was to find a place small enough so that you could talk to
the owner. If the man had just taken something as a trade-in that
he wasn't particularly fond of, cash could be attractive. He
wouldn't have a price he had to get back, and once the car was
off the lot, he could put any figure he wanted down in his books.
But for Wolf's purposes, the car had to be right. He ended up
with an '83 Dodge Colt that hadn't even been put out on the line
with the others yet, because they hadn't had time to spot-paint
the nicks on the doors and roll back the odometer. It was plain,
unassuming and unmemorable, and it ran well enough. It was
a little below the scale for his new neighborhood, but not so
much that it attracted attention. He started it, backed out of his
driveway and had shifted into first before he caught something
in his rearview mirror: Elizabeth Waring's Mazda wasn't moving.

As Wolf let the car drift forward, he steered it so that his rearview mirror would show him what was going on. The Mazda was stalled, and she was walking quickly toward the back of his car, waving her arms. It was too late, and the appeal was too blatant, to drive off and pretend that he didn't see her. In the mirror she seemed to be staring right into his eyes, which meant she must have seen him move his head to spot her. He had to pretend he had seen her all along.

Wolf stopped, backed up until his car was in front of hers, then got out and talked to her over the roof of his Colt. "Hi. I see you've got troubles. Anything I can do to help?"

Elizabeth Waring threw up her arms, her brows knitted in despair. "Anything. It just died."

Wolf turned off his engine and walked to her car. It was unbelievable that he had let this happen to him. He went over it in his mind. He had seen her come out of her house, turn to wave to the Spanish maid and the baby and walk to the garage. Then he had put on his coat and checked the doors of his rented house. If she'd had any trouble starting the Mazda, that's when it must have happened, because when he had returned to look out the window again, she was already backing out of her driveway. Then he had stopped looking.

He reached under her dashboard and popped the hood, then went around, lifted it and looked at the engine for any obvious sign of trouble. If he could just get the damned thing going before she had time to get bored with her trouble and start looking at his face, he might be able to get through this. Nothing under the hood was disconnected or leaking, but everything looked a little grimy for a car this age. He walked back to the driver's side, slid in and tried to start the car. He heard the ignition click, but the starter motor didn't engage, and he smelled gas.

He got out again. "Your carburetor got flooded and your battery gave out—not necessarily in that order. Do you have jumper cables?"

Elizabeth seemed to be thinking about something else. "Look," she said. "I know you've got to get to work. Thanks for trying, but I'll just call a gas station."

Wolf decided he had better look at his watch before answering, and he did so. "It's no problem. Honestly, I don't have to be there for another hour."

But she persisted. "No, it's not right. I'm not one of those women who just assume that any man who happens to be within screaming distance is there to be used. Or at least I don't want to be.''

"It just takes a minute," he said. "It's not hard or dirty or anything. We'll just see if we can get it started. Have you got cables?''

"Yes," she said. "They're in the trunk."

He pulled her keys from the ignition, opened her trunk and surveyed the mess. There were toys, a child's car seat, a whole package of diapers that looked about the size of a bale of hay, a couple of umbrellas and, at the bottom, a pair of jumper cables whose plastic wrapping was still intact. He unraveled them, hooked the alligator clips to her battery terminals and then turned his car around. When the two cars were nose-to-nose, he unlatched his own hood, connected the cables to his own battery terminals and restarted his car. "Okay," he said, handing her the keys. "Try it."

The car started immediately, but as he disconnected the cables, he could hear that the Mazda wasn't running evenly. It sounded as though the cylinders weren't all firing. He closed the hood and said, "You got a garage you can take it to?"

"Yes," she answered. "I take it this means it isn't healed."

"That's right. I can get the heart to beat, but it takes a mechanic to get it off life support. Tell me where it is and I'll follow you in case it stalls."

"That's all right," she said, and this time she looked worried. "The only reason this happened is that I kept putting off taking it in. I'm guilty."

"So buy it a new wax job and apologize. If you stall out in a major intersection you're liable to get hammered."

"I'd have to be pretty unlucky to have it happen at an intersection."

Wolf shook his head. "They only stall when you slow down, and you only do that when you're coming to a corner."

She seemed to see a vision of it, like a premonition. "It's on Millwood. The corner of Millwood and Fanshawe."

"See you there," he said, and walked back to his car. This was going to change everything.

In an hour Wolf was watching her walk through the doorway of the Justice Department. He pulled away from the curb and drove down Constitution Avenue toward the Federal Triangle. This morning he was on his way to look for tourists. There was no use kidding himself: every day that he spent in the United States was making it more dangerous for him. He would have to see if he could find a British citizen and separate him from the herd. If he got the right one and hid the body well enough, it might be weeks before his relatives made enough noise to get the authorities to do anything about putting him on a list, and by then Michael Schaeffer would be sitting at home again.

He felt a strange reluctance to get out this way, and he weighed and examined the feeling. If he'd had to explain it to somebody he would have had to say that he wasn't in the mood to do the work. He felt tired. Eddie had always said that if it didn't feel right, it wasn't. It had been Eddie's theory that some little part of the subconscious mind had caught a danger signal—maybe seen something, or figured out a flaw, or even smelled something it didn't like—but hadn't yet been able to formulate it into a package the conscious mind would accept. Eddie always said that ninety percent of the brain was never used. Actually, in his case it had probably been more. He had once had himself hypnotized by a dentist because he couldn't remember any of the words to "Annie Had a Baby" except ". . . his name was sunny Jim. She put him in the bathtub to see if he could swim."

But Wolf wasn't nervous. He was just tired. He had spent most of the last ten years hoping that he would never have to do this kind of thing again, but here he was, up to his armpits in blood and not even working, just hunting for some harmless stranger so that he could live long enough to get home. He drove into the city with the rest of the world and looked for a place to park that Vico hadn't bought simply for the chance to have his people slip a slim-jim into the door and pop the locks.

Paul Martillo was in a lousy mood because people treated him like dirt. He wasn't some chump; he was a registered lobbyist. He wore tailored suits and fine silk ties, and talked to congressmen and even cabinet officers on business involving the limits of civil rights and the responsible exercise of free speech by the electronic media. He represented a confederation of reputable organizations, notably the Italian-American Anti-Libel League, Citizens for Fair Reporting, and the Dorothea Gorro Scholarship Foundation, named after a dead olive-oil heiress but subscribed to by many fine people who were still alive.

Martillo had just left the office of a congressman from New Jersey named Ameroy. He had been told by the congressman's secretary that he should wait in the outer office and that Ameroy would see him as soon as he got off the phone. Ameroy had kept him waiting two hours, and then, as soon as he had gotten into the private office, the man had started to look at his watch. In fact, before he even shook hands with him, Ameroy was looking at his watch. Martillo hadn't invented the system. It wasn't his fault that it cost four or five million dollars to run for Congress. The ambitious jerks had dug their own hole, each time they ran for office putting a little more into the campaign, getting themselves on television a little more often. All that Martillo did was go among them and try to make friends. Then he would make a list of the friends and turn the list over to the groups he represented. When it was time for congressmen to run for reelection, the friends were not forgotten.

This making of friends was not a clandestine activity. It was a growing profession engaged in by about twenty thousand people. There was no corporation of any size, no charity, no union, no city that didn't have somebody like Paul Martillo on the Hill; so where did a two-bit hack politician who ran for office because he couldn't make it as a lawyer get off treating him like he was still a bag man making his way around Detroit for Toscanzio? The answer was that somebody had told Ameroy what Martillo was going around talking about this week.

Martillo hadn't liked bringing it up any more than the congressman had liked hearing it, but he had to say it, and Ameroy damned well had to listen to it, because they were both taking their money from the same place. Ameroy didn't want to have anybody say anything specific in his presence, so Martillo had to play the stupid kid's game too. He did it because it meant that Ameroy wanted to be able to continue to take the money. Martillo had said that the members of the organizations Martillo represented continued to be pleased that Ameroy was a leader in the fight for equal justice, so of course he would be interested in the strange case of a man imprisoned for murder on the flimsiest kind of circumstantial evidence just because he was a well-known and prosperous businessman of Italian descent. The man in question continued, in fact, to be a large contributor to the Dorothea Gorro Foundation in spite of the fact that he had been in a federal prison for eight years. This was how his case had come to the attention of the Foundation, which, as the congressman knew, was nominally dedicated to the promotion of parochial education.

What it came down to was that Victor Toscanzio had ordered Martillo to go around and pull some strings. On the face of it this was an odd thing for him to do, but Toscanzio was not a frivolous man, so if he was doing it, Balacontano must have offered him something substantial. The whole lobbying business was something Toscanzio ran for the old men. It wasn't his to jeopardize on some whim, and he knew it. But he also had a reputation for incredible luck. Only a few old paisans like Martillo knew what kind of luck it was. Toscanzio had the uncanny gift of sensing when a change was going to take place, and getting in before the bell rang. Carl Bala was obviously an active commodity again. Also there were the rumors. From time to time people had said that Carl Bala had gone crazy in prison, and maybe Toscanzio had decided it was going to be important soon to be one of the people who had tried hard to get him out.

Martillo didn't have any objection to letting his fate ride on Toscanzio's bet, whatever it was. He had done pretty well so far. Now he was in his black Lincoln Town Car on his way to have a lunch briefing from a senator from Florida. This was the kind of holdup that was getting to be increasingly popular, and he resented it. The bastards would send out invitations to go to lunch at a thousand dollars a plate, and there would be maybe forty or fifty lobbyists paying to sit there and listen to the windbag talk about what his committee was doing to help the ivory-billed woodpecker. It was an attempt to extort money, and it worked up to a point. Most of the lobbyists had some interest they had to protect from the sudden indifference of an incumbent senator. Martillo almost felt sorry for them. His organizations didn't have a bunch of jobs to protect, or even any real members, only about twenty anonymous donors, so today's lunch was going to be a little different for the senator. If he didn't find a way to spend a few minutes alone with Martillo, he was going to watch two million bucks walk out of his campaign fund and into the challenger's.

Martillo looked out the window of the car as his driver pulled away from the Sam Rayburn Office Building. As usual, the first twenty tourists in line for the tour were Japs. The movement of capital in the world was still a miracle to Martillo, although he had studied it for twenty years the way a bear studies bee swarms. Everything seemed to be the same as it always had been; it was just that there was all this floating money. It was qualitatively different from regular money, which stayed pretty much where you put it. This was like gambling money because it didn't seem to really belong to anybody. It moved in and out of the markets and financial centers of the world in huge quantities every day.

But without warning the floating money had transferred itself out of the country and into the markets of foreigners, primarily towel-heads, Japs and Krauts. At the moment the Japanese were the big spenders, but what they were spending wasn't the floating money. It was a kind of by-product of having so much of the floating money trapped in one place for a time. It was like the wetness that formed on the outside of an icy glass on a hot day.

This reminded Martillo that what he really wanted right now was a drink. Making the rounds would have been easier if he had been able to loosen his tongue a little. But this was out of the question; you didn't just gulp down alcohol when you were on an errand for Vincent Toscanzio. When you were done with work, you could drink yourself into a stupor, or shoot heroin into your jugular if you felt like it, but while you were on his business you were his. In the old days he had once seen Toscanzio explain this to a numbers runner with a sawed-off pool cue.

Stuck in traffic, Martillo watched another busload of tourists forming a new line to wander through the halls of the Capitol building. This group looked like Europeans. Why the hell did any of these people care about looking at another public building? You could take them to an insurance company and tell them it was the Supreme Court. He looked at their faces and watched the way they walked. Foreigners walked different, and he studied them to see if he could figure out where they came from. This bunch was taller than most, very white and they had bad teeth, so they were probably English.

But then Martillo saw something that made the skin on his arms tighten, and his right foot try to stomp an imaginary brake on the floor of the car. "Pull over," he said. "Let me out." It was *him*. He couldn't imagine what the hell he would be doing standing in line with a bunch of Limey tourists, but it was worth his life to find out. "Use the car phone to call Mr. Vico. I need five, ten guys right here as fast as he can get them, and maybe four cars."

Wolf moved with the queue of English couples gathering for a mass invasion of the Capitol building. There didn't seem to be any of the usual ill-behaved British children in short pants chasing each other in circles, which was promising. Children had preternaturally sharp senses, and they lived at the three-foot level, where anything he did would be right in front of their eyes. He had to move slowly enough to keep from spooking the herd, but quickly enough so that he wouldn't give any of its members the uneasy feeling that he was being stalked. He tried to get a sense of who was carrying what. If they had all left their valuables inside suitcases in the keeping of the bus driver, he had better know it now. As he passed a couple in their late forties, he heard the woman say, "Not again."

The man said peevishly, "It's not my fault. It's the damned water. I'm sure there'll be one inside the tube station over there."

The Englishman started a purposeful march away from the herd, his long, skinny legs straight and stiff as he headed for the subway station. Wolf had been wrong when he had told himself that killing E. V. Waring was as far as he could skid; the real end of the line was when you were following a sick tourist to a public restroom so that you could whack him for his wallet and passport. He had walked in the same direction that the herd of tourists was moving so that he could come up behind them; now he was going to have to reverse directions without letting any of them notice. He waited a few moments, until what he did wouldn't be connected with the man's departure, then turned and crossed the street.

Wolf timed the cars and dodged between two of them to make it to the other side. But as he reached the curb he wasn't thinking about the British tourist anymore, but about the man who had gotten out of a black Lincoln behind him, then pivoted and reversed directions when he had. It was a rare advantage to be able to walk along facing the man who had been following him. The man was tall and trim, but not young, and the dark suit he wore appeared to be the regulation uniform of lawyers and politicians in this town when they weren't playing golf. The fact that his hair was long and wavy didn't mean anything; it could belong to the director of the FBI. He had the build of a cop, but somehow Wolf couldn't see the suit as belonging to one. Also, the shoes were wrong; they were some sort of thin, bumpy leather like alligator, and too pointed for a cop's. The soles were thin and slippery, and the heels gave off a shine when the man walked, as though they were made of a substance harder than rubber. As Wolf proceeded down the street, he never took his eyes off the man. He knew that if there were others, he would never see them unless the man did something to acknowledge them. But then the man did something unexpected: He slowed down, turned and glanced over his shoulder directly at Wolf.

When their eyes met, Wolf saw the alarm in the man's face. Immediately the man pretended to look past him, but he must

have known it was too late. The face was familiar. It took Wolf
a few seconds to bring it back because it was buried somewhere
deep in his memory, in Chicago or somewhere—no, it was Detroit. It was Pauly the Bag Man. His throat tightened in a feeling
of regret and disappointment that was like pain. He had been
very young in Detroit, maybe nineteen, and he had let them use
his face for a few months. If somebody didn't pay his nut one
week, the next week he would be in his store or on his way
home from the office, trying to think of something to tell Pauly
the Bag Man, but the one who showed up to ask him about it
wasn't the friendly Pauly, but the boy. He would simply arrive
quietly and give the man an inquiring look. People knew who
he was, and told each other things that made them sweat when
they saw him.

What the hell was Pauly the Bag Man doing in Washington,
D.C., wearing a tailored suit and women's shoes? They must
have closed the bars and chased out everybody who had ever
laid eyes on him in the old days. Hell, they must have dredged
the lake for corpses. He had to get out of this man's sight. He
looked for a way to disappear, but the sheer size of the lawns
and the sidewalks, like airport runways leading up to broad,
high steps, made it hard to imagine how he was going to do it.
He could see for a mile in any direction. He hadn't been expecting to do anything chancy here, just to find a tourist and
wait until he was alone. He kept walking toward the subway
entrance. If he could make it that far, he could probably step
onto the first train before somebody like Pauly the Bag Man
overcame his natural caution and followed.

As he walked, Pauly walked along on the other side of the
street a few paces ahead. It puzzled Wolf that he would do this.
Could he possibly imagine that Wolf hadn't spotted him? He
resisted the temptation to reach into his coat to touch the reassuring weight and solidity of Little Norman's pistol. Pauly
wouldn't try to take him out on his own, which meant that there
must be others somewhere in the stream of people walking along
the sidewalks. But as he thought about it, he decided that if there
really were others, Pauly wouldn't be here at all. The man was
hanging around to see where he went, which meant that there
was going to be somebody he could tell. Somebody was on the
way, and Pauly must be expecting him to arrive soon. Directions
wouldn't work if they were an hour old. He walked along the
broad avenue knowing that each step was taking him into some
kind of ambush. People were on the way, and when they got

here, Pauly would see them and he wouldn't. When enough of them had gotten into position, Pauly would stop walking, turn and point his finger.

Wolf was beginning to feel hot, and his heart began to pound in his chest as he thought about it. He had made a decision a long time ago that he wasn't going to let something like this happen to him. His jaw tightened and started to chew on nothing. He wasn't going to walk along like some loser who was preparing to defend himself. They still didn't get it, and it still astonished him. He wasn't going to lie down and wait until they took their turn before he took his. He watched Pauly stroll along the sidewalk across the street from him and started to drift toward him.

Wolf was at the curb, then a second later he was in the traffic, slipping into the backstream of one car and out of the lane before the next one arrived. He made it to the double white line in the middle before something about the sound of the cars changed enough to make Pauly turn his head. When he did, Wolf could see his eyes widen. His hands came up and a nervous tremor started to grip him. His head shook so hard that he seemed to be nodding. He was already backing away, and he almost fell as he turned to break into a run.

Pauly the Bag Man was over fifty years old and hadn't needed to run from anyone since the February night in 1972 when the brain of a man named Fritz Hinckel short-circuited in Pastorelli's Family Restaurant, and that time it hadn't been personal. Pauly had been just one of fifty or sixty people whom Hinckel was trying to stick with a steak knife, and he had only needed to run five or six steps before an anonymous diner dropped Hinckel with five shots from a Colt Cobra that happened to be part of his evening wear. Pauly was long-legged, but his muscles were slack and slow from riding in the Town Car, and the leather soles of the new three-hundred-dollar shoes he was wearing hadn't been scraped against anything but floor wax and carpeting until a few minutes ago. He was still striving to attain what he hoped was sufficient speed when he began to hear the Butcher's Boy's footsteps.

Pauly kept his head up and elongated his strides, pumping his arms and hitting the pavement with the balls of his feet like a quarter-miler. He had a terrible sense that the Butcher's Boy was about to put a bullet into his spine, and that he wasn't going to hear it first. There would be a horrible, wrenching pain, and then he would be down, but the lower part of his body would

already be limp and dead. Or maybe the top part. Why not the
top part? Just because you never heard about—

Wolf watched Pauly offering a credible imitation of a sprint
as he abandoned the concrete and headed out across the wide
green lawn. He could see that Pauly wasn't running toward anything or anybody, which meant that nobody had arrived yet. He
was simply a one-man stampede, like a man running from a
hornet's nest. There was no point in going after him. Wolf didn't
slow down; he merely changed directions. Where Pauly had
veered to the right onto the lawn, he turned to the left, darted
across the street again and sidestepped into the crowd. In a
second he was walking in the other direction.

He joined a group of men and women who were walking up
the steps of the first big building he came to. He put on the same
bored, resigned expression they all wore. The sign said HEALTH
AND HUMAN SERVICES, so he stayed with them. He was reasonably confident that he wasn't about to stroll into the beam of a
metal detector. As soon as he was inside the doorway, he looked
back out the glass door at Independence Avenue and saw a car
pull up near the spot where the tourists had assembled in front
of the Rayburn Building. Three doors opened, three men got
out and the car pulled away. As the three men stood on the
sidewalk, each of them made a slow 360-degree turn, then picked
a favorite point on the horizon and stared at it.

Wolf turned and moved deeper into the hallway. He walked
until he came to a corridor that turned off toward Fourth Street,
and stayed on it until he could see another, smaller entrance.
He ignored the people to the right and left of him, and never
paused to look inside an open door. But then without warning a
woman coming toward him looked up from a file she was carrying and gave him a perfunctory smile. It was only then that
he realized he had been smiling too.

He paused and looked out at the street before going through
the door, but there seemed to be nobody out there whom Pauly
the Bag Man would ask for if he needed help, so he set off down
Fourth Street with his head down and his legs matching the pace
of the busy civil servants around him. He was going to have to
make it to the car after all. There was no telling what Pauly the
Bag Man was doing in Washington, but the three men on Independence Avenue must belong to Vico. If Vico thought he
had a reason to send three men to stand around in sight of the
Capitol scanning the crowd for somebody to kill, he wouldn't
be shy about sending twenty more. Wolf had to get out of here.

The car was in the garage at the Gateway Tour Center on Fourth and E streets. It was only a couple of blocks, but there was no way to get there except by the sidewalk, and nothing to hide him but the bodies of the other people walking the street. They were a mixed group. The ones who looked like college students or lawyers were in a hurry, moving along in both directions without letting their eyes rest on the ones that looked like derelicts, even when they had to weave a course among them. The ones who complicated the mixture most were in pairs, most of them elderly and from East Jesus, Kentucky, or Marrowbone, Texas, stopping without warning to give the Capitol a proprietary survey or to study the grass on the lawn to see if their employees had given it the proper dose of fertilizer. Each time they did so, one of the quick ones had to do a strange little dance to get around them without stepping on their heels. Wolf did his best to imitate the quick ones.

He was in trouble now. Vico was a scavenger. He had come up in the forties with the Castigliones, and been sent off to Washington to see what he could do about cashing in on the war-surplus business. A lot of Castiglione people had been in the army and seen the unimaginably huge hoards of every known commodity that had been built up in four years, and somebody had been curious enough to wonder what was going to happen to all of it later. The idea had been that a man with a supply of cash could probably pick up some useful stuff cheap. Vico had been the man with the cash, and he had found that it went a long way. He had bought up gigantic lots consisting of everything from unassembled motorcycles packed in oil to leather bridles for a cavalry that didn't exist anymore to tinned K rations so cheap that he could make money opening them up just to salvage the cigarettes inside. From then on, the story went, he had been the organization's man in Washington.

Wolf hadn't even been born then, and by the time he ran into Vico, Washington had been sewn up. The capital was a huge place that had hundreds of thousands of people getting paid for producing nothing. All day and night trucks, trains and planes brought in everything they used, and Vico took whatever was spilled in the process: appliances taken off freight cars, percentages of the food brought in for the markets, even the gasoline left in the hulls of tanker trucks after they had shorted the stations to which they had made deliveries. He would take the money and multiply it by supplying the drugs, whores and gambling the residents needed, and by lending them money to pay for these necessities at fifty percent interest. Vico had an army of vultures working the streets all the time, looking for ways to make money that he hadn't thought of yet.

Wolf had met Vico only for a moment in the year before he'd had to leave the country. He had been hired to kill a man named McPray, who had recently moved to Washington. He had been a Texas businessman who acted like an oil man. It was said that he had some connection with people in oil, but in those days everybody in that part of the world knew somebody who was in oil. Somehow he had been involved in the buying of supplies for the public schools in a large area of the state. It was never explained to Wolf exactly how he had gained a say in the matter, but he had one. For several years he had steered the contract for paper to a company owned by Mike Mascone, but one year, without warning, when Mascone had a huge inventory he had collected in an Amarillo warehouse in anticipation, McPray had simply changed vendors: some relative of his had gone into business. This put Mascone into a bind, and he had made some semipublic threats about having relatives of his own. The truth was that Mascone was a genuine made guy, but he was also of no importance. He wasn't even very rich. After some stewing, he decided that the only way he was ever going to be rich was to have McPray killed. By now McPray had moved to Washington on some other scheme, and Mascone wanted him killed in a way that would make certain people in Texas believe that Mascone was some kind of serious Mafioso with connections everywhere. After a number of inquiries, he had found out whom to call, and the Butcher's Boy had collected his money in advance and gone to Washington.

Being isolated in Amarillo, Mascone had an idealistic view of how the world worked. He thought he should call Vico and tell him what was going on because it was a courtesy. Vico was true to his reputation. He sent three men to the Butcher's Boy's hotel to demand a third of the price for McPray. It was, they said, the overhead for doing that kind of business in Vico's territory. The Butcher's Boy had said he understood, and started to pack his suitcase in front of them. When they asked what he was doing, he said, "I'm not going to do that kind of business in Vico's territory." Then he had called Mascone in front of them and told him that calling Vico had cost him twenty-five thousand dollars.

This had created a problem for Vico's men, who had been told to pick up eighty-three hundred dollars. The Butcher's Boy was in the airport when he saw them again, only this time Vico was with them. He had been about sixty then and fat. He had sat waiting in the airport coffee shop while his men pointed him out to the Butcher's Boy, who went in to listen to what Vico had to say. He had said that eight thousand dollars wasn't the point. It had to do with the way things had always been done. The local capo got a cut of everything that went on, and this covered the aggravation, bad publicity and protection if it was necessary. It was simply overhead. The Butcher's Boy had answered that he understood, but said that he was keeping Mascone's money because he too charged for overhead, aggravation and bad publicity. Then he excused himself, stood up from the table and got on his plane. A month later he read that McPray had been found in the Potomac suitably mutilated, and without thinking about it very hard he knew who had done it. He also knew that Vico would have seen it as an opportunity to charge at least fifty thousand.

If Vico thought he had a chance to collect on the contract for the Butcher's Boy, he would probably come out and walk the streets himself, even though he must have been over seventy by now and had more money than some state treasuries. The fact that it was unseemly for a man in his position to expect money for what the other old men would have considered a favor would not bother him; he would demand it. If Wolf got hit by lightning in the next ten minutes, Vico would send a man to see Carl Bala in prison on the grounds that it was his lightning.

When Wolf was finally inside the garage, he had to control an impulse to run. There was something about getting out of the open that made him feel light and optimistic. He walked quickly toward the stairway, climbed to the first landing and then up to the second level. He moved cautiously. There was no telling where he had been when Pauly the Bag Man had first seen him. If he had been in the car, then he could be walking into something now. He stopped at the doorway onto the second level and waited. He listened to the distant sound of cars on the ramps above, then walked back to the head of the steps and held his breath.

Paul Martillo was dizzy and gasping for breath. The coat of his suit had big sweat spots under the armpits, and his new shoes were scuffed from trying to catch himself when he slipped on the sidewalk, but what was most annoying was that his ears felt like they were plugged up. He had a vague suspicion that having your ears feel pressure must be a sign of heart trouble, but he couldn't remember ever hearing anybody say it. He still couldn't believe he wasn't running anymore. He had gone all the way to Constitution Avenue and was making the turn up Louisiana before he realized he had outrun the son of a bitch. Then Vico's men had come along in a car, made a U-turn in the middle of Louisiana and picked him up. As he thought about it now, getting into the car probably had been a mistake. In the first place, his leg muscles were certainly going to stiffen up because you were supposed to walk around for a while and stretch your muscles after a dash like that. In the second place, just in case there was one person inside the Beltway who had not seen him running like a madman across the damned Capitol lawn chased by a hit man, he had given them a good chance to see him getting into a brand-new Cadillac with four of the most obvious-looking hoods that he had ever seen. Two of them had even had guns in their hands when they had picked him up.

Now that he had his wind back, he began to think about the fact that this was going to be over in a few minutes, and Paul Martillo still had to live here. In fact, until this interruption, he had been on his way to see a senator. It was hard enough around here. At least the bastards had a phone in their Cadillac so that he could call Bart, his driver, and tell him where to meet him. When he hung up he even made a little joke to hide the way he felt. "I was afraid I was going to have to call the cops and get them to activate the Thiefbuster on the Lincoln."

Sitting in the back seat of the Cadillac, he had tolerated the questions from Carmine, the leader of the crew. "So what's he got on?"

Martillo thought. "I don't know. A sport coat, a pair of pants. He doesn't look like anything. Doesn't Vico have anybody out here who met him?"

"Sure," said Carmine, "but that was a long time ago."

"Not long enough," said Martillo.

There was a little snort that stood for laughter from one of the others. Sure, these jerk-offs thought they were better than Paul Martillo. It was like the guy who came to fix your toilet thinking he was smarter than you because you had to hire him to do it.

At last the car pulled over beside the parking garage. Martillo opened the door and nearly fell out, straightened his tie, pulled his cuffs so that they showed a little beyond the coat and walked into the dark concrete structure. He was a little more upset than he had let Vico's men see. As he thought about it, he realized it

was just possible that Vincent Toscanzio was only doing what
the old men had told him to do. They probably figured that if
they got Balacontano out, from then on the Butcher's Boy would
be his problem. Carl Bala was a nasty, arrogant maniac in his
own right, and he would be capable of getting this one little guy.
The old men were smart that way. They thought ahead, which
was why they were the old men, and the ones who had come up
with them were all buried. On the other hand, this development
was good luck for Carl Bala. If somebody didn't pull some
strings in Washington, he was going to sit in jail for a hell of a
long time. He would be like the Birdman of Alcatraz, one of
those ancient, clean old guys who took up needlepoint or something.

As he walked to the staircase to meet Bart in the Town Car,
Martillo noted that the Cadillac was driving up and down the
aisles looking for a parking space. This was why those guys
were still being sent around town in threes and fours, carrying
guns. Given Washington on a day like this at one o'clock, anybody with a brain knew that the lower levels would be filled. It
was the only public lot for about ten blocks, for Christ's sake,
and anybody who was ever going to make something of himself
would take the ramp to at least the third floor to save some time.
That was the real difference between the schmucks and the winners: the winners could think ahead, while the schmucks went
around and around the track like donkeys.

Paul Martillo leaned hard on the railing as he started to climb
the steps. He knew his shoes must be making a loud noise on
the metal steps, but the clanks sounded distant and hollow. He
was going to have his ears looked at.

Wolf heard the footsteps, then moved ahead again and looked
onto the floor of the garage. The black Lincoln with the driver
still in it pretending to read a newspaper wasn't more than fifty
feet from Wolf's Dodge. He took three deep breaths as he pulled
Little Norman's pistol out of his coat, held it down beside his
thigh and turned back to the stairwell. There just wasn't anywhere to go.

Carmine Fusco had worked for Vico for a long time and he knew
what the Butcher's Boy meant to him. Vico could pick up a
couple of million bucks in one morning, just for popping one
man. If Vico had a crew working the hotels that was good enough
to lift a couple of thousand dollars' worth of cameras and jew-

elry every single day, and a guy who trucked it all to another town to sell it for a thousand, which was pretty good, it would still take more than three years to gross a million from the operation. Then you had to add another three years to pay off all those guys. That was how Vico thought, so it was how Fusco thought.

He had let Martillo off at the bottom of the garage and the jerk had stood for it. That was the joke about having somebody like him come to town from someplace like Detroit and not work for Mr. Vico like everybody else. He wasn't born here, so he didn't know the city well enough to figure out that anybody who had been spotted in this part of town on foot only had a couple of places where he could have parked.

As Fusco's brother-in-law, Gilbert, drove slowly up each aisle and turned down the next, Carmine kept the window open and listened. If the Butcher's Boy was looking for Martillo, he was going to have a chance at him, but if he made any noise it was going to cost him. You had to take some risks to get a guy like this, but Carmine wasn't about to risk anybody who belonged to Mr. Vico.

Then he heard the pop. It sounded more like something blew up than a gunshot, because the concrete made it reverberate for a second. He poked Gilbert. "Hit it."

The Cadillac didn't make much noise when it accelerated, so there was just a scream of tires as the car floated around the corner like a sailboat in a high wind. It was one big, fat slob of a car. In a few seconds it was on its way up the ramp. Now there was a second shot, this one even louder than the first, and it made Carmine see yellow for a second. So much for Martillo. It had to be the coup de grâce, the guy putting a hole in his head to make sure he stayed dead. "Stop," he said. "Let us out, and get ready to block the ramp."

He and Castelli and Petri climbed out, and then Carmine had a vision of black and silver. With a roar the front of Martillo's Lincoln skidded around the bend, the rear end swinging about so that the grille and headlights were no more than ten feet in front of him. As he realized that it wasn't going to stop, he took three steps back to get up on the railing and out of its way. It passed him so close that he felt the wind. He somehow knew that there was a bullet hole with a big crack in the driver's side window without knowing how he saw it because the car was moving so fast. As it tilted down the ramp it seemed to be flying, and when it hit the first floor it bottomed out and sent up a spray of sparks.

Fusco gave Castelli a push toward the stairs, then looked at Petri and pointed to the left. Fusco walked up the ramp himself. It was good for his status to have the others think that he had all the guts, but the truth was that it was the safest place to be. This guy wasn't going to shoot the man in the middle first. You might shoot the one on the right, or the one on the left, but you never shot the one in the middle. It was one of those odd things.

Fusco was a little suprised when he made it to the top of the ramp without hearing another shot. But then he saw Martillo's driver, who was dead as a can of tuna. When he turned his head, he could see Castelli bending over another body in the stairwell. It was Martillo, which left only one likely candidate for the driver of the Lincoln.

"Carmine," said Petri.

"Wait a minute," Fusco said. "I'm thinking."

"Didn't that guy Martillo say his car had a Thiefbuster?"

Fusco smiled. It figured that Petri would have picked up on that. Ever since those things had gone on the market, Mr. Vico had been on Petri's butt to think of a way to locate and disconnect them. They were making it dangerous and nerve-racking to boost a car.

Wolf finally found the button that rolled down the window and pushed it. It went only halfway down before the place where his bullet had punched through stuck in the slot and the electric motor hummed without moving it. When he rested his elbow and forearm on the window and leaned, it rolled all the way in. This didn't help make him feel any more comfortable, but it did make the car look normal from the outside. On the inside it wasn't normal at all. He had walked up to the driver and shot him through the window. The bullet had gone through his forehead and out the back of his skull, and he had fallen across the front seat. The problem with head wounds was that they produced a lot of blood. Even though he had pushed the body out the passenger side within a few seconds, there was blood all over the interior; the leather upholstery of the passenger seat had a pool of blood on it that sloshed onto the floor every time he applied the brake, and seeped backward when he stepped on the gas pedal.

The only thing on his mind now was getting onto I-395 and back to Alexandria before somebody spotted him. He had to find a way to slow everything down. It was as though the pace of things had changed in his absence. Events happened too quickly now, which made it seem as though they didn't have any relationship to each other. He needed an hour or two in a place where he didn't have to look over his shoulder. He would have to duck under the surface again and come up someplace else where *he* could be the one who made things happen. He wished now that he had killed Little Norman instead of talking to him. He had considered it carefully, and thought he'd had nothing to lose. If everybody he had ever known was already eagerly looking for him so that they could get rich, then there was no way he could make things worse, so he had offered a rational, measured bargain: in effect, he would cease to exist, and all they had to do was to let him. But they hadn't let him, and this was why things were happening so fast.

He reached Alexandria with a small feeling of surprise. He had managed to sedate himself with the simple mechanical task of keeping the car between the lines. He turned onto his street, then into the driveway, opened the garage door, drove the car in and shut the door with the briefest, most economical movements he could manage. As he walked to the front door, he glanced across the street at the house of E. V. Waring. Tonight was going to have to be the night. If he left her body inside the trunk of Pauly the Bag Man's car and parked it in the right place, maybe he could cause some trouble for them.

As he opened his front door, he saw a piece of paper stuck in the mail slot. When he plucked it out, he could see the engraving that he had selected: "E. V. Waring." It read, "Please stop by around eight for coffee and dessert. It's the only way I can thank you for your help this morning, and my pride demands it. The least I can do is welcome you to the neighborhood. Sincerely, E."

18

"**Y**ou know, this wasn't necessary," said Wolf. "It's wonderful, but you didn't have to do it." He gestured vaguely at the long dinner table. The dark, polished hardwood stretched for at least five feet past the zone covered with white linen, china, silverware and the remnants of a peach torte. She must have bought it in some other time, when she thought she was going to be cooking for her whole FBI squad, or whatever they called them.

Elizabeth smiled. At least somebody had taught him to compliment the hostess. He seemed to be nice enough, but he was boring—unbelievably, thunderously boring. He didn't appear to have any interests or experiences that he could be induced to tell her about. Why did she always feel that she had to do this kind of thing? "It's nothing. I just wanted to thank you for helping with the car and giving me a ride to work. I hope you didn't get into trouble . . ."

"Trouble?"

"You were late, weren't you?"

"Not at all. I was making cold calls."

"Cold calls?"

"No appointment, no warning. You just drop in on them and see if they're interested in what you're selling."

"What are you selling?" she asked brightly.

"At the moment, advertising space. Want some?"

"I don't think so." No wonder he didn't talk about it. Even he wasn't interested. "Would you like some more of this torte?"

Wolf looked at the pastry and shook his head. "Save some for your kids. Where are they, anyway?"

"They had dinner at six tonight. If you can call it dinner. Amanda throws it, mostly, and Jimmy evades it. Amanda goes

271

to bed around seven-thirty, and tonight Jimmy fell asleep at eight—a big day at preschool, I guess.'' She pointed to the little box on the sideboard that looked like a transistor radio. "If you listen carefully, you can hear Amanda snoring. I'm afraid you won't get to meet them.''

"Oh. Too bad.'' He began to search his mind for a way of killing her so that they wouldn't see it happen, or walk out here in the morning and find the body. He didn't want to kill them, and he wanted the maid to find the body.

"Do you like children?'' Elizabeth asked. She regretted it instantly, and a wave of something that felt like heat swept over her. It was the sort of question that somebody—somebody very crude and desperate—might ask a single man if she wanted to determine whether he was a suitable prospect. Now he would think that she was pathetic. Then it occurred to her that there was a worse possibility. What if he misinterpreted the whole invitation? She had dragged him over here alone in the evening—well, not alone, because the kids were here, but without any other adults—and he could easily think it was because she wanted to seduce him. Of course he would, when in reality the impulse had been exactly the opposite. She had wanted to assert the fact that she was an independent person who repaid a kindness with an appropriate gesture of thanks. But he could understand this and still imagine that she thought the appropriate gesture of thanks was . . .

It took him a moment to come back to the conversation. "Uh . . . I guess so. I mean, I don't really know much about them, except for remembering being one. But it would be sort of odd not to like them, wouldn't it? It would put me in a strange position: not liking the members of my species until they were fully grown. So I guess I do.''

She smiled again. She had been imagining it all. He had managed to block another avenue of conversation in the process of reassuring her, but that was no loss; she had been known to drone on about the kids.

Wolf said, ''It must be kind of hard taking care of them by yourself. I see you going off to work every day.'' At last he had found a way to bring up the husband. Was he at a military base on Guam, or was he going to come through the door in ten minutes to pick up his mail or pay his alimony?

"I have a baby-sitter. She's a nice woman and the kids like her. But it *is* hard. You feel guilty for leaving them, and you feel guilty at work because you sometimes have to miss a day or go home early because they're sick, or whatever. What it is, really, is that when you have kids you need to work more than you ever did, but even when you're at work, you're not always thinking about your job, and if it comes down to a choice, the job always comes second.''

If the job came second, she must be a hell of a mother. He had been in the trade for more than fifteen years before he had left, and he had never had to think about the federal government. But now he did. ''What do you do at the Justice Department?''

''I'm sort of a bureaucrat, I guess.''

''You mean you're a lawyer, or an FBI agent?''

''Lawyer,'' she said. ''My husband was the FBI agent. He got to do the glamorous stuff, and I sit in an office.''

''Was. You're divorced.'' He tried again.

''No such luck,'' she said. ''Jim died of cancer about a year ago.''

''Oh. I'm sorry.'' He noted the way she said it. It would be better if he could be alive. She loved him, or had reached the stage where he had a rosy glow around him and she was telling herself that she did. But she was in luck; she was going to be one of those widows who didn't last long after her husband died.

''Don't be,'' she said. ''Everybody loses somebody; if it's not a husband it's parents, grandparents. And we had the kids. I'm lucky.''

He nodded. ''That's a nice way to think about it.''

''You sound like you think I'm deluding myself.''

''I didn't mean to,'' Wolf said. ''I meant it. We don't have a whole lot of choice about certain things, and death is one of them. But you do have a choice about how you think about it.''

''That's true. But I've thought about it in a lot of different ways, and I think this is the right one—not because it's the most useful, but because it's the most accurate. Most of the time I don't feel sad. I just miss him.''

Wolf wasn't really listening now. Something strange was happening. From his seat at the end of the table he could see a red glow through the curtains. It was the brake lights of a car pulling up in front of his house across the street. After a second or two the lights went out. He hadn't seen any headlights. He listened for the thumps of doors slamming so he could count them, but he couldn't pick up a sound. ''Tell me about him,'' he said. ''I mean, if it doesn't bother you.''

It was strange the way he focused his eyes on some point beyond the wall, almost like a blind person. Maybe he was remembering something of his own. There was more to him than she had thought. "Well, we had fun together. . . ."

"You mean he had a sense of humor."

"Not exactly. I mean, he did, but it was sort of an FBI agent's sense of humor. I know it's not fair, but they're in a mostly male sort of world, so most of the jokes are inside jokes, and the ones that aren't are kind of simple. Somebody famous once said that the difference between men and women is that women don't like Falstaff."

What the hell was she talking about? He still hadn't heard the doors. He tried to concentrate. "I thought it was The Three Stooges."

She grinned. "That was a different famous person."

He hadn't heard the doors, but a car went by on the street, and he saw that for just a second the brake lights went on as it passed his house. "Maybe so."

"I guess what I mean about Jim was that he had a capacity for fun. The way we got together was that ten years ago we were each assigned to the same case. It was a bad case, and the outcome was awful. Afterward I took six months in Europe. One morning, really early, I was asleep in my hotel when the concierge woke me up to tell me I had a visitor. It was Jim. We hadn't been dating or anything; he simply showed up."

It must be the police. How could they have followed him here from the parking structure without him seeing? Why hadn't they just grabbed him as he had pulled into his driveway? He realized that some reaction was expected, but he hadn't heard any of it, so he smiled.

"Then later, about two years ago, he came home one day with three tickets for a flight to London."

"A flight to London?"

"That's right. He did it because it had been eight years since the first time."

"Very nice," he said. "That is fun."

"He was always doing unexpected things like that. When I say he was an FBI agent, you probably picture a fullback with a big neck. He wasn't. In fact, he looked enough like you to be a relative. He was perfectly normal, about your size, and had an intelligent look in his eyes. He had a perfectly good law degree, and we always talked about going into practice together someday."

Was it possible that she had somehow identified him? Maybe she was going on like this to give her people time to surround the place. She would go out to the kitchen again to get more coffee, then slip out the back while the SWAT team came bursting in through every door and window. No, she had actually made herself feel sad. He wanted to look out the window at the people across the street, but he couldn't take the chance. "Here," he said. "Let me help you take the plates and stuff." He picked up a plate and the glass serving dish with the torte on it and stood up. He decided that if she was conning him he would crack the serving dish on the edge of the counter and bring it across her throat.

As they walked to the kitchen, he had to think of something to say. "It's too bad the kids were so young. They didn't get to see much of him."

"I know," said Elizabeth. "I think it's going to be hardest on Jimmy. He'll remember him a little bit. Then there's all that stuff the psychologists put in their books to scare mothers. . . ."

"What stuff?"

"About little boys needing men to identify with."

"I wouldn't take that too seriously."

"I don't know. I find myself stuck being a combination of the strong, domineering mother and the cold, distant father." She looked at him mischievously. "I run into the product a lot professionally."

She couldn't see that he had stepped sideways through the door because she was looking the other way. He surveyed the kitchen, but there was nothing. The place looked like the kitchens he remembered seeing on television when he was a kid, with curtains on the window over the sink and a lot of cookie jars and salt-and-pepper shakers that looked like fish and fruit and little people in rows on the shelf. It was also a mess. There were pots and pans and knives and spills on the counter, and even a couple of slippery spots on the floor where something had dripped while she was cooking the kids' dinner. Eddie's kitchen had looked like an operating room in a hospital, with a gleaming stainless-steel cutting table in the middle of the floor that he had bought from the same wholesaler he dealt with at the butcher shop. But Eddie had been a rotten cook, so they had eaten at diners whenever they could think of an excuse.

He followed her back to the dining room for another load of dishes. He had to get a look out that window. "Did you take any pictures of England?"

"Sure," she said. "But you don't want to see them."

"Yes, I do."

"Jim took almost all of them, so it's Elizabeth and Jimmy in front of this and Elizabeth and Jimmy in front of that."

"What's wrong with that?"

She shrugged. "You have to promise that as soon as you're bored you'll stop looking. They're what you might call priceless family treasures. That means we're always in focus, but the monuments and cathedrals aren't. I put them away in Jimmy's closet because I knew that someday he and Amanda will want to look at them."

"If it's too much trouble, don't bother. I just thought that sometime I might like to go there. I've never been out of this country."

"I don't mind showing them to you. It's just that looking at pictures of somebody else's vacation is sort of a yawn."

"I promise not to."

Carmine Fusco sat in the dark in the living room of the house where the Butcher's Boy had parked Martillo's car. He had been sitting in a comfortable chair to the side of the door and about fifteen feet away from it, but now he was restless and he stood up. Imagine a man like that living in this kind of a house for all these years. It was going to be an embarrassment to Mr. Vico if anybody found out that the Butcher's Boy had been living quietly in the Washington suburbs for ten years.

He walked across the room. There was something about the darkness that made you more quiet. He could hear every creak of the floor. "Castelli?" he whispered.

"Yeah?"

"See anything?"

"No. Maybe he's got a date."

"If he can get it up after what he's been through today, I'd like to meet her."

"Jesus, if *I* can get it up after what *I've* been through I'd like to meet her."

Carmine moved to the window and held up his wrist beside the curtain, but he still couldn't see his watch. He knew it should have been comforting, because it meant the rest of him wasn't going to be easy to see either, but it was just frustrating. It was bad enough waiting to blow away somebody you were scared of, but losing track of time made it seem longer.

Wolf waited until she kicked off her shoes and slipped into the hallway. He noticed that she didn't tiptoe, but placed her feet flat on the floor to keep her weight from making the floorboards creak. When she turned and opened a door on her left he quickly stepped to the window and moved the curtain aside half an inch. He could see that the cars that had stopped in front of his house had pulled away immediately. They must have expected to find him there, so they had all arrived at once to storm the place. When they had found that he wasn't inside, they had made the cars disappear and sat down to wait. That didn't seem to him to be the way cops usually operated. They would kick in the door, flip on all the lights and rush him. But if they found the house empty, they would spend the next five hours tearing it apart and taking pictures and fingerprints. It occurred to him that he was with somebody who knew what cops would do, but that there wasn't any way to get her to tell him.

Elizabeth returned with a disturbingly large box, set it on the couch between them, untied a string around it, lifted the lid and handed him the first pile of photographs. She looked apologetic and shy and a little sad. "These are London."

As Wolf glanced at the first few they made his head ache. He had stood on the Embankment right where a younger Elizabeth Waring was standing, only he had been with The Honourable Meg. He was hiding in this woman's living room because across the street there were men waiting to kill him. He had no clear idea what he was going to do; all he wanted was somehow to be magically transported into those photographs and stand there in the soft British light.

Elizabeth glanced at the pictures as he shuffled through them. He really seemed to be studying them. What a peculiar man. At first he had seemed so empty and dull, but he was sensitive in an odd, quiet way. Maybe he was quiet because he was so intensely interested in other people. Suddenly, without warning, this train of thought reversed itself and she felt a chill move up her spine. Maybe the interest wasn't healthy; maybe he was some kind of voyeur. It had been so long since anyone had been interested in anything about her life, her world, that maybe she was exposing herself to something awful that she couldn't name. He had encouraged her to go on a lot longer and more openly than anyone else ever had about things that she had always kept private. It hadn't started out that way, and it hadn't seemed peculiar at the time, so how had it happened? Maybe she was becoming—had become—one of those widows who ended up signing over their life insurance to a con man because he had paid attention to her. Maybe even to somebody she just *imag-*

ined was paying attention to her—say, a television preacher with a wig that looked like a monkey pelt. No, she told herself; I was just being polite. She pretended to go through the box, but kept him in the corner of her eye. He's nothing out of the ordinary. If you look at him objectively, he's already giving signs that he's restless.

When the telephone rang, she sprang to her feet. "Got to grab that before it wakes the kids," she explained. She managed to snatch it up before the second ring. "Hello?"

Richardson's voice came to her. "Elizabeth. Sorry to call now, but it's important."

"Something happen?"

"Yeah. The police just identified two bodies they picked up in the parking garage at the Gateway Tour Center. One was your basic LCN infantry. His name was Jerry Bartolomeo. The other was a surprise, a guy named Paul Martillo. He was a lobbyist for a bunch of nonprofit organizations, one of them being the Italian American Anti-Libel League."

"What's that? Is it legitimate?"

There was a blast of air across the receiver that must have been a kind of laugh. "I forgot you haven't been on the mailing list for a while. It was founded by Peter Cuccione about thirty years ago to threaten the television networks because he didn't like having his kids see *The Untouchables*. Since then it's been run out of Detroit by the Toscanzio family."

"Then it's a definite possibility."

"I don't know if this has anything to do with the rest of it, but a guy like Martillo . . . I thought you'd better know."

"You bet I want to know. You think it's him?"

Richardson was cautious. "Well, I don't know. Martillo wasn't a big deal, but he worked for people who are a very big deal. And shooting the guy in the middle of a workday near the Federal Triangle is kind of bizarre."

"It is. Richardson, we've got to get somebody down there. Jack's in Chicago, and I can't go just like that. I've got the kids sleeping."

"Can't they . . . oh, yeah, they're little, aren't they?"

"Four and eleven months."

"How about a neighbor?"

Elizabeth eyes moved to Wolf reflexively, and then away. A minute ago she had been trying to figure out if he was a con man, an emotional vacuum cleaner or a sexual sadist. "No."

Richardson sighed. "Okay. I guess I'll drive in myself. I'll try to get as much from the D.C. police and the FBI as they'll give me, and I'll ask them to send you copies of whatever gets committed to paper.''

"Thanks,'' she said. "Sorry I can't do it, but—''

"I know,'' he interrupted. "I forgot about the kids.''

Wolf picked up the fourth packet of photographs and recognized a shot of Milk Street in Bath. But beneath it, at the bottom of the box, was a pile of papers, tags and things held together with a rubber band. There were long envelopes with the British Airways logo and a couple of receipts that somebody had just tossed in. As he looked at the photographs, he felt the packet with his other hand. It was stiff, and a corner of something blue was sticking out. He recognized its texture and size. She had said they had gone two years ago. It wouldn't expire for five. He looked at her as she prepared to hang up the phone. In a second she would turn away to put it on the cradle. He gripped the corner hard with his thumb and forefinger. Come on, turn. Come on. Now!

But she didn't turn. She picked up the whole telephone, brought it around her without looking at it, set the receiver down and returned to the couch. "Sorry. It was work.''

Sorry. He nodded. It was work, all right. Since the start of all this he had been reduced to doing everything the hard way. "Look, I couldn't help overhearing. If you have to go somewhere . . .''

She shook her head. "No, thanks. I can't leave the kids.''

"I'll keep an eye on them for you. I don't mind.''

She smiled. "That's very kind, but they don't know you. If they woke up, they'd be terrified.''

Jack Hamp sat in his motel room and listened to the big jet engines roaring along the runway at O'Hare, louder and louder as their pilots throttled them up, and then thundering off into the sky before they made the wide turn to bank into their prescribed compass headings.

The Washington report was virtually incoherent. This was one more time when he wished that computers would either take over the world completely so that people would know precisely and promptly what the hell was happening, or else just go away. The combination of human being and machine hadn't worked out too well. The report had two people dying who at first glance didn't seem to have much to do with each other, let alone with the Butcher's Boy, until they both were found lying in a Wash-

ington parking ramp. Their occupations were listed as "Driver"
and "Lobbyist." To Hamp's practiced eye, it looked like a report where one or both of the bodies were misidentified. All it
told him was that something had happened in Washington today,
and that some people had died. He could have learned as much
from the flashing light of his silenced phone beeper.

He glanced at his watch, picked up his suitcase and then
walked the room a last time to be sure he hadn't left anything.
That was another thing: The goddamned machines put out so
much paper that you practically had to bundle it like a week of
newspapers before you could throw it away. Not that you *could*
throw it away, because it was always full of sensitive information
that didn't answer any of the questions any sensible cop would
ask.

As Hamp walked into the airport, he considered calling Elizabeth Waring. It wasn't because she was the person in the home
office to whom he was supposed to be reporting. Twenty years
of police work didn't make you more respectful of hierarchies;
it only made them one more thing you found out you could live
with, like carbon monoxide and bird shit. Ninety-nine percent
of the time you were out on your own, driving around town in
a car and trying to solve people's problems by asserting an au-
thority that, if only they knew it, consisted of nothing more than
your ability to persuade people that whatever they were contemplating wasn't worth it. He wanted to call Elizabeth because
after a couple of weeks of talking to her two or three times a
day, he was fairly sure she would be able to sort the report out
for him.

But it was after eleven o'clock in Washington, and young
widows with kids had enough to do in the evening without having to explain to somebody who the hell Paul Martillo was, and
what he was doing in a parking ramp without a car or a set of
keys. There would be time enough for that in the morning, after
she'd had her meeting. She probably didn't know she was having
one yet, but this kind of thing always caused morning meetings.
All bureaucracies worked the same.

Wolf put the photographs back in the box. "Let me help you
with the dishes." It was going to have to be the hard way. He
couldn't even use Little Norman's gun because the whole neighborhood would hear it, and when the men across the street heard
it, they would know what it was. He was going to have to take
the serrated bread knife off the counter and slit this woman's

throat while her two children slept. He would have to hold her over the sink while she bled to death, and then grab the passport out of the box. The worst part of it wasn't that it was messy; it was that he had gone to a lot of trouble to find Elizabeth Waring, and now what he really felt like doing was just leaving her alone. It had probably been the telephone call. She was no threat to him; she wasn't even capable of going out at night to do whatever her boss had wanted her to do. In fact she had probably been hoping to be in bed by now. She was simply a nice woman with no husband who had a job that she was good at, and today she had met a man who was polite and didn't scare her. She wouldn't go out looking for a man, but if she met one by accident, it would seem all right to her. Women like her probably didn't get laid very often, and something like this wouldn't have done any harm. She was smart and sensible enough to know that she was still attractive to men, and if things had been different, he would have liked to accommodate her. Cutting her throat with a kitchen knife wasn't going to throw the FBI into confusion; it wasn't going to accomplish anything.

"Anyway," Elizabeth was saying, "the whole point of this was to thank you for helping me this morning. You're not doing any dishes in my house."

Wolf stood, and the moment came and went. "All right, then," he said. "But I'll take the garbage out for you on my way home."

"A deal," she said. "Going out there at night gives me the creeps."

Wolf carried the garbage bag out to the side of Elizabeth's garage, where there were four big cans. He set the bag in a can carefully so that it didn't make any noise, then fit the lid back on. He looked at the kitchen door, and then at the window. At least she wasn't standing there to watch him walk down the driveway and across the street to whatever was waiting for him. He could go through the back yard to the next street and then circle around.

Carmine stood up again and walked through the house to the back door, where Petri was waiting. "See anything move out there?"

Petri grunted.

"What the hell does that mean?"

"I was shaking my head. The answer is no."

"What time is it?" He hated asking Petri for the time, but it was so dark in here that he couldn't read his watch, and so he had to keep making up excuses to ask the others. He would have to start eating carrots, or else get a watch that glowed in the dark.

"About a quarter after eleven."

Carmine thought about it. "I don't like it."

"What do you mean?"

"I mean what if he's not coming? I mean I don't want to sit around in here until dawn with a car in the garage that doesn't belong to him, and sure as hell won't have his fingerprints on it, and has blood splashed all over the inside of it. If he knew we were here, all he'd have to do is call the cops and say somebody had broken into his house, and I'm not sure I want to bet my life he can't figure that out."

"He doesn't know we're here, Carmine."

"I'm not sure I want to bet my life on that either. Where's the phone?"

"What phone?"

"His phone."

"There is no phone."

"No phone at all?"

"No. We went through the place. If there'd been one, I'd have seen it."

Carmine's heart began to pound, and then the pressure seemed to move upward to his head. "You went through this whole fucking place, there was no fucking telephone and you didn't tell me?"

Petri said defensively, "So what?"

"I guarantee you this man had a telephone this morning. You can't live without a telephone. That means he took it out."

"Not necessarily. My grandmother didn't have a phone."

"This guy isn't your grandmother, you dumb shit. That's the first thing you do in a war; you cut the enemy off and isolate him. He's severed our communications. He knows we're here, and he's going to do something about it."

"So use the car phone."

"Huh?"

"The car phone. Martillo had a phone in his car. That's how he called Mr. Vico when he saw the guy in the first place."

Fusco's mind scurried back and forth, looking for something that would negate Petri's suggestion, but he kept coming up with nothing. Finally he muttered, "I didn't want to have to do that.

But now I haven't got any choice." He pulled out his pistol, stepped to the back door and whispered, "Keep your eyes open. This is where he'll make his move if he's out there."

Wolf walked through the yard of the house beside his, staying in the shadows and moving slowly, then stopping to listen. He scanned the back of his house. There were no lights on inside, and he couldn't detect any broken windows. Suddenly he saw his back door open. He froze, then slowly brought Little Norman's pistol up in line with the doorknob. He couldn't quite discern the shape of what was pushing it open, but when the door began to close again, the silhouette of a man materialized against the white clapboards.

Wolf moved his eyes away from the man; maybe they were trying to see if he was out here. He watched the windows and the door itself, but could discern no shape or motion. Then the man began to walk, and since the man wasn't coming toward him, Wolf watched. The man went to the garage door, opened it, then ducked inside. What he did then was mystifying: he closed the garage door behind him.

That was no cop. At this stage there was no such thing as one cop. There would have been about five of them around Pauly the Bag Man's car trying to get prints, samples of blood and hair and whatever else they collected these days. But if it wasn't a cop, it must be Vico's people, and if this man wasn't doing what cops did, what *was* he doing?

Wolf stood still and watched the house. Vico's crews still seemed to consist of three soldiers and a driver. In the old days he had sent three men to try to hold Wolf up for money. This afternoon Wolf had seen three men get out of a car on Independence Avenue, and then he had seen three men on the parking ramp. Most likely there were two more men inside his house, and one in a car somewhere nearby.

He stood still for another moment. There was still a chance he could simply turn around and walk away. He had enough money on him even now. He could go back the way he had come, walk a mile or so to a liquor store away from the neighborhood and call for a cab. The chances were pretty good that the driver who would come for him would have nothing to do with Vico, and even if he was wrong, the man wouldn't know who he was. There was no reason for him to go back into that house. He had rented it with the expectation that he was going to kill the woman who lived across the street, then disappear, so he hadn't touched anything with his bare hands, or left anything that could be traced to him. He had even cut the labels out of his clothes.

But he was angry. What Vico was doing was pure opportunism. Wolf had done nothing to him, and before that, Michael Schaeffer had done nothing to anybody for ten years except sit in his house in Bath and go to an occasional concert with his girlfriend. These guys were waiting inside the house to collect on the Butcher's Boy. He wondered if they were really prepared to see him face-to-face.

If there were two men inside, one of them would be watching the street. That left the other, and he would be at the kitchen door to cover his companion's path to the garage. Wolf moved to the side of his house, staying within six inches of the clapboards as he sidestepped to the back door. He crawled across the steps, then sidestepped again to get to the garage door. He quietly slipped the bolt on the garage door to lock the man inside, then stepped to the back door, knocked quietly on it and whispered, "Let me in. It's me."

The door opened inward an inch and he threw his weight against it so that it hit the man hard in the face. The man's hands went up to cover his bleeding nose and mouth, and he staggered backward. Before he could lower them, Wolf was inside and pushing Little Norman's pistol against his head. Wolf whispered in his ear, "Lie down on your face. If you make a noise, you're dead."

The man sank to the floor. Wolf looked around for the man's gun and saw it on the floor at his feet. It was a Browning 9 millimeter, with a silencer screwed onto the end of it. He knelt down on the floor and picked it up, but as he did, the kitchen doorway seemed to fill with darkness. It was the shape of a big man looking down at them. "What are you doing on the floor?" Wolf raised his arm and pulled the trigger three times as quickly as he could. There were three hoarse spitting sounds, and the man took a step backward and toppled over into the dining room.

The one on the floor pushed himself upward with his arms and kicked out at Wolf with his feet. Wolf danced to the side to avoid the swinging legs, then fired down into the man's back. He took his time aiming the second shot, and it went into the top of the man's head. He walked cautiously into the dining room and shot the other one in the temple.

Wolf sighed. It hadn't gone well; he had wanted them alive. He turned on the lights, went to the bathroom, gathered all the towels and pushed them under the two men to catch the blood. Then he frisked the man on the kitchen floor to see if he had any more 9-millimeter ammunition. He found a second clip in the man's right pants pocket, dug it out, pulled the one he had used out of the pistol and inserted the full one.

He went to the kitchen door, stepped outside to the garage and listened. The man inside was already tugging on the garage door to get out. Wolf waited until he heard the man step away, then slipped the bolt on the door and stepped back around the corner of the garage. The man was standing inside a small square enclosure with a car. There were no windows, and the only door was the one he had raised to get inside. Wolf had a certain morbid interest in what the man was going to do.

Carmine was sweating. When he had called, Mr. Vico had yelled at him. Mr. Vico was a fat old man with a heart condition, and he probably hadn't yelled at anyone since the Eisenhower administration, but what he had said had been worse than the yelling. At least yelling got rid of some of the anger before he did anything about it. Carmine might survive the yelling, but the other thing was trouble. He'd said that the way car telephones worked was that they billed you for each call, put the number and time you had called on the bill, just like long distance, and that the guy who owned the car had been dead for hours; the police had already scraped his body up off the parking lot for an autopsy.

This had started Carmine sweating. Then, when he had tried to get out of the garage to tell Petri, whose fault it all was, he had found he couldn't open the damned door. He had practically gotten a hernia tugging on the thing, and still it wouldn't go up. Now he was getting scared. The first thing he had thought of was to call Castelli and Petri to tell them to come open the door, but the reason he was stuck in here was that there wasn't any phone in the house for them to answer. Then he had thought of calling Mr. Vico back and asking him to send somebody to tell Castelli and Petri to get him out, but he knew that wasn't a good idea. Then he had tried to think of who else he could call, but remembered what Mr. Vico had said about the phone numbers being recorded. Anybody he called might know what Mr. Vico knew about phone bills; anyway, at some point they were going to hear, and then they would know he had put their phone numbers on a short list that had been called after Martillo was dead. Also, he had ordered his brother-in-law Gilbert not to drive that big-assed Caddy back to this street. Gilbert would be sitting in the car now, playing the radio and waiting for Carmine to get this over with and walk with the others to the liquor-store parking lot on foot. Except that Carmine wasn't about to walk anywhere.

Carmine was gradually getting around to admitting to himself that there was only one way out: he was going to have to hot-wire Martillo's car, start the engine and ram his way out the door. He had no idea how long it took to fill up a tiny garage like this with enough carbon monoxide to smother him if he failed. He also worried about what would happen later. Crashing through the door would make a hell of a lot of noise, so he would have no choice but to keep on going, because Petri and Castelli would assume that any big-time disturbance had to be caused by somebody other than Carmine and would open fire. But if he did take off, it would leave Castelli and Petri inside the Butcher's Boy's house with the cops on the way and no car in sight. It would be hard to explain, and he sure as hell wasn't going to get protection from Mr. Vico.

He opened the car door and turned on the headlights, then looked around. There had to be a crowbar or something, but all he could see was a network of studs over bare tar paper. It was weird; what kind of man had a garage with nothing in it but his car? He turned off the lights and went to the door again; he had to get the damned thing open or he was going to regret it. He bent his knees and got down as far as he could. You had to get your legs into it.

Wolf heard the garage door roll up into the roof with incredible violence. It sounded as though it were going to jump the track. Then he heard the hiss of the man's breathing. It sounded as though his chest were heaving. He let the man walk out of the garage and stagger to the kitchen door. Then the man stopped and wondered why the lights were on inside. Wolf raised the pistol with the silencer on it and put Carmine's mind at rest.

19

Wolf dragged the last one into the garage. He was the one lying in the dining room, and he had been at least six feet three and heavy. Wolf closed the garage door, lifted the body into the back seat and propped it up with the other one, then looked at his little display. The three men sat in the car in three different postures of leisured comfort. He moved the last one's right arm to the back of the seat so it looked as though he were resting it behind the other one's head, and that helped to hide the hole and the blood.

Wolf opened the garage door again, got into the car, started it and pulled out into the driveway before closing the door again. He backed out as quietly as he could, letting the big car coast down the driveway to the street, then slowly accelerated away. As he drove, he made an inventory. He had cleaned the floors thoroughly, put the towels onto the car seats to soak up some of the blood and then prepared his companions for the ride. He still had two pistols with full loads and silencers, one under his coat and another at his feet under the driver's seat. He had stuck Little Norman's in the coat of the corpse in the passenger seat beside him. If he didn't make any sudden stops or reckless turns, his companions would remain sitting in fairly natural positions. It had been at least three hours since the last of them died, and by now the beginnings of rigor mortis would help. It always started in the jaws and neck, then spread to the torso and legs.

It had taken a long time, but he had probably done as well as he needed to. If the police really went through the place they would undoubtedly find blood, hair and threads from these three, and from him and from the family that owned the house, and their dogs and cats. But they wouldn't look.

After all these years Wolf wasn't squeamish about handling

bodies, but he didn't want these three toppling over while he
was on the highway. He had taken the precaution of searching
their wallets to be sure they weren't some kind of police, but all
he had found was money and credit cards. Their names were
Castelli, Petri and Fusco, but by now he didn't remember which
was which. They had all lived in Washington, and none of them
had any kind of card that entitled them to medical or dental care.
Vico obviously didn't pay the employer's share.

He had checked when he had come to town to see whether
any of Vico's businesses still had the same names, and some of
them did. They were all called Acme or Apex or AAA or ABC,
so that his contacts didn't have to learn the whole alphabet to
figure out where to drop things. Wolf had gone to a lot of trouble
to be sure he didn't run into Vico's people by accident, but it
hadn't done him much good. He had even driven by the big
house Vico lived in just so he would know where it was.

Vico had just finished making a formal complaint to the telephone company's business representative. He had received a
crank telephone call this evening, and had demanded a new
unlisted number. While he was talking he could hear the woman
clicking away on the keyboard, duly noting his request in the
company's computers in case his lawyer needed it later. He
hadn't decided what to do about Fusco yet. Carmine was the
loyal-dog type, and once in a while he needed a rap on the nose
with a newspaper, but you couldn't expect a dog to climb trees
for you. He was good enough at what he was expected to do,
and right now he was making Vico a hero.

Vico sat back in his favorite chair and stared at the fire. He
had always liked a fire. He had a vague sense that there were
things he should be doing, but he wasn't going to move. He was
waiting for a call. He had at least two hundred people out there
right now actively looking for the Butcher's Boy, and that was
part of his agitation. He had always believed that he had inherited a little bit of his mother's witch quality. In her youth she
had been one of those young girls who dreamed of train crashes
and ships going down, and then when she was older she had
been the one all the pregnant women in the neighborhood had
gone to and asked if their children would be boys or girls. What
he was feeling was probably the eagerness of all his people out
there—a little bit scared, a little bit excited—as they turned the
city into a tiger hunt.

The telephone at his elbow beeped patiently, and he picked it up. "Yeah?"

It was Toscanzio, of course. "You know who this is?" Of course he did; he had been waiting.

"Yes. I was sorry to hear about it. Is your family well?"

"I'll tell them you asked. We have a little problem, eh?"

"I want you to know I've made arrangements for Paul's . . . remains to be sent to his family out there. It's all in their name, just as though they had picked the undertaker out of a phone book, but the bill . . . where do you want it sent?"

There was a long silence on the other end.

"Well, I'll have it sent to you, and you can decide how you want to handle it." That ought to give him the hint. Martillo never should have been operating in Vico's town and not reporting to Vico.

"There's going to be fallout from this."

"What do you mean?"

"Our friend in California. Pauly was talking to important people to see if he could work out something in the way of clemency. But the way he went . . . I don't see how we can send somebody else to walk into some senator's office and start all over again. They get skittish when the last guy got a bullet in the head."

"Have you talked to anybody else?"

"Some people in Chicago."

"You know what I mean. Did you call anybody in New York?"

"I didn't think that was a good idea. Look, he's going to get out sooner or later. When he does, I don't want to be the one who said we gave up on his problem. Do you?"

Vico's smile was audible. "I didn't. I'm working on it right now. By morning I should have something to ship to his people in New York."

"Really?"

"Really."

Vico could tell that Toscanzio was already trying to figure out if he should call the Balacontano family in New York, or whether there was some way of talking directly to Carl Bala in prison. Let him. If Vico did get the body, he would make sure Bala knew where it came from. If he didn't, Toscanzio would be the one Bala hated for getting his hopes up.

"That's good news."

"I'll let you know when it's done."

"Thank you. My best to your family."

"Good-bye."

Vico hung up the telephone and went back to staring at the fire. It was a good feeling. It was as though the whole world—not just the people, but the natural forces, the wind and the stars—were working for him.

Wolf switched off the headlights before he turned the car into the driveway, and stopped it before it could trigger the electric eye that would buzz the intercom inside. He turned off the engine, popped the hood and went around to the front of the car. In the last few days he had found that he wasn't as good with cars as he used to be. They had changed a lot while he was gone, without changing at all. But he still knew how to yank out wires and hoses.

When he was satisfied, he closed the hood quietly and turned his attention to the electric eye. There was a little light and a receptor on each side of the driveway. If he didn't disconnect both sides of it at once, a light was going to stop hitting a receptor and it would buzz. The way to handle this kind of system was to put a mirror at exactly the right angle in front of each box so that it detected its own light, but he wasn't prepared to screw around with that. He studied the system carefully. The wiring would be steel-jacketed and buried inside a pipe, and some of it must run under the driveway. But the vulnerability of a system that had lights was that there must be a way to change a bulb without setting it off.

He stepped over the beam of light and knelt beside the gate. There was a lever that was designed to permit the electric motor that moved the gate to be disengaged in case it jammed, so he pressed the lever and pushed the gate open on its rails. It wasn't hard to find the circuit box. It was mounted on the brick wall just inside the yard, with a holly bush planted in front of it. He opened the box and watched the electric eyes go out as he flipped the circuit breaker.

He went back to the car, released the brake, shifted into neutral and then hurried to the back to push. In the old days a Lincoln had been a hell of a lot of metal, and he had been wondering if he would be able to move this one up the incline by himself. At first it was hard to get it to budge, but finally it rolled through the gate and ten feet inside before the front wheels turned a little and it headed onto the lawn. He stopped pushing it near a birdbath with a naked nymph pirouetting in the center.

Then he went around, reached inside the window, yanked out the keys and put them in his coat pocket with the wires he had taken out of the engine. He took out one of the pistols with a silencer and waited. After a minute or two, the light changed on a street somewhere nearby, and the driver of a big truck began to goad his diesel engine up through its gears. It was the only sound as Wolf walked toward the driveway.

He stopped at the gate. It was big and heavy and made of wrought iron, but it would be hard to keep somebody from moving it the way he had. He decided such a fine gate was worth a few more minutes. Following the dead line from the circuit box to the electric eye, he pulled a few feet of it out of the ground, cut it and stripped the insulation away for two inches. He wrapped the two bare wires around the bottom rung of the gate, then returned to the box and switched the circuit breaker back on. As he climbed over the wall to get back onto the street, he wasn't sure how the sequence would work, but somebody was going to realize that it was important not to leave Martillo's car in Vico's yard, and that the only way to get it out was through the gate. When the button inside didn't open it, somebody was going to touch the gate.

Wolf had walked half a mile before he found the right place to call for a taxi. On another night he might have stopped in one of the bars he had passed, but tonight Vico would have his army of collectors and parasites out looking for him, and it was always possible that he would run into someone who had seen his face in the old days. He had never had much to do with Vico's people, but he was through with letting himself be surprised.

The safest sort of place was a telephone booth beside a closed gas station, and he waited until he found one. There were six or seven diseased cars parked beside the building, and he decided that his was one of them. It was the new Chevy on the end, and he had pulled it in there and left it, in case the cab driver was curious. But when the driver arrived, he wasn't curious. He was young and a little bit frightened because this was the way cab drivers got robbed. Somebody called them from a public address where there weren't any other people and there wasn't much light. Then there would be a gun against the driver's neck, a whole night's receipts went up some guy's arm and the driver probably got killed. But this one was okay. He was old—at least thirty-five—and he wanted to go to Alexandria, and he only seemed tired, and looked as though he had some money.

* * *

Jack Hamp's flight from Chicago was within inches of touching down at Washington National just as a freak tail wind blew in from nowhere, and in order to keep the wing from dipping, the pilot had to give the engines another punch. There was no doubt in Hamp's mind what was happening because when the wheels touched the ground the tires gave a screech like a buzz saw, and the plane rattled along the runway taking the regularly spaced bumps at about twice the normal speed. He barely had time to brace himself for the drag of the brakes before he felt his head go forward in a bow so that he was looking at his knees. He wasn't particularly concerned, because a hot-wheels landing wasn't unusual, but he was impatient because now the plane would have to sit on the runway until the brakes cooled. To pass the time he read over the preliminary report from the Washington office again, occasionally glancing out the window beside him at the men in coveralls down on the tarmac playing flashlight beams over the tires and undercarriage.

He'd seen the whole procedure a few times in his days as a birdwatcher at LAX. The ground crew always stood fore or aft of the wheels because on the rare occasions when they did pop, the hot debris and metal would tear straight out along the wings. There wasn't a hell of a lot anyone could do until the night air cooled the wheels down to a temperature that would at least let the ground crew move a portable gangway up to get the passengers out.

As he read, he thought about Elizabeth Waring. She might not know who these victims were any more than he did. That was what bothered him most about this case. You had to be an organized criminal yourself to know who these guys Bartolomeo and Martillo were—and a well-organized criminal at that. It didn't make any sense as an offensive move. The only thing that might help the Butcher's Boy right now was noise; the victim had to be big enough to cause a stir. If he was in Washington, it would have to be Jerry Vico, or at least somebody who had made his bones with Vico.

The Butcher's Boy was in a special sort of fix right now. He had to do things which weren't predictable, but which made some kind of sense in retrospect. If they were predictable, there would be people waiting for him, but if they didn't make sense when you thought about them later, then they wouldn't help him get out. The organization would assume that he was completely round the bend, like a rabid animal. If this happened, he was dead, because you couldn't see something like that and figure you would just wait until it wandered away. You wanted to know exactly where it was during every second until you killed it. If the report said he was popping unknowns who hadn't done anything to him, then something was missing.

Elizabeth could probably help him out on this one. As he thought about her he felt a shudder of regret and embarrassment. He never should have made that joke about her being ugly; what if she really *was* ugly? No, it was worse than that. Just about every woman he had met who was worth anything thought that she was ugly. It was some kind of mass delusion. What on earth had led him to trigger a reaction he would have known was likely if he had stopped to think? But there was something about the anonymous present that bothered him. At first it had surprised him and made him feel panicky because maybe he was supposed to have sent her a present and hadn't known it, so he had pushed it away with the first smart-ass remark that came to mind. He had even said something about its being a bomb, as though nobody would send her anything unless he wanted to . . .

Hamp could feel his scalp begin to tighten, as though his hair were actually going to stand up. Martillo and Bartolomeo were such little fish that only a criminal would recognize them, and one had. The Butcher's Boy had seen those guys in Washington and they had seen him, so he had shut them up. It all made perfect sense, but only afterward. Hamp unbuckled his seat belt, stood up and started to sidestep his way into the aisle. The stewardess saw him and hurried up the aisle toward him to let him know he was busted. "Sir—"

But he took out his identification wallet and held it up in front of her face. "My name is Jack Hamp, and I'm a special investigator for the Justice Department. I have a car waiting in that airport, and I need to get to it now."

"I'm sorry, sir, but it will be a few more minutes before we can deplane. It isn't something we can do anything about. It's an FAA regulation."

Hamp took a step forward and she sensed that she had to move with him or step aside, so she came with him. "The wheels are hot," he said. "If they were going to blow, they'd have done it by now, but we'll sit here an hour or more just to be safe. Explain to the pilot that I've got an emergency."

"But, sir. Mr.—"

"Hamp. Do it. Because if you don't I'm going to crank that hatch open myself."

* * *

Hamp couldn't believe it. Elizabeth had actually told him about it the minute she had gotten the damned present, and he hadn't figured it out. He drove fast along Jefferson, changing lanes and keeping the pedal down as far as he dared. He was what might have been called a professional speeder, since that was what cops in L.A. had to be to get anywhere while the bodies were still warm. He instantly wished he hadn't thought it in those words. Because now it all made sense, and he hoped this didn't mean that it was already over.

The mistake was in thinking that the Butcher's Boy was just wandering around slaughtering the big bosses because they were big. He wasn't in any position to take on something like that. All he was doing was what Jack Hamp would have done in his place: trying to stay alive. Though to a man like the Butcher's Boy it meant that you figured out who was giving you the most trouble, and then you killed him. So now he was in Washington, but he hadn't come here to find a pair of nonentities like Martillo and Bartolomeo. That had just been an accident. Somehow he had figured out who was giving him the worst trouble, the one who had kept him from leaving the country in the first place and would keep closing in on him until he couldn't move at all—Elizabeth Waring.

Wolf had the cab driver go all the way up the block past his house before he told him to stop at the end of the street and got out. He waited for the driver to disappear before walking back down the block. He was still watching for the fourth man. Somebody had brought those three to his house this evening, and he still hadn't spotted the man or his car in the neighborhood. But he wasn't in a position to spend any time looking for him. He had started the sequence, and now he had to finish it and get out.

As he went to E. V. Waring's kitchen door, he tried to remember the exact layout of the house. There were no alarms or even serious locks to stop him, and she had cleaned the place before he had come to dinner, so there wouldn't be eight hundred toys on the floor to trip over in the dark.

He reached into his pocket, found a credit card from one of the men he had left in Vico's yard, slipped it between the door and the jamb and moved it up and down until he found the plunger. He depressed the plunger, but the door wouldn't move. He could feel that another bolt somewhere near the knob was engaged. He got down on his knees on the concrete steps and pushed on the rubber flap of the cat door that was cut into the lower panel. He measured the length of his arm from the cat door to the doorknob, and judged that it was long enough. Lying on his back on the steps, he stuck his arm inside all the way to the shoulder and felt for the bolt. The tips of his fingers barely touched it, but he managed to turn it and pull it out. Opening the door, he crawled inside, then closed it carefully.

Wolf stood up and made his way slowly into the dining room, where they had eaten, then glided silently across the living room where the thick carpet muffled his steps. He could feel his left knee brush against the couch where they had sat, and this helped him orient himself. He stood absolutely still so that he could let his mind work without distraction. He was inside, but he still wasn't sure what he was going to do. At any other time of his life he would have gone down the hallway to her bedroom and put a hole in her temple before even attempting to do anything else. He might make a noise in the next few minutes, and she would wake up. Or there might be some blood at his house that he had missed, and then she would be alive to give the FBI an accurate description of him. But while he constructed the argument for it, he already knew that he wasn't going to do it. He was not here to kill this woman. He might have to do it to survive, but he was determined to at least try it the other way first. If he could just get into the room, take what he wanted and get out, there would never be any reason for her to tell anyone what he looked like. He began to move again, but at the entrance to the hallway he stopped. When she had walked onto this floor, she had taken off her shoes, so he did the same.

Inside the door he could hear the sound of a child breathing slowly and deeply. He stepped to the side and felt his way along the wall until he identified the woodwork that framed the closet door. He groped for the knob and squeezed it tightly in his fist to swing it open without making any noise. He reached up to the top shelf and felt something made of leather. A baseball glove. Then there was the soft texture of cloth. Sure, a baseball cap. Now the smooth, sharp corner of the box. He reached both hands up to the shelf to be sure he could lift it without sliding it across the wood.

"Who are you?" came a little voice.

It was high and piping, and there was something shaky about it, like a bird. Oh, God, he thought. I don't want to kill this kid. "Mr. Richardson," Wolf said softly.

"Oh," said the boy. He waited for the kid to say something else, but there was no sound. He lifted the box and turned. "What are you doing here? I was asleep."

"I'm sorry, but I had to come. I'll be gone in a minute."

"Where's my mother?"

"She's asleep. If we're quiet, she won't wake up. She needs her rest."

The light came on and the click sounded like a hammer hitting a piece of metal. He was a tiny little boy, skinny, with his hair standing up on his head. He still had his hand on the lamp beside his bed, and he was squinting. "What are you doing with that?"

"It's for work. We need one of these pictures of your trip to England at the office right away."

"Which one?"

Wolf opened the lid. "London. The Parliament building. We're going to enlarge it so we can see what's going on inside."

"How can you do that?"

Wolf regretted having said it. How old was this kid—four? "We blow up the part we want so we can see in the window, and we transfer it to a computer. Then we can make a three-dimensional image and turn it around every which way." He made a slow rotating motion with both hands.

"What for?"

"I shouldn't tell you," Wolf said. Jimmy looked at him skeptically. "Well, we think somebody in Parliament isn't who he says he is."

"Who is he?"

"We don't know yet. That's why we need the picture."

Jimmy seemed to contemplate the plan, and finally to enlist, but he was a little worried. "You can't see much."

"We have to try. Can you show me which one?" Wolf took the sheaf of papers out of the box as he set it down on the kid's bed. While the little boy shuffled through the pictures, he worked the rubber band off the papers with one hand.

"This one," said Jimmy, and he held out a picture of his mother standing in front of the Houses of Parliament.

Wolf felt the passport now, and in a second he had it in his coat pocket with the pistol. He took the picture and scrutinized it. "It's perfect," he said. "Thanks, Jimmy." He stood up, returned the photographs and packet of papers to the box and put it back in the closet. Then he turned to the little boy. "I'm sorry I had to wake you up. You'd better turn the light out and go back to sleep now."

"Okay." Jimmy clicked the light off and lay back on his pillow.

As Wolf made his way into the hall and closed the door, he could hear the boy stirring. He walked quickly out of the hallway to the living room, stepped into his shoes and moved to the front door. As he opened it, he sensed that he wasn't alone. He was going to have to kill him.

This time the voice was a tiny whisper. "Good night."

"Good night, Jimmy." He stepped outside and closed the door, then hurried down the steps and across the lawn to get to the sidewalk and the place where the darkness began. In an hour he could be on a plane to London.

Jack Hamp crouched in the bushes across the street from the Waring house and watched the lone man walk toward him. The man was cautious, first turning his head to look at Elizabeth's house, then at the one beside it and finally at the one where Hamp was hiding. He walked slowly, but there was nothing casual or leisurely about it. He had sensed that something wasn't the way he wanted it, and he was scanning for some sign of another person. It was mesmerizing to watch him. He was going to assure himself that the whole block was clear before he made an attempt to break in on Elizabeth. Attempt? Hell, he still couldn't overcome his years of talking like a cop. If this guy decided to do it, Elizabeth was going to have a visitor.

Hamp slowly pulled his big .45 out of his coat, trying to keep the movement steady and silent. He had the hammer cocked and the safety engaged. The man was already moving toward the lawn in front of Hamp; in a second or two he would be on top of him. Hamp spent part of the second remembering that the Butcher's Boy was probably more than a match for him in the dark. By temperament, training and experience, Hamp desperately wanted not to have to squeeze a trigger on anybody, and this would make him hesitate.

Hamp disengaged the safety with his thumb, straightened his legs enough to bring the pistol up above the top of the bush and hoped that it was all that the Butcher's Boy could see clearly. "Justice Department. Keep your hands where I can see them."

It was exactly as he had seen it a dozen times in his imagination. The man didn't stop to think and didn't hesitate. In the second that it took Hamp to see that his right hand was going to his coat, it was already there and coming back out. Hamp fired. The report of the heavy military pistol clapped the air and the man took the round square in the center of his chest. As the man flopped backward onto the sidewalk, Hamp could see that he had almost gotten the barrel clear of his coat. It slid off his chest onto the pavement and Hamp walked over to pick it up. He stared down at the man. He was about the right age, and he was nondescript and ordinary enough to have survived for a long time while people were looking for him. Hamp could also see that the hollow-point round had made a terrible mess of his chest.

Hamp looked around him at the lights going on in upstairs windows all along the block. He noticed that his mouth had gone all dry and cottony. The last time this had happened, he had thought it was the shock from taking the bullet in his leg, but it must have been another reaction. He began the process of composing himself for the first of the conversations he would have to go through now: you know the fellow you've been trying to find? Yes, the one you've wanted for ten years. I'm afraid he can't tell you anything now. I just killed him. My name is Jack Hamp.

Elizabeth looked at the two sets of fingerprints, and then at the report from the FBI. She had been awake half the night waiting for this, and she wondered if the strain, surprise and sheer fatigue had simply obliterated her ability to comprehend. But it hadn't. She moved past the standard preprinted paragraph about the required thirteen points of comparison and read the conclusion again. It was positive. Suddenly she remembered that Jack had been waiting even before she had begun, and it was thoughtless to make him wait any longer.

"His name is Gilbert O'Mally. He has four arrests: grand theft, assault, aggravated assault and a parole violation."

"That isn't what I'd figured," said Jack. "I didn't think they'd even have him on file." It was going to take him some time to give this the proper amount of reflection. Elizabeth Waring didn't look the way he thought she would at all, but she was exactly the way he had hoped she would be. The suspect looked pretty much as he had expected, but nothing else about him was right. "I expected no arrests, no convictions."

"You were right," said Elizabeth. "Ten years ago was when this man was serving his time for aggravated assault. He's a local criminal." She waited for this to sink in, but Jack didn't say anything. What was he feeling—disappointment, relief? "It isn't him. This isn't the Butcher's Boy. He's still out there."

20

It's happening again,'' said Elizabeth.

Richardson shook his head. ''We don't think so.'' He looked at Hillman, the deputy assistant, for a sign of agreement, but the deputy assistant was staring at something that had besmirched his shirt cuff without actually becoming visible. Elizabeth wondered if this was a rebuff for Richardson's being presumptuous enough to postulate a ''we'' that included a deputy assistant attorney general of the United States of America. It was possible; short men were protective of their right to speak for themselves, as though if they were not heard, they would disappear. But Richardson was pressing on. ''Martillo worked for Detroit. He was here at the sufferance of Vico, and that sufferance simply wore itself out. Is that hard to believe?''

''Yes.''

Richardson's lips didn't quite smile. ''The phone company says a call was made on Martillo's car phone after he was dead. You know who the call went to? Vico.''

''Does Vico have a car phone?''

''Yes.''

''Then he'd know that they list all the outgoing calls.''

''He was caught literally red-handed. The car was found full of blood in his back yard, for Christ's sake.''

''With three of his own men inside.''

''It was a reprisal. Toscanzio's people were telling him that he shouldn't have killed their boy.''

''Okay,'' said Elizabeth. ''Let me get this straight. You honestly think that Vico had Martillo killed, and then his soldiers called him on Martillo's car phone to tell him that the deed was done. Then Toscanzio's people arrived from Detroit and killed the three killers. Then what? Did they put the bodies in the car and deliver them to Vico's back yard, or did Vico do that himself?''

"Choice number one. They also booby-trapped the fence so that whoever touched it would be electrocuted.''

"Was anybody?''

"Two people, actually,'' said Richardson. "Both of them soldiers of Vico's, and both heavily armed, incidentally, as though they were expecting trouble.''

"And you're going to try to bring Vico to trial on the basis of this evidence?''

Without warning, the deputy assistant suddenly satisfied himself that he had found the fault on his cuff. He straightened his short arms so that the cuffs would retract into the sleeves of his jacket, then raised his eyes. He never let them move to Richardson, but instead let them gaze into space for a moment, then settled them on Elizabeth. "What do you think happened, Elizabeth?''

"Ten years ago the Butcher's Boy got into trouble with the Mob. Specifically, Carlo Balacontano hired him, then tried to have him killed instead of paying him. What he did in response was to lash out violently and senselessly, killing several people who had little or nothing to do with the dispute. Since the various families were all suspicious of each other anyway, this created confusion and allowed him some breathing space. What he did with the time he had won was to kill a man named Arthur Fieldston and bury his head and hands on the estate of the man who had betrayed him in the first place.''

"Who was convicted in a court by a jury,'' snapped Richardson. "And the conviction held up under appeal.''

The deputy assistant restored silence by staring straight ahead without acknowledging that he had heard Richardson. Then he looked once more at Elizabeth. "And that's what you think is happening again?''

"Yes. I know he killed Talarese, and I think he killed Mantino and Fratelli. Two of them were creatures of Carlo Balacontano. I think he made an attempt at somebody in Gary, Indiana—maybe Cambria or Puccio—and the policeman, Lempert, got killed in the scuffle. I don't know what Martillo had to do with anything, except that I'm told he worked for Toscanzio in Detroit, which would add to the mess. I think that Vico didn't do any of this, and that he's been framed just like Carl Bala was ten years ago.''

"Here's the crux," said the deputy assistant. "It's Occam's razor."

"It is?"

"You have two possibilities. First, that we're witnessing the periodic internal strife that occurs inside the Mob for the usual reasons of fear and greed, and that they're using their many foot soldiers to pursue a power struggle. The other possibility is that one man, for no known reason, comes back after ten years and kills lots of heavily armed and protected people in different places in different ways, and then frames still another for some of the killings. One theory is simple and based on familiar behavior; the other is complicated and based on unknown quantities. One is likely and the other is unlikely. No?"

"Not this time."

"Why not?"

"Because a man like Vico isn't stupid. You're accusing him of killing Martillo, which would start a gang war, and then forgetting about it long enough to let the man's car be delivered to his back yard with his own casualties inside. He doesn't make mistakes like that."

The deputy assistant's face seemed to soften with a kind of paternal sympathy. "You have to look at this logically, Elizabeth. We're in the business of taking men like Vico off the street. In order to do this, we have to wait until he makes a mistake. When he finally makes one, can we say we won't prosecute because we don't believe he'd make that mistake?"

"This time, yes. Because this, all of it, has happened before—ten years ago—and Vico had nothing to do with it."

"So if what you say is accurate, what the Butcher's Boy will now do is to use the confusion he's caused to disappear, possibly forever."

"I don't know that, but I do think Vico's innocent."

"I don't think so," said the deputy assistant. "Logically I can't think so and still do my job. I'd like to have everyone in this room working on preparing this case."

It was happening again. Ten years ago the people who had sat in this room had made the decision to believe that the one who had disposed of Arthur Fieldston must be the big, powerful gangster, rather than the solitary killer. Their logic had brought them promotions and public notice, and eventually had elevated them right out of the Justice Department. Now the ones who had replaced them were making the same decision. The Butcher's Boy was going to disappear again. She tried not to think about Jack Hamp, waiting downstairs to hear where he was going next. Home was where he would be going.

Elizabeth cleared her throat. "I . . . I'd like to be excused, if I could. I've been on loan from my own office, and I've got cases of my own coming to trial."

The deputy assistant looked at Richardson, whose face was expressionless. "I hope it's not hurt feelings?"

"Me?" said Elizabeth. "No. I think you're wrong, but I always do my job. It's just that my regular job is the one I ought to be doing, and I've probably been away too long." She added, "Besides, my son has heard Richardson's name so many times that he's been having bad dreams about him."

21

The Immigration officer at Heathrow Airport studied James Hart's face, then compared it to the photograph on the passport. The gentleman in front of him looked notably older than the one in the two-year-old photograph. Perhaps it was the fact that he had changed his spectacles, or that he had allowed his hair to grow a little. His flight bag had been vetted by the X-ray machine, his pockets had been emptied, and clearly he was bringing nothing into the country but two thousand American dollars, all declared as required. This Mr. Hart didn't fit any of the profiles of undesirables. The money was sufficient for him to have a short holiday, but not enough to do anything that was not on. The Immigration officer applied his stamps to the passport: "Given leave to enter the United Kingdom for six months," which was five and three-quarters months longer than Mr. Hart had said he intended to stay; and the other, "13 September Heathrow (3)." The officer handed the passport back and watched Mr. Hart take two steps away from the counter. He had considered suggesting that Mr. Hart have another photograph taken, but it would have been absurd. The next three people on the same flight from Kennedy would undoubtedly have restyled and dyed their hair and be wearing contact lenses that changed their eye color.

James Hart stopped at the door and looked out at the cool, damp, gray morning, and then ceased to exist. Michael Schaeffer walked out along the asphalt pavement to the red double-decker Airbus and gave his fare to the Pakistani conductor on the steps.

Schaeffer settled into his seat and let the vaguely familiar sights of the ancient western suburbs go by. He liked Hammersmith particularly. It had something to do with the profusion of wet brick that always reminded him of cities in the northeastern United States. It began to rain as they moved into London, and the architectural trophies that the Empire had awarded itself began to appear, all of them old and built on top of foundations that were even older.

When the bus pulled to a stop on the street outside the huge barn of Victoria Station, Schaeffer got off with the others, moved quickly through the doors and down to the tube, looking at nothing and at no one, maneuvering himself into the right stream of people. He took the Circle Line to Paddington Station. When the train came to a stop, he went upstairs, walked over to the BritRail window and bought a ticket to Bath.

"Schubert, Octet in F Major for Strings and Winds, D. 803." The concert in the Deanery Gardens was exactly what Schaeffer had expected, merging in his mind with a hundred others he had sat through in the ten years in various green spots around Bath. Since they had moved to the north, he had let Meg drag him into York only for an occasional shopping trip. After all, you couldn't hire somebody to try on clothes for you. But now that life had settled down a little, he didn't mind concerts. All he required was that they park the car west of the River Ouse, beyond the medieval city walls, so that they wouldn't have to cross any of the little bridges to get out to the A59.

Schaeffer knew that Eddie Mastrewski would have told him he was crazy. "Are you telling me you're going to sit here on your ass in the sunshine like a superannuated tortoise listening to a bunch of Germans playing violins? Look at you, for Christ's sake. You're practically dead already, because let me tell you they don't forget. You're not trying to save your life; you're just waiting to sell it at the top market price."

There was an explosion of applause, and Schaeffer added his few pats to the general uproar. He missed Eddie. He still liked to argue with him, and Eddie's arguments had improved in the years since he had died.

Between concerts he forgot about music, but whenever he went to another concert it felt as though it were continuous, one long book that he was picking up where he had stopped last time. He was learning more about music, but he had trouble associating the dry, meaningless numbers that served as titles with the little tunes that entered his head. He would sit and listen, and by now he could form the themes and changes into complex spatial structures in his mind. But then, amid the obfuscating blare and blast, he would hear a little melody begin to form, tentatively at first and then gradually taking over, until it obscured the rest. Then he would realize that he had heard it before, recognize it like an old acquaintance and feel frustrated. It was as though he had opened the book and read two or three pages before discovering that he had read them already. Once, when Meg had asked him to take her to a concert, he had asked what they were going to play. She had recited a bewildering string of B flat majors and opus 106's, and when he had said, "What's that?" she had hummed them to him, one after the other, as though they were popular songs.

The Honourable Margaret Holroyd glanced at Schaeffer beside her. He looked as though he were in suspended animation, sitting comfortably in his folding chair with the gentle sun warming him. He really was a remarkable man. He had apparently had less formal education than the average saddle horse, but lots of Americans gave this impression, and ever since he had settled whatever business he'd had in America, he had seemed different. For one thing, he had become studious. He had been so willing to read books that nobody else actually read that she had been tempted to give him something like the *Dictionary of National Biography* to see how far his dedication went.

At one time she would have done this, but she had changed too since the business with the Bulgarians. She always called it this when she thought about it because that was the only lie he had given her. They had never spoken about it since. He had simply shown up at her door one day, about ten pounds thinner and looking exhausted, and said, "You're not married or anything, are you?" She had thrown herself at him and hugged him so hard that she had probably squeezed the breath right out of him, but of course he would never have let her know. That was how it had happened. She had made a huge, irreversible decision without actually deciding anything.

While Michael was away, Margaret had bought American newspapers and tried to figure out what he was really doing. There had even been a few nasty days when she had wondered if she had already read about his death. After all, there was no reason to imagine that she knew his real name. He might have had one of those names that were in the papers—Fratelli, Talarese, Vico and so on. There had been a surprising number of them in the month that he was gone. But that gangster business had just been Meg's penchant for making up ridiculous stories,

and she had turned it on herself because she hadn't had anyone
to tell the stories to. Gwendolyn's detestable aunt would have
said it was her punishment on earth for being a liar, to be followed in due course by more severe and exquisite punishments
in the afterlife.

In any event, Margaret could see that it was over. It wasn't
unheard of, after all. There were all those men who went off to
wars and saw and did unspeakable things, and then after a year
or two they were perfectly fine—or at least they appeared to be.
She looked at Schaeffer and felt good about the decision she had
not made. It was possible he was going to be one of those tough
men who surprised you by being doting fathers. To look at him
now, you could imagine that he was a professor, or even an
artist. He never fidgeted or moved, and there was nothing in his
face to register any change in the music. Only his eyes were in
motion, gliding from one person in the audience to another,
then upward to the top of the city walls where the walkway was,
then over to the gardens and the Minster, then back to the atten-
tive group of tourists and local gentry seated in the folding chairs
on the lawn.

Jack Hamp walked along the thick carpet of grass and looked
out over the fence across the track. It was an odd little place.
With the short season here, all the horses had returned to their
paddocks for the winter. Today you could as easily imagine that
this was the site of the Santa Maria County Fair as a place where
people laid down serious money on horses.

The desk sergeant had said that B. Baldwin's betting booth
had stood sixty meters to the left of the stands, ten meters back
from the rail. That would be about here. Hamp turned and
looked at the grandstand, then beyond it toward the road. From
this spot you couldn't even see the top of the walnut tree where
the Bentley with the bodies in it had been parked. So it wasn't
a question of an enterprising bookmaker noticing a couple of
rich young men and deciding that it would be safe to get together
a crew to kill them for their walking-around money. The victims
hadn't even gotten close enough to the track for Baldwin to see
them; there had been no betting slips in their pockets, no turf
on their shoes.

So if anybody had picked them out, it had to be Lucchi or
young Talarese. It was odd that the nephew of a New York
underboss would be reduced to starting his career as a street
thief, or even as a bookie who happened to see a couple of easy

marks. What good could the family imagine that his experience as a British bookie would do him in New York? There was no possibility of useful contacts in the barns or on the street; there wasn't even the same monetary system.

Hamp decided to ask the Brighton police about the stolen-car market in England. He couldn't imagine that anybody might have hoped to sell a hot Bentley in a country that wasn't more than four hundred miles from end to end, but it was something you had to ask about before eliminating it. For all he knew, Talarese might have been serving an apprenticeship in pinching Rolls-Royces and using the Mafia's channels to sell them in Asia or someplace.

But he had an instinct about this. He was fairly confident that when he had done all the footwork and checked out every angle, what he was going to end up with was essentially the same story. The two Limeys had only been unexpected witnesses. Talarese had been out here one fine day at the Brighton racetrack, doing whatever he was supposed to be doing, when he had happened to see a man who, among all the people milling around at this track, he and only he could possibly have recognized. Then with the sun making the bright silks on the horses and jockeys glow, and the birds singing—they were sure as hell singing today, so they probably had been then too—he had started feeling lucky.